Joy Fie novels, including *Kiss Mommy Goodbye* and *See Jane Run*:

'Finely tuned and convincing . . . suspense is maintained at a high level . . . sharply drawn articulate characters' *Publishers Weekly*

'Compulsive reading' *Company*

She lives with her lawyer husband and two daughters, dividing her time betwen Toronto, Ontario and Palm Beach, and Florida.

Also by Joy Fielding

Missing Pieces
Don't Cry Now
See Jane Run
Kiss Mommy Goodbye
The Other Woman
Life Penalty
The Deep End
Good Intentions
The Best of Friends
The Transformation
Trance

Tell Me No Secrets

Joy Fielding

HEADLINE
FEATURE

First published in Great Britain in 1993
by HEADLINE BOOK PUBLISHING

First published in paperback in 1993
by HEADLINE BOOK PUBLISHING

A HEADLINE FEATURE paperback

10 9 8 7

ISBN 0 7472 4163 5

Printed and bound in Great Britain

HEADLINE BOOK PUBLISHING
A division of Hodder Headline PLC
338 Euston Road
London NW1 3BH

For Renee

ACKNOWLEDGEMENTS

I would like to thank the following people for the help, they gave me in the writing of this book: Neil Cohen, who provided me with a crash course in the law and generously gave of his time and expertise – he is not only a lawyer, but a poet as well; Dean Morask, Chief of The Criminal Prosecutions Bureau for Cook County, who took time from his busy schedule to grant me a prolonged interview and answer some pretty far-out questions; the Honourable Judge Earl Strayhorn, who allowed me into his courtroom and showed me how justice is best served.

I would also like to thank Julie Rickerd for knowing just the right things to say just when I needed to hear them.

My deepest gratitude and appreciation to all of you.

Chapter One

He was waiting for her when she got to work. Or so it seemed to Jess, who spotted him immediately, standing motionless at the corner of California Avenue and Twenty-Fifth Street. She felt him watching her as she left the parking garage and hurried across the street toward the Administration Building, his dark eyes colder than the late October wind that played with his straggly blond hair, his bare hands clenched into tight fists outside the pockets of his well-worn brown leather jacket. Did she know him?

His body shifted slightly as Jess drew closer, and she saw that his mouth was twisted into an eerie little half-grin that pulled at one side of his full lips, as if he knew something that she didn't. It was a smile devoid of warmth, the smile of one who, as a child, enjoyed pulling the wings off butterflies, she thought with a shudder, ignoring the almost imperceptible nod of his head that greeted her as their eyes connected. A smile full of secrets, she understood, turning away quickly, and running up the front steps, suddenly afraid.

Jess felt the man move into position behind her, knew without looking that he was mounting the stairs after her, the deliberateness of his steps vibrating throughout her body. She reached the landing and pushed her shoulder against the heavy glass revolving door, the stranger stopping at the top of the steps, his face appearing and reappearing with each rotation of the glass, the sly smile never leaving his lips.

I am Death, the smile whispered. *I have come for you.*

Jess heard a loud gasp escape her lips, understood from the shuffling along the marble floor behind her that she had attracted the attention of one of the security guards. She spun around, watching the guard, whose name was Tony, approach cautiously, his hand gravitating toward the holster of his gun. 'Something wrong?' he asked.

'I hope not,' Jess answered. 'There's a man out there who . . .' Who what? she demanded silently, staring deep into the guard's tired blue eyes. Who wants to come in out of the cold? Who has a creepy grin? Was that a crime now in Cook County? The guard looked past her toward the door, Jess slowly tracking his gaze. There was no one there.

'Looks like I'm seeing ghosts,' Jess said apologetically, wondering if this were true, grateful that whatever the young man was, he was gone.

'Well, it's the season for it,' the guard said, checking Jess's identification even though he knew who she was, waving her through the metal detector, as he'd been doing routinely every morning for the past four years.

Jess liked routine. Every morning she got up at 6:45, quickly showered and dressed in the clothes she had carefully laid out the night before, gobbled a piece of Pepperidge Farm frozen cake directly from the freezer, and was behind her desk within the hour, her calendar open to the day's events, her case files ready. If she was prosecuting a case, there would be details to go over with her assistants, strategies to devise, questions to formulate, answers to determine. (A good attorney never asked a question to which she didn't already know the answer.) If she was preparing for an upcoming trial, there would be information to gather, leads to run down, witnesses waiting upstairs to be interviewed, police officers to talk to, meetings to attend, timetables to coordinate. Everything according to schedule. Jess Koster didn't like surprises outside the courtroom any better than she liked them inside it.

After she had a full grasp of the day that lay ahead, she would sit back with a cup of black coffee and a jelly donut and study the morning paper, starting with the obituaries. She always checked the obituaries. *Ashcroft, Pauline, died suddenly in her home, in her 67th year; Barrett, Ronald, passed away after a lengthy illness, age 79; Black, Matthew, beloved husband and father, no age given, donations to be sent to the Heart and Stroke*

Foundation of America. Jess wasn't sure when she'd started making the obituaries part of her regular morning routine, and she wasn't sure why. It was an unusual habit for someone barely thirty years old, even for a prosecutor with the Cook County State's Attorney's Office in Chicago. 'Find anyone you know?' one of her partners once asked. Jess had shaken her head, no. There was never anyone she knew.

Was she searching for her mother, as her ex-husband had once suggested? Or was it her own name she expected to see?

The stranger with the unruly blond hair and evil grin pushed his way rudely into her mind's eye. *I am Death*, he teased, his voice bouncing off the bareness of the office walls. *I have come for you*.

Jess lowered the morning paper and let her eyes glance around the room. Three desks in varying degrees of scratched walnut sat at random angles against dull white walls. There were no framed pictures, no landscapes, no portraits, nothing but an old poster from Bye Bye Birdie haphazardly tacked onto the wall across from her desk by a few random pieces of yellowing scotch tape. Law books filled strictly utilitarian metal shelves. Everything looked as if it could be picked up and moved out with only a minute's notice. Which it could. Which it often was. Assistant State's Attorneys were rotated on a regular basis. It was never a good idea to get too comfortable.

Jess shared the office with Neil Strayhorn and Barbara Cohen, her second and third chair respectively, who would be arriving within the half hour. As first chair, it was up to Jess to make all major decisions as to how her office was run. There were 750 State's Attorneys in Cook County, over 200 of them in this building alone, eighteen attorneys to every wing, three attorneys to every room, each watched over by a wing supervisor. By eight-thirty, the labyrinth of offices that made up the eleventh and twelfth floors of the Administration Building would be as noisy as Wrigley Field, or so it often seemed to Jess, who usually relished these few moments of peace and quiet before everyone arrived.

Today was different. The young man had unnerved her,

thrown her off her usual rhythm. What about him was so familiar? she wondered. In truth, she hadn't gotten a good look at his face, hadn't seen much past the eerie grin, would never have been able to describe him for a police sketch artist, could never have picked him out of a line-up. He hadn't even spoken to her. So why was she obsessing on him?

Jess resumed her scanning of the obituaries: *Bederman, Marvin, 74, died peacefully in his sleep after a lengthy illness; Edwards, Sarah, taken in her 91st year . . .*

'You're here early.' The male voice travelled easily to her desk from the open doorway.

'I'm always here early,' Jess answered without looking up. No need to. If the heavy scent of Aramis cologne wasn't enough to give Greg Oliver away, the confident swagger in his voice would. It was an office cliché that Greg Oliver's winning record in the courtroom was surpassed only by his record in the bedroom, and for that reason, Jess had always made sure to keep her conversations with the forty-year-old prosecutor from the next office strictly professional. Her divorce from one lawyer had taught her that the last thing she ever wanted to do was get involved with another. 'Is there something I can do for you, Greg?'

Greg Oliver traversed the distance to her desk in three quick strides. 'Tell me what you're reading.' He leaned forward to peer over her shoulder. 'The obits? Christ, what some people won't do to get their name in print.'

Jess chuckled in spite of herself. 'Greg, I'm really busy . . .'

'I can see that.'

'No, really,' Jess told him, taking quick note of his conventionally handsome face, made memorable by the liquid chocolate of his eyes. 'I have to be in court at nine-thirty.'

He checked his watch. A Rolex. Gold. She'd heard rumors that he'd recently married money. 'You've got lots of time.'

'Time I need to get my thoughts in order.'

'I bet your thoughts are already in order,' he said, straightening up only to lean back against her desk, openly checking his reflection in the glass of the window behind her, his hand brushing against a stack of carefully organized paperwork. 'I bet your mind is as neat as your desk.' He laughed, the motion tugging at one corner of his mouth, reminding Jess instantly of the stranger with the ominous grin. 'Look at you,' Greg said, misreading her response. 'You're all uptight because I accidentally moved a couple of your papers.' He made a great show of straightening them, then whisked some imaginary dust from the ragged surface of her desk top. 'You don't like anybody touching your stuff, do you?' His fingers caressed the wood grain in small, increasingly suggestive circles. The effect was almost hypnotic. A snake charmer, Jess thought, wondering momentarily whether he was the charmer or the snake.

She smiled, amazed at the way her mind seemed to be working this morning, and stood up, moving purposefully toward the book shelves, though, in truth, she had no purpose in mind. 'I think you better go so I can get some work done. I'm delivering my closing argument this morning in the Erica Barnowski case and . . .'

'Erica Barnowski?' His eyes reflected the path of his thoughts. 'Oh, yes. The girl who says she was raped . . .'

'The *woman* who *was* raped,' Jess corrected.

His laugh invaded the space between them. 'Jesus Christ, Jess, she wasn't wearing panties! You think any jury in the land is going to convict a guy of raping some woman he meets in a bar when she wasn't wearing panties?' Greg Oliver looked toward the ceiling, then back at Jess, automatically smoothing back several hairs he'd displaced. 'I don't know, but her not wearing panties to a pick-up bar smacks of implied consent to me.'

'And a knife at her throat is your idea of foreplay?' Jess shook her head, more in sadness than disgust. Greg Oliver was notoriously accurate in his assessments. If she couldn't manage to persuade her fellow prosecutors that the man on trial was guilty, how could she hope to convince a jury?

'I don't see a panty line under that short skirt,' Greg Oliver was saying. 'Tell me, counsellor, you wearing panties?'

Jess's hands moved to the sides of the grey wool skirt that stopped at her knees. 'Cut it out, Greg,' she said simply.

The mischief in Greg Oliver's voice spread to his eyes. 'Tell me, counsellor, just what would it take to get into those panties?'

'Sorry, Greg,' Jess told him evenly, 'but I'm afraid there's only room in these panties for *one* asshole.'

The liquid chocolate of Greg Oliver's eyes hardened into brown ice, then immediately melted as the sound of his laughter once again filled the room. 'That's what I love about you, Jess. You're so damn feisty. You'll take anybody on.' He walked toward the door. 'I'll give you this much – if anybody can win this case, you can.'

'Thanks,' Jess said to the closing door. She walked to the window and stared absently out at the street eleven stories below. Large billboards shouted up at her: *Abogado*, they announced. Lawyer, in Spanish, followed by a name. A different name for every sign. Open 24 hours a day.

There were no other high buildings in the area. At fourteen stories tall, the Administration Building stuck out like the sore thumb it represented. The adjoining Court House was a mere seven stories high. Behind them stood the Cook County Jail, where accused murderers and other alleged criminals, who either couldn't make bail or were being held without bond, were kept until their cases came to court. Jess often thought of the area as a dark, evil place for dark, evil people.

I am Death, she heard the streets whisper. *I have come for you.*

She shook her head, glancing up at the sky, but even it was a dirty shade of grey, heavy with the threat of snow. Snow in October, Jess thought, unable to recall the last time it had snowed before Halloween. Despite the weather forecast, she hadn't worn boots. They leaked and had unsightly salt rings around the toes, like the age lines of a tree. Maybe she'd go out later and buy herself a new pair.

The phone rang. Barely past eight o'clock and already the phone was ringing. She picked it up before it had a chance to ring again. 'Jess Koster,' she said simply.

'Jess Koster, Maureen Peppler,' the voice said, with a girlish giggle. 'Am I interrupting anything?'

'Never,' Jess told her older sister, picturing the woman's crinkly smile and warm green eyes. 'I'm glad you called.' Jess had always likened Maureen to one of those delicate sketches of ballet dancers by Edgar Degas, all soft and fuzzy around the edges. Even her voice was soft. People often said the sisters looked alike. But while the two women shared basic variations of the same oval face, and were both tall and slender, there was nothing fuzzy around the edges about Jess. Her brown shoulder-length hair was darker than Maureen's, her eyes a more disturbing shade of green, her small-boned frame less curvaceous, more angular. It was as if the artist had drawn the same sketch twice, then rendered one in pastels, the other in oil. 'What's doing?' Jess asked. 'How are Tyler and the twins?'

'The twins are great. Tyler's still not thrilled. He keeps asking when we're sending them back. You didn't ask about Barry.'

Jess felt her jaw tighten. Maureen's husband, Barry, was a successful accountant, and the vanity license plates on his late-model Jaguar spelled EARND IT. Did she really need to know more? 'How is he?' she asked anyway.

'He's fine. Business is terrific despite the economy. Or maybe because of it. Anyway, he's very happy. We want you to come to dinner tomorrow night, and please don't tell me you already have a date.'

Jess almost laughed. When was the last time she'd had a date? When was the last time she'd been anywhere socially that wasn't connected, in some way, to the law? Where had she gotten the idea that only doctors were on call twenty-four hours a day? 'No, I don't have a date,' she answered.

'Good, then you'll come. I don't get to see nearly enough of you these days. I think I saw more of you when I was working.'

'So go back to work.'

'Not on your life. Anyway, tomorrow at six. Dad's coming.'

Jess smiled into the phone. 'See you tomorrow.' She replaced the receiver to the sound of a baby's distant cry. She pictured

Maureen running toward the sound, cooing over the cribs of her six-month-old twins, changing their diapers, seeing to their needs, while making sure that the three-year-old at her feet was getting the attention he craved. A far cry from the hallowed halls of Harvard Business School where she'd earned her MBA. Jess shrugged. We all make choices, she thought. Her sister had obviously made hers.

She sat back down at her desk, trying to concentrate on the morning that lay ahead, praying she would be able to prove Greg Oliver wrong. She knew that securing a conviction in this case would be next to impossible. She and her partner would have to be very convincing.

The State's Attorney's office always tried jury cases in pairs. Her second chair, Neil Strayhorn, was set to deliver the initial closing argument, recounting for the jury the straight, unpleasant facts of the case. This would be followed by the defense attorney's closing remarks, and then Jess would handle the rebuttal, a position that allowed ample room for creative moral indignation. 'Every day in the United States, 1,871 women are forcibly raped,' she began, rehearsing the words in the safety of her office. 'That translates to 1.3 rapes of adult women every minute and a staggering 683,000 rapes each year.' She took a deep breath, tossing the sentences over in her mind, like errant pieces of lettuce in a large unwieldy salad. She was still tossing them over when Barbara Cohen arrived some twenty minutes later.

'How's it going?' At five feet eleven inches, and with bright red hair that cascaded halfway down her back in frenzied ripples, Barbara Cohen often seemed the anthropomorphic version of a carrot. She was almost a head taller than Jess, and her long, skinny legs gave the impression that she was standing on stilts. No matter how bad Jess was feeling, just looking at the young woman who was her third chair always made her smile.

'Hanging in there.' Jess checked her watch. Unlike Greg Oliver's, it was a simple Timex with a plain black leather band.

'Listen, I'd like you and Neil to handle the Alvarez drug case when it comes to trial.'

The look on Barbara Cohen's face reflected a mixture of excitement and apprehension. 'I thought you wanted to take that one.'

'I can't. I'm swamped. Besides, you guys can handle it. I'll be here if you need any help.'

Barbara Cohen tried, and failed, to keep the smile that was spreading across her face from overtaking her more professional demeanor. 'Can I get you some coffee?' she asked.

'If I drink anymore coffee, I'll be excusing myself from the courtroom every five minutes to pee. Think that would win me any sympathy points with the jury?'

'I wouldn't count on it.'

'How could she not wear panties, for God's sake,' Jess muttered. 'At the very least, you'd think she'd worry about discharge.'

'You're so practical,' Barbara stated, and laughed, readying her cart with files for the judge's morning call.

Neil Strayhorn arrived a few minutes later with the news that he thought he was coming down with a cold, then went straight to his desk. Jess could see his lips moving, silently mouthing the words to his opening closing statement. All around her, the offices of the State's Attorneys for Cook County were coming to life, like a flower opening to the sun.

Jess was aware of each new arrival, of chairs being pushed back, pulled in, computers being activated, Fax machines delivering messages, phones ringing. She unconsciously monitored the arrival of each of the four secretaries who serviced the eighteen lawyers in the wing, was able to distinguish the heavy steps of Tom Olinsky, her trial supervisor, as he walked toward his office at the end of the long hall.

'Every day in the United States, 1,871 women are forcibly raped,' she began again, trying to refocus.

One of the secretaries, a pear-shaped black woman who could

have passed for either twenty or forty, stuck her head through the doorway, her long, dangly red earrings falling almost to her shoulders. 'Connie DeVuono's here,' she said, then took a step back, as if she half expected Jess to hurl something at her head.

'What do you mean she's here?'

'I mean she's outside the door. Apparently, she walked right past the receptionist. She says she has to talk to you.'

Jess scanned her appointment calendar. 'Our meeting isn't until four o'clock. Did you tell her I have to be in court in a few minutes?'

'I told her. She says she has to see you now. She's very upset.'

'That's not too surprising,' Jess said, picturing the middle-aged widow who'd been brutally beaten and raped by a man who'd subsequently threatened to kill her if she testified against him, an event that was scheduled for ten days from today. 'Take her to the conference room, will you, Sally? I'll be right there.'

'Do you want me to talk to her?' Barbara Cohen volunteered.

'No, I'll do it.'

'Think it could be trouble?' Neil Strayhorn asked as Jess stepped into the hall.

'What else?'

The conference room was a small, windowless office, taken up almost entirely by an old walnut table and eight low-backed, mismatched brown chairs. The walls were the same dull white as the rest of the rooms, the carpet a well-worn beige.

Connie DeVuono stood just inside the doorway. She seemed to have shrunk since the last time Jess saw her, and her black coat hung on her body as if on a coat rack. Her complexion was so white, it appeared tinged with green, and the bags under her eyes lay in soft, unflattering folds, sad testament to the fact that she probably hadn't slept in weeks. Only the dark eyes themselves radiated an angry energy, hinting at the beautiful woman Connie DeVuono had once been. 'I'm sorry to be disturbing you,' she began.

'It's just that we don't have a lot of time,' Jess said softly, afraid that if she spoke above a whisper, the woman might shatter, like glass. 'I have to be in court in about half an hour.' Jess pulled out one of the small chairs for Connie to sit in. The woman needed no further encouragement. She collapsed, like an accordion, inside it. 'Are you all right? Would you like some coffee? Some water? Here, let me take your coat.'

Connie DeVuono waved away each suggestion with shaking hands. Jess noticed that her nails were bitten to the quick and her cuticles had been picked raw. 'I can't testify,' she said, looking away, her voice so low as to be almost inaudible.

Still, the words had the force of a shout. 'What?' Jess asked, though she'd heard every word.

'I said I can't testify.'

Jess lowered herself into one of the other chairs and leaned toward Connie DeVuono, so that their knees were touching. She reached for the woman's hands and cupped them inside her own. They were freezing. 'Connie,' she began slowly, trying to warm them, 'you're our whole case. If you don't testify, the man who attacked you goes free.'

'I know. I'm sorry.'

'You're sorry?'

'I can't go through with it. I can't. I can't.' She started crying.

Jess quickly drew a tissue from the pocket of her grey jacket and handed it to Connie, who ignored it. Her cries grew louder. Jess thought of her sister, the effortless way she seemed able to comfort her crying babies. Jess had no such talents. She could only sit by helplessly and watch.

'I know I'm letting you down,' Connie DeVuono continued, her shoulders shaking. 'I know I'm letting everybody down . . .'

'Don't worry about us,' Jess told her. 'Worry about you. Think about what that monster did to you.'

The woman's angry eyes bore deeply into her own. 'Do you think I could ever forget it?'

'Then you have to make sure he isn't in a position to do it again.'

'I can't testify. I just can't. I can't. I can't.'

'Okay, okay, calm down. It's okay. Try to stop crying.' Jess leaned back in her chair and tried to crawl inside Connie's mind. Something had obviously happened since the last time they spoke. At each of their previous meetings, Connie, though frightened, had been adamant about testifying. The daughter of Italian immigrants, she had grown up in a household that believed fiercely in the American system of justice. Jess had been very impressed with that belief. After four years with the State's Attorney's Office, Jess thought it probably stronger than her own. 'Has something happened?' she asked, watching Connie's racking shoulders shudder to a halt.

'I have to think about my son,' Connie said forcefully. 'He's only eight years old. His father died of cancer two years ago. If something happens to me, then he has no one.'

'Nothing's going to happen to you.'

'My mother is too old to look after him. Her English is very poor. What will happen to Steffan if I die? Who will take care of him? Will you?'

Jess understood the question was rhetorical, but answered anyway. 'I'm afraid I'm not very good with men,' she said softly, hoping to elicit a smile, watching Connie DeVuono struggle to oblige.

'But, Connie, nothing is going to happen to you once we put Rick Ferguson behind bars.'

The very mention of the man's name caused Connie's body to visibly tremble. 'It was hard enough for Steffan to lose his father at so young an age. What could be worse than losing his mother too?'

Jess felt her eyes instantly well up with tears. She nodded. There could be nothing worse.

'Connie,' she began, surprised by the trembling in her voice, 'believe me, I hear what you're saying. I understand what you're going through. But what makes you think that if you don't testify, you'll be safe? Rick Ferguson already broke into your apartment once and raped you. He beat you so badly you could barely open your eyes for a month. He didn't know that your son wasn't home. He didn't care. What makes you think he won't try it again? Especially once he knows that he can get away with it, because you're too frightened to stop him. What makes you think that the next time, he won't hurt your son too?'

'Not if I refuse to testify.'

'You don't know that.'

'I only know he said I'd never live to testify against him.'

'He made that threat months ago and it didn't stop you.' There was a moment's silence. 'What happened, Connie? What's frightening you? Has he contacted you in any way? Because if he has, we can have his bail revoked . . .'

'There's nothing you can do.'

'There's plenty we can do.'

Connie DeVuono reached inside her floppy black leather purse and pulled out a small white box.

'What's that?'

Connie DeVuono said nothing as she handed the box to Jess.

Jess opened it, gingerly working her way through layers of tissues, feeling something small and hard beneath her fingers.

'The box was in front of my door when I opened it this morning,' Connie said, watching as Jess pulled away the final tissue.

Jess felt her stomach lurch. The turtle that lay lifeless and exposed in her hands was missing its head and two of its feet.

'It was Steffan's,' Connie said, her voice flat. 'We came home a few nights ago and it wasn't in its tank. We couldn't understand how it could have gotten out. We looked everywhere.'

Instantly Jess understood Connie's terror. Three months ago, Rick Ferguson had broken into her apartment, raped her, sodomized her, beaten her, then threatened her life. Now, he was showing her how easy it would be to make good on his threats. He'd broken into her apartment again, as effortlessly as if he'd been handed the key. He'd killed and mutilated her child's pet. No one had seen him. No one had stopped him.

Jess rewrapped the dead turtle in its shroud of tissues and placed it back in its cardboard casket. 'Not that I think it'll do any good, but I'd like to show this to forensics.' She walked to the door and quickly signalled for Sally. 'Get this over to forensics for me, will you?'

Sally took the box from Jess's hands as carefully as if she were handling a poisonous snake.

Suddenly Connie was on her feet. 'You know as well as I do you'll never be able to connect this to Rick Ferguson. He'll get away with it. He'll get away with everything.'

'Only if you let him.' Jess returned to Connie's side.

'What choice do I have?'

'A clear choice,' Jess told her, knowing she had only a few minutes left to change Connie's mind. 'You can refuse to testify, that way ensuring that Rick Ferguson walks away scot-free, that he never has to be held accountable for what he did to you, for what he's *still* doing to you.' She paused, giving her words time to register. 'Or you can go to court and make sure that that bastard gets what he deserves, that he gets put behind bars where he can't hurt you or anyone else for a very long time.' She waited, watching Connie's eyes flicker with indecision. 'Face it, Connie. If you don't testify against Rick Ferguson, you're not helping anyone, least of all yourself. You're only giving him permission to do it again.'

The words hung suspended in the space between them, like laundry someone had forgotten to take off the line. Jess held her breath, sensing Connie was on the verge of capitulating, afraid to do anything that might tip the delicate balance in the other direction. Another speech was already working its way to the tip of her tongue. There's an easy way to do this, it began, and there's a hard way. The easy way is that you agree to testify as planned. The hard way is that I'll have to force you to testify. I'll get the judge to issue a bench warrant for your arrest, force you to come to court, force you to take the stand. And if you still refuse to testify, the judge can, and will, hold you in contempt, send you to jail. Wouldn't that be a tragedy – you in jail and not the man who attacked you?

Jess waited, fully prepared to use these words if she had to, silently praying they wouldn't be necessary. 'Come on, Connie,' she said, giving it one last try. 'You've fought back before. After your husband died, you didn't give up, you went to night school, you got a job so that you could provide for your son. You're a fighter, Connie. You've always been a fighter. Don't let Rick Ferguson take that away from you. Fight back, Connie. Fight back.'

Connie said nothing, but there was a slight stiffening of her back. Her shoulders lifted. Finally, she nodded.

Jess reached for Connie's hands. 'You'll testify?'

Connie's voice was a whisper. 'God help me.'

'We'll take all the help we can get.' Jess checked her watch, rose quickly to her feet. 'Come on, I'll walk you out.'

Neil and Barbara had already left for court, and Jess ushered Connie along the corridor of the State's Attorneys' offices, past the display of cut-off ties that lined one wall, symbolizing each prosecutor's first win before a jury. The halls were decorated in preparation for Halloween, large orange paper pumpkins and witches on broomsticks taped across the walls, like in a kindergarten class, Jess thought, accepting Greg Oliver's 'good luck' salutations, and proceeding through the reception area to the bank of elevators outside the glass doors. From the large window at the far end of the six elevators, the whole west side and northwest side of the city was visible. On a nice day, O'Hare Airport could be easily discerned. Even faraway Du Page County seemed within reach.

The women said nothing on the ride down to the main floor, knowing everything important had already been said. They exited the elevator and rounded the corner, pointedly ignoring the Victim-Witness Services Office with its large picture-laden poster proclaiming *We Remember You . . . In Loving Memory of . . .* and proceeded to the glassed-in, rectangular hallway that connected the administration building to the courthouse next door. 'Where are you parked?' Jess asked, about to guide Connie through the airport-like security to the outside.

'I took the bus,' Connie DeVuono began, then stopped abruptly, her hand lifting to her mouth. 'Oh, my God!'

'What? What's the matter?' Jess followed the woman's frightened gaze.

The man was standing at the opposite end of the corridor, leaning against the cold expanse of glass wall, his lean frame heavy with menace, his blunt features partially obscured by the thick mass of long, uncombed, dark blond hair that fell over the collar of his brown leather jacket. As his body swivelled slowly around to greet them, Jess watched the side of his lips twist into the same chilling grin that had greeted her arrival at work that morning.

I am Death, the grin said.

Jess shuddered, then tried to pretend it was from a gust of cold air that had sneaked into the lobby through the revolving doors.

Rick Ferguson, she realized.

'I want you to take a taxi,' Jess told Connie, seeing one pull up to drop somebody off, guiding Connie through the doors onto California Avenue, and thrusting ten dollars into her hand. 'I'll take care of Rick Ferguson.'

Connie said nothing. It was as if she had expended all her energy in Jess's office, and she simply had no more strength to argue. Tightly clutching the ten-dollar bill, she allowed Jess to put her in the cab, not bothering to look back as the car pulled away. Jess remained for a moment on the sidewalk, trying to still the loud thumping in her chest, then turned around and pushed her way back through the revolving doors.

He hadn't moved.

Jess strode toward him across the long corridor, the heels of her black pumps clicking on the hard granite floor, watching as Rick Ferguson's features snapped into sharper focus with each step. The vague generic menace he projected – white male, early twenties, five feet ten inches tall, 170 pounds, blond hair, brown eyes – became more concrete, individualized – shoulders that stooped slightly, unkempt hair pulled into a loose pony tail, deeply hooded cobra-like eyes, a nose that had been broken several times and never properly reset, and always that same unnerving grin.

'I'm warning you to stay away from my client,' Jess announced when she reached him, not giving him the chance to interrupt. 'If you show up within fifty yards of her again, even accidentally, if you try to speak to her or contact her in any way, if you leave any more gruesome little presents outside her door, I'll have your bail revoked and your ass in jail. Am I making myself clear?'

'You know,' he said, speaking very deliberately, as if he were in the middle of an entirely different conversation, 'it's not such a great idea to get on my bad side.'

Jess almost laughed. 'What's that supposed to mean?'

Rick Ferguson shifted his body weight from one foot to the other, then shrugged, managing to appear almost bored. He looked around, scratched at the side of his nose. 'It's just that people who annoy me have a way of . . . disappearing.'

Jess found herself taking an involuntary step back. A cold shiver, like a drill, snaked its way through her chest to her gut. She had to fight the sudden urge to throw up. When she spoke, her voice was hollow, lacking resonance. 'Are you threatening me?'

Rick Ferguson pushed his body away from the wall. His smile widened. *I am Death*, the smile said. *I have come for you.*

Then he walked away without a backward glance.

Chapter Two

'Every day in the United States, 1,871 women are forcibly raped,' Jess began, her eyes tracking the seven men and seven women who made up the two rows of twelve jurors and their two alternates sitting in courtroom 706 of the State Court House at 2600 California Avenue. 'That translates to 1.3 rapes of adult women every minute and a staggering 683,000 rapes each year.' She took a brief pause to let the sheer volume of her statistics sink in. 'Some are attacked in the streets; others are set on in their own homes. Some are raped by the proverbial stranger in a dark alley, far more by people they know: an angry ex-boyfriend, a once-trusted friend, a casual acquaintance. Perhaps, like Erica Barnowski,' she said, indicating the plaintiff with a nod of her head, 'by someone they met in a bar. The women, like the men who attack them, come in all shapes and sizes, all religious denominations and cultural backgrounds, all ages and colors. The only trait they have in common is their sex, which is very ironic when you think about it, because rape is not about sex. Rape is a crime of violence. It is not about passion, or even lust. It is about power. It is about domination and humiliation. It is about control. It is about the infliction of pain. It is an act of rage, an act of hate. It has nothing to do with sex. It only uses sex as its weapon of choice.'

Jess surveyed the majestic old courtroom, its high ceilings and large side windows, the dark panelling along the walls, the black marble framing its large wooden doors. A sign to the right of the judge proclaimed loudly over the rear door: Positively! NO VISITING in courtroom or cell block. To the left another sign declared: QUIET. No Smoking, Eating, Children, Talking.

The visitors' block, which contained eight rows of graffiti-carved benches, was distinguished by an old black and white tile floor. Just like in the movies, Jess thought, grateful to have been assigned to Judge Harris's court for the past eighteen months instead of one of the newer, smaller courtrooms on the lower floors.

'The defense would have you believe otherwise,' Jess continued, making deliberate eye contact with each of the jurors, before gradually switching her focus to the defendant. The defendant, Douglas Phillips, white, ordinary, quite respectable-looking in his dark blue suit and quiet paisley tie, made a small pout with his lips before looking toward the brown-carpeted floor. 'The defense would have you believe that what happened between Douglas Phillips and Erica Barnowski was an act of consensual sex. They have told you that on the night of May the thirteenth, 1992, Douglas Phillips met Erica Barnowski in a singles' bar called the Red Rooster, and that he bought her several drinks. They have called several witnesses who testified seeing them together, drinking and laughing, and who have sworn that Erica Barnowski left the bar with Douglas Phillips of her own free will and by her own accord. Erica Barnowski, herself, admitted as much when she took the stand.

'But the defense would also have you believe that after they left the bar, what transpired was an act of runaway passion between two consenting adults. Douglas Phillips explains the bruises on the victim's legs and arms as the unfortunate byproduct of making love in a small, European car. He dismisses the victim's subsequent hysteria, witnessed by several people in the parking lot, and later observed by Dr. Robert Ives at Grant Hospital, as the ravings of an hysterical woman furious at being picked up and discarded, in his sensitive phrase, "like a piece of used Kleenex".'

Jess now devoted her full attention to Erica Barnowski, who sat beside Neil Strayhorn at the prosecutors' table, directly across from the jury box. The woman, 27 years old and very pale, very blonde, sat absolutely still in her high-backed brown leather chair. The only thing about her that moved was her bottom lip, which had been trembling throughout the trial, and which had occasionally made her testimony almost indecipherable. Still, there was little about the woman that was soft. The hair was too yellow, the eyes too small, the blouse too blue, too cheap. There was nothing to inspire pity, nothing, Jess knew, to trigger automatic compassion in the hearts of the jurors.

'He has a little more trouble explaining the cuts on her neck and throat,' Jess went on. 'He didn't mean to hurt her, he says. It was just a little knife, after all, barely four inches long. And he only brought it out when she started getting feisty. It even seemed to excite her, he told you. He thought she liked it. How was he supposed to know that she didn't? How was he supposed to figure out that she didn't want the same things he wanted? How was he supposed to know *what* she wanted? After all, hadn't she come to the Red Rooster looking for a man? Hadn't she let him buy her drinks? Hadn't she laughed at his jokes and let him kiss her? And don't forget, ladies and gentlemen, she wasn't wearing any panties!'

Jess took a deep breath, returning her gaze to the members of the jury, who were now hanging on her every word. 'The defense has made a big deal of the fact that when Erica Barnowski went to the Red Rooster that night, she wasn't wearing any underwear. An open invitation, they would have you believe. Implied consent. Any woman who goes to a pick-up bar and doesn't wear panties is obviously asking for whatever she gets. Consent before the fact. Erica Barnowski was looking for action, the defense tells you, and that's exactly what she got. Oh, she may have gotten a little more than she bargained for, but hey, she should have known better.

'Well, maybe she should have. Maybe going to a bar like the Red Rooster and leaving her panties at home wasn't the smartest thing Erica Barnowski could have done. But don't think for a moment that a lack of common sense on one person's part eliminates the need for common decency on another's. Don't believe for a second that Douglas Phillips got his signals crossed. Don't be hoodwinked into accepting that this man, who repairs state-of-the-art computers for a living, who has no difficulty whatsoever decoding sophisticated software terminology, has trouble understanding the difference between a simple yes and no. What part of "no" is so difficult for a grown man to understand? No, quite simply, means no!

'And Erica Barnowski said no loud and clear, ladies and gentlemen. She not only *said* no, she *screamed* it. She screamed it so loud and so often that Douglas Phillips had to hold a knife to her throat to silence her.'

Jess found herself directing her remarks to a juror in the second row, a woman in her late fifties with auburn hair and strong, yet curiously delicate, features. There was something about the woman's face she found intriguing. She'd become aware of her early in the trial, and had occasionally found herself speaking almost exclusively to her. Maybe it was the intelligence that was obvious in her soft grey eyes. Maybe it was the way she tilted her head when trying to come to terms with a difficult point. Maybe it was simply the fact that she was better dressed than most of the jurors, several of whom wore blue jeans and baggy, ill-fitting sweaters. Or maybe it was just because Jess felt she was getting through to her, and that through her, she might be able to reach the others.

'Now, I don't claim to be an authority on men,' Jess stated, and heard her inner voice laugh, 'but I have a very hard time accepting that any man who has to hold a knife to a woman's jugular honestly believes she's consenting to intercourse.' Jess paused, choosing her next words very carefully. 'I suggest to you that, even in today's supposedly enlightened times, the double standard looms very large in Cook County. Large enough for the defense to try to convince you that the fact Erica Barnowski wasn't wearing panties that night is somehow more damning than the fact Douglas Phillips held a knife to her throat.'

Jess's eyes travelled slowly down the double row of jurors and two alternates, all of whom wore a red adhesive strip with white letters that said JUROR. 'Douglas Phillips claims he thought Erica Barnowski was consenting to sex,' she stated.

'Well, isn't it time we stopped looking at rape from the rapist's point of view? Isn't it time we stopped accepting what men are *thinking*, and started listening to what women are *saying*? Consent is not a unilateral concept, ladies and gentlemen. It cuts both ways, requires agreement from both parties. What happened between Erica Barnowski and Douglas Phillips on the night of May the thirteenth was decidedly *not* an act of consensual sex.

'Erica Barnowski might be guilty of an error in judgement,' Jess said simply in conclusion. 'Douglas Phillips is guilty of rape.'

She returned to her seat, gently patted Erica Barnowski's surprisingly warm hands. The young woman thanked her with a hint of a smile. 'Well done,' Neil Strayhorn whispered. No such acknowledgements were forthcoming from the defense table, where Douglas Phillips and his lawyer, Rosemary Michaud, stared resolutely ahead.

Rosemary Michaud was five years older than Jess but looked at least twice that. Her dark brown hair was pulled into a severe bun, and if she wore any make-up, it had been applied so subtly as to be invisible. Jess had always thought she resembled the stereotype of a maiden aunt, although this maiden aunt had been married three times and was rumored to be having an affair with a senior official in the police department. Still, in law, as in life, what was important wasn't the way things actually were, but the way they were *perceived* to be. Image, as the ads stated, was everything. And Rosemary Michaud looked like the kind of woman who would never defend a man if she truly believed him to be guilty of so vile an act as rape, or aggravated criminal sexual assault, as the state was now calling it. In her conservative blue suit and unadorned face, Rosemary Michaud looked as if the very idea of defending such a man would offend her to the bone. Douglas Phillips had been smart to hire her.

Rosemary Michaud's motives in accepting Douglas Phillips for a client were harder to fathom, although Jess well understood that it was not the lawyer's job to determine guilt or innocence. That was what the jury system was all about. How many times had she heard argued, had *herself* argued, that if lawyers started acting as judges and jurors, the entire system of justice would fall apart? The presumption of innocence, after all; everyone was entitled to the best possible defense.

Judge Earl Harris cleared his throat, signalling he was about to deliver his instructions to the jury. Judge Harris was a handsome man in his late sixties, his light black skin framed by a close-cropped halo of curly grey hair. There was a genuine kindness to his face, a softness to his dark eyes, that underlined his deep commitment to justice. 'Ladies and gentlemen of the jury,' he began, managing somehow to make even these words sound fresh, 'I want to thank you for the attention and respect you have shown this courtroom over the past several days. Cases like this one are never easy. Emotions run very high. But your duty as jurors is to keep your emotions out of the jury room, and concentrate on the facts.'

Jess, herself, concentrated less on the message being delivered than in how it was being received, her focus returning to the members of the jury, all of whom were leaning forward in their brown leather swivel chairs, listening attentively.

Which side's vision of the truth were they most likely to adopt as their own? she wondered, aware that juries were notoriously difficult to read, their verdicts almost impossible to predict. When she first came to work at the State's Attorney's office four years ago, she'd been surprised to discover how wrong she could be, and how often.

The woman juror with the intelligent eyes coughed into the palm of her hand. Jess knew that women jurors in a rape trial were often harder to win over than their male counterparts. Something to do with denial, she supposed. If they could convince themselves that what had happened was somehow the victim's fault, then they could assure themselves that they would never meet a similar fate. After all, *they* would never be so careless as to walk alone after dark, accept a ride with a casual acquaintance, pick up a man in a bar, *not wear any panties*. No, they were much too smart for that. They were too aware of the dangers. They would never be raped. They would simply never put themselves in so vulnerable a position.

The woman juror became aware of Jess's scrutiny, and twisted self-consciously in her seat. She drew her shoulders back and lifted herself just slightly out of her chair before settling in comfortably again, her eyes riveted on the judge's mouth. In profile, the woman seemed more formidable, her nose sharper, the shape of her face more convex. There was a familiarity about her that Jess hadn't noticed before: the way she occasionally tapped her lips with her finger; the way her neck arched forward on certain key phrases; the slant of her forehead; the thinness of her eyebrows. She reminded Jess of someone, Jess realized, drawing in an audible intake of air, trying to block out the thoughts that were taking shape in her mind, trying to banish the picture that was quickly developing. No, she wouldn't do this, Jess thought, scanning the courtroom, a dreaded tingling creeping in her arms and legs. She fought the urge to flee.

Calm down, she castigated herself silently, feeling her breathing constrict, her hands grow clammy, her underarms become moist. Why now? she wondered, fighting the growing panic, trying to will herself back to normalcy. Why was this happening now?

She forced her eyes back to the woman juror, who was leaning forward in her chair. As if aware of Jess's renewed interest and determined not to be intimidated by it, the woman turned to look her squarely in the eye.

Jess caught the woman's gaze with her own, held it suspended for an instant, then closed her eyes with relief. What had she been thinking of? she wondered, feeling the muscles in her back start to uncramp. What could have possibly triggered such an association? The woman looked like no one she knew, no one she had ever known. Certainly nothing at all like the woman she had fleetingly imagined her to be, Jess thought, feeling foolish and a bit ashamed.

No, nothing remotely like her mother at all.

Jess lowered her head so that her chin almost disappeared into the pink collar of her cotton blouse. It had been eight years since her mother disappeared. Eight years since her mother had left the house to keep a scheduled doctor's appointment and was never seen again. Eight years since the police gave up searching for her and declared her the probable victim of foul play.

In the first few days, months, even years after her mother disappeared, Jess had often thought she'd seen her mother's face in a crowd. It used to happen all the time: she'd be grocery shopping and her mother would be pushing an overflowing cart down the next aisle; she'd be at a baseball game when she'd hear her mother's distinctive voice cheering for the Cubs from her seat on the other side of Wrigley Field. Her mother was the woman behind the newspaper at the back of the bus, the woman in the front seat of the taxi going the other way, the woman struggling to catch up to her dog as they ran along the waterfront.

As the years progressed, the sightings had diminished in frequency. Still, for a long while, Jess had been the victim of nightmares and panic attacks, attacks that struck whenever, wherever, attacks so virulent they robbed her of all feeling in her limbs, all strength in her muscles. They would start with a mild tingling sensation in her arms and legs and develop into virtual paralysis as waves of nausea swept over her. They would end – sometimes in minutes, sometimes after hours – with her sitting powerless, overwhelmed, defeated, her body bathed in sweat.

Gradually, painfully, like someone learning to walk again after a stroke, Jess had regained her equilibrium, her confidence, her self-esteem. She had stopped expecting her mother to come walking through the front door, stopped jumping every time the phone rang, expecting the voice on the other end to be hers. The nightmares had stopped. The panic attacks had ceased. Jess had promised herself that she would never be that vulnerable, that powerless, again.

And now the familiar tingle had returned to her arms and legs.

Why now? Why today?

She knew why.

Rick Ferguson.

Jess watched him push through the doors of her memory, his cruel grin surrounding her like a noose around her neck. 'It's not such a great idea to get on my bad side,' she heard him say, his voice tight, his hands forming fists at his sides. 'People who annoy me have a way of . . . disappearing.'

Disappearing.

Like her mother.

Jess tried to refocus, concentrate all her attention on what Judge Earl Harris was saying. But Rick Ferguson kept positioning himself directly in front of the prosecutor's table, his brown eyes daring her to provoke him into action.

What was it about her and men with brown eyes? Jess wondered, a collage of brown-eyed images filling her brain: Rick Ferguson, Greg Oliver, her father, even her ex-husband.

The image of her ex-husband quickly relegated the others to the back corners of her mind. So typical of Don, she thought, to be so dominant, so overpowering, even when he wasn't there. Eleven years her senior, Don had been her mentor, her lover, her protector, her friend. *He won't give you room to grow*, her mother had cautioned when Jess first announced her intention to marry the brash bulldozer of a man who'd been her first year tutorial instructor. *Give yourself a chance*, she'd begged. *What's the rush?* But, like any rebellious daughter, the more her mother objected, the more determined Jess became, until her mother's opposition was the strongest bond between Jess and Don. They married soon after she disappeared.

Don immediately took charge. During their four years together, it was Don who picked the places they went, selected the apartment they lived in and the furniture they bought, decided who they saw, what they did, even what food she ate, what clothes she wore.

Perhaps it had been her fault. Perhaps that was what she'd wanted, needed, even begged for, in the years immediately following her mother's disappearance: the chance not to have to make any major decisions, to be taken care of, looked after, catered to. The chance to disappear herself, inside someone else.

In the beginning, Jess had made no objections to Don running her life. Didn't he know what was best for her? Didn't he have her best interests at heart? Wasn't he always there to wipe away her tears, nurse her through each crippling panic attack? How could she survive without him?

But increasingly, perhaps even unwittingly, Jess had struggled to reassert herself, picking fights, wearing colors she knew he despised, filling up on junk food before they were to go out to his favorite restaurant, refusing to see his friends, applying for a job at the State's Attorney's office instead of joining Don's firm, ultimately moving out.

Now she lived on the top floor of a three-storey brownstone in an old part of the city, instead of in the glassed-in penthouse of a downtown highrise, and she ordered pizza instead of room service, and her closest friend, outside of her sister, was a bright yellow canary named Fred. And if she was no longer the carefree spirit she'd been before her mother vanished, at least she was no longer the invalid she'd allowed herself to become during much of her marriage to Don.

'You are here to see that justice is done,' Judge Harris was concluding. 'It is only by your act of being fair and impartial, of refusing to be swayed by either sympathy for the victim or the accused, but by deciding the case strictly on facts, that you will turn this dark, dank, dreary building into a true, shining temple of justice.'

Jess had heard Judge Harris deliver this speech many times in the past, and it never failed to move her. She watched its effect on the jury. They filed out of the courtroom as if being guided by a shining star.

Erica Barnowski said nothing as the courtroom emptied out. Only after the defendant and his lawyer had left the room did she stand up and nod toward Jess. Neil Strayhorn explained that she would be contacted when the jury returned with a verdict, that it could be hours or possibly days, that she should keep herself available.

'I'll get in touch with you as soon as I hear anything,' Jess said instead of goodbye, watching the younger woman walk briskly down the hall toward the elevators. Unconsciously, her eyes drifted toward Erica Barnowski's full hips. ('I don't see a panty line,' she heard Greg Oliver repeat.) Roughly, she snapped her head back, then shook it, as if trying to clear her mind of all such unpleasant musings. 'You did a great job,' Jess told her second chair. 'You were clear; you were focused; you gave the jurors all the facts they needed to take with them into the jury room. Now, go get your cold some chicken soup,' she continued before Neil could reply. 'I think I'll grab some of that fresh October air.'

Jess opted for the stairs over the elevator, despite the seven flights. She could use the exercise. Maybe she'd take a long walk, buy those winter boots she needed. Maybe she'd even treat herself to a new pair of shoes.

Maybe she'd just grab a hot dog from the vendor at the curb, then go back upstairs to her office to wait out the verdict and start working on her next case, she decided, walking across the granite floor of the foyer.

The cold air hit her like a slap to the face. She hunched her shoulders up around her ears and pressed forward down the steps to the street, surreptitiously peeking toward the busy corner, assuring herself that Rick Ferguson was nowhere to be seen. 'A hot dog with everything on it,' she shouted with relief, watching as the vendor expertly tossed a giant kosher hot dog into a sesame seed bun and smothered it with ketchup, mustard and relish. 'That's great, thank you.' She deposited a fistful of change into his hand, then took a large bite.

'How many times do I have to tell you those things are deadly?' The voice, full, cheery, masculine, came from somewhere to her right. Jess turned toward the sound. 'They're solid fat. Absolutely lethal.'

Jess was tempted to rub her eyes in disbelief. 'My God, I was just thinking about you.'

'Good thoughts, I hope,' Don Shaw stated.

Jess stared at her ex-husband as if she couldn't quite decide if he were real or something her mind had conjured up to confuse her. He was such a remarkable presence, she thought, watching the rest of the street disappear into a soft blur around him. Although he was only of average height, everything about him seemed oversized: his hands; his chest; his voice; his eyes, their lashes the envy of all the women he met. What was he doing here? she wondered. She'd never run into him like this before, despite the fact they frequented the same turf. She hadn't spoken to him in months. And now she had only to think of him and he was here.

'You know I can't stand watching you eat this crap,' he was saying, grabbing the hot dog out of her hands and tossing it into a nearby trash bin.

'What are you doing?!'

'Come on, let me buy you some real food.'

'I can't believe you did that!' Jess signalled the vendor for another hot dog. 'Touch this one, you'll lose your hand,' she warned, only half in jest.

'One of these days you're going to wake up fat,' he cautioned, then smiled, the kind of loopy grin that made it impossible not to smile back.

Jess stuffed half the new hot dog into her mouth, thinking it wasn't as good as the first. 'So, how've you been?' she asked. 'What's this I hear about a new girlfriend?' She felt immediately self-conscious, whisked some imaginary crumbs off the front of her jacket.

'Who said anything about a girlfriend?' They started walking slowly toward twenty-sixth Street, falling into the casual rhythm of each other's steps, as if this impromptu walk had been carefully choreographed in advance. Around them swirled an indifferent chorus of police and pimps and drug dealers.

'Word gets around, counsellor,' she said, surprised to find that she was genuinely curious about the details of his new romance, perhaps even a little jealous. She'd never counted on him getting involved with anyone else. Don was her safety net, after all, the one she thought would always be there for her. 'What's her name? What's she like?'

'Her name is Trish,' he answered easily. 'She's very bright, very pretty, has very short, very blond hair, and a very wicked laugh.'

'That's a lot of verys.'

Don laughed, volunteering no further information.

'Is she a lawyer?'

'Not a chance.' He paused. 'And you? Seeing anyone special?'

'Just Fred,' she answered, gulping down the rest of her hot dog, crumpling its wrapper in the palm of her hand.

'You and that damn canary.' They reached the corner, waited while the light went from red to green. 'I have a confession to make,' he said, taking her elbow and guiding her across the street.

'You're getting married?' She was surprised by the urgency in the question she hadn't meant to ask.

'No,' he said lightly, but his voice betrayed him. It carried serious traces just beneath its surface, like a dangerous undertow beneath a deceptively smooth ocean. 'This is about Rick Ferguson.'

Jess stopped dead in the middle of the road, the hot dog wrapper dropping from her open palm. Surely she hadn't heard right. 'What?'

'Come on, Jess,' Don urged, tugging on her arm. 'You'll get us run over.'

She stopped again as soon as they reached the other side of the street. 'What do you know about Rick Ferguson?'

'He's my client.'

'What?'

'I didn't just run into you today, Jess,' Don told her sheepishly. 'I called your office. They said you were in court.'

'Since when have you been representing Rick Ferguson?'

'Since last week.'

'I don't believe it. Why?'

'Why? Because he hired me. What kind of a question is that?'

'Rick Ferguson is an animal. I can't believe you'd agree to represent him.'

'Jess,' Don said patiently, 'I'm a defense attorney. It's what I do.'

Jess nodded. While it was true that her ex-husband had built a very lucrative practice out of defending such low life, she would never understand how such a kind and thoughtful man could champion the rights of those whose thoughts precluded kindness, how a man of such fierce intelligence could use that intelligence on behalf of those who were merely fierce.

While she knew that Don had always been fascinated by the marginal elements of society, the years since their divorce had magnified this attraction. Increasingly he took on the kind of seemingly hopeless cases that other lawyers shunned. And won more often than not, she realized, not relishing the thought of facing her ex-husband in court. That had happened on two occasions in the last four years. He'd won both times.

'Jess, has it ever occurred to you that the man might be innocent?'

'The man, as you generously refer to him, has been positively identified by the woman he attacked.'

'And she couldn't be mistaken?'

'He broke into her apartment and beat her almost unconscious. Then he made her undress, one item at a time, nice and slow, so she had lots of time to get a good look at his face before he raped and sodomized her.'

'Rick Ferguson has an airtight alibi for the time of the attack,' Don reminded her.

Jess scoffed. 'I know – he was visiting his mother.'

'The woman put her house up as collateral for his bail. She's fully prepared to testify for him in court. Not to mention that there are thousands of men matching Rick Ferguson's description in this city. What makes you so sure Rick Ferguson is your man?'

'I'm sure.'

'Just like that?'

Jess told him about Rick Ferguson waiting for her when she arrived at work that morning and their subsequent altercation in the courthouse lobby.

'You're saying he threatened you?'

Jess saw Don struggling to stay neutral, to pretend she was just another Assistant State's Attorney, and not someone he obviously still cared deeply about. 'I'm saying I don't understand why you waste your precious talent on such obvious low-lifes,' she told him gently. 'Weren't you the one who told me that a lawyer's practice is ultimately a reflection of his own personality?'

He smiled. 'Nice to know you were listening.'

She reached over and kissed him lightly on the cheek. 'I better get back to work.'

'I take it that means you won't consider dropping the charges?' His statement curled into a question.

'Not a chance.'

He smiled sadly, taking her hand and walking her back toward the Administration Building, squeezing her thin fingers inside his massive palm before releasing her.

Watch to make sure I get inside safely, she urged silently as she raced up the concrete stairs.

But when she reached the top and turned around, he was already gone.

Chapter Three

The nightmare always started the same way: Jess was sitting in the sterile reception area of a doctor's office reading an old magazine while somewhere beside her a phone was ringing. 'It's your mother,' the doctor informed her, pulling a phone out of his large black doctor's bag and handing it over.

'Mother, where are you?' Jess asked. 'The doctor's waiting for you.'

'Meet me in the John Hancock Building in fifteen minutes. I'll explain everything when I see you.'

Suddenly Jess stood before a bank of elevators, but no matter how many times she pressed the call button, no elevator came. Locating the stairs, she raced down the seven flights only to find the door to the outside locked. She pushed; she pulled; she begged; she cried. The door wouldn't budge.

In the next instant, she was in front of the Art Institute on Michigan Avenue, the sun bouncing off the sidewalk into her eyes. 'Come inside,' an auburn-haired woman with grey eyes called from the top step of the impressive structure. 'The tour's about to begin, and you're keeping everybody waiting.'

'I really can't stay,' Jess told the crowd, whose faces were a blur of brown eyes and red mouths. The group paused for several minutes in front of Seurat's masterpiece, Sunday Afternoon in the Park.

'Let's play connect the dots,' Don called out, as Jess broke free and hurried outside in time to leap on board a bus that was pulling away. But the bus headed in the wrong direction and she ended up in Union Station. She hailed a cab, only to have the driver misunderstand her instructions and take her to Roosevelt Road.

He was waiting for her when she stepped out of the taxi, a

faceless figure all in black, standing perfectly still by the side of the road. Immediately, Jess tried to get back in the car, but the taxi had disappeared. Slowly, the figure in black advanced toward her.

Death, Jess understood, bolting for the open road. 'Help me!' she cried, the shadow of Death advancing effortlessly behind her as she raced up the steps of her parents' home. She pulled open the screen door, pushing it shut after her, desperately trying to secure the latch as Death's hand reached for the door, his face coming into clear view.

Rick Ferguson.

'No!' Jess screamed, lurching forward in her bed, her heart pounding, the bedding soaked in sweat.

No wonder he'd felt so familiar, she realized, drawing her knees to her chin and sobbing, her breath slamming against her lungs, as if someone were playing racquetball in her chest. A product of her darkest imaginings, he'd stepped, quite literally, out of her dreams and into her life. The nightmares that used to haunt her were back, and the figure had a name – Rick Ferguson.

Jess pushed away the wet sheets and struggled to her feet, only to feel her legs give way beneath her. She collapsed in a crumpled heap on the floor, trying to catch her breath, afraid she was going to throw up. 'Oh, God,' she muttered, addressing the panic as if it were a physical presence in the room. 'Please stop. Please go away.'

Jess stretched toward the white china lamp on the night table beside her bed and flipped on the light. The room snapped into focus: soft peaches mixed with delicate greys and blues, a double bed, a Drury rug, a white wicker chair over which hung her clothes for the next day, a chest of drawers, a small mirror, a poster by Niki de Saint Phalle, another by Henri Matisse. She tried to will herself back to normalcy by concentrating on the wood grain of the light oak floor, the stitching on the pale peach curtains, the white duvet, the expanse of high ceiling. One of the nice things about living in an old brownstone, she tried to remind herself, was the high ceilings. You didn't find that in modern glass highrises.

It wasn't working. Her heart continued to race as her breath curled into a tight little ball in the middle of her throat. Once again she forced herself to her feet, teetering on legs that threatened to send her sprawling, toward the tiny, purely functional bathroom that the landlord had laughingly described as ensuite when she'd moved in just after her divorce. She ran the tap and threw cold water across her face and shoulders, letting the water sneak down underneath her pink nightshirt and onto her breasts and belly.

She rested against the side of the tub and stared into the toilet bowl. There was nothing she hated worse than throwing up. Ever since she was a small child and had overdosed on red licorice sticks and banana splits at Allison Nichol's birthday party, she'd dreaded throwing up. Every night for years afterward, she'd gone to bed asking her mother, 'Will I be all right?' And every night her mother had answered patiently that yes, she'd be fine. 'Do you promise?' the child had persisted. 'I promise,' had come the immediate reply.

How ironic then that it had been the mother, and not the child, who'd been in danger.

And now the nightmare that had plagued her after her mother's disappearance was back, along with the shortness of breath, the trembling hands, the paralyzing, nameless dread that permeated every fiber in her body. It wasn't fair, Jess thought, leaning over the toilet bowl, gritting her teeth against the possibility of what might follow, clutching at the pain that stabbed repeatedly at her chest, like the dull blade of a long knife.

She could call Don, she thought, resting her cheek against the cool lid of the toilet. He always knew what to do. So many nights he'd held her trembling against him, his hands softly stroking the damp hair away from her forehead as he engulfed her inside his large arms, and assured her, as her mother had, that she would be all right. Yes, she could call Don. He'd help her. He'd know exactly what to do.

Jess pushed herself back toward the bedroom, perched precariously on the edge of her bed, and reached for the phone, then stopped. She knew all she had to do was phone Don and he would dash right over, leave whatever he was doing, whomever he was with, and race to her side, stay with her as long as she needed him. She knew Don still loved her, had never stopped. She knew that, and that was why she knew she couldn't call him.

He was involved with someone else now. Trish, she repeated, examining the name in her mind. Probably short for Patricia. Trish with the wicked laugh. The *very* wicked laugh, she heard him say, recalling the proud twinkle in his eyes. Had the possibility that she might be losing Don to another woman been enough to precipitate this anxiety attack?

The attack was over, she realized with a start. Her heart was no longer racing; her breathing had returned to normal; her body was no longer awash in perspiration. She fell back against her pillow, luxuriating in the sense of renewed well-being. Surprisingly, she discovered she was hungry.

Jess shuffled through the darkened hallway to the kitchen, heading directly for the freezer. She opened it, recoiling from the sudden flash of light, and drew out a box of frozen pizzas, quickly tearing at the cellophane around each individual pie and popping one stiff disk into the microwave oven that sat on the side counter. She pressed the necessary buttons and listened to the soft whir of the micro rays as they circled their frozen prey, careful not to stand directly in front of the oven.

Don had warned her against standing directly in its path when it was on. But surely these things are perfectly safe, she had argued. Why take chances? had come his instant rebuttal. He was probably right, she'd decided, adopting his precautions as her own. You never knew what harmful rays might be lurking about, just waiting for their chance to feast on larger game.

Jess watched the microwave silently ticking down its seconds, then defiantly thrust her body directly in its path.

'Come and get me,' she cried, then laughed again, feeling almost giddy. Was she really standing in her small galley kitchen at three o'clock in the morning challenging her microwave oven?

The timer beeped five times, announcing her pizza was ready, and Jess gently lifted the now hot piece of pie into her hands and carried it into the large combination living and dining area. She loved her apartment, had from the first moment she'd walked up the three flights to its door. It was old and full of interesting angles, the bay windows of its west wall looking out onto Orchard Street, only a block and a half away from where she'd lived as a child, and a far cry from the modern three-bedroom apartment on Lake Shore Drive she'd shared with Don.

It was the sharing part of her life she missed the most: having someone to talk to; to be with; to cuddle up next to at the end of the day. It had felt nice to share big ideas, small triumphs, needless worries. It had felt comforting to be part of a couple, safe to be part of *Jess and Don.*

Jess switched on the stereo that rested against the wall across from the old tie-dyed velvet sofa she'd found in a second-hand store on Armitage Avenue, and listened as the ineffably beautiful strains of César Franck's violin and piano concerto filled the room. Beside her, her canary, his cage covered for the night, started to sing. Jess sank into the soft swirls of her velvet sofa, listening to the sweet sounds, and eating her pizza in the dark.

'Ladies and gentlemen of the jury, have you reached your verdict?' the judge asked, and Jess felt a rush of adrenaline surge through her body. It had been nearly twenty-four hours since she had delivered her closing argument. The jury had deliberated for almost eight hours before deciding that no consensus was immediately forthcoming, and Judge Harris had impatiently ordered them to a hotel for the night, under careful instructions not to discuss the case with anybody. They had resumed their deliberations at nine o'clock this morning.

Surprisingly, an hour later, they were ready.

The jury foreman said yes, they had reached their verdict, and Judge Harris instructed the defendant to please rise. Jess listened, her breathing stilled, as the jury foreman intoned solemnly, 'We, the jury, find the defendant, Douglas Phillips . . . not guilty.'

Not guilty.

Jess felt a pin prick her side, sensed her body slowly losing air.

Not guilty.

'My God, they didn't believe me,' Erica Barnowski whispered beside her.

Not guilty.

Doug Phillips embraced his attorney. Rosemary Michaud gave Jess a discreet victory smile.

Not guilty.

'Damn it,' Neil Strayhorn said. 'I really thought we had a chance.'

Not guilty.

'What kind of justice is this?' Erica Barnowski demanded, her voice gaining strength through indignation. 'The man admitted holding a knife to my throat, for God's sake, and the jury says he isn't guilty?'

Jess could only nod. She'd been part of the justice system too long to harbor any delusions about its so-called justice. Guilt was a relative concept, a matter of ghosts and shadows. Like beauty, it was in the eye of the beholder. Like truth, it was subject to interpretation.

'What do I do now?' Erica Barnowski was asking. 'I lost my job, my boyfriend, my self-respect. What do I do now?' She didn't wait for an answer, fleeing the courtroom before Jess had time to think of a suitable response.

What could she have said? Don't worry, tomorrow is another day? Things will look brighter in the morning? It's always darkest before the dawn? How about, what goes around comes around? He'll get his? If it's meant to be, it's meant to be? Of course, there was always, tough luck, better luck next time, heaven helps those who help themselves. And for added comfort, give it time, you did the right thing, it only hurts for a little while, life goes on.

There it was in a nutshell, she thought: the wisdom of the ages condensed into three small words – life goes on.

Jess gathered her papers together, glancing over her shoulder as the defendant shook hands with each of the jurors in turn. The jury members carefully avoided making eye contact with her as they filed from the courtroom minutes later, the woman juror with the intelligent face and soft grey eyes being the only one to say goodbye to Jess. Jess nodded in return, curious as to what part this woman had played in the jury's final decision. Had she been convinced of Douglas Phillips's innocence all along, or had she been the reason for the lengthy deliberations, the final hold-out for a guilty verdict, giving in only when her obstinacy threatened to force a mistrial? Or had she sat there, impatiently tapping her foot, waiting for the others to come to their senses and see things her way?

Not guilty.

'Do you want to talk about it?' Neil asked.

Jess shook her head, not sure whether she was more angry or sad. Later there would be plenty of time to analyze and discuss whether they could have done things differently. Right now, there was nothing anyone could do. It was over. She couldn't change the outcome of the case any more than she could change the facts of the case, and the fact, as Greg Oliver had clearly stated the day before, was that no jury in the land was going to convict a man of rape when the woman wasn't wearing panties.

Jess knew she wasn't ready to return to the office. Quite apart from the unpleasant certainty of having to acknowledge Greg Oliver's superior savvy, she needed time alone to come to terms with the jury's decision, time to accept it before moving on, time to deal with her anger and frustration. With her loss. Time to get her mind ready for her next case.

Ultimately that was the biggest truth about the American justice system: one person's life was just another person's case.

Jess found herself on California Avenue with no clear

memory of having left the Court House. It was unlike her not to know exactly what she was doing, she thought, feeling the cold through her thin tweed jacket. The weather forecasters were still predicting the possibility of snow. Predicting a possibility, she repeated silently, thinking this an interesting concept. She bundled her jacket around her, and started walking. 'I might as well be naked,' she said out loud, knowing nobody would be paying attention. Just another casualty of the justice system, she thought, a sudden impulse guiding her aboard a number 60 bus, heading for downtown Chicago.

'What am I doing?' she muttered under her breath, taking a seat near the driver. It wasn't like her to act on impulse. Impulses were for those who lacked control over their lives, she thought, closing her eyes, the steady hum of the motor vibrating through her.

She wasn't sure how long the bus had been in motion before she reopened her eyes, or when she first realized that the woman juror with the auburn hair and soft grey eyes was sitting at the back of the bus. She was even less sure at what moment she decided to follow her. It was certainly nothing she had consciously planned. And yet, here she was, approximately half an hour later, exiting the bus several paces behind the woman, following her onto Michigan Avenue, trailing her from a distance of perhaps twenty feet. What on earth was she doing?

Several blocks down Michigan Avenue, the woman stopped to look in a jewelry store window and Jess did the same, gazing past the display of precious gems and gold bracelets, finding her shivering, quizzical reflection in the glass, as if her image were trying to figure out who she was. She'd never been into jewelry. The only jewelry she'd ever worn had been her simple gold wedding band. Don had given up buying her trinkets during their marriage when he found them inevitably consigned to the back of her dresser drawer. It just wasn't her style, she'd explained. She always felt like a little girl playing dress-up in her mother's things.

Her mother, she thought, realizing that the woman juror had

moved on. How could she have considered, even for an instant, that the woman looked anything like her mother? This woman was approximately five feet five inches tall and 140 pounds; in comparison, her mother had been almost four inches taller and ten pounds heavier. Not to mention the differences in the color of their eyes and hair, or in the amount of make-up they wore, Jess thought, confident that her mother would never have worn lipstick that pink or blush that obviously applied. Unlike her mother, this woman was clearly skittish and insecure, her heavy make-up a mask against time. No, there was nothing similar about the two women at all.

The woman juror stopped in front of another shop, and Jess found herself staring at an ugly assortment of leather bags and cases. Was the woman going to go inside the store? Buy herself a little treat? A reward for a job well done? Well, why not? Jess thought, turning her head discreetly away as the woman pushed open the door and headed for the center of the store.

Should she follow her inside? Jess wondered, thinking she could use a new briefcase. Hers was very old; Don had bought it for her when she graduated from law school and, unlike his jewelry purchases, he certainly couldn't complain about this gift's lack of use. The once shiny black leather had grown scratched and smudged, its stitching frayed, the zipper forever catching on some wayward threads. Maybe it was time to give it up, buy a new one. Sever her ties with the past once and for all.

The woman emerged from the store with only the brown handbag she'd been carrying when she went in. She gathered the collar of her dark green coat around her chin and stuffed her gloved hands inside her pockets. Jess found herself mimicking the woman's actions, following several paces behind.

They crossed the Chicago River, the Wrigley Building looming high on one side of the wide street, the Tribune Tower on the other. Downtown Chicago was a wealth of architectural splendors, boasting skyscrapers by the likes of Mies Van der Rohe, Helmut Jahn, and Bruce Graham. Jess had often contemplated taking a lecture cruise along Lake Michigan and the Chicago River. Somehow she'd never gotten around to it.

The woman continued for several more paces then stopped abruptly, spinning around. 'Why are you following me?' she demanded angrily, tapping impatient fingers against the sleeve of her coat, like a schoolteacher questioning an errant pupil.

Jess felt herself reduced in stature to that of a small child, terrified of getting her knuckles rapped. 'I'm sorry,' she stammered, wondering again what she was doing. 'I didn't mean to . . .'

'I saw you on the bus, but I didn't think anything of it,' the woman said, clearly flustered. 'Then I saw you by the jewelry store, but I thought, well, everybody has the right to look in the same window, I'm sure it's just a coincidence. But when you were still there when I came out of that leather goods store, I knew you had to be following me. Why? What do you want?'

'I don't want anything. Really, I wasn't following you.'

The woman's eyes narrowed, challenged her own.

'I . . . I'm not sure why I was following you,' Jess admitted after a pause. She couldn't remember a time she'd felt more foolish.

'It wasn't you, you know,' the woman began, relaxing slightly. 'If that's what you wanted to know. It wasn't anything you said or did.'

'I beg your pardon?'

'We thought you were wonderful,' she continued. 'The jury . . . we thought what you said about a lack of common sense not excusing a lack of common decency, well, we thought that was wonderful. We argued about it for a long time. Quite vehemently.'

'But you didn't accept it,' Jess stated, surprised by how eager she was to understand how the jury had arrived at its verdict.

The woman looked toward the sidewalk. 'It wasn't an easy decision. We did what we thought was right. We know that Mr Phillips was wrong in what he did, but, in the end, we decided that to put the man in prison for years, to make him lose his job and his livelihood . . . for an error in judgement, like you said . . .'

'I wasn't talking about the defendant's lack of judgement!' Jess heard the horror in her voice. How could they have misunderstood?

'Yes, we knew that,' the woman quickly explained. 'We just thought that it could apply to both sides.'

Wonderful, Jess thought, catching a gulp of cold air, finding it hard to appreciate the irony of the situation, harder still to exhale.

'We loved your little suits,' the woman continued, as if trying to cheer her up.

'My little suits?'

'Yes. The grey one in particular. One of the women said she was thinking of asking you where you bought it.'

'You were looking at my suit?'

'Appearances are very important,' the woman said. 'That's what I'm always telling my daughters. First impressions and all that.'

She reached out and patted Jess's hand. 'You make a very good impression, dear.'

Jess wasn't sure whether to curtsy or scream. She felt her heart starting to pound against the tweed fabric of her jacket.

'Anyway,' the woman was saying. 'You did a very good job.'

How could someone with such intelligent eyes be so stupid? Jess asked herself, finding it difficult to catch her breath.

'I really should get going,' the woman said, obviously uncomfortable with Jess's silence. She took a few steps, then stopped. 'Are you okay? You're looking a little pale.'

Jess tried to speak, could only nod, forcing her lips into what she hoped was a reassuring smile. The woman smiled in return, then walked briskly down the street, taking several quick peeks over her shoulder to where Jess remained standing. She probably wants to make sure I'm not following her, Jess thought, wondering again what had possessed her. What had she been doing trailing after this woman, for God's sake? What was she doing now?

Having a goddamn panic attack, she realized. 'Oh, God,' she moaned, fighting off the anxiety that was making her head too light to hold down even as it made her legs too heavy to lift. 'This is ridiculous. What am I going to do?'

Jess felt her eyes fill with tears, and brushed them angrily aside. 'I can't believe I'm crying in the middle of goddamn Michigan Avenue,' she berated herself. 'I can't believe I'm *talking to myself* in the middle of goddamn Michigan Avenue!' Unlike the drug pushers and crazies along California Avenue, the well-heeled shoppers along Michigan Avenue were much more likely to notice, although no more likely to do anything about it.

She forced her feet toward a nearby bus stop, leaned against its side. Even through her jacket, it felt cold against her skin. She wouldn't give in to this, she thought angrily. She would not let these stupid attacks get the better of her.

Think pleasant thoughts, she told herself. Think about getting a massage; think about a holiday in Hawaii; think about your baby nieces. She imagined their soft heads nestled against her cold cheeks, realized she was supposed to be at her sister's house for dinner at six o'clock.

How could she go to her sister's for dinner? What if she were still in the throes of an anxiety attack? What if she had another one in front of everybody? Did she really want to inflict her neuroses on those she loved most?

What's family for? Maureen would undoubtedly ask.

Jess felt the bile rise in her throat. God, was she going to throw up? Throw up in the middle of goddamn Michigan Avenue? She counted to ten, then twenty, swallowing rapidly, once, twice, three times, before the feeling finally disappeared. 'Take deep breaths,' Don used to tell her, so she did, filling her lungs with air, trying to keep from doubling over with the pain.

Nobody noticed her suffering. Pedestrians continued to file past, one even asked her the time. Not so different from California Avenue after all, she thought as a bus pulled to a halt in front of her and opened its doors, disgorging several people, who pushed past her as if she weren't there. The driver waited several seconds for her to step in, shrugged his shoulders when she didn't, closed the doors and drove on. Jess felt the warm gust of dirty air from the bus's exhaust against her face as the bus departed. It filled her eyes and nostrils. She found it oddly soothing.

Soon, her breathing started to normalize. She felt the color returning to her cheeks, the paralysis beginning to lift. 'You're okay now,' she told herself, pushing one leg in front of the other, stepping gingerly off the curb, as if stepping into a too hot bath. 'You're okay now. It's over.'

The car came out of nowhere.

It happened so fast, was so unexpected, that, even as it was happening, Jess had the strange feeling it was happening to someone else. She was somewhere outside her body, watching the events alongside the half dozen spectators who quickly gathered at the scene. Jess felt a rush of air beside her, saw her body spinning like a top, took fleeting note of the white Chrysler as it disappeared around the corner. Only then did she return to the body kneeling on the side of the road. Only then did she feel the stinging at her knees and palms. Only then did she hear the voices.

'Are you all right?'

'My God, I thought you were a goner for sure.'

'He came this close! Missed you by not more than two inches!'

'I'm fine,' someone said, and Jess recognized the voice as her own. 'I guess I wasn't paying attention.' She wondered momentarily why she was accepting responsibility for something that was clearly not her fault. She'd almost been run down by a maniac in a white Chrysler who'd sped by and hadn't even bothered to stop; she'd bruised her hands and scraped her legs when she hit the pavement; her tweed jacket was streaked with grime; her panty hose were shredded at the knees. And she was feeling guilty about causing a scene. 'I must have been daydreaming,' she apologized, rising shakily to her feet. 'But it's okay now. I'll be fine.

'I'll be fine,' she repeated, limping toward the opposite corner and hailing a passing taxi, crawling inside. 'I'll be fine.'

Chapter Four

Jess pulled her red Mustang into the driveway of her sister's large, white, wood-frame house on Sheraton Road in Evanston at precisely three minutes before six o'clock. 'You'll be fine,' she told herself, turning off the ignition and gathering up the shopping bag containing wine and gifts from the seat beside her. 'Stay calm, stay cool, don't let Barry draw you into any silly arguments,' she continued, sliding out of the car and walking up the front walk to the large glass-panelled door. 'Everything will be fine.'

The door opened just as her hand reached for the bell.

'Jess,' Barry said, his voice blowing down the tree-lined street, like a gust of wind. Leaves swirled at her feet. 'Right on time, as always.'

'How are you, Barry?' Jess stepped into the large cream-colored marble foyer.

'Never better,' came the instant reply. Barry always said 'never better'. 'How about you?'

'I'm fine.' She took a deep breath, thrust the bottle of wine in his direction. 'It's from Chile. The man in the liquor store said it came highly recommended.'

Barry examined the label closely, clearly sceptical. 'Well, thank you, although I hope you won't mind if we save it for another time. I already have some expensive French on ice. Here, let me help you off with your coat.' He discarded the wine on the small antique table to the left of the front door, and started awkwardly pulling at her sleeve.

'It's okay, Barry. I think I can manage on my own.'

'Well, at least let me hang it up for you.'

Jess decided against playing tug-of-war with Barry for her coat. 'Is Maureen upstairs?'

'She's putting the twins to bed.' He hung her coat in the closet and led her toward the predominantly rose- and white-colored living room, accented by strong blocs of black: a black concert grand piano that took up much of the front part of the room, although nobody played; a black marble fireplace, in which a fire already roared.

'I'll go upstairs and say hello. I bought them something.' Jess indicated the Marshall Field's shopping bag in her hand.

'They'll be awake again in a few hours. You can give it to them then.'

'Jess, is that you?' Maureen called from upstairs.

'Coming right up,' Jess answered, her body gravitating toward the center hall.

'Don't you dare,' Maureen called back. 'I've just got everybody settled. Stay and talk to Barry. I'll be down in two minutes.'

'She'll be down in two minutes,' Barry parroted. 'So, what do you say? Think you can spend two minutes talking to your brother-in-law?'

Jess smiled, and sat down in one of two white wing chairs across from Barry, who perched on the edge of the rose-colored sofa, as if ready to hang on her every word. Ready to pounce, more likely, Jess thought, wondering why she and Barry had never been able to connect. What was it about the man that rubbed her the wrong way? she wondered, conscious of his clear blue eyes recording her every gesture. He wasn't ugly. He wasn't stupid. He wasn't overtly unpleasant.

Why could she only think of him in the negative? Surely there was more to the man than what he wasn't.

She had tried to like him. When he'd married her sister some six years ago, Jess had assumed she would like anyone who made her sister happy. She'd been wrong.

Maybe it was the sneaky way he tried to mask his receding hairline by combing his thinning hair from one side of his head to the other that bothered her. Or the fact that his nails were better manicured than her own, that he boasted of flossing his teeth after every meal. Maybe it was his habit of always wearing a shirt and tie, even under a casual cardigan sweater, like tonight.

More likely it was the thinly veiled chauvinism of his remarks, she decided, his casually dismissive ways, the fact that he could never admit he was wrong. Or maybe it was the fact that he had taken a bright young graduate of the Harvard Business School and turned her into Total Woman, someone who was so busy decorating their home and producing babies that she had no time to think about resuming her once promising career. What would their mother have thought?

'You look nice,' Barry told her. 'That's a lovely sweater. You should wear blue more often.'

'It's green.'

'Green? No, it's blue.'

Were they really arguing about the color of her sweater? 'Can we settle for turquoise?' she asked.

Barry looked sceptical, shook his head. 'It's blue,' he pronounced, looking toward the fire. Barry always lit a perfect fire.

Jess took a deep breath. 'So, Barry, how's business?'

He tossed aside her inquiry with a wave of his hand. 'You don't really want to hear about my business.'

'I don't?'

'Do you?'

'Barry, I asked you a simple question. If it's going to get too complicated, then . . .'

'Business is great. Terrific. Couldn't be better.'

'Good.'

'Not good.' He laughed. 'Great. Terrific. Couldn't be better.'

'Couldn't be better,' Jess repeated, looking toward the stairs. What was keeping her sister?

'Actually,' Barry was saying, 'I had quite a spectacular day today.'

'And what made it so spectacular?' Jess asked.

'I stole a very important client away from my former partner.' Barry chuckled. 'The son-of-a-bitch never saw it coming.'

'I thought you two were friends.'

'So did he.' The chuckle became a laugh. 'Guy thinks he can

screw me and get away with it.' He tapped his finger against the side of his head. 'I never forget. I get even.'

'You get even,' Jess repeated.

'Hey, I didn't do anything illegal.' He winked. 'By the way, some information about a new type of individual retirement account crossed my desk this afternoon. It's something I think you should take a look at. If you'd like, I could send the information on to you.

'Sure,' Jess said. 'That'd be great.'

'I think I'll mention it to your Dad as well.'

They both checked their watches. What was keeping her father? He knew how much she worried whenever he was late.

'How was *your* day?' Barry asked, managing to look as if he cared.

'Could have been better,' Jess replied sardonically, using Barry's words, not really surprised when he failed to notice. I lost a case I was desperate to win, I had an anxiety attack in the middle of Michigan Avenue, and I was almost killed by a hit-and-run driver, but hey, a woman said she liked my suit, so the day wasn't a total loss, she continued silently.

'I don't know how you stand it,' Barry was saying.

'Stand what?'

'Day after day of dealing with scum,' he said succinctly.

'I'm the one who gets to put the scum in jail,' she told him.

'When you win.'

'When I win,' she agreed sadly.

'I've got to hand it to you, Jess,' he said, jumping to his feet. 'I never thought you'd stick it out this long. What can I get you to drink?' He said the two sentences as if one naturally flowed from the other.

'What do you mean?'

'I mean, would you like some wine or something more substantial?'

'Why wouldn't you think I'd stick it out?' Jess asked, genuinely bewildered by his earlier remark.

He shook his head. 'I don't know. I guess I thought that you'd have opted for something more lucrative by now. I mean, with your grades, you could have gone anywhere you wanted.'

'I did.'

Jess saw the confusion settle behind Barry's eyes. Clearly, her career choices were beyond his comprehension. 'So, what can I get you to drink?' he asked again.

'A Coke would be great.'

There was a moment's silence. 'We stopped buying soft drinks,' he said. 'We figure if we don't keep soft drinks in the house, then Tyler won't be tempted. Besides, you're the only one who ever drinks them.'

It was Jess's turn to look confused.

There was a sudden cascade of footsteps down the stairs and through the hallway. Jess saw an explosion of dark hair, enormous blue eyes, and small hands waving frantically in the air. In the next instant, her three-year-old nephew was across the pink and white carpet and in her arms. 'Did you buy me a present?' he said instead of hello.

'Don't I always?' Jess reached beside her into the Marshall Field's bag, trying to avoid the realization that her nephew was wearing a shirt and tie, similar to his father's.

'Just a minute.' Barry's voice was swift, stern. 'We don't get any presents until we've said our proper hellos. Hello, Auntie Jess,' he coached.

Tyler said nothing. Ignoring the boy's father, Jess pulled a model airplane out of the bag, and deposited it in her nephew's waiting hands.

'Wow!' Tyler dropped off her lap onto the floor, studying the toy plane from all angles, whirling it through the air.

'What do we say?' Barry said, trying again, his voice tight. 'Don't we say, thank you, Auntie Jess?'

'It's okay, Barry,' Jess told him. 'He can thank me later.'

Barry looked as if the collar under his silk tie had suddenly shrunk two sizes. 'I don't appreciate your attempts to undermine my authority,' he pronounced.

'My attempts to what?' Jess asked. Surely, she must have misunderstood.

'You heard me. And don't give me that innocent look. You

know damn well what I'm talking about.'

Tyler ran happily between his father and his aunt, dipping his new plane between their hips and the floor, oblivious of the tension in the room.

Neither Barry nor Jess moved. Both stood in their respective positions, Barry by the sofa, Jess by her chair, as if waiting for something to happen, someone to interrupt.

'Isn't the doorbell supposed to ring now or something?' Jess asked, grateful when she saw Barry's jaw relax into a close approximation of a smile. If there was going to be an argument, and there was always an argument when she and Barry got together, it would not be her fault. She had promised herself that on the thirty-minute drive from her apartment to the upper class suburb.

'Oh, good,' Maureen said, suddenly appearing in the doorway. 'You two are getting along.'

Barry was immediately at his wife's side, kissing her cheek. 'Nothing to it,' he assured her.

Maureen gave her husband and sister one of her luminous smiles. Despite the fact that she had to be exhausted, she looked radiant in a crisp white shirt over black wool pants. Her figure was almost back to normal, Jess noticed, wondering if Barry had talked his wife into resuming her strict exercise routine. As if looking after a big house and three small children wasn't enough to keep her busy.

'You look wonderful,' Jess told her sister truthfully.

'And you look tired,' Maureen said, giving her sister a hug. 'You getting enough sleep?'

Jess shrugged, recalling her recent nightmare.

'Look what Auntie Jess gave me,' Tyler said from the floor, proudly brandishing his new airplane.

'Isn't that wonderful! I hope you said thank you.'

'Your sister doesn't believe in thank-yous,' Barry said, walking across the room to the wet bar and pouring himself a scotch and water. 'Can I get anybody anything?'

'Not for me,' Maureen said. 'That's a great sweater, Jess. You should wear blue more often. It's a great color for you.'

'It's green,' Barry corrected, lifting his eyebrows toward his sister-in-law. 'Isn't that what you said, Jess?'

'Oh, no, it's definitely blue,' Maureen said flatly. 'No question.'

'Are the twins asleep?' Jess asked.

'For the moment. But that never lasts very long.'

'I bought them a little something.'

'Oh, Jess, you don't have to buy them something every time you come over.'

'Of course I do. What are Aunties for?'

'Well, thank you.' Maureen took the Marshall Field's bag from Jess's hand and peeked inside.

'It's just some bibs. I thought they were kind of cute.'

'They're adorable.' Maureen held up the small white terry cloth bibs festooned with bright red apples and berries. 'Oh, look at these. Aren't they sweet, Barry?'

Jess didn't hear Barry's reply. Could this really be her sister? she was wondering, trying not to stare. Could they really have shared the same mother? Could the woman she'd watched graduate with honors from one of the top colleges in the land be so enthralled with a couple of five-dollar bibs from Marshall Field's? Could she really be proffering them forward for her husband's approval? From Summa Cum Laude to Stepford Wife?

'So, what happened in court today?' Maureen asked, as if sensing Jess's discomfort. 'You get a verdict?'

'The wrong one.'

'You were kind of expecting that, weren't you?' Maureen took Jess's hands and led her to the sofa, not relinquishing her hands even after they were both seated.

'I was hoping.'

'It must be tough.'

'So's your sister,' Barry said, taking a long sip of his drink, not releasing it from his lips until the glass was almost empty. 'Aren't you, Jess?'

'Something wrong with that?' Jess heard the dare escape her voice.

'Not as long as it's confined to the courtroom.'

Don't bite, she thought. Don't let him get to you. 'I see,' she said, despite her best efforts. 'It's okay to be strong when I'm fighting someone else's battles, just not my own.'

'Who says you always have to be fighting?'

'I don't think Jess is tough,' Maureen offered, her voice questioning.

'Tell me, Jess,' Barry asked, 'why is it that as soon as a woman gets a little power, she loses her sense of humor?'

'And why is it that whenever a man fails at being funny, he attacks a woman's sense of humor?' Jess shot back.

'There's a big difference between being strong and being tough,' Barry said, returning to his original point, and emphasizing it with a nod of his head, as if this were one of those constitutional truths supposed to be self-evident. 'A man can afford to be both; a woman can't.'

'Jess,' Maureen intervened softly, 'you know Barry's just teasing you.'

Jess jumped to her feet. 'Bullshit, he's teasing!'

Tyler's head snapped toward his aunt.

'Kindly watch your language in this house,' Barry admonished.

Jess felt the sting of his rebuke sharper than a slap across the face. She desperately hoped she wouldn't cry. 'So now we don't swear either, is that right?' she said, using her voice to keep the tears at bay. 'We don't drink Coke and we don't swear.'

Barry looked at his wife, his hands in the air, as if giving up.

'Jess, please,' Maureen implored, tugging on her sister's hand, trying to draw her back down on the couch.

'I just want to make sure I have all your husband's rules straight.' Jess glared at her brother-in-law, who was suddenly a poster boy for reason and calm. He'd gotten to her again, she realized, disgusted and ashamed of herself. 'I don't know how you do it,' she muttered dejectedly. 'It must take some special skill.'

'What are you fulminating about now?' Barry asked, a look of genuine puzzlement in his eyes.

'Fulminating?' Jess gasped, abandoning any further attempts at control. 'Fulminating?'

'Tyler,' Maureen began, rising and gently steering her son out of the room, 'why don't you take your new toy upstairs and play with it there?'

'I want to stay here,' the boy protested.

'Tyler, go play in your room until we call you for dinner,' his father instructed.

The boy jumped into immediate action.

'His master's voice,' Jess said as the youngster scampered up the stairs.

'Jess, please,' Maureen urged.

'I didn't start it.' Jess heard the hurt child in her voice, was angry and embarrassed that they could hear it too.

'It doesn't matter who started it,' Maureen was saying, speaking as if to two children, refusing to make eye contact with either of them. 'What matters is that it stops before it goes any further.'

'Consider it stopped.' Barry's voice filled the large room.

Jess said nothing.

'Jess?'

Jess nodded, her head swimming with anger and guilt. Guilt for her anger, anger for her guilt.

'So, what's next on the prosecutor's agenda?' Maureen's words were full of forced joviality, as if she were visiting a terminally ill patient in the hospital. Her normally soft voice was a shrill half octave higher than usual. She returned to the rose-colored sofa and patted the seat beside her with an intensity approaching desperation. Neither Jess nor Barry moved.

'A few drug charges I'm hoping we can plead out,' Jess told her, 'and I go to trial the week after next on another assault case. Oh, and I have a meeting on Monday with the lawyer who's representing that man who shot his estranged wife with a cross-bow.' Jess massaged the bridge of her nose, disturbed by the matter-of-factness in her tone.

'With a cross-bow, my God!' Maureen shuddered. 'How barbaric.'

'You must have read about it in the paper a few months back. It made all the front pages.'

'Well, that explains why I missed it,' Maureen stated. 'I never read anything in the papers these days but the recipes.'

Jess struggled to keep her dismay from registering on her face, knew she was failing.

'It's just too depressing,' Maureen explained, her voice as much apology as explanation. 'And there's only so much time.' Her voice trailed off to a whisper.

'So, what special treat have you concocted for us for tonight?' Barry joined his wife on the couch, taking her hands in his.

Maureen took a deep breath, pulling her eyes away from Jess and staring straight ahead, as if she were reading from an imaginary blackboard. 'To start with, there's a mock turtle soup, followed by a honey-glazed chicken with sesame seeds, candied yams and grilled veggies, then a green salad with pecans and gorgonzola cheese, and finally, a pear mousse with raspberry sauce.'

'Sounds fabulous.' Barry gave his wife's hand an extra squeeze.

'Sounds like you've been cooking all week.'

'Sounds like much more work than it actually is,' Maureen said modestly.

'I don't know how you do it,' Jess said, sputtering over the 'how' when what she really wanted to say was 'why'.

'Actually, I find it very relaxing.'

'You should try it, Jess,' Barry said.

'You should stuff it, Barry,' Jess said in return.

Once again both Jess and Barry were on their feet. 'That's it,' he was saying. 'I've had enough.'

'You've had more than enough,' Jess told him. 'And for much too long. At my sister's expense.'

'Jess, you're wrong.'

'I'm not wrong, Maureen.' Jess began pacing the room.

'What's happened to you? You used to be this fabulous, smart woman who knew the morning paper backwards and forwards. Now, you only read recipes? For God's sake, you were on your way to a vice-presidency! Now you're on your way to the kitchen! This man has you up to your eyeballs in dirty dishes and dirty diapers and you're trying to convince me that you like it!'

'She doesn't have to convince you of anything,' Barry said angrily.

'I think my sister is perfectly capable of speaking for herself. Or is that another new rule around here? She only speaks through you.'

'You know what I think, Jess?' Barry asked, not waiting for an answer. 'I think you're jealous.'

'Jealous?'

'Yes, jealous. Because your sister has a husband and a family, and she's happy. And what have you got? A freezer full of frozen pizzas and a goddamn canary!'

'Next you'll tell me all I really need is a good fuck!'

'Jess!' Maureen looked toward the stairs, her eyes filling with tears.

'What you really need is a good spanking,' Barry said, walking to the piano by the large picture window, and slamming his knuckles against the keys. The sound, an unpleasant fistful of sharps and flats, swept through the house, like a sudden brushfire. From upstairs, the twins started to cry, first one, then the other.

Maureen lowered her head into her chest, crying into the crisp white collar of her blouse. Then without looking at either Jess or Barry, she bolted from the room.

'Dammit,' Jess whispered, her own eyes filling with tears.

'One day,' Barry said quietly, 'you'll go too far.'

'I know,' Jess said, her voice dripping sarcasm. 'You never forget. You get even.' In the next instant, she was on the stairs behind her sister. 'Maureen, please, wait. Let me talk to you.'

'There's nothing you can say,' Maureen told her, opening the door to the lilac- and white-papered nursery to the right of the stairs. The smell of talcum powder immediately invaded Jess's nostrils, like a heavy narcotic. She hung back, newly dizzy and lightheaded, clinging to the doorway, watching as Maureen ministered to her infant daughters.

The cribs stood at right angles against the opposite wall, mobiles of tiny giraffes and teddy bears swirling gently above them. There was a large Bentwood rocking chair in the middle of the room and an overstuffed chair in bold white and purple stripes off to one side, as well as a changing table and a large flower-printed diaper pail. Maureen leaned over the cribs and cooed at her children, speaking over her shoulder at Jess with a gentle lilt in her voice that belied the strength of her words. 'I don't understand you, Jess. I really don't. You know Barry doesn't mean half of what he says. He just likes to give you a hard time. Why do you always have to rise to the bait?'

Jess shook her head. A million excuses fought their way to the tip of her tongue, but she swallowed them all, allowing only an apology to escape. 'I'm sorry. Really I am. I shouldn't have lost control like that. I don't know what happened,' she continued, when the apology didn't seem to suffice.

'Same thing that always happens when you and Barry get together. Only worse.'

'It's just that no matter how hard I try, he always finds a way to get to me.'

'You get to yourself.'

'Maybe.' Jess leaned against the doorway, listening to the babies settle down at the sound of their mother's voice. Maybe she should tell Maureen about Rick Ferguson's threat, and the nightmare and anxiety attacks that threat had subsequently unleashed. Maybe Maureen would cradle her in her arms and tell her that everything would be all right. How she needed to be held; how she longed to be comforted. 'I've had a really rotten day.'

'We all have rotten days. They don't give you the right to be mean and unpleasant.'

'I said I was sorry.'

Maureen lifted one of the twins out of her crib. 'Here, Carrie, go spit up on your mean Auntie Jessica.' She deposited the baby in Jess's arms.

Jess hugged the infant to her breast, feeling the softness of the baby's head against her lips, inhaling her sweet smell. If only she could go back, start all over again. There were so many things she'd do differently.

'Come to Mommy, Chloe.' Maureen lifted the second baby into her arms. 'Not everything has to be a confrontation,' she told Jess, rocking the baby gently back and forth.

'That's not what they taught us in law school.'

Maureen smiled, and Jess knew all was forgiven. Maureen had never been able to stay angry for long. She'd been like that since they were children, always eager to make things right, unlike Jess, who could nurse a grudge for days, a trait that drove their mother to distraction.

'Do you ever think . . .' Jess began, then hesitated, not sure whether to continue. She had never broached this subject with Maureen before.

'Do I ever think what?'

Jess began rocking the baby in her arms back and forth. 'Do you ever think you've seen Mommy?' she asked slowly.

A look of shock passed across Maureen's face. 'What?'

'Do you ever imagine that you've seen . . . Mother?' Jess repeated, straining for formality, avoiding her sister's incredulous gaze. 'You know, in a crowd. Or across the street.' Her voice trailed to a halt. Did she sound as ridiculous as she felt?

'Our mother is dead,' Maureen said firmly.

'I just meant . . .'

'Why are you doing this to yourself?'

'I'm not doing anything to myself.'

'Look at me, Jess,' Maureen ordered, and Jess reluctantly turned toward her sister's voice. The two women, each cradling an infant in her arms, stared into each other's green eyes from across the room. 'Our mother is dead,' Maureen repeated, as Jess felt her body grow numb.

They heard the doorbell ring. 'That's Daddy,' Jess said,

desperate to escape her sister's scrutiny.

Maureen's eyes refused to release her. 'Jess, I think you should talk to Stephanie Banack.'

Jess heard the front door open, listened as her father and Barry exchanged pleasantries in the front foyer. 'Stephanie Banack? Why would I want to talk to her? She's *your* friend.'

'She's also a therapist.'

'I don't need a therapist.'

'I think you do. Look, I'm going to write out her phone number before you go. I want you to call her.'

Jess was about to argue, but thought better of it when she heard her father's footsteps on the stairs.

'Well, look at this,' her father bellowed from the doorway. 'All my gorgeous girls together in one room.' He walked to Jess and engulfed her in his arms, kissing her cheek. 'How are you, doll?'

'I'm fine, Daddy,' Jess told him, and felt, for the first time that day, that maybe she was.

'And how's my other doll?' he asked Maureen, hugging her against him. 'And my little dolls?' he asked, drawing them all together. He lifted Chloe from her mother's arms, smothering her face with kisses. 'Oh you sweet thing. You sweet thing,' he chanted. 'I love you. Yes, I do.' He stopped, smiling at his own two daughters. 'I said that to a bigger girl last night,' he told them, then stood back and waited for their reaction.

'What did you say?' Maureen asked.

Jess said nothing. Maureen had taken the words right out of her mouth.

Chapter Five

Jess spent the first hour after she left her sister's house driving around the streets of Evanston trying not to think about the things her father had said at dinner. Naturally, she could think of nothing else.

'I said that to a bigger girl last night,' he'd announced, sounding so calm, so pleased, so sure of himself. As if falling in love was no big deal, as if he made that sort of declaration every day.

'Tell us all about her,' Maureen had urged at the dinner table, ladling out the mock turtle soup as Jess struggled to banish the image of a child's decapitated turtle from her mind. 'We want to hear absolutely everything. What's her name? What's she like? Where did you meet? When do *we* get to meet her?'

No, Jess thought. Don't say another word. Don't tell us a thing. Please, don't say anything.

'Her name is Sherry Hasek,' her father stated proudly. 'She's just a little bit of a thing. Not too tall, a little on the skinny side, dark hair, almost black. I think she colors it . . .'

Jess forced a spoonful of hot soup into her mouth, felt it numb the tip of her tongue, sear the roof of her mouth. Her mother had been tall, bosomy, her brown hair attractively sprinkled with grey. She'd always hated dyed black hair, said it looked so phony. Her father had agreed. Could he possibly have forgotten? she wondered, swallowing the urge to remind him, feeling the soup burn a path to her stomach. Pictures of headless turtles swam their way back up the path to her brain.

'We met at my life drawing class about six months ago,' he continued.

'Don't tell me she was a model.' Barry laughed into his soup.

'No, just a fellow student. Always liked to draw, never had the time. Like me.'

'Is she a widow?' Maureen asked. 'What's the matter, Jess? Don't you like the soup?'

She wasn't a widow. She was divorced. Had been for almost fifteen years. She was fifty-eight, the mother of three grown sons, and she worked in an antique store. She liked bright colors, dressed in long flowing skirts and Birkenstock sandals, and she had been the one to suggest coffee after class. Evidently she knew a good thing when she saw it. Art Koster was definitely a good thing.

Jess turned a corner and found herself back on Sheridan Road, stately homes to one side, Lake Michigan to the other. How long had she been circling the dark streets of Evanston? Long enough for it to have started raining, she realized, activating the car's windshield wipers, seeing one of them stick, drag itself across the car's window in what was obviously a Herculean effort. Rain then, not snow, she thought, not sure which she preferred. A fog was rolling in from the lake.

October was always the least dependable of months, she thought, full of ghosts and shadows.

People always raved about the glorious colors of autumn, the reds, oranges and yellows that disrupted, then replaced, the omnipresent green of summer. Jess had never shared their enthusiasm. For her, the change in colors meant only that the leaves were dying. And now, the trees were almost bare. What leaves were left were faded, shrivelled, drained of energy. Cruel reminders of their once buoyant selves. Like people abandoned in old age homes, death the only visitor they could rely on. Lonely people left too long without love.

Certainly her father deserved to find love, Jess thought, turning right and finding herself on a street she didn't recognize. She looked for a sign, didn't see one, turned left at the next corner. Still no street sign. What was the matter with people who lived in the suburbs? Didn't they want anyone to know where they were?

She'd always lived in the heart of the city, always in the same three-block radius, except during her marriage to Don. When she was little, and her father had worked as a buyer for a chain of women's clothing stores, they'd lived in a duplex on Howe Street. They'd moved when she was ten, her father then the successful manager of his own store, to a fully detached home on Burling Street, only a block away. Nothing fancy. Nothing particularly innovative or compelling in its architecture. Decidedly no Mies van der Rohe or Frank Lloyd Wright. It was just comfortable. The kind of house one felt good about coming home to. They'd loved it, planned on staying in it forever. And then one afternoon in August, her mother left for a doctor's appointment and never came back.

After that, everybody went their separate ways – Maureen back to Harvard, Jess back to law school and into marriage with Don, her father on increased buying trips to Europe. The once loved house sat empty. Eventually, her father worked up the necessary resolve to sell it. He could no longer bear to live in it alone.

And now her father had a new woman in his life.

It shouldn't have come as such a surprise, Jess realized, turning another corner and finding herself back on Sheraton Road. What was truly surprising was that he had waited eight long years. Women had always found him attractive. True, he was only average in appearance and his hairline had receded into nothingness, but there was still a twinkle in his brown eyes, and a ready laugh in his voice.

For a long while, there had been no laughter.

In the days, even months, after Laura Koster went missing, Art Koster had been the chief, and only, suspect in his wife's disappearance. Despite the fact he'd been out of town on a buying trip when she vanished, the police had refused to rule out his potential involvement. He could have hired someone, after all, they pointed out, delving into the couple's marriage, asking questions of neighbors and friends, probing into his business and financial affairs.

How had the couple been getting along? Did they argue? How

frequently? About money? The time he spent away from home? Other women?

Of course they argued, Art Koster had told them. Not often, but possibly more often than he realized. Not about anything important. Not about money. Not about his occasional business trips. Certainly not about other women. There were no other women, he told the police. He insisted on taking a polygraph test. Passed. The police seemed disappointed. Ultimately, they'd had no choice but to believe him.

There had never been any question as far as Jess was concerned. Her father was innocent. It was that simple. Whatever had happened to her mother, her father had had nothing to do with it.

It had taken Art Koster years to resume the rhythm of his daily life. For a time, he lost himself in his work. He drifted apart from old friends, then away. He rarely socialized, didn't date. He moved to an apartment on the waterfront, spent hours staring at Lake Michigan, seeing only Jess and Don and Maureen. Everyone coaxing everyone else. Come on, it'll be good for you. You need to get out. We need to see you. We're all we've got.

It was probably the combination of Maureen's marriage and Jess's divorce that brought Art Koster back to his normal pace. He'd been as upset by the news that Jess and Don were separating as he'd been by their engagement. Not that he didn't like Don. He did. Very much. He'd just wanted Jess to wait a little while. She was still so young. She was just starting law school. Don was eleven years her senior, already so well established. Jess needed time to be on her own, he'd told her, echoing her mother's sentiments, as he always did.

Still, he later confessed he'd been grateful that she'd had somewhere to turn after her mother vanished. It had taken some of the burden off him. And Don had taken good care of Art Koster's younger child. He was genuinely sorry when the marriage ended. Sorry, but supportive. As always. There for Jess when she needed him, resuming the fatherly role, taking her to dinner, the theater, the opera. Making sure she didn't hide out in her apartment, that she didn't bury herself in her work, as he had done. Trying to see that she ate properly. A losing battle.

And then Maureen had given birth to his first grandchild, and suddenly everything seemed to fall into place. Maybe it was just a question of time, Jess thought, continuing her drive north, away from the city, away from her problems. Not that time was the great healer that everyone promised. Just that time did indeed have a way of marching on. Ultimately you had no choice but to march with it. And now her father was in love.

The campus of Northwestern University appeared suddenly on her right. Jess passed the observatory with its giant telescope looking off into space, the frat houses, the drama building, the art center, the rain-soaked tennis courts. She continued past Lighthouse Beach, squinted past her defective windshield wiper at the old lighthouse that once warned sailors of dangerous rocks, then turned left on Central Street, driving the few blocks to Ridge Road, slowly ascending to the top of the steep incline, past the El stop, which Barry claimed was transporting crime back into the suburbs, past the hospital, past the Municipal Golf Course, over the bridge at the Chicago River, past Dyche Stadium, where the Northwestern University football team served as perennial losers to a variety of visiting teams, past the kosher hot dog outlet known as Custard's Last Stand, till she reached the Evanston Theaters, all in all a tour of less than a mile.

The street was crowded with parked cars. Jess had to circle the block before she found a parking spot. It was almost ten o'clock. The pizza parlor down the street was half empty, the ice cream store deserted. Not exactly a night for ice cream, she thought, recalling the taste of Maureen's exotic pear mousse with raspberry sauce.

No, she wouldn't think about Maureen, she decided, jumping out of her car and running toward the movie theater. She didn't know what movies were playing. She didn't care. Whatever was playing beat going home and having to deal with the revelations of this evening. Her sister's life was her own, as was her father's. She would have to let them live their lives as she had demanded the freedom to live hers.

'Which movie?' a young girl in a pink- and white-striped shirt and oddly angled red bow tie inquired as Jess pushed her money across the wicket.

Jess tried to focus on the list of films printed in white letters on the black slate behind the girl, but the names blurred, then ran together, disappearing before they reached her brain. 'Doesn't matter,' she told the girl. 'Whatever is starting next.'

'They've all already started.' The girl managed to look bored and confused at the same time.

'Well, then, you pick one. I'm having trouble . . .' She stopped, allowing the thought to dangle.

The girl shrugged, took the money, punched some figures into her cash register, and handed Jess a ticket. '*Hell Hounds*. Theater one, to your left,' she stated. 'It started ten minutes ago.'

There was no one waiting in the lobby to take Jess's ticket, no one to ensure she didn't wander into the wrong screening room, no one who cared what she did.

She opened the door to theater one and plunged into immediate, total darkness. Whatever was happening on the screen had to be happening in the dead of night. She couldn't see a thing.

Jess waited a few minutes for her eyes to adjust, was surprised by how little of the auditorium she could make out even after the screen filled with light. She proceeded slowly down the aisle, peering across rows of bodies, searching for a seat.

For a few minutes, it looked as if there weren't any. Sure, Jess thought, she sells me a ticket to the one movie that's all sold out. But then she saw it – a single seat in the middle of the fourth row from the front. Of course, it's Friday night, she reminded herself. Date night. Everybody a couple, she thought, carrying her aloneness like a bright neon sign as she tried to squeeze her legs between recalcitrant feet to get to the vacant seat.

'Will you sit down,' someone hissed from behind her, a command, not a question.

'Jeez, how long you gonna take, lady?'

'Excuse me,' Jess whispered, stepping over knees that refused to budge.

In the next instant, she was in her seat, afraid to take off her coat, lest she create a further disturbance. Around her, angry voices fluttered like autumn leaves, then settled into stillness.

On the screen, a young man, whose blue eyes were pierced through with fear, was fleeing an angry mob. The mob, individual faces contorted with rage, raised fists pummeling the air, was shouting obscenities at him, laughing when he tripped and fell, setting their snarling pit bulls after him. Seconds later, the dogs caught up with the hapless young man as he was clambering to his feet, and dragged him screaming back to the ground. Jess watched as a giant claw scratched across the young man's jugular, blood spurting from the wound to soak the screen. The audience cheered.

What on earth was she watching?

She closed her eyes, opened them again to see the same young man in bed with a beautiful woman whose curly blond hair draped teasingly along the tops of her bare breasts. Either a flashback or a very speedy recovery, Jess thought, watching their tongues disappear into each other's mouths.

Whatever happened to dialogue? she wondered. For as long as she'd been sitting here, nobody on the screen had said a word. They kissed, they killed, they fled, they fornicated. But nobody talked.

Maybe it was better that way, she decided. Think how much better off they'd all be if nobody ever said anything. It would certainly make her job as an Assistant State's Attorney a whole lot easier. She'd simply shoot the bad guys instead of trying to convince a peevish jury. As for family problems, a well-executed left hook to the jaw would put an end to her tiresome brother-in-law. Her father's disquieting announcement would be something she'd never have to hear.

Her father in love, she thought again, witnessing his image

jump onto the screen, suddenly larger than life, as he stepped into the young man's place, assumed his starring role. It was her father who now gathered the naked young woman into his arms, kissed her full on the lips, twisted her silky blond hair between his fingers. Jess tried to turn her head away, couldn't, sat transfixed, powerless, a prisoner to her own imaginings. She saw her father cup the young woman's face in his large hands, watching, with Jess, as her blond hair turned brown, dusted over with grey. Creases of wisdom appeared around the young woman's eyes and mouth. Her eyes deepened from light blue to navy to forest green. She turned and peered through the screen at Jess.

Her mother, Jess realized, as the woman's slow smile enveloped her. Her beautiful mother.

Jess leaned forward in her seat, her arms reaching around herself, holding her body tight.

And then another woman, smaller, thinner, her hair shoe polish black, dressed in flowing chiffon and Birkenstocks, dancing into the frame, into her father's arms, her father oblivious of his change in co-stars, her mother clinging precariously to the side of the screen, her image growing weaker, fading, disappearing.

Gone.

Jess gasped, her head dropping to her knees, clutching her stomach as if she'd been shot.

'What now?' someone muttered.

Jess tried to sit back up, aware of a tightening in her chest. She twisted her shoulders, arched her back, wondered if there was some subtle way she could unhook her bra, decided there wasn't. She felt hot, flushed, dizzy.

Well, of course she was dizzy. Of course she was hot. She was wearing her coat, for God's sake. The theater was crowded. They were packed in like sardines. Small wonder she could scarcely breathe. It was a miracle she hadn't already fainted. Jess threw her shoulders forward and pulled at her sleeves, wrenching the coat free of her arms as if it was on fire.

'For God's sake,' a voice beside her complained. 'Can't you sit still?'

'Sorry,' Jess whispered. She was still hot, flushed, dizzy. Taking off her coat had accomplished nothing. She began pulling at her sweater. Blue, green, turquoise – whatever color the damn thing was, it was too warm. It was choking her, denying her air. Why couldn't she breathe?

Jess looked around frantically for the exit sign, her head bouncing from her right to her left, her eyes darting in all directions simultaneously, her stomach pushing against her ribs. The turtle soup mocking me, she thought, pulling at the neck of her turtleneck sweater, picturing herself suddenly surrounded by a sea of headless turtles.

Was she going to be sick? Oh, no, please don't throw up. Please don't throw up. She looked back at the screen. The young man lay dead on the ground, his face so savaged by the dogs he was no longer recognizable. Barely human. The mob, satisfied, abandoned him to the deserted stretch of highway.

Had her mother met a similar fate? Savaged and abandoned on some desolate stretch of road?

Or was she sitting somewhere in a theater much like this one, watching some equally grotesque concoction and wondering if she could ever go home, if her daughters could ever forgive her for abandoning them?

'*I don't need this, Jess,*' she had shouted the morning of her disappearance. '*I don't need this from you!*'

Jess felt the bile rise in her throat. She tasted mock turtle soup mixed with honey-glazed chicken and Gorgonzola cheese. No, please don't throw up, she prayed, clenching her jaw, gritting her teeth.

Take deep breaths, she told herself, remembering Don's advice. Lots of deep breaths. From the diaphragm. In. Out. In. Out.

It wasn't working. Nothing was working. She felt the perspiration break out on her forehead, felt it trickle down the side of her face. She was going to be sick. She was going to throw up in the middle of a movie in the middle of a packed theater. No, please, she couldn't do that. She had to get out. She had to break free.

She jumped to her feet.

'Oh, no. Sit down, lady!'

'What the hell's going on?'

Jess grabbed for her coat, pushed her way through the row to the aisle, stepping on toes, knocking against the shoulders of the people in the row ahead, almost tripping over someone's damp umbrella. 'Excuse me,' she whispered.

'Ssh!'

'Don't come back!'

'Excuse me,' she repeated to no one in particular, racing for the lobby, gulping down the outside air. The girl behind the ticket window eyed her suspiciously, but said nothing. Jess ran along the street toward her car. It was still raining, now harder than before.

She fumbled through her purse for the car key, then fumbled with it again trying to put it in the lock. By the time she got behind the wheel, she was soaked through, her hair dripping into her eyes, her sweater clinging clammily to her body, like a cold sweat. She threw her coat into the back seat, then spread out across the front, letting the dampness cool her. She swallowed the cold night air, savouring it in her mouth as if it were a fine wine. She lay like this until, gradually, her breathing returned to normal.

The panic subsided, then died.

Jess sat up, quickly turned on the car's ignition. The windshield wipers shot immediately into action. Or, at least, one of them did. The other one merely sputtered into approximate position, then dragged itself along the window, like chalk across a blackboard. She'd definitely have to get it taken care of. She could barely see to drive.

She pulled the car out of her parking space onto the street, heading south on Central. She flipped on the radio, listened as Mariah Carey's high whine reverberated throughout the small car, ricocheting off the doors and windows. Something about feeling emotions. Jess wondered absently what else there was to feel.

She didn't see the white car until it was coming right at her. Instinctively, Jess swerved her car to the side of the road, the wheels losing their grip on the wet pavement, the car spinning to a halt as her foot frantically pumped the brake. 'Jesus Christ!' she shouted over Mariah Carey's oblivious pyrotechnics. 'You moron! You could have gotten us both killed!'

But the white car was long gone. She was screaming at air.

That was twice today she'd barely missed being demolished by a white car, the first a Chrysler, this one . . . she wasn't sure. Could have been a Chrysler, she supposed, trying to get a fix on the car's basic shape. But it had sped by too quickly, and it was raining and dark. And one of her windshield wipers didn't work. And what difference did it make anyway? It was probably her fault. She wasn't concentrating on what she was doing, where she was going. Too preoccupied with other things. Too preoccupied with not being preoccupied. About her sister. Her father. Her anxiety attacks.

Maybe she *should* give Maureen's friend, Stephanie Banack, a call. Jess felt in the pocket of her black slacks for the piece of paper on which her sister had written the therapist's address and phone number.

Jess recalled Stephanie Banack as a studious, no-frills type of woman whose shoulders stooped slightly forward and whose nose had always been too wide for the rest of her narrow face. Stephanie and her sister went all the way back to high school, and they still kept in frequent touch. Jess hadn't seen her in years, had forgotten she'd become a therapist, decided against seeing her now. She didn't need a therapist; she needed a good night's sleep.

Central Street became Sheraton Road, then eventually Lake Shore Drive. Jess started to relax, feeling better as she approached Lincoln Park, almost normal when she turned right onto North Avenue. Almost home, she thought, noting that the rain was turning to snow.

Home was the top floor of a three-story brownstone on Orchard Avenue, near Armitage. The old, increasingly gentrified area was lined with beautiful old houses, many of them semi-detached, most having undergone extensive renovations during the last decade. The homes were an eclectic bunch: some large, some tiny, some brick, others painted clapboard, a hodgepodge of shapes and styles, rental units next to single family dwellings, few with any front yard, fewer still with attached garages. Most residents, an equally eclectic mix, parked on the street, their parking permits prominently displayed on the dashboards of their cars.

The red brick façade of the house Jess lived in had been sandblasted over the summer and its wood shutters had received a fresh coat of shiny black paint. Jess felt good every time she saw the old house, knew how lucky she'd been to be able to rent its top floor. If only it had an elevator, she wished, though normally she thought nothing of the three flights of stairs. Tonight, however, her legs felt tired, as if she'd spent the last few hours jogging.

She hadn't jogged since her divorce. She and Don had regularly run the distance between the North Avenue and Oak Street beaches when they'd lived on Lake Shore Drive. But the jogging had been at Don's insistence, and she'd given it up as soon as she'd moved out, along with three balanced meals a day and eight hours sleep a night. It seemed she'd given up everything that was good for her. Including Don, she thought now, deciding that tonight was one of those nights when it would have been nice not to have to come home to an empty apartment.

Jess parked her old red Mustang behind the new metallic grey Lexus of the woman who lived across the street, and ran through the light drizzle – was it actually snow? – to the front door. She unlocked the door and stepped into the small foyer, switching on the light and relocking the door behind her. To her right was the closed door of the ground floor apartment. Directly ahead were three flights of dark red-carpeted stairs. Her hand tracing an invisible line along the side of the white wall, she began her ascent, hearing music emanating from the second floor apartment as she passed by.

She rarely saw the other tenants. Both were young urban professionals, like herself, one a twice-divorced architect with the city planning commission, the other a gay systems analyst. Whatever that was. Systems analyst was one of those jobs she would never understand, no matter how often and in how much detail it was explained to her.

The systems analyst was a jazz fan, and the plaintive wail of a saxophone accompanied her to her door. The hall light, which was on an automatic timer, turned off as she stretched her key toward the lock. Once inside, the saxophone's mournful sounds gave way to the happier song of her canary. 'Hello, Fred,' she called, closing the door and walking directly to the bird's cage, bringing her lips close to the slender bars. Like visiting a friend in prison, she thought. Behind her, the radio, which she left on all day along with the most of the lights, was playing an old Tom Jones tune. 'Why, why, why, Delilah . . .?' she sang along as she headed for the kitchen.

'Sorry I'm so late, Freddy. But trust me, you're lucky you stayed home.' Jess opened the freezer and pulled out a box of Pepperidge Farm vanilla cake, cutting herself a wide slice, then returning the box to the freezer, the cake already half-eaten by the time she shut the freezer door. 'My brother-in-law was in top form, and I got sucked in again,' Jess stated, returning to the living room. 'My father is in love, and I can't seem to be happy for him. It looks like it's actually starting to snow out there and I seem to be taking it as a personal affront. I think I'm having a nervous breakdown.' She swallowed the rest of the cake. 'What do you think, Fred? Think your mistress is going crazy?'

The canary flitted back and forth between his perches, ignoring her.

'Exactly right,' Jess said, approaching her large front window and staring down onto Orchard Street from behind antique lace curtains.

A white Chrysler was parked on the street directly across

from her house. Jess gasped, instantly retreating from the window and pressing her back against the wall. Another white Chrysler. Had it been there when she arrived?

'Stop being silly,' she said over the loud pounding of her heart, the canary bursting into a fresh round of song. 'There must be a million white Chryslers in this city.' Just because in the course of a single day, one had almost run her down, another had almost plowed into her car, and a third was now parked outside her apartment, that didn't necessarily add up to more than coincidence. Sure, and it never snowed before Halloween, she thought, reminding herself that she wasn't even sure that the car that had almost collided with her own in Evanston had been a Chrysler.

Jess edged back toward the window, peering out from behind the lace curtains. The white Chrysler was still there, a man sitting motionless behind the wheel, shadows from the street lights falling across his face. He was staring straight ahead, not looking in her direction. The darkness, the weather, and the distance combined to throw a scrim across his features. 'Rick Ferguson?' she asked out loud.

The sound of his name on her lips sent Jess scurrying out of the living room, down the hall, and into her bedroom. She threw open her closet door, falling to her hands and knees, and rifling through her seemingly endless supply of shoes, many still in their original boxes. 'Where the hell did I put it?' she demanded, getting off the floor, stretching for the top shelf where she kept still more shoes, old favorites not currently in fashion, but too precious to throw away. 'Where did I hide that damn gun?'

She ejected the boxes from the high shelf with one grand sweep of her hand, protecting her head as it rained shoes around her. 'Where is it?' she cried, spying something shiny and black beneath some crumpled white tissue paper.

A pair of black patent high-heeled shoes, she discovered, wondering what had ever possessed her to purchase shoes with four-inch heels. She'd worn them exactly once.

Jess finally discovered the small snub-nose revolver hidden

behind the enormous cloth flowers that adorned a pair of pewter pumps, the bullets painstakingly lodged inside the shoes' toes. Her hands shaking, Jess loaded six bullets into the barrel of the .38 caliber Smith and Wesson that Don had insisted she take with her when she moved out on her own. 'Call it my divorce present,' he'd told her, brooking no further discussion.

It had sat in the shoe box for four years. Would it still work? Jess thought, wondering if guns carried the same sort of 'Best if used before' warning that came with dairy products and other perishable items. She let the gun lead her back into the living room, tapping its short barrel against the light switch and throwing the room into darkness. The canary abruptly stopped singing.

Jess approached the window, the gun at her side. 'Just don't shoot yourself in the foot,' she cautioned, feeling as foolish as she did frightened, parting the lace curtains with trembling hands.

There was nothing there. No white Chrysler. No white car of any kind. Nothing white except the snow that was gradually peppering the grass and pavement. Nothing but a quiet residential street. Had there been a white car at all?

'Your mistress is definitely going crazy,' Jess told her canary, leaving the room in darkness. She covered the bird's cage with a dark green cloth and turned off the radio, carrying the gun back to her bedroom, freshly carpeted with shoes. Why couldn't she collect stamps? she wondered, surveying the mess. Stamps definitely took up less space, were less messy, less subject to the frivolous dictates of fashion. Certainly, nobody would have criticized Imelda Marcos for collecting three thousand pairs of stamps.

She was getting giddy, she realized, squatting on the floor and starting to tidy up. There was no way she'd be able to sleep when the floor of her bedroom looked like it could be declared a national disaster area. Assuming she could sleep at all.

'What a night!' she said, staring at the gun in her hand. Would she have actually been able to use it? She shrugged, grateful not to have been put to the test, and returned it to the shoe box behind the large cloth flowers of her old pewter pumps. Guns 'N' Roses, she thought, immediately lifting the gun back out.

Maybe it would be a better idea to hide it somewhere a little more accessible. Even if she wasn't ever going to use it. Just to make her feel better.

Opening the top drawer of her night table, Jess tucked the gun into the rear corner behind an old photograph album. 'Just for tonight,' she said out loud, picturing herself trying to outrun a pack of blood-thirsty pit bulls.

Just for tonight.

Chapter Six

Jess was the first of her party to arrive at Scoozi, located on Huron Street in River West. Unlike the small, dark bars along California Street, where Jess and her fellow prosecutors were more used to hanging out, Scoozi was an enormous old warehouse that had been converted into a restaurant and bar, with huge, high ceilings, and old Chicago-style windows lined with shelves of wine bottles. A giant Art-Deco chandelier hung down into the center of the ersatz Tuscany-style room. To the back sat a big clay pot filled with bright, artificial flowers, to the front an always crowded bar. The main floor of the restaurant was filled with well-lacquered wooden tables; to either side were raised decks with booths and still more tables. Jess estimated the large room could easily accommodate over three hundred people. Italian music played loudly from invisible speakers. All in all, the restaurant was the perfect choice for celebrating Leo Pameter's forty-first birthday.

Jess hadn't seen Leo Pameter in the year since he'd left the State's Attorney's Office to go into private practice. She was sure the only reason she'd been invited to his birthday celebration was because the entire eleventh and twelfth floors had been asked. She was less sure why she'd chosen to accept.

It was something to do, she supposed, smiling knowingly when the maître d' told her no one else from her party was here yet, asking if she'd like to wait at the bar. The bar was already crowded, despite the fact it was barely six o'clock. Jess checked her watch, more for something to do than for the information it could provide, and wondered again why she was here.

She was here, she told herself, because she'd always liked Leo Pameter, although they'd never had the time to get really close, and she'd been sorry to see him leave. Unlike many of the other state prosecutors, Greg Oliver among them, Leo Pameter was soft-spoken and respectful, a calming influence on those around him, possibly because he never let his ambitions got the better of his good manners. Everyone liked him, which was one of the reasons everyone would be here tonight. Jess wondered how many people would show up if the birthday party were for her.

She grabbed a fistful of pretzels and some kind of cheese crackers in the shape of little fish, and stuffed them into her mouth, watching as several of the fish tumbled from her hand onto the front of her brown sweater.

'Let me get that for you,' a male voice said playfully from the seat beside her.

Jess quickly brought her hands to her chest. 'Thank you, I can do it myself.'

The young man had a thick neck, close-cropped blond hair, and a big barrel chest that stretched against the silk of his kelly green shirt. He looked like a football player.

'Are you a football player?' Jess asked without meaning to, picking the wayward fish off her sweater.

'Can I buy you a drink if I say yes?'

She smiled. He was kind of cute. 'I'm waiting for someone,' she told him, turning away. She had no room in her life for kind of cute.

What was the matter with her? she wondered, grabbing another handful of fish crackers. Everyone kept telling her what an attractive woman she was, how smart, how clever, how talented. She was young. She was healthy. She was unattached.

She hadn't had a date in months. Her sex life was non-existent. Her *life*, outside of the office, was non-existent. And here was this nice-looking guy, maybe a little big for her taste, but nice-looking nonetheless, and he was asking her if he could buy her a drink, and she was saying no. Was this what Nancy Reagan had in mind?

She turned back toward the would-be football player, but he was already engaged in conversation with a woman on his other side. That was quick, Jess thought, coughing into her hand so that no one could see her blush. What had she been thinking? Had she seriously considered letting some stranger in a bar pick her up because he was kind of cute and she was kind of lonely? 'Kind of stupid,' she muttered.

'Sorry?' the bartender asked, although it was hardly a question. 'Did you say you wanted something to drink?'

Jess stared into the bartender's somber blue eyes. 'I'll have a glass of white wine.' She took another handful of fish and stuffed them into her mouth.

'God, would you just look at the crap she eats.'

Jess spun round, spilling a small school of fish onto the lap of her brown skirt, jumping off the bar stool to her feet. 'Don! I don't believe this.' His arms quickly encircled her, drawing her into a warm, comforting embrace. She was disappointed when he pulled away after only several seconds.

'Once again, it's not quite the coincidence you think it is,' he explained. 'Leo and I went to law school together. Remember?'

'I'd forgotten,' Jess admitted. Or had she? Had she suspected Don might be here tonight? Was that at least part of the reason she had come? Was he the someone she'd told the would-be football player she was waiting for?

'I knew you'd be the first one here. Thought we'd come early to keep you company.'

We? The word fell, like a blunt instrument, on Jess's ears.

'Jess, this is Trish McMillan,' Don was saying. He pulled a pretty woman with short blond hair and a wide smile to his side. 'Trish, this is Jess.'

'Hi, Jess,' the woman said. 'It's nice to meet you. I've heard a lot about you.'

Jess muttered something inane, conscious of the woman's deep dimples, and the fact that her arm was round Don's waist.

'What are you drinking?' Don asked.

Jess reached behind her for her drink. 'White wine.' She took a long sip, tasted nothing.

Trish McMillan laughed, and Don beamed. Jess felt confused. She hadn't said anything funny. She surreptitiously checked her sweater to determine whether any stray fish might be clinging to her breasts. There weren't any. Maybe Trish McMillan was just one of those sickeningly happy people who didn't need a reason to laugh out loud. Don had been right. Her laugh *was* wicked, as if she knew something the rest of the world didn't, as if she knew something that Jess didn't. Jess took another long sip of her drink.

'Two house wine,' Don told the bartender. 'You here alone?'

Jess shrugged. The question didn't require a response. Why had he asked?

'I haven't seen Leo since he left the department,' Jess said, feeling she had to say something.

'He's doing very well,' Don told her. 'He went with Remington, Faskin, as you know.' Remington, Faskin, Carter and Bloom was a small, but very prestigious, Chicago law firm. 'Seems very happy there.'

'What do *you* do?' Jess asked Trish McMillan, trying not to notice that her arm still encircled Don's waist.

'I'm a teacher.'

Jess nodded. Nothing too impressive about that.

'Well, not just a teacher,' Don embellished proudly. 'Trish teaches over at Children's Memorial Hospital. In the brain ward and dialysis unit.'

'I don't understand,' Jess said. 'What do you teach?'

'Everything,' Trish answered, laughing over the rapidly increasing din of the restaurant.

Jess thought: Everything. Of course.

'I teach kids in grades one through twelve, who are hooked up to dialysis machines and can't get to school, or kids who've had brain operations. The ones who are in hospital for the long haul.'

'Sounds very depressing.'

'It can be. But I try not to let it get me down.' She laughed again. Her eyes sparkled. Her dimples crinkled. Jess was having a hard time not hating her. Mother Teresa with short blond hair and a wicked laugh.

Jess took another sip of her drink, realized with some surprise that there was nothing left, signalled the bartender for another, insisted on paying for it herself.

'I understand you had a rather heated session this afternoon,' Don said.

'How'd you hear?'

'Word gets around.'

'Hal Bristol has a hell of a nerve trying to get me to go for involuntary manslaughter two weeks before the trial.' Jess heard the anger in her voice. She turned to Trish so suddenly, the woman jumped. 'Some bastard shoots his estranged wife through the heart with a crossbow, and his lawyer tries to convince me it was an accident!'

Trish McMillan said nothing. The pupils of her dark eyes grew larger.

'Bristol's claiming it was an accident?' Even Don sounded surprised.

'He says his client didn't mean to shoot her, only frighten her a little. And why not? I mean, she'd provoked the poor guy beyond reason. Right? What other options did he have but to buy a bow and arrow and shoot her down in the middle of a busy intersection?'

'Bristol was probably just trying to get you to settle for some middle ground.'

'There is no middle ground.'

Don smiled sadly. 'With you, there never is.' He hugged Trish McMillan closer to his side.

Jess finished her second glass of wine. 'I'm glad you're here,' she announced in as businesslike a tone as she could muster. 'I wanted to ask you something.'

'Shoot.'

Jess pictured herself behind the antique lace curtains of her apartment window, staring onto Orchard Street, gun in hand. She wished Don had chosen another word.

'What kind of car does Rick Ferguson drive?'

Don cupped his hand to his ear. 'Sorry. I didn't hear you.'

Jess raised her voice. 'Does Rick Ferguson drive a white Chrysler?'

Don made no effort to hide his obvious surprise. 'Why?'

'Does he?'

'I think so,' Don answered. 'I repeat, why?'

Jess felt her glass start to shake in her hand. She brought it to her lips, steadied it with her teeth.

There was a sudden explosion of sound, voices raised in greetings and congratulations, backs being slapped, hands being shaken, and in the next instant Jess found herself on one of the raised decks at the side of the room, another drink in hand, a party in full steam around her.

'I hear you really let old Bristol have it,' Greg Oliver was bellowing above the din.

Jess said nothing, searching through the crowd for Don, hearing Trish's wicked laugh mocking her from the far end of the deck.

'I guess word gets around,' she said, using Don's earlier phrase, catching sight of her ex-husband as he introduced his new lady to the rest of the gathering.

'So, what's the story? Are you going to settle for murder two? Save the taxpayer the expense of a hung jury?'

'I take it you don't think I'll get a conviction,' Jess stated, despair gnawing at the pit of her stomach. Did he always have to tell her what she didn't want to hear?

'For murder two, probably. Murder one? Never.'

Jess shook her head in disgust. 'The man murdered his wife in cold blood.'

'He was half out of his mind. His wife had been having an affair. She'd taunted him for weeks about his failings as a man. It got to be too much. They had a horrendous fight. She said she was leaving him, that he'd never see his kids again, that she'd take him for everything he owned. He just snapped.'

'The man was an abusive bully who couldn't stand the fact that his wife had finally worked up the courage to leave him,' Jess countered. 'Don't try to tell me this was a crime of passion. It was murder, pure and simple.'

'Not so pure,' Greg Oliver stated. 'Anything but simple.' He paused, possibly waiting for Jess to say something, continued when she didn't. 'She ridiculed his sexual prowess, remember.

A lot of male jurors are going to understand and sympathize with his response.'

'So, let me get this straight,' Jess said, finishing her drink and grabbing another from a passing waiter. 'You think it's acceptable for a man to kill his wife if she insults his precious manhood?'

'I think Bristol might be able to convince a jury of that, yes.'

Jess shook her head in disgust. 'What is it – open season on women?'

'Just warning you. I was right about the Barnowski case, remember.'

Jess scanned the room, hoping to find someone she could wave to, someone she could gravitate toward. Anyone. But there was no one. It seemed that everyone was either paired off or already engaged in pleasant conversation. No one even glanced her way.

It was her own fault, she realized. She didn't make friends easily. Never had. She was too serious, too intense. She frightened people, put them off. She had to work hard to establish friendships, harder to maintain them. She'd given up the pretense. She worked hard enough at the office.

'You're looking very delectable tonight,' Greg was saying, leaning closer, his lips brushing against the side of her hair.

Jess spun round, whisking her hair none too gently across Greg Oliver's cheek, seeing him wince. 'Where's your wife, Greg?' she asked, loud enough to be heard by those in the immediate vicinity. Then she turned and walked away, though she had no idea where she was headed.

She spent the next fifteen minutes in earnest conversation with one of the waiters. She couldn't make out most of what he was saying – the room was starting to sway slightly – but she managed to look interested and nod politely at appropriate intervals.

'Go easy on the drinks,' Don whispered, coming up behind her.

Jess stretched her head back against his chest. 'Where's Mother Teresa?' she asked.

'Who?'

'Teresa,' Jess repeated stubbornly.

'You mean Trish?'

'Trish, yes. Sorry.'

'She went to the washroom. Jess, why did you ask me about Rick Ferguson's car?'

Jess told him. About her narrow escape on Michigan Avenue, her near collision in Evanston, the white car waiting outside her apartment. Don's face registered interest, concern, then anger, in rapid succession. His response was characteristically direct.

'Did you get the license plate number?'

Jess was horrified to realize she hadn't even thought of it. 'It all happened so fast,' she said, the excuse sounding lame even to her ears.

'There are a lot of white Chryslers in Chicago,' Don told her, and she nodded. 'But I'll check it out, talk to my client. I can't believe he'd do anything so stupid so close to trial.'

'I hope you're right.'

Jess heard Trish's laugh, saw her arm snake round Don's waist, reclaim her territory. She turned away, watching the room spin to catch up. A young woman was striding purposefully across the floor toward the deck, a large portable cassette player in her hands. There was something off-kilter about her. She looked wrong, displaced. There was a kind of desperation to her heavy make-up, as if she were trying to hide who she really was. Her legs wobbled on a pair of too-high heels. Her trench coat was old and ill fitting. And something else, Jess thought, watching the young woman as she approached the birthday boy. She looked scared.

'Leo Pameter?' the girl asked, her voice that of a lost child.

Leo Pameter nodded warily.

The young woman, whose face was surrounded by a huge mass of unruly black curls, pushed a button on her tape cassette and suddenly the room reverberated to the traditional bump and grind music of a striptease show.

'Happy birthday, Leo Pameter!' the young girl shouted,

throwing off her trench coat and skipping around the deck in a white push-up bra and panties, complete with matching garter belt and stockings.

There were loud hoots from the men and embarrassed laughter from the women as the stripper shook her larger-than-life breasts in their direction before concentrating her energy on the hapless birthday boy.

'Jesus Christ,' Jess moaned, burying her eyes in her glass of wine.

'Those can't be real,' Trish exclaimed from somewhere beside her.

Jess looked up only when the music stopped. The young woman stood nude except for a G-string in front of Leo Pameter, who had the good grace to look embarrassed. She leaned over and planted a hot pink kiss on his forehead. 'From Greg Oliver,' she said, then quickly gathered up her things, threw her coat over her shoulders and fled to a smattering of self-conscious applause.

'How enlightened,' Jess muttered as Greg approached.

'It's you who have to lighten up, Jess.' Greg's eyes directly challenged hers. 'You have to learn to have fun, let yourself go, tell a few jokes.'

Jess downed the remainder of her drink, took a deep breath, and struggled to keep her eyes from crossing. 'Did you hear about the miracle baby that was born at Northwestern Memorial Hospital?' she asked, feeling all eyes turn toward her.

'Miracle baby?' Greg repeated, clearly wondering what this had to do with him.

'Yes,' Jess said loudly. 'It had brains *and* a penis!'

In the next instant, the room was spinning, and Jess was on the floor.

'Really, Don, this isn't necessary,' Jess was saying. 'I can take a cab.'

'Don't be silly. I'm not letting you go home alone.'

'What about Mother Teresa?'

'*Trish*,' Don emphasized, 'will meet me back at my apartment.'

'I'm sorry. I didn't mean to ruin your evening.'

'You aren't, and you didn't, so don't worry about it. Just get in the car.'

Jess crawled into the front seat of the black Mercedes, heard the car door shut after her. She leaned against the soft black leather, eyes closed, feeling Don assume his place behind the wheel, start the engine, pull away from the curb. 'I'm really sorry,' she began again, then stopped. He was right. She wasn't sorry.

No sooner had they started, but they stopped. She heard a car door open, then close. Now what? she thought, opening her eyes.

They were in front of her brownstone. Don came round to her side of the car, opened her door, and helped her out.

'That was fast,' she heard herself say, wondering how much time had elapsed.

'Think you can walk?' Don asked.

Jess said yes, though she wasn't at all sure. She leaned against Don, felt his arm slip round her waist, allowed him to guide her from the car toward the front door of the large house. 'I can do the rest on my own,' she told him, watching him search through her purse for her key.

'Sure you can. You don't mind if I just stand here and watch, do you?'

'Could you do me a favor?' she asked once they were inside the foyer, three flights of stairs stretching before her.

'You want me to leave?'

'I want you to carry me up.'

Don laughed, draping her left arm round his right shoulder and supporting her weight with his own. 'Jess, Jess, what am I going to do with you?'

'I bet you say that to all the girls,' she muttered as they began their slow climb.

'Only to girls named Jess.'

What on earth had possessed her to drink so much? Jess

wondered as she groped for the stairs. She wasn't a drinker, rarely had more than a single glass of wine. What was the matter with her? And why did she seem to be asking herself that question so often lately?

'You know,' Jess said, recalling the sneer in Greg Oliver's voice when he told her to lighten up, 'it's not that I don't like men. It's lawyers I have a problem with.'

'Are you trying to tell me something?' Don asked.

'And accountants,' Jess added.

They opted for silence the rest of the way. By the time they reached the top of the stairs, Jess felt as if she had conquered Mount Everest. Her legs were like jelly, her knees refusing to lock into place. Don continued propping her up as he twisted the key in the lock. Somewhere a phone was ringing.

'Is that your phone?' Don asked, pushing the door open. The ringing got louder, grew more urgent.

'Don't answer it,' Jess instructed her ex-husband, closing her eyes against the lights as he lowered her to the couch.

'Why not?' He looked toward the kitchen where the phone continued its insistent ring. 'It could be important.'

'It isn't.'

'You know who it is?'

'My father,' Jess told him. 'He's been trying to set up a good time for me to meet his new friend.' I've met enough new friends for one night, she thought, but didn't say.

'Your father has a girlfriend?'

'Well, I'd hardly call her a girl.' Jess curled up inside her sofa, drawing her knees against her chest. 'I'm an awful person,' she moaned into the velvet cushion. 'Why can't I just be happy for him?' The phone continued to ring, then suddenly, mercifully, stopped. She opened her eyes. Where was Don?

'Hello,' she heard him say from the kitchen, and for a minute, she thought maybe someone else had entered the apartment. 'I'm sorry,' he continued. 'I can't understand what you're saying. Can you speak slower?'

'I told you not to answer it,' Jess said, wobbling into the kitchen, holding her hand toward the telephone.

Don handed her the phone, his forehead creasing into a series of worried folds. 'It's a woman, but I can't make out a word she's saying. She has a very thick accent.'

Jess felt sobriety tugging at her consciousness. She didn't want to be sober, she thought, putting the phone to her ear, her mellowness seeping away from her, like a slow leak.

The woman's voice assaulted her ears before she had time to say hello. 'I'm sorry. What? Who is this?' Jess felt a terrible sinking feeling in the pit of her stomach. 'Mrs Gambala? Is this Mrs Gambala?'

'Who's Mrs Gambala?'

'Connie DeVuono's mother,' Jess whispered, her hand across the receiver. 'Mrs Gambala, you have to calm down. I can't understand you . . . What? What do you mean she didn't come home?'

Jess listened to the rest of what Mrs Gambala had to say in stunned silence. When she hung up the phone, her whole body was shaking. She turned to Don, watching his eyes narrow with unasked questions. 'Connie didn't pick up her son at her mother's house after work,' she said, dread audible in every word. 'She's disappeared.'

Chapter Seven

'I can't believe I was so stupid!'

'Jess . . .'

'So stupid, and so damned self-centered!'

'Self-centered? Jess, for God's sake, what are you talking about?'

'I just assumed he was talking about me.'

'Who? What are you talking about?'

'Rick Ferguson!'

'Rick Ferguson? Jess, slow down.' Don pushed some imaginary hairs away from his forehead, his expression hovering between curiosity and exasperation. 'What has Rick Ferguson got to do with this?'

'Come on, Don.' Jess made no attempt to hide her impatience with her ex-husband. 'You know as well as I do that Rick Ferguson is responsible for Connie DeVuono's disappearance. Don't try to tell me you don't. Don't play games with me. Not now. This isn't a courtroom.' Jess marched out of the kitchen into her living room, pacing restlessly in front of the bird cage, her canary hopping back and forth between perches, as if consciously mimicking her strides.

Don was right behind her, hands in the air, trying to get Jess to slow down. 'Jess, if you would just calm down for half a second.' He grabbed hold of her shoulders with both hands. 'If you would just stop moving for half a second.' The pressure of his palms forced her to a standstill. Don stared into her eyes until she had no choice but to look back. 'Now, can you tell me exactly what happened?'

'Rick Ferguson—' she began.

Immediately, he cut her off. 'Not what you *think* happened, what you *know* happened.'

Jess took a deep breath, shrugged her shoulders free of his strong grip. 'Connie DeVuono called her mother at approximately four-thirty this afternoon to say she was leaving work, she'd be there in twenty minutes to pick up her son, could she please have him dressed and ready to go. Her son has hockey practice every Monday at five-thirty, and it's always a bit of a rush.'

'Connie's mother looks after her son?'

Jess nodded. 'He goes to her house after school, waits there for Connie to pick him up when she's finished work. Connie always calls before she's leaving. Today, she called. But she never showed up.'

Don's eyes told Jess he expected more.

'That's it,' Jess said, hearing Don scoff, though in truth he made no sound.

'Okay. So, what we *know*,' Don emphasized, 'is that Connie DeVuono didn't pick her son up after work.'

'After she called and said she was on her way,' Jess reminded him.

'And we don't know whether or not anybody saw her leave work, or what kind of a mood she might have been in, or if she told anybody she had to stop off somewhere, or—'

'We don't know anything. The police won't officially start investigating until she's been missing for twenty-four hours. You know that.'

'We don't know if she was depressed or anxious,' Don continued.

'Of course she's depressed and anxious. She was raped. She was beaten. The man who attacked her convinced a judge he's a model citizen with deep roots in the community, the sole support for his aged mother, and other assorted crap, so they let him out on bail. Connie DeVuono's supposed to testify in court next week. And your client has threatened to kill her if she tries. You're damn right she's depressed and anxious! In fact, she's scared to death!' Jess heard the shrillness in her voice. Her canary started singing.

'Scared enough to just take off?' Don underlined the importance of his question with a furrowing of his brow.

Jess was about to answer, then stopped, swallowing her words before they could leave her mouth. She recalled the sight of Connie in her office the previous week, how frightened she'd been, how adamant that she wouldn't testify. Jess had convinced her otherwise. Persuaded her to go against her better judgement, to challenge her tormentor in a court of law.

Jess had to admit at least the possibility that Connie might have changed her mind again, decided she couldn't go through with testifying, that the risks were too great. She could easily have felt too embarrassed to inform Jess of her change of heart, too afraid Jess might be able to convince her otherwise, too guilty for being such a coward. So strange, Jess thought, how often it was the innocent who suffered the most guilt.

'She wouldn't leave her son,' Jess said quietly, the words half out of her mouth before she realized she was speaking.

'She probably just needs time to clear her head.'

'She wouldn't leave her son.'

'She's probably in a hotel somewhere. In a day or two, when she's calmed down, had a bit of a rest, decided what she wants to do, she'll call.'

'You're not hearing me.' Jess walked toward the window, stared out onto the street. Patches of snow lay across the grass and sidewalks, like torn doilies.

Don came up behind her, massaged the back of her neck with his strong hands. Suddenly he stopped, resting his palms on her shoulders. Jess could feel him thinking, formulating the words he wanted to say. 'Jess,' he began, speaking in slow, measured tones, 'not everyone who doesn't show up on time disappears for ever.'

Neither moved. In the background, Jess's canary hopped from perch to perch to the beat of an old Beatles melody. Jess tried to speak, couldn't for the sudden constriction in her chest. She finally managed to force the words out.

'This isn't about my mother,' she told him carefully.

Another silence.

'Isn't it?'

Jess maneuvered her body away from him, coming round to the front of the sofa, dropping lifelessly into its soft pillows, burying her face in her hands. Only her right foot betrayed her anxiety, twitching restlessly beneath her. She looked up only when she felt the cushion beside her sag, felt Don take her hands in his own.

'It's all my fault,' she began.

'Jess—'

'No, please don't try to tell me otherwise. It is my fault. I know it. I accept it. I'm the one who convinced her she had to testify when she really didn't want to; I'm the one who pressured her, who promised her everything would be all right. "Who will look after my son?" she asked me, and I made some silly joke, but she was serious. She knew that Rick Ferguson meant what he said.'

'Jess—'

'She knew he'd kill her if she didn't drop the charges.'

'Jess, you're really jumping the gun here. The woman's been missing less than six hours. We don't know that she's dead, for God's sake.'

'I was so proud of myself, too. So proud of my ability to turn things around, to convince this poor frightened woman that she had to testify, that she'd only be safe *if* she testified. Oh yes, I was very proud of myself. It's a big case for me, after all. Another potential winner for my files.'

'Jess, you did what anybody would do.'

'I did what any *prosecutor* would do! If I'd had an ounce of real compassion for that woman, I'd have told her to drop the charges and run. Jesus!' Jess jumped to her feet, though she had nowhere to go. 'I talked to that animal! I stood there in the lobby of the Administration Building and I warned him to keep away from Connie. And that bastard told me, told me right out, though I was too full of myself to really hear him, he told me that people who annoyed him had a way of disappearing. And I assumed it was me he was threatening! Who else would he be threatening? Doesn't the universe revolve around Jess Koster?' She laughed, a harsh, cold sound that stuck in the air. 'Only it *wasn't* me he was talking about. It was Connie. And now she's gone. Disappeared. Just like he threatened.'

'Jess–'

'So don't you dare sit there and try to tell me that your client had nothing to do with her disappearance! Don't you dare try to convince me that Connie would leave her son, even for a day or two, because I know she wouldn't. We both know that Rick Ferguson is responsible for whatever's happened to Connie DeVuono. And we both know that, barring a miracle, she's already dead.'

'Jess–'

'Don't we both know that, Don? Don't we both know she's dead? We do. We know that. And we have to find her, Don.' Involuntary tears traced the length of Jess's cheeks. She wiped the back of her hand across her face, trying to rub them away, but the tears only came faster.

Don was on his feet beside her, but she moved quickly out of his reach. She didn't want to be comforted. She didn't deserve it.

'We have to find her body, Don,' Jess continued, starting to shake. 'Because if we don't, that little boy will spend the rest of his life wondering what happened to his mother. He will spend years searching through crowds for her, thinking he sees her, wondering what he did that was so awful she went away and never came home. And even when he's all grown up, and he rationally accepts the fact she's dead, he'll never quite believe it. A part of him will always wonder. He'll never know for sure. He'll never be able to put it behind him, to grieve for her the way he needs to grieve for her. The way he needs to grieve for himself.' She stopped, allowed Don to take her in his arms, hold her. 'There has to be a resolution, Don. There has to be.'

They stood that way for several minutes, so close their breath seemed to emanate from one body. It was Don who finally broke the stillness. 'I miss her too,' he said quietly, and Jess knew he was talking about her mother.

'I thought it was supposed to get easier with time,' Jess said, allowing Don to guide her back to the sofa. She sat cradled in his arms as he gently rocked her to and fro.

'It only gets farther away,' he said simply.

She smiled sadly. 'I'm so tired.'

'Lay your head on my shoulder,' he said, and she did, grateful to be told what to do. 'Now close your eyes. Try to sleep.'

'I can't sleep.' She made a feeble attempt to get up. 'I should really go over to Mrs Gambala's.'

'Mrs Gambala will call you when she hears from Connie.' He pressed her head back against his shoulder. 'Ssh. Get some sleep.'

'What about your friend?'

'Trish is a big girl. She'll understand.'

'Yes, she's very understanding.' Jess heard the thinness in her voice, knew she was close to losing consciousness. Her eyes fluttered closed. She forced them open again. 'Probably because she works in a hospital.'

'Ssh.'

'She seemed like a very nice person.'

'She is.'

'I don't like her,' Jess said, closing her eyes and allowing them to stay shut.

'I know you don't.'

'I'm not a very nice person.'

'You never were,' he said, and Jess felt his smile against the side of her face.

She would have smiled in return, but she was having trouble controlling the muscles in her face. They were sinking toward her chin, giving in to the pull of gravity.

In the next second, she was asleep and a phone was ringing.

She opened her eyes to find she was in the sterile reception area of a doctor's office. 'The phone's for you,' the doctor said, producing a plain black phone from his bag. 'It's your mother.'

Jess took the phone. 'Mother, where are you?'

'There's been an accident,' her mother told her. 'I'm in the hospital.'

'The hospital?'

'I'm in the brain ward. They have me hooked up to all these machines.'

'I'll be right there.'

'Hurry. I can't wait for long.'

Jess was suddenly in front of Northwestern Memorial Hospital, lines of angry picketers blocking her way.

'What are you protesting?' Jess asked one of the nurses, a young woman with very short blond hair and dimples so deep they all but overwhelmed her face.

'Duplicity,' the woman said simply.

'I don't understand,' Jess muttered, transported in the next second to a busy nurses' station. Half a dozen young women in crisp white caps and garter belts and stockings stood behind the counter engaged in earnest conversation. No one looked her way. 'I'm here to see my mother,' Jess shouted.

'You just missed her,' one of the nurses said, though no lips moved.

'Where did she go?' Jess spun round, grabbing a passing orderly by the sleeve.

Greg Oliver's face glowered before her. 'Your mother is gone,' he told her. 'She disappeared.'

In the next instant, Jess was standing on the street in front of her parents' home. A white stretch limousine was idling on the corner. Jess watched as a man opened the car door and stepped onto the sidewalk. It was dark and Jess couldn't make out his face. But she could feel his long slow strides as he moved toward her, felt him mounting the front stairs after her, his hand reaching for her as she pulled open the door and slammed it shut. His face pressed heavily against the screen, his hideous grin seeping slowly through the wire mesh.

She screamed, her cried piercing the dimension between sleep and consciousness, waking Jess up with the sudden sharpness of an alarm clock. She jumped to her feet, flailing madly in the darkness. Where was she?

Don was immediately at her side. 'Jess, it's all right. It's all right. It was just a bad dream.'

It all came back to her: the party; the wine; Trish; Mrs Gambala; Don. 'You're still here,' she acknowledged gratefully, falling back into his arms, wiping the combination of sweat and tears from her cheeks, trying to still the frantic beating of her heart.

'Take deep breaths,' he advised, as if he could see the chaos growing inside her body. His voice was groggy, full of sleep. 'That's a girl. In, now out. Steady. That's right. You've got it.'

'It was the same dream I used to have,' she whispered. 'Remember? The one where Death is waiting for me.'

'You know I'd never let anyone hurt you,' he assured her, control returning to his voice. 'Everything's going to be all right. I promise.'

Just like her mother, she thought, settling comfortably into his arms.

Approximately half an hour later, he slipped his arm round her waist, and led her gingerly toward her bedroom. 'I think it's time to go to bed. Will you be all right if I leave you alone?'

Jess smiled weakly as Don tucked her, fully clothed, between the covers of her double bed. Part of her wanted him to stay; part of her wanted him to go, the way it always was when they were together. Would she ever figure out what she wanted? Would she ever grow up?

Without a mother, how could she?

'I'll be fine,' she assured him, as he bent over to kiss her forehead. 'Don?'

He didn't move.

'You're a nice man,' she told him.

He laughed. 'Think you'll remember that a few days from now?'

She was too tired to ask what he meant.

'You bastard!' she was screaming barely forty-eight hours later. 'You turd! You miserable piece of shit!'

'Jess, calm down!' Don was circling the oblong wooden table

backwards, trying to keep an arm's length from his angry ex-wife.

'I can't believe you'd pull a stunt like this!'

'Can you at least keep your voice down?'

'You shit! You creep! You . . . *shit*!'

'Yes, point taken, counsellor. Now, do you think you can calm down so that we can discuss this like the two rational attorneys-at-law we are?'

Jess folded her arms in front of her and stared at the blood-red concrete floor. They were in a small, windowless room on the second floor of the police station that serviced Chicago's downtown core. Recessed, high-wattage lights emanated from the dull, acoustic tile ceiling. A bench lay across one wall; a formica table was bolted into the floor on another, several uncomfortable chairs beside it. In the next room, which was smaller and even more claustrophobic, sat Rick Ferguson, sullen and silent. He hadn't said a word since the police had brought him in for questioning earlier that morning. When Jess had tried to question him, he'd yawned, then closed his eyes. He hadn't opened them even after they'd manacled his hands to the wall. He'd feigned indifference, then indignation, when they asked him what he'd done with Connie DeVuono. He'd looked interested in the proceedings only when his attorney, Don Shaw, arrived, apoplectic about what he deemed the deliberate abrogation of his client's rights, threatening to break down the door if he wasn't allowed in to confer with his client.

'You have no right to be here,' Jess told him, keeping her voice low and steady. 'I could report you to the attorney disciplinary committee.'

'If anybody's going to report anybody to the attorney disciplinary committee,' he shot back, 'it'll be me.'

'You?!' Jess was almost too flabbergasted to speak.

'You're the one who violated the canon of ethics,' he told her.

'What?!'

'You violated the canon of ethics, Jess,' Don repeated. 'You had no right to arrest my client. You certainly had no right to try to question him without his attorney present.'

Jess struggled to keep her voice calm. 'Your client is not under arrest.'

'I see. He's sitting in a locked room manacled to the wall because he likes it. Is that what you're trying to tell me?'

'I don't have to tell you anything. I am perfectly within my rights here.'

'What about Rick Ferguson's rights? Or have you decided that because you don't like him, he doesn't have any?'

Jess clenched, then unclenched, her fist, grabbing the back of a chair to anchor herself, give her head time to clear, her thoughts a chance to settle. She glared at her ex-husband with barely concealed fury. He ignored the message in her eyes, continued his lecture.

'You have the police pick up my client at work; you don't read him his rights; you don't let him call his attorney. And it's not like you don't know he's got a lawyer. A lawyer who's already advised you that his client has nothing to say, that he's executing his legal right to remain silent. You already know that's the position we've taken. It's on the record. But it doesn't stop you from embarrassing him at work, dragging him down here, handcuffing him to the wall . . . Jess, for Christ's sake, was that really necessary?'

'I thought so. Your client is a dangerous man. He wasn't being very cooperative.'

'It's not his job to cooperate. It's *your* job to make sure he's treated fairly.'

'Did he treat Connie DeVuono fairly?'

'That's not the issue here, Jess,' Don reminded her.

'Did you treat *me* fairly?'

There was a moment's silence.

'You used me, Don.' Jess heard the combination of hurt and disbelief in her voice. 'How could you do that to me?'

'How could I do what? What is it you think I've done to you?' A look of genuine confusion filled Don's face.

Jess shook her head. Were they really having this conversation? 'You were with me the night Connie DeVuono disappeared,' she began. 'You knew I suspected Rick Ferguson, that we were planning to pick him up.'

'I knew you suspected him. I had no idea you were planning to pick him up,' Don told her.

'What else would I be planning?'

'At the very least, I thought you might wait a few more days. Jess, it's been less than forty-eight hours since the woman disappeared.'

'You know as well as I do that she's not coming back,' Jess said.

'I know no such thing.'

'Oh, please! Don't insult my intelligence.'

'Don't insult mine,' Don parried. 'What do you expect me to do, Jess? Allow you free rein because you used to be my wife? Am I supposed to let my feelings for you override my responsibilities to my client? Am I?'

Jess said nothing. She looked toward the wall that separated the two small rooms. She'd seen the smirk on Rick Ferguson's face when she'd left the room to deal with Don. She knew he understood what was going on, that he was enjoying her discomfort.

'Now, either charge my client or release him.'

'Release him?! No way am I releasing him.'

'Then you're arresting him? On what grounds? On what evidence? You know you have absolutely nothing to link Rick Ferguson to Connie DeVuono's disappearance.'

Jess brought her hands to her lips, breathed deeply against her fingers. He was right, and she knew it. She had no hard evidence to justify holding him. 'For God's sake, Don, I don't want to arrest him. I just want to talk to him.'

'But my client doesn't want to talk to you.'

'He might if his lawyer would stop interfering.'

'You know I'm not going to do that, Jess.' It was Don's turn to take a deep breath. 'As far as I'm concerned, you've violated the fifth and sixth amendments guaranteeing the accused the right to counsel, and the accused the right to remain silent, under the fifth. I have every right to be here.'

Jess could scarcely believe what she was hearing. 'What are you trying to pull? You know the recent Supreme Court ruling as well as I do. The Miranda warning, the right to have an attorney present, they only apply the first time an arrest is made. They don't apply to a subsequent offense.'

'Maybe yes, maybe no. Maybe we should let the attorney disciplinary commission determine the propriety of your actions, and let a court of law decide what rights my client still has. If any. Let the courts decide whether the constitution is still alive and well in Cook County!'

'A truly bravura speech, counsellor,' Jess told him, impressed despite herself.

'In any event, Jess,' Don continued, his voice softening, 'you have to have probable cause to arrest my client. You simply haven't got it.' He paused. 'Now, is my client free to leave, or isn't he?'

Jess looked toward the wall separating the two interrogation rooms. Even through the locked door, she could feel the force of Rick Ferguson's contempt. 'How did you find out we'd picked him up?' She hoped the defeat wasn't too evident in her voice.

'His mother phoned my office. Apparently she called Rick at work, and his foreman told her what happened.'

Jess shook her head. Wasn't that always the way? It was probably the first time the woman had called her son at work in years, and it *would* be today. 'What, did she run out of booze?'

'I want to talk to my client, Jess,' Don said, ignoring her sarcasm. 'Now, are you going to let me talk to him or not?'

'If I let you talk to him, you'll tell him to keep quiet,' Jess acknowledged.

'And if you hold him, you have to let him have counsel.'

'Is this what they call a Catch-22?'

'It's what they call the law.'

'I don't need you to teach me the law,' Jess said bitterly, knowing it was futile to continue. She walked into the hall and knocked on the next door. It was opened almost immediately by a uniformed police officer. Jess and Don moved quickly inside. Another detective, wearing plain clothes and an expression of resignation, as if he had known what the outcome of her conference would be all along, stood against the far wall, sucking on the end of an unlit cigarette. Rick Ferguson, in black jeans and brown leather jacket, sat on a small wooden chair, his hands manacled to the wall behind him.

'Take those things off now,' Don commanded impatiently.

'I didn't say a thing, counsellor,' Ferguson told him, staring at Jess.

Jess signalled to the detective, who, in turn, nodded at the uniformed police officer. In the next instant, Rick Ferguson's hands were freed.

Rick Ferguson didn't rub his wrists, or jump to his feet as most prisoners would have done. Instead he rose slowly, almost casually, and stretched, as if he were in no hurry, like a cat awakened from a nap, as if he were thinking of sticking around. 'I told her I had nothing to say,' he repeated, staring at Jess. 'She didn't believe me.'

'Let's go, Rick,' Don advised from the doorway.

'Why is it you never believe me, huh, Jess?' Ferguson held on to the final s of her name, so that it emerged as a hiss.

'That's enough, Rick.' The edge to Don's voice was unmistakable.

'Almost made me miss Halloween,' he said, his lips stretching into the familiar, evil grin, his tongue flicking obscenely between his teeth. 'Trick or treat,' he said.

Without a word, Don brusquely steered his client out the door.

Jess heard the echo of Rick Ferguson's laugh long after he had left the room.

Chapter Eight

'I want him charged with murder,' Jess told her trial supervisor.

Tom Olinsky peered across his desk from behind small, circular, wire-rimmed glasses much too small for his round face. He was an enormous man, close to six feet six inches tall and at least two hundred and fifty pounds. As a result, he seemed to overpower almost everything that crossed his path. The granny glasses, a tribute to growing up in the sixties, while decidedly incongruous, humanized him, rendered him more accessible.

Jess fidgeted in the large leather wing chair across from Tom Olinsky's oversized desk. Like the man himself, all the furniture in the small office at the end of the hall was too big for its surroundings. Whenever Jess set foot in this office, she felt like Alice after eating the wrong mushroom. She felt diminished, insignificant, inadequate. She invariably compensated for these feelings by speaking louder, faster, and more often than was necessary.

'Jess . . .'

'I know what you've told me before,' she said stubbornly. 'That without a body—'

'Without a body, we'll be laughed right out of court.' Tom came around to the front of his desk, his wide girth threatening to squeeze Jess out of the room. 'Jess, I know you think this guy committed murder, and you're probably right. But we just don't have any evidence.'

'We know he raped and beat her.'

'Which was never proved in court.'

'Because he killed her before she could testify against him.'

'Prove it.'

Jess threw her head back, stared at the ceiling. Hadn't she

already had this conversation? 'Rick Ferguson threatened Connie, told her she'd never live to testify.'

'For which we have only her word.'

'What about what he said to me?' Jess asked. Too loud. Too desperate.

'Not strong enough.'

'Not strong enough? What do you mean, not strong enough?'

'It's just not strong enough,' Tom repeated, not bothering to embellish. 'We wouldn't get past a preliminary hearing. You know that as well as I do.'

'What about a grand jury?'

'Even a grand jury is going to want some proof the woman is dead!'

'There have been numerous instances of people being charged with murder without a body ever being recovered,' Jess reminded him stubbornly.

'And how many convictions?' Tom paused, leaned against his desk. Jess felt the wood groan. 'Jess, do I have to remind you that the man has an alibi for the time Connie DeVuono disappeared?'

'I know – his sainted mother!' Jess scoffed. 'He keeps her supplied with booze; she keeps him supplied with alibis.'

Tom returned to his side of the desk and lowered himself slowly into the oversized leather chair. He said nothing, his silence more intimidating than words.

'So, we just let him get away with it,' Jess said. 'Is that what you're telling me?' She threw her hands in the air, standing up and turning her head so that he wouldn't see the tears forming in her eyes.

'What's going on, Jess?' Tom asked as Jess walked toward the door.

She stopped, wiped at her eyes before turning to face him. 'What do you mean?'

'You're more involved in this case than you should be. Don't get me wrong,' he continued, without prompting. 'One of the things that makes you so special as a prosecutor is the empathy you seem to develop with most of the victims. It makes you see things the rest of us sometimes miss, gives you an edge, makes you fight that much harder. But I'm sensing something more here. Am I right? And are you going to tell me what it is?'

Jess shrugged, trying desperately not to picture her mother's face. 'Maybe I just hate loose ends.' She tried to smile, failed. 'Or maybe I just like a good fight.'

'Even you have to have something to fight with,' Tom told her. 'We just don't have it here. A good defense lawyer – and your ex-husband is a very good defense lawyer – would make mincemeat out of us. We need evidence, Jess. We need a body.'

Jess recalled the image of Connie DeVuono, eyes ablaze, sitting across from her in the small conference room – 'Who will look after my son?' she'd demanded. 'Will you?' – and tried to imagine the woman lying lifeless and cold on some deserted stretch of road. The image came easier than Jess anticipated. It made her want to gag. Immediately, she clamped down on her jaw, gritting her teeth until they ached.

Jess said nothing, nodding her head in acknowledgement of the stated facts, and left her trial supervisor's office. The Halloween decorations along the corridors had been removed and replaced by an assortment of turkeys and pilgrims in anticipation of Thanksgiving. Jess returned to her office only long enough to pick up her coat and say goodbye to her cohorts, whose faces registered their surprise at seeing her leave so early, despite the fact it was after five o'clock.

Not that she wanted to leave work early. Not that she didn't have a lot to do. Not that she had any choice, she told herself. She'd given her word. After ten days of *I really can't, I'm up to my eyeballs,* Jess had finally given in to her sister's exhortations to meet Sherry Hasek, the new woman in their father's life. Dinner at seven. Bistro 110. *Yes, I'll be there. I promise.*

Her brother-in-law and her father's new love, all in one evening, two headaches for the price of one. 'Just what I need,' Jess moaned out loud, relieved at finding the elevator to herself. 'Just what I need to cap off the end of a perfect day.'

The elevator stopped at the next floor and a woman got on,

catching Jess in mid-sentence. Jess quickly twisted her mouth into a yawn.

'Long day?' the woman asked, and Jess almost laughed.

The day's events replayed quickly in her mind, like a video on fast forward. She saw herself standing in front of Judge Earl Harris, her ex-husband at her side, demanding his client's right to a speedy trial for assaulting Connie DeVuono. 'Justice delayed is justice denied,' he'd intoned.

She saw Rick Ferguson's mocking grin, heard her own weak response: 'Judge, we're forced to take a motion state because our witness isn't available for trial today.'

'What day do you want?' Judge Harris asked.

'Judge, give us thirty days,' Jess requested.

'Getting awfully close to Christmas,' the Judge reminded her.

'Yes, Your Honor.'

'Thirty days it is.'

'Sure hope the old lady shows up in thirty days,' Rick Ferguson said, not bothering to disguise the laughter in his voice. 'I hate to keep dragging my butt down here for nothing.'

Jess leaned back against the elevator wall, scoffed out loud, pretended to cough. 'You all right?' the woman beside her asked.

'Fine,' Jess said, recalling her later frustration with the auto body shop to which she'd taken her car first thing that morning. 'What do you mean, my car won't be ready by tonight? It's just a windshield wiper, for God's sake!' Now she'd have to take the El home, and it would be crowded and unpleasant, and she'd never get a seat. And she'd have to rush to make the restaurant by seven.

She could take a cab, she thought, knowing that no cabs would be waiting anywhere in the vicinity. Cabs hated coming even remotely near 26th Street and California, especially after dark. Of course she could have called for a taxi from her office, but that would have been too easy. Or she could have called Don. No, she'd never do that. She was angry with him, even furious. For what? For being objective? For believing there was a chance that Rick Ferguson might be innocent? For refusing to let his feelings for her trample over his client's rights? For being such a good lawyer? Yes, all those things, she realized.

So, she wasn't really fine, after all, Jess thought as the elevator stopped on the fourth floor to admit a bunch of tall, black men in an assortment of multi-colored wool hats. She was frustrated and fed-up and furious. 'Fuck it,' one of the tall, black men uttered as the elevator doors opened to the ground floor.

My sentiments exactly, Jess thought, tucking her purse underneath her coat as she hurried through the lobby toward the revolving doors.

It was very cold outside. Those fearless Chicago weather forecasters had predicted an unusually bitter November, and so far they'd been right. The possibility of lots of snow for December, they heralded. Jess still hadn't bought new winter boots.

She approached the bus stop at the corner, momentarily overwhelmed by what the darkness couldn't hide: the bag ladies, wearing their lives in layers against the cold; the crazies, raging against invisible demons, wandering around aimlessly, bottles in hand, no shoes on their feet; the kids, so stoned they didn't have either the energy or the inclination to pull the needles from their skinny arms; the pimps; the hookers; the dealers; the disenchanted. It was all there, Jess knew, and getting bigger every year. Like watching a cancer grow, she thought, grateful when a bus approached.

She rode the bus to California and Eighth, took the subway to State Street, transferred to the El, all with a minimum of fuss and bother. If Don could only see her now, Jess thought, and almost laughed. He'd have a fit. 'Are you nuts?' she could hear him yell. 'Don't you know how dangerous the El is, especially at night? What are you trying to prove?'

Just trying to get myself home, she answered silently, refusing to be intimidated by someone who wasn't there.

The El platform was crowded, littered, noisy. A youth bumped into Jess from behind, didn't bother with an 'excuse me' as he hurried past her. An elderly woman stepped on her toes as she edged in front of Jess, then glowered as if Jess owed *her* the apology. Black faces, brown faces, white faces. Cold faces, Jess thought, her mind painting everyone in winter blue. Bodies shivering against the night. Everyone just a little afraid of everyone else. Like watching a cancer grow, she thought again, seeing her mother's face suddenly appear in the front window of the approaching train.

The train stopped, and Jess felt herself being pushed toward its doors, barely conscious of her feet touching the ground. In the next instant, she was swept up and deposited into a cracked vinyl seat, squished between a large black man on her right and an elderly Mexican woman with a large shopping bag on her left. Across the crowded aisle sat a Filipina trying to keep a squirming white child on her lap. A whistle blew. The train lurched, then started. Torsos swayed to the rhythm of the moving train. Winter coats, like heavy curtains, fell across Jess's line of vision. Hot breath filled the air around her.

Jess closed her eyes, saw herself as a small child, holding on to her mother's hand as they stood on a platform waiting for the El. 'It's just a train, honey,' her mother had said, scooping the terrified youngster into her arms as the train barrelled toward them. 'You don't have to be afraid.'

Where was I when *you* were so afraid? Jess wondered now. Where was I when *you* needed me?

'I don't need this from you, Jess!' she heard her mother cry, tears streaking her beautiful face.

The train screeched to a halt at its next stop. Jess kept her eyes closed, heard the doors open, felt the exchange of passengers, the additional weight of more people pressing against her knees. The whistle sounded. The doors closed. The train began slowly resuming speed. Jess kept her eyes shut as the train raced through the center of the city.

She was remembering the morning of the day her mother disappeared.

It had been very hot, even for August, the temperature stretching toward ninety degrees before ten a.m. Jess had come down to the kitchen wearing shorts and an old T-shirt emblazoned with the head of Jerry Garcia. Her father was away on a buying trip. Maureen was at the library, preparing for her return to Harvard in the fall. Her mother was standing by the phone in the kitchen, dressed in a white linen dress, her make-up carefully applied, her hair neatly combed away from her face. She was obviously ready to go out. 'Where are you going?' Jess had asked.

Her mother's voice had emerged as if on pinpricks. 'Nowhere,' she'd said.

'Since when do you get so dressed up to go nowhere?'

The words reverberated to the rhythm of the train. *Since when do you get so dressed up to go nowhere? Since when do you get so dressed up to go nowhere? Since when do you get so dressed up to go nowhere?*

The train jerked, then twisted, and Jess felt someone fall across her knees. She opened her eyes, saw an elderly black woman struggling to regain her footing. 'I'm so sorry,' the woman said.

'Don't worry about it,' Jess told her, grabbing one of the woman's hands and trying to assist her, about to offer her her seat.

It was then that she saw him.

'My God!'

'Did I hurt you?' the old woman asked. 'I'm really sorry. The train jerked so suddenly, I lost my balance. Did I step on your foot?'

'I'm fine,' Jess whispered, pushing the words out of her mouth, staring past the woman at the sullen young man who stood several feet behind her, arms at his side, stubbornly refusing to hold onto anything, his defiance supporting him, holding him up.

Rick Ferguson stared back. Then he disappeared behind a wave of bodies.

Maybe she hadn't seen him at all, Jess thought, peering through the crowded car, trying to relocate him, recalling her experience with the white Chrysler in front of her brownstone. Maybe she hadn't seen anything. Maybe it was her imagination having cruel fun with her. Or maybe not.

Definitely not, Jess told herself, tired of pretending things were other than the way she knew them to be. She pushed herself to her feet. Immediately, her seat was occupied by someone else. She worked her way to the other side of the car.

He was backed against the door, wearing the same blue jeans and brown leather jacket he'd worn to court that morning, his long, dirty blond hair pulled back into a pony tail, his eyes an opaque brown that contained his entire past: the broken home; the abusive father; the alcoholic mother; the soul-destroying poverty; the frequent trouble with the law; the succession of back-breaking factory jobs; the frequent dismissals; the failed stream of relationships with women; the anger, the bitterness; the contempt. And always the smile, tight-lipped, joyless, *wrong*.

'Excuse me,' Jess whispered to a frail-looking gentleman blocking her path, and the man immediately backed out of her way. Rick Ferguson smiled as Jess stepped directly into his line of vision.

'Well, well,' he said. 'As I live and breathe.'

'Are you following me?' Jess demanded, her voice loud enough to be heard by everyone in the crowded car.

He laughed. 'Me? Following you? Why would I be doing that?'

'You tell me.'

'I don't have to tell you anything,' he said, looking over her head toward the window. 'My lawyer said so.'

The train slowed in preparation of its next stop.

'What are you doing on this train?' Jess persisted.

No answer.

'What are you doing on this train?' she said again.

He scratched the side of his nose. 'Takin' a ride.' His voice was lazy, as if the act of speaking was almost too great an effort.

'Where to?' Jess demanded.

He said nothing.

'What stop are you getting off at?'

He smiled. 'I haven't decided yet.'

'I want to know where you're going.'

'Maybe I'm going home.'

'Your mother lives on Aberdeen. That's the other way.'

'What if I'm not going to my mother's?'

'Then you're in violation of your bail. I can have you arrested.'

'The conditions of my bond state that I have to live with my mother while I'm out on bail. They don't say anything about what El trains I can, or can't, take,' he reminded her.

'What have you done with Connie DeVuono?' she asked, hoping to catch him off guard.

Rick Ferguson looked up toward the ceiling, as if he might actually be considering a response. 'Objection!' he suddenly taunted. 'I don't think my lawyer would approve of that question.'

The train lurched to a stop. Jess moved to secure her feet against the sudden motion, to reach for something to grab onto, but there was nothing, and she lost her balance, falling forward, crashing against Rick Ferguson's chest. He grabbed her, his hands gripping the sides of her arms so hard Jess could almost feel bruises starting to form.

'Let go of me,' Jess shouted. 'Let go of me this instant!'

Ferguson lifted his hands into the air. 'Hey, I was only trying to help.'

'I don't need your help.'

'You looked like you were headed for a rather nasty fall,' he said, straightening his jacket and shrugging his shoulders. 'And we wouldn't want anything to happen to you. Not now. Not when things are just starting to get interesting.'

'What does that mean?'

He laughed. 'Well, what do you know?' he said, looking past her again toward the window. 'This is my stop.' He pushed his way toward the door. 'See you around,' he said, sneaking through the doors of the train just as they were closing.

As the train pulled away from the station, Jess watched Rick Ferguson waving goodbye from the open platform.

She was sitting on the bed, naked, her clothes laid out carefully beside her, unable to move. She wasn't sure how long she'd been sitting like this, how much time had passed since she'd emerged from her shower, how many minutes had elapsed since her legs had gone numb and her breathing had become labored and heavy. 'This is ridiculous,' Jess told herself. 'You can't do this. Everyone's expecting you. You'll be late. You can't do this.'

She couldn't do anything.

She couldn't move.

'Come on, Jess,' she said. 'Don't be silly. You have to get moving. You have to get dressed.' She looked at the black silk dress that lay beside her. 'Come on. You already know what you want to wear. All you have to do is put it on.'

She couldn't. Her hands refused to leave her lap.

The panic had started as a prickly feeling in her side as she stepped out of the shower. At first she'd tried rubbing it away with her towel, but it had quickly spread to her stomach and chest, then to her hands and feet. She became light-headed, lost the feeling in her legs, was forced to sit down. Soon, it hurt to breathe. It hurt to think.

Beside the bed, the phone began to ring.

Jess stared at the phone, unable to reach for the receiver. 'Please help me,' she whispered, her body shivering from the cold. 'Please, somebody, help me.'

The phone rang once, twice, three times . . . stopped at ten. Jess closed her eyes, swayed, felt her fear rising in her throat, like a mouthful of saliva. 'Please help me,' she cried again. 'Please help me.' She stared into the mirror across from her bed. A small, frightened child stared back. 'Please help me, Mommy,' the little girl wailed. 'Promise me I'll be all right.'

'Oh, God,' Jess moaned, doubling over, her forehead touching her knees. 'What's happening to me? What's happening to me?'

The phone began ringing again. Once, twice, three times.

'I have to answer it,' she said. 'I have to answer it.'

Jess forced herself back into an upright position, hearing her body crack, like a corpse stiff with rigor mortis. Four rings, five. 'I have to answer it.' She willed her hand toward the phone, watched it as if it belonged to someone else as it brought the receiver to her ear.

'Hello, Jess? Jess, are you there?' the voice demanded, not waiting for a hello.

'Maureen?' Jess expelled the word from her mouth in a desperate whisper.

'Jess, where have you been? And what are you doing at home? You're supposed to be here!' Maureen sounded vaguely frantic.

'What time is it?'

'It's almost eight o'clock. We've been waiting since seven. Everybody's starving, not to mention worried half to death. I've been calling and calling. What's going on? You're never late.' The sentences emerged almost as one.

'I just got home,' Jess lied, still unable to feel her legs.

'Well, get right over here.'

'I can't,' Jess told her.

'What?!'

'Please, Maureen. I just can't. I'm not feeling very well.'

'Jess, you promised.'

'I know, but—'

'No buts.'

'I can't. I just can't.'

'Jess—'

'Please tell Dad I'm really sorry, but I'll have to meet his lady another time.'

'Don't do this, Jess.'

'Honestly, Maureen, I think I'm coming down with something.'

She could hear her sister crying.

'Please don't cry, Maureen. This wasn't anything I planned. I have my dress laid out and everything. I just can't make it.'

There was a second's silence. 'Suit yourself,' her sister said. The line went dead in her hand.

'Shit!' Jess screamed, slamming the receiver back into its carriage, her crippling lethargy suddenly gone. She jumped to her feet. What the hell was going on? What was she doing to herself? To her family?

Didn't she hate it when people were late? Didn't she make a point of always being on time? Wasn't she always the first one to arrive? Eight o'clock, for God's sake! She'd been sitting on her bed for ninety minutes. Sitting naked, her clothes laid out beside her, unable to put them on, unable to move.

Ninety minutes. An hour and a half. The worst attack yet. Certainly the longest. What would happen if these attacks were to follow her to work, spill over into the courtroom, paralyze her during an important cross-examination? What would she do?

She couldn't take that chance. She couldn't let that happen. She had to do something. She had to do something now.

Jess walked to her closet, pulled out her black slacks and fished through the pockets, locating the slip of paper on which her sister had scrawled the phone number of her friend, Stephanie Banack.

'Stephanie Banack,' Jess read out loud, wondering whether the therapist could be of any help. 'Call her and find out.'

Jess punched in the appropriate buttons, suddenly remembering the lateness of the hour. 'You'll just get her answering machine.' Jess was debating whether or not to leave a message when the phone was answered on its first ring.

'Stephanie Banack,' the voice said instead of hello.

Jess was nonplussed. 'I'm sorry. Is this a recording?'

Stephanie Banack laughed. 'No, it's the real thing, I'm afraid. How can I help you?'

'It's Jess Koster,' Jess said. 'Maureen's sister.'

There was a second's silence. Then, 'How are you, Jess? Is everything all right?'

'Maureen's fine, if that's what you're asking. It's me,' she continued quickly, afraid that if she slowed down, she'd stop altogether. 'I was wondering if you might have some time to see me . . . soon.'

'I'll make time,' the therapist said. 'How about noon tomorrow?'

Jess hesitated, stammered. She hadn't been expecting such immediate action.

'Come on, Jess. I don't give up my lunch hour for just anybody.'

Jess nodded into the phone. 'Twelve o'clock,' she agreed. 'I'll be there.'

Chapter Nine

Stephanie Banack's office was located on Michigan Avenue in the core of the downtown shopping district. 'She's obviously doing very well for herself,' Jess whispered into her coat collar as she waited for an elevator to take her to the fourteenth floor. She hadn't seen Stephanie Banack in years, hadn't felt the slightest desire to see her, had never understood her sister's abiding friendship with the woman. But then there was much about Maureen that Jess didn't understand. Especially these days. But that was another matter. Something that had nothing to do with why she was here.

Why *was* she here?

Jess looked around the mirror-lined, black and white marble lobby, trying to come up with a suitable response. Immediately, she concluded there was none. She had no good reason to be here. She was wasting valuable time and energy on something that required neither. She checked her watch, noted that it was five minutes to twelve, that she still had time to call upstairs and cancel her appointment without seriously inconveniencing her sister's friend. The woman had said she was giving up her lunch hour to accommodate her. Now she wouldn't have to. She wouldn't be inconveniencing her at all: she'd be doing her a favour.

Jess was searching the mirrored walls for a phone when the elevator closest to her opened. It stood there empty and waiting. Well, it seemed to be saying, what are you going to do? There's no phone and I won't wait for ever. Shit or get off the pot, it hummed impatiently. What are you going to do?

'I guess I'm coming with you,' Jess answered, glad there was no one in the lobby to overhear her. 'I'm talking to elevators, and I have to ask what I'm doing here?' She stepped inside, the elevator doors closing behind her.

The interior of the elevator was lined on three sides with the same mirrors as the lobby, and Jess discovered that, no matter how she turned her head, it was almost impossible to avoid her own reflection. Was this a deliberate ploy on the part of the therapists who occupied much of the building? Were they subtly forcing their reluctant patients to confront themselves? 'Give me a break,' Jess said out loud, refusing to be intimidated by her own image, staring past her worry-filled eyes, and securing her hair behind her ears.

The elevator doors opened on the fourteenth floor. Jess stayed pressed against the rear wall, feeling the elevator vibrate against her back, nudging her gently forward. First you won't come in; now you won't leave, it seemed to say. Jess defiantly pushed herself out into the hall, biting down hard on her tongue to keep from saying goodbye. 'You have now crossed the boundary from relative neurotic to total fruitcake,' she said, walking across the soft blue and grey carpeting to the appropriate door at the far end of the corridor. *Stephanie Banack*, the embossed gold lettering proclaimed across the dark oak, followed by an impressive number of degrees.

Too impressive, Jess thought, recalling the awkward teenager who'd often seemed glued to her sister's side, unable to imagine her as a woman capable of amassing so many initials after her name: BA; MSW; PhD. Obviously, the woman suffers from low self-esteem, Jess decided. All those expensive degrees to bolster her confidence, when a nose job was probably all she really needed.

Jess was reaching for the door knob when the door opened, and a young woman with a blond ponytail and deep purple eye shadow emerged. She smiled, the kind of loopy grin that went in all directions at once. 'Are you Jess Koster?' she asked.

Jess took a step back, silently debating whether or not to take ownership of her identity. She nodded without speaking.

'I'm Dr Banack's receptionist. Dr Banack is expecting you. You can go right in.'

She held the door open for Jess to enter, and Jess gamely stepped inside the office, holding her breath. All she had to do was wait a few seconds until she was sure the receptionist had gone, then she could leave. She'd find a pay phone somewhere on the street, call Stephanie Banack, BA, MSW, PhD, and tell her there was no need for a consultation after all. She didn't need anyone to tell her she was nuts; she'd figured it out all by herself. No need to waste time. No need to go hungry.

The reception area was pleasant enough, Jess observed, listening for the sound of an elevator door opening and closing down the hall. The walls and carpet were a soft shade of grey, the two tub chairs against one wall a pleasing mint green and grey stripe. There was a glass coffee table stacked with the latest in news and fashion magazines. The receptionist's desk was a light oak; the computer resting on it top of the line. Several posters by Calder and Miro hung on the walls, as well as a mirror next to a small closet. A large benjamin plant filled one corner. All in all, very warm and inviting. Even reassuring. You make a very good first impression, dear, she acknowledged silently, hearing the woman juror from the Erica Barnowski case whisper in her ear.

'I have to get out of here,' Jess told herself.

'Jess, is that you?' The voice coming from the inner office was clear, friendly, in command.

Jess said nothing, her eyes glued to the half-open door.

'Jess?'

Jess heard movement, felt Stephanie Banack's presence in the doorway even before she appeared.

'Jess?' Stephanie Banack asked tentatively, forcing Jess's eyes to her own.

'My God, you're beautiful,' Jess exclaimed, the words out of her mouth before she had a chance to consider them.

Stephanie laughed, a rich sound full of solid mental health, Jess thought, reaching forward to shake her outstretched hand.

'I guess you haven't seen me since I had my nose done.'

'You had your nose done?' Jess asked, striving for sincerity.

'And my hair lightened. Here, let me have your coat.'

Jess allowed Stephanie to help her off with her coat and hang it in the closet. She felt suddenly naked, despite the heavy wool of her black skirt and sweater.

The therapist motioned toward the inner office with a sweep of her hand. 'Let's go inside.'

The soft greys and greens of the reception area continued into the inner office, as did the posters and plants. A large oak desk, its top covered with numerous framed photographs of three grinning boys, sat against one wall, a paisley swivel chair in front of it. Light from the window cast an almost eerie glow on the series of framed degrees that hung on the opposite wall. But the room was dominated by the large grey leather recliner that sat at its center.

'It's been a long time since I've seen you,' Stephanie said. 'How've you been?'

'Fine.'

'Still with the State's Attorney's Office?'

'Yes.'

'You're happy there?'

'Very.'

'You're not on the witness stand, Jess. You don't have to confine your answers to one word.' Stephanie patted the high back of the grey leather chair as she walked toward her desk and sat down, immediately swivelling her chair in Jess's direction. 'Why don't you have a seat?'

Jess stubbornly remained standing, noting the proud thrust of Stephanie's shoulders, her effortlessly perfect posture, the warmth and directness of her smile. Surely Jess was in the wrong office. Or maybe she was in the right office but with the wrong therapist. The Stephanie Banack Jess had been expecting to see was stoop-shouldered and grim. She wore ill-fitting hand-me-downs, not sleek Armani pantsuits and stylish Maud Frizon shoes. This woman must be a *different* Stephanie Banack. It was not altogether outside the realm of possibility that there were two therapists named Stephanie Banack practising in downtown Chicago. Maybe they were *both* good friends of her sister. Or maybe this woman was an imposter, a patient who had murdered the real Stephanie Banack and assumed her identity. Maybe Jess should get the hell out of here as quickly as possible.

Or maybe she should just check herself into the nearest psychiatric hospital. She was obviously certifiable, a definite wacko. Where were these crazy ideas coming from? 'This was probably a mistake,' she heard herself say, disassociating herself from even the sound of her own voice.

'What was?'

'My coming here.'

'What makes you say that?'

Jess shook her head, said nothing.

'Jess, you're already here. Why don't you sit down? You don't have to tell me anything you don't want to.'

Jess nodded, didn't move.

'When you phoned last night,' the therapist ventured, 'you sounded very distraught.'

'I was overreacting.'

'To what?'

Jess shrugged. 'I'm not sure.'

'You never struck me as the type who overreacts.'

'Maybe I never used to.'

'Maybe you aren't now.'

Jess took a few tentative steps forward, touched the soft leather of the high-backed reclining chair. 'Have you spoken to Maureen?'

'I usually speak to her every week or so.'

Jess hesitated. 'I guess what I really meant to ask was, has she spoken to you?'

The therapist cocked her head. Jess was reminded immediately of a friendly cocker spaniel. 'I'm not sure I understand the question.'

'About me,' Jess stated. 'Has she said anything to you about me?'

'She mentioned some weeks back that you might call,' Stephanie said simply. 'That you were having some problems.'

'Did she say what they were?'

'I don't think she knows.'

Jess came round to the front of the large recliner, slowly lowering herself into it, pushing against the back of the chair, feeling it surround her, like a cupped hand. The chair moved with her, a foot stool miraculously rising as the chair reclined. Jess lifted her feet, rested them on the much needed support. 'This chair's great.'

Stephanie nodded.

'So, tell me, what do you think of my sister these days?' Jess asked, deciding that since she was already sitting down, she might as well be friendly, make small talk. Play nice, as her mother used to say.

'I think she's wonderful. Motherhood suits her.'

'You think so?'

'You don't?'

'I think it's a bit of a waste.' Jess looked toward the window. 'Not that I think looking after children is a waste,' she clarified. 'Just that someone with Maureen's ability and brains, not to mention the job she gave up, well, it just seems like she should be doing something more with her life than diapering babies and catering to her husband's every whim.'

Stephanie leaned forward. 'You think that Maureen caters to Barry's every whim?'

'You don't?'

Stephanie smiled. 'That's my line.'

'I mean, it's not like my parents put her through all those years of school – and you know how much Harvard costs, even on a partial scholarship – only to see her throw it all away.'

'You think your father is disappointed?'

'I don't know.' Jess looked toward the floor. 'Probably not. He's thrilled about his grandchildren. Besides, even if he were disappointed, he'd never say anything.'

'What about your mother?'

Jess felt her back stiffen. 'What do you mean?'

'Well, you implied that your parents wouldn't be happy with the choices Maureen has made recently.'

'What I said was that I didn't think they'd put her through all those years of school so that she could stay home and make babies.'

'How *do* you think your mother would feel?'

Jess turned her head to one side, pressed her chin toward her shoulder. 'She'd be furious.'

'What makes you say that?'

Jess felt her feet twitching impatiently on the footstool. 'Come on, Stephanie, you were always over at our house. You knew my mother. You knew how important it was to her that her girls get a good education, that they make something of their lives, that they learn to stand on their own two feet.'

'A woman ahead of her time. I remember.'

'Well then, you should know how she'd feel about what Maureen is doing.'

'How would she feel?'

Jess searched the air for the proper adjectives. 'Angry. Confused. Betrayed.'

'Is that how you feel?'

'I'm telling you how I think my mother would feel.'

'You don't think your mother wanted Maureen to have a family?'

'That's not what I'm saying.'

'What are you saying?'

Jess looked up at the ceiling, toward the window, at the series of framed degrees on the far wall, finally at the woman across from her. 'Look, you must remember how upset my mother was when I told her I was going to marry Don.'

'The circumstances were very different, Jess.'

'How? How were they different?'

'Well, for one thing, you were very young. Don was so much older than you. He was a practising attorney. You were just finishing your first year law school. I don't think it was marriage, per se, that your mother was objecting to, so much as the timing.'

Jess began chipping away at the clear polish of her fingernails. She said nothing.

'But Maureen had already finished her education,' Stephanie

continued. 'She was well established when she met and married Barry. I don't think your mother would have had any objections to her taking some time off to raise a family.'

'I'm not saying my mother wouldn't have wanted Maureen to marry and have children,' Jess stated, anger propelling her words. 'Why wouldn't she? My mother loved having children. She loved being married. She'd dedicated her life to being the best wife and mother anybody could hope for. But . . .'

'But what?'

'But she wanted more for her daughters,' Jess said. 'Is that so awful? Is there something wrong with that?'

'It depends on what the daughter wants for herself.'

Jess squeezed her upper lip between the fingers of her right hand, waiting till her heart stopped racing before trying to speak. 'Look, I didn't come here to talk about Maureen or my mother.'

'Why *did* you come?'

'I really don't know.'

There was a moment's silence. For the first time, Jess became aware of the clock on Stephanie's desk. She watched the minute hand jerk to its next stop. Another minute lost. Time passing, she thought, thinking of all the things she should be doing. She had an appointment with the Medical Examiner's Office at one-thirty, an interview with an eyewitness to the crossbow killing at three, a meeting with several police officers at four. She could have used this time to prepare. What was she doing wasting a precious hour here, accomplishing nothing?

'What were you doing when you called last night?' Stephanie asked.

'What do you mean, what was I doing?'

Stephanie looked confused. 'It's a pretty straightforward question, Jess. What were you doing immediately before you phoned me last night?'

'Nothing.'

'Nothing? And out of the blue you just decided, gee, I haven't seen Stephanie Banack in years. I think I'll give her a call?'

'Something like that.'

Another silence. 'Jess, I can't help you if you won't even give me a chance.'

Jess wanted to speak, couldn't.

'Why did you ask your sister for my number?'

'I didn't.'

'So she's the one who suggested that you call?'

Jess shrugged.

'Why is that?'

'You'll have to ask her.'

'Look, maybe the fact that I'm your sister's friend is what's getting in the way here. You must know that anything you say to me will be held in the strictest confidence. But maybe you'd prefer that I recommend someone else.'

'No,' Jess said quickly. 'It's not you. It's me.'

'Tell me about you,' Stephanie said gently.

'I've been having these anxiety attacks.'

'What do you mean by anxiety attacks?'

'Feelings of panic.'

'What happens when you get these feelings?'

Jess stared into her lap, saw the chips of her nail polish resting on the surface of her black skirt like sparkling sequins. 'Shortness of breath. Numbness. My legs won't move. They get tingly, weak. My head feels light, then heavy. My heart starts racing. My chest feels like someone's got me in a hammerlock. Paralysis. I literally can't move. I feel like I'm going to throw up.'

'How long have you been having these attacks?'

'They started again a few weeks ago.'

'Again?'

'What?'

Stephanie crossed, then uncrossed her legs. 'You said they started *again* a few weeks ago.'

'Did I?'

'Yes.'

'I guess that's what they call a Freudian slip.' Jess laughed bitterly. Was her subconscious so ready to reveal all her secrets?

'So these attacks aren't something new.' The comment was

more statement than question.

'No.' Jess paused, then pressed on. 'I had them after my mother disappeared. Almost every day for at least a year, then frequently for several years after that.'

'Then they stopped?'

'I hadn't had any attacks in about four years.'

'And now they've started again.'

Jess nodded. 'They've started happening with increasing frequency. Lasting longer. Getting worse.'

'And this started again, you said, a few weeks ago?'

'Yes.'

'What do you think triggered this latest round?'

'I'm not sure.'

'Is there some sort of pattern to the attacks?'

'What do you mean by pattern?'

Stephanie paused, rubbed her fingers against the side of her perfectly sculpted nose. 'Do they happen at any particular time of the day or night? Do they happen at work? When you're alone? In any particular place? Around specific people?'

Jess's mind raced through all the questions in turn. The attacks happened at all hours of the day or night. They happened at work, at her apartment, when she was alone, when she was walking along a busy street, when she was at the movies, when she was stepping out of the shower. 'There's no pattern,' she said hopelessly.

'Were you having an attack before you called last night?'

Jess nodded.

'What were you doing?'

Jess told her about getting ready to go out. 'I knew what I was going to wear,' Jess heard herself whisper. 'I had it all laid out and everything.'

'You were supposed to meet the new lady in your father's life?'

'Yes,' Jess admitted.

'I imagine that would be a fairly anxiety-provoking situation.'

'Well, it's not something I was exactly looking forward to,

which, I guess makes me a pretty horrible person.'

'Why do you say that?'

'Because I'm supposed to want my father to be happy.'

'And you don't?'

'I do!' Jess felt tears forming in her eyes. She struggled to contain them. 'That's what I don't understand. I *do* want him to be happy. Of course, I want him to be happy. What makes him happy should make me happy.'

'Why?'

'What?'

'Since when does what makes another person happy have to make us happy too? You're demanding a great deal of yourself, Jess. Maybe too much.'

'Maureen doesn't seem to be having any trouble with the situation. '

'Maureen isn't you.'

Jess sifted quickly through all that had been said. 'But it can't just be my father. The attacks started before I even knew that he was involved with anyone.'

'When exactly did they start?'

Jess thought back to the night she woke up to find her body shaking and her bed sheets soaking wet. 'I was in bed, asleep. I had a nightmare. It woke me up.'

'Do you remember what the nightmare was about?'

'My mother,' Jess said. 'I kept trying to reach her, but I couldn't.'

'Had you been thinking about your mother before you went to sleep?'

'I don't remember,' Jess lied. The whole day had been filled with thoughts of her mother. In fact, her first attack hadn't followed her nightmare at all. It had happened earlier in the day, in the courtroom during the Erica Barnowski rape trial, when she thought she recognized her mother behind a juror's face.

She didn't want to talk anymore about her mother.

'Look, I think I know why this is happening,' Jess announced. 'I think it has to do with a man I'm prosecuting.' She saw Rick

Ferguson's face in the reflection of the glass protecting Stephanie Banack's framed degrees. 'He's made some threats.'

'What kind of threats?'

People who annoy me have a way of disappearing . . .

Disappearing.

Like her mother.

I don't need this, Jess. I don't need this from you!

She didn't want to think about her mother.

'Look, I really don't think it's as important to know why these attacks are happening so much as what I can do to stop them.'

'I can give you some simple relaxation exercises to work on, some techniques that may take the edge off the attacks,' Stephanie told her, 'but I think that in order to really get rid of them, you have to deal with the underlying problems that are causing these attacks.'

'You're talking long-term therapy?'

'I'm talking some therapy, yes.'

'I don't need therapy. I just need to put this guy behind bars.'

'Why do I think it's not as simple as that?'

'Because that's how you've been trained to think. It's your job.' Jess checked her watch, though she already knew the time. 'And speaking of jobs, I have to get back to mine.' She pushed herself out of the comfortable recliner and walked briskly to the door of the reception room, as if responding to a silent fire drill.

'Jess, wait.'

Jess continued into the reception area without pausing, retrieving her coat from the closet and throwing it over her shoulders as she headed for the door to the hallway. 'It's been nice seeing you again, Stephanie. Take care of yourself.' She marched into the corridor and proceeded with purposeful strides toward the elevators.

'I'm here any time, Jess,' Stephanie called after her. 'All you have to do is call.'

Don't hold your breath, Jess wanted to reply, but didn't. She didn't have to. Her silence said it all.

Chapter Ten

'Can I help you?'

'I'm just looking, thank you.'

What was she doing now? Jess wondered, examining a pair of green suede Bruno Magli flats. What had possessed her to come into this store? The last thing she needed was another pair of shoes.

She checked her watch. Almost twelve-thirty. She had an appointment with the Chief Medical Examiner in one hour. The medical examiner's office was over on Harrison Street, a drive of at least twenty minutes, and she still didn't have her car back from the shop. They'd called first thing this morning; something about another minor, though very necessary, repair. She'd have to take a taxi.

'If you give me some idea of the type of shoe you have in mind,' the salesman persisted.

'I really don't have anything in mind,' Jess said curtly. The salesman, a short, middle-aged man with an ill-fitting brown toupee, bowed with exaggerated politeness and moved quickly toward a woman who was just coming in the door.

Jess let her eyes travel down a long table covered with an astonishing array of casual shoes in a variety of colorful suedes and leathers. She lifted a pair of mustard-yellow loafers into her palms and turned them over with her fingers. Nothing like a new pair of shoes to make the problems of the world disappear, she thought, stroking the soft suede. That was all the therapy she really needed. Certainly cheaper, she decided, staring at the price ticket stuck to the bottom of the heel. Ninety-nine dollars as opposed to . . .

As opposed to what?

She'd never even discussed price with Stephanie Banack,

never thought to inquire as to her hourly rate, walked out on the woman without so much as asking what she owed her. Not only did the woman not get lunch, she didn't get paid either. Two indignities for the price of one.

Jess returned the shoe to the table, shaking her head in dismay. It was one thing to be rude; it was something else to be presumptuous. She'd treated her sister's friend very badly. She'd have to apologize, maybe send the woman flowers and a brief thank you note. And say what? Thanks for the memories? Thanks for nothing? Thanks but no thanks?

'I think that in order to really get rid of your anxiety attacks,' she heard Stephanie Banack repeat, *'you have to deal with the underlying problems that are causing them.'*

There are no underlying problems, Jess insisted silently, approaching the next table, covered with more formal footwear, running her fingers across the toes of a series of black patent high-heeled shoes.

There was only one problem, and she knew exactly what that problem was.

Rick Ferguson.

Not that he was the first felon who had threatened her. Hate, abuse, intimidation – they were all part of her job description. For the last two years, she had received a Christmas card from a man she had successfully prosecuted and put away for ten years. He'd threatened to come after her as soon as he got out. The Christmas cards, innocuous as they appeared on the surface, were his not-so-subtle way of reminding her he hadn't forgotten.

In truth, such threats were rarely carried out. They were uttered; they were received; they were eventually forgotten. By both sides.

Rick Ferguson was different.

The man of her dreams, she thought ironically, recalling the nightmare that began with her frantically trying to find her mother and ended with her finding Death. Somehow Rick Ferguson had been able to reach into her most secret self, to accidentally trigger long-dormant feelings of guilt and anxiety.

Anxiety, yes, Jess acknowledged, lifting a shiny black shoe

into her hand, squeezing its toe so hard she felt the leather crack. Not guilt. What did she possibly have to feel guilty about? 'Don't be silly,' she muttered under her breath, again recalling Stephanie Banack's words. 'There *are* no underlying problems.' She began banging the sharp end of the high heel into the palm of her hand.

'Hey, be careful,' a voice called from somewhere beside her. A hand reached out and stopped the movement of her own. 'It's a shoe, not a hammer.'

Jess stared first into her bruised palm, then at the crumpled shoe in her other hand, and finally up at the man with light brown hair and worried brown eyes whose hand rested lightly on her arm. The tag pinned to his dark blue sports jacket identified him as Adam Stohn. White male, early to middle thirties, six feet tall, approximately one hundred and eighty pounds, she summed up silently, as if reading from a police report. 'I'm so sorry,' she began. 'Of course I'll pay for them.'

'I'm not worried about the shoe,' he said, gently lifting it from her hand and returning it to the table.

Jess watched it wobble, then fall over on its side, as if it had been shot. 'But I've ruined it.'

'Nothing a quick polish and a good shoe tree won't fix. What about your hand?'

Jess felt it throbbing, saw the round purple splotch that sat, like a discolored quarter, in the center of her palm. 'It'll be okay.'

'Looks like you might have broken a blood vessel.'

'I'll be fine. Really,' she assured him, understanding that he was genuinely concerned. Was the store liable?

'Can I get you a drink of water?'

Jess shook her head.

'How about a candy?' He pulled a red and white striped mint from his pocket.

Jess smiled. 'No, thank you.'

'How about a joke?'

'Do I look that desperate?' She sensed his reluctance to leave her to her own devices.

'You look like someone who could use a good joke.'

She nodded. 'You're right. Go ahead.'

'Clean or mildly risqué?'

Jess laughed. 'What the hell. Let's go for broke.'

'Mildly risqué, it is.' He paused. 'A man and woman are making love when they hear someone coming up the stairs and the woman cries, "My God, it's my husband!" Her lover immediately jumps out of the window into a clump of bushes. So, here's this guy, he's outside hiding in this sorry clump of bushes, he's naked, and he doesn't know what to do, and naturally, it starts raining. Suddenly, a bunch of joggers go jogging by, and the guy sees his chance, and leaps into the middle of the joggers, running along with them. After a few seconds, the jogger beside him looks over and says, "Excuse me, but do you mind if I ask you a question?" And the guy says, "Go ahead." And the jogger says, "Do you always jog naked?" And the guy says, "Always." And the jogger asks, "Do you always wear a condom when you jog?" And the guy says, "Only when it's raining." '

Jess found herself laughing out loud.

'That's better. Now, can I sell you a pair of shoes?'

Jess laughed even harder.

'That wasn't supposed to be funny. The funny part's over.'

'I'm sorry. Are you as good at selling shoes as you are at telling jokes?'

'Try me.'

Jess checked her watch. She still had a little time. Surely one pair of shoes wouldn't hurt. She probably owed the store that much, having murdered that poor black pump. Besides, she found herself curiously reluctant to leave. It had been a long time since a man had made her laugh out loud. She liked the sound. She liked the feeling. 'Actually, I could use a new pair of winter boots,' she said, remembering, relieved at finding a legitimate reason to stay.

'Right this way.' Adam Stohn directed her toward a display of leather and vinyl boots. 'Have a seat.'

Jess lowered herself into a small rust-colored chair, for the first time taking note of her surroundings. The store was very modern, all glass and chrome. Shoes were everywhere, on glass tables, on mirrored shelves, along the brown and gold carpeted floor, reflected in the high mirrored ceiling. She realized she'd shopped here several times before, though she had no memory of Adam Stohn.

'Are you new here?' she asked.

'I started this summer.'

'You like it?'

'Shoes are my life,' he said, his voice a sly smile. 'Now, what sort of boot can I show you?'

'I'm not sure. I hate to spend a lot of money on a leather boot that's only going to get ruined by the snow and salt.'

'So don't buy leather.'

'But I like some style. And I like my feet to be warm.'

'The lady wants style *and* warmth. I believe I have just what you need.'

'Is that so?'

'Have I ever lied to you?'

'Probably.'

He smiled. 'I see we have a cynic in our midst. Well then, allow me.' He reached over to a small display of sleek and shiny black boots. 'These are vinyl, fleece-lined, waterproof, absolutely no-maintenance winter boots. They are stylish; they are warm; they are guaranteed to withstand even the worst Chicago winter.' He handed Jess the boot.

'And they're very expensive,' Jess exclaimed, surprised at the two hundred dollar price tag. 'I can buy real leather for that price.'

'But you don't want real leather. You have to spray it; you have to take care of it. And real leather leaks and marks and does all the things you want to avoid. This boot,' he said, tapping its shiny side, 'you wear and forget about. It's indestructible.'

'You *are* as good at selling shoes as you are at telling jokes,' Jess said.

'Are you saying you'd like to try them on?'

'Size eight and a half,' Jess said.

'Be right back.'

Jess watched Adam Stohn disappear through a door at the back of the store. She liked the casual determination of his gait, the straightness of his shoulders. Confidence without arrogance, she thought, her eyes drifting back along the mirrored walls.

Was there no escape from one's own reflection? Were people really so interested in seeing themselves every second of the day? Jess caught the disappointed glare of the middle-aged salesman with the ill-fitting toupee in the glass. She closed her eyes. I know, she thought, responding to his silent admonishment, I'm shallow and easily swayed. A pretty face and a good joke get me every time.

'You're not going to believe this,' Adam Stohn said upon his return, his arms filled with two wide boxes, 'but I'm out of size eight and a half. I have a size eight and a size nine.'

She tried them. Predictably, the eight was too small, the nine too big.

'You're sure you have no eight and a halfs?'

'I looked everywhere.'

Jess shrugged, checked her watch, stood up. She couldn't afford to waste any more time.

'I can call one of our other stores,' Adam Stohn offered.

'All right,' Jess answered quickly. What was she doing?

He walked to the counter at the front of the store, picked up the black telephone, punched in some buttons, and spoke into the receiver, shaking his head, then repeating the process two more times. 'Can you believe it?' he asked upon his return. 'I called three stores. No one has size eight and a half. But,' he continued, his finger poking the air for emphasis, 'one store has several on order and will call me as soon as they come in. Would you like me to call you?'

'I beg your pardon?' Was he asking her out?

'When the boots come in, would you like me to call you?'

'Oh, oh, sure. Yes, please. That would be great.' Jess realized she was talking to cover her embarrassment. What had she been thinking of? Why had she thought he might be asking her out? Because he'd offered her a candy and told her a joke about condoms? Because the idea appealed to her? Just because she thought he was attractive and charming, did that necessarily mean the reverse was true?

Don't be an idiot, Jess, she scolded herself, following him to the counter at the front of the store. The man was a shoe salesman, for God's sake. Hardly the world's prize catch.

Don't be such a snob, a little voice admonished. At least he's not a lawyer.

'Name?' he asked, reaching for a nearby pad and pencil.

'Jess Koster.'

'Phone number where you can be reached during the day?'

Jess gave him her number at work. 'Maybe I better give you my home number too,' she said, not believing the words coming out of her mouth.

'Sure.' He copied the numbers down as she recited them. 'My name is Adam Stohn.' He indicated the tag on his jacket, pronouncing the Stohn as Stone. 'It shouldn't be more than a week.'

'That's great. Hopefully, it won't snow before then.'

'It wouldn't dare.'

Jess smiled and waited for him to say more, but he didn't. Instead, he looked just past her to where a woman stood admiring a pair of tomato-red Charles Jourdan pumps. 'Thanks again,' she said on her way out, but he was already moving toward the other woman, and all Jess got was a perfunctory wave.

'I can't believe I did that,' Jess muttered as she slid into the back seat of a yellow taxi. Could she have been any more obvious? Why didn't she just wear a large sign round her neck that stated *Lonely and Deeply Disturbed*?

The cab reeked of cigarette smoke, although there was a large sign prominently displayed across the back of the front seat thanking people for not smoking. She gave the taxi driver the address of the Chief Medical Examiner on Harrison Street, and sank back into the scuffed and torn black vinyl seat. Probably what my new boots will look like by the end of the season, Jess thought, running her hand across the rough surface.

What had possessed her? That was twice in the last month she'd almost allowed a handsome stranger to pick her up. Had she learned absolutely nothing from the Erica Barnowski case? And this time the man in question hadn't even come on to her. He'd offered her a glass of water, a candy, and some amusing repartee, all in pursuit of a hoped-for commission. He'd been trying to get into her purse, not her pants, when he told the joke about the naked jogger. And she'd let him in without even a struggle, committing herself to the most expensive pair of rubber boots ever made. 'Not even leather,' she chastized herself, picking at a tear that sliced through the seat's cheap upholstery like a large, gaping wound.

'Sorry?' the cab driver said. 'You say something?'

'Nothing. Sorry,' Jess apologized in return, continuing silently. Just talking to myself again. Something I seem to be doing with alarming frequency these days.

Two hundred dollars for a pair of vinyl boots. Was she crazy?

Well, yes, actually, she thought. That fact had been pretty much established.

'Nice day,' Jess commented, struggling for normalcy.

'Sorry?'

'I said it's nice to see the sun again.'

The cab driver shrugged, said nothing. Jess rode the rest of the way to the Medical Examiner's Office in silence, punctuated only by the instructions and static coming over the driver's two-way radio.

The office of the Chief Medical Examiner was a nondescript three-story building on a block full of such structures. Jess paid the cab driver, exited the taxi, and walked briskly toward the entrance, gathering her coat tightly round her, preparing her body for the approaching chill.

Anderson, Michael, age 45, died suddenly as the result of a car accident, Jess recited in her mind, recalling the morning obituaries as she strode through the front lobby toward the glassed-in receptionist's corner. *Clemmons, Irene, died peacefully in her sleep in her 102nd year, remembered fondly by her fellow residents at the Whispering Pines Lodge. Lawson, David, age 33. He's gone on to other things. Mourned by his mother, his father, his sisters and his dog. In lieu of donations to your favorite charities, lots and lots of flowers would be gratefully appreciated.*

Why was it that some people barely made it past the first bloom of youth, when others hung on into their second century? Where was the fairness? she wondered, surprising herself. She thought she had given up on fairness a long time ago.

'I'm here to see Hilary Waugh,' she told the gum-chewing young woman behind the receptionist's window.

The woman, whose straight brown hair looked as if it could use a good washing, cracked her gum, and dialed the appropriate extension. 'She says you're early,' the receptionist informed Jess a few seconds later, her voice a rebuke. 'She'll be with you in a few minutes. If you want to have a seat . . .'

'Thank you.' Jess backed away from the small reception area toward a faded brown corduroy sofa that sat against one beige wall, but she didn't sit down. She could never sit down anywhere in this building. In fact, she could barely stand still. She hugged her arms round her, rubbed them in a vain effort to generate warmth.

Mateus, Jose, taken suddenly in his fifty-fourth year, survived by his mother, Alma, and his wife Rosa, and their two children, Paolo and Gino, Jess's memory recited. Neilsen, Thomas, a retired civil servant, of a heart attack in his 77th year. Mr Neilsen is survived by his wife, Linda, his sons Peter and Henry, his daughters-in-law Rita and Susan, his grandchildren Lisa, Karen, Jonathan, Stephen, and Jeffrey. The family will be receiving visitors at J. Humphrey's Funeral Home all this week.

Not like those unfortunates resting in Boot Hill, Jess thought, unwillingly conjuring up the image of that section of the morgue where rows of heavy grey metal drawers stored unidentified, unclaimed bodies. The only people who ever came to visit these lost souls were people like herself, people whose professional curiosity demanded their presence, if not their respect.

Doe, John, black male, suspected drug dealer, died of a gunshot wound to the head in his 22nd year; Doe, Jane, white female, suspected prostitute, suddenly in her 18th year, strangled and left for dead near the shore of the Chicago River; Doe, John, white male and probable pimp, dead of three stab wounds to the chest, age 19; Doe, Jane, black female, longtime crack addict, in her 28th year, beaten to death after being sexually assaulted. Doe, John—

'Jess?'

Jess's head snapped to the sound of her name.

'I'm sorry,' Hilary Waugh was saying, moving toward her. 'I didn't mean to startle you.'

Jess shook the outstretched hand. She never failed to be surprised by how fit and fresh the Chief Medical Examiner for Cook County always appeared, despite the unpleasantness and long hours of her job. Hilary Waugh had to be close to fifty, yet she had the skin of a woman half her age, and her posture, accentuated by her white lab coat, was impeccable. She wore her dark shoulder-length hair pulled back into a French braid, and her hazel eyes were framed by large glasses.

'Thank you for seeing me,' Jess said, following Hilary through the door that led from the lobby to the inner offices.

'Always a pleasure. What can I do for you?'

The long corridor was sterile and white and smelled faintly of formaldehyde, although Jess suspected any odors she was picking up were part of her overactive imagination. The morgue was in the basement, safely out of olfactory range.

'Have a seat,' Hilary said, stepping inside the tiny white cubby-hole that served as her office and motioning toward the empty chair across from her desk.

'If you don't mind, I'll stand.' Jess looked around the tiny cubicle that was the office of the Chief Medical Examiner of Cook County. It was sparsely furnished with an old metal desk and two chairs, one on either side of the desk, the deep wine of the seat covers fraying at the seams. File cabinets lined the walls, alongside precarious stacks of papers. A tall green plant flourished despite the fact that it was crammed into a corner and all but hidden by books. There was no window, fluorescent lighting taking the place of the sun. 'You obviously have a very green thumb,' Jess remarked.

'Oh, it's not real,' Hilary said, laughing. 'It's silk. Much less trouble that way. Much more pleasant. I see enough dead things as it is. Which is, I'm sure, the point of your visit.'

Jess cleared her throat. 'I'm looking for a woman, mid-forties, Italian-American, about five feet six inches tall, 135 pounds, maybe less. Actually, here,' Jess reached inside her purse, 'this is her picture.' She held out an old photo of Connie DeVuono standing with her arms proudly around her son, Steffan, then age 6. 'The picture's a few years old. She's lost some weight since then. Her hair's a bit shorter.'

The Chief Medical Examiner took the picture, spent several seconds looking at it. 'A very attractive woman. Who is she?'

'Her name is Connie DeVuono. She's been missing over two weeks.'

'This is the woman you called me about last week?' Hilary Waugh asked.

Jess nodded sheepishly. 'I'm sorry to be such a pest. It's just that I keep thinking of her little boy.'

'Looks just like his mother,' the Medical Examiner remarked as Jess reclaimed the photograph, carefully returning it to her purse.

'Yes. And it's very hard on him . . . not knowing exactly what happened to her.' Jess swallowed the catch in her throat.

'I'm sure it is. And I wish I could help.'

'No bodies matching Connie DeVuono's description have turned up?'

'At the moment we have three unidentified white females in Boot Hill. Two are teenagers, probably runaways. One died of a drug overdose; the other was raped and strangled.'

'And the third?'

'Just came in this morning. We haven't run any tests yet. But the state of decomposition indicates she's only been dead a few days.'

'It's possible,' Jess stated quickly, although she found it highly unlikely. Rick Ferguson would hardly have been foolhardy enough to kidnap Connie, then wait several weeks before killing her. 'About how old is she? *Was* she?' Jess corrected, hearing the word *decomposition* ricochet inside her brain.

'Impossible to say at the moment. She was beaten beyond all recognition.'

Jess felt her stomach turn over. She fought to stay steady. 'But you don't think it's Connie deVuono.'

'The woman on the table downstairs has blond hair and is approximately five feet nine inches tall. I'd say that eliminates her as the woman you're looking for. Are you sure you wouldn't like to sit down?'

'No, I really should get going,' Jess said, taking several tentative steps to the office door. Hilary pushed back her chair, rose to her feet. 'No, you don't have to get up,' Jess told her, not sure whether she was relieved or disappointed that the unidentified woman wasn't Connie DeVuono. 'Will you call me if anything . . .' She stopped, unable to complete the sentence.

'I'll call you if anyone even remotely resembling Connie DeVuono turns up.'

Jess stepped into the hall, hesitated, then turned back to Hilary. 'I'm going to get hold of Connie's dental records, have them sent over here,' she said, thinking of the woman lying downstairs. *Beaten beyond all recognition.* 'Just so you'll have them on hand if . . .' She stopped, cleared her throat, started again. 'It might speed things up a bit.'

'That would be very helpful,' Hilary agreed. 'Assuming we find her body.'

Assuming we find her body. The words followed Jess down the corridor and into the lobby. *Assuming we find her body.* She pushed open the door to the outside, and ran down the steps to the street. She threw her head back and inhaled a deep breath of fresh air, feeling the cold sun warm on her face.

Assuming we find her body, she thought.

Chapter Eleven

'Four hundred and eleven dollars?!' Jess yelled. 'Are you crazy?'

The young black man behind the high white counter remained calm, his face impassive. He was obviously used to such outbursts. 'The bill is carefully itemized. If you'd care to take another look—'

'I've looked. I still don't understand what could possibly have cost over four hundred dollars!' Jess realized that her voice was becoming dangerously shrill, that the other patrons of the auto body shop where she had taken her car to be serviced almost three weeks ago were staring at her.

'There was a lot that had to be done,' the young man reminded her.

'There was a windshield wiper!'

'Both wipers, actually,' the man, whose name tag identified him as Robert, stated. 'You recall we phoned you, told you that both would have to be replaced, along with the catalytic converter and the alternator,' Robert expanded patiently. 'Your car hadn't been serviced in some time.'

'There was never any need.'

'Yes, well, you were very lucky. The problem with these old cars is that they require a lot of maintenance . . .'

'Three weeks' worth?'

'We had to order the parts. There was some delay in getting them in.'

'And what's all this?' Jess said, desperately pointing to a host of other items at the bottom of the list.

'Winterizing, tune-up, valve changes. Actually, you got off pretty cheaply, considering.'

'That's it!' Jess exploded. 'I want to talk to the manager.'

Jess looked helplessly from side to side. A middle-aged man waiting at the next counter turned quickly away; a young woman giggled; an elderly woman waiting beside her husband raised her fist to her breast in a covert salute.

'He's not in yet,' Robert explained as Jess checked the large clock on the wall. 7:55, it read.

Normally, she'd have been in her office ten minutes ago. She'd be going over her calendar, making her notes, deciding on what more had to be done in preparation for her day in court. Now, instead of rehearsing her opening statement for the most high-profile murder case of her career, she was arguing with somebody named Robert about her car.

'Look, I really don't have time for this. What if I simply refuse to pay?'

'Then you don't get your car back,' Robert said, equally simply.

Jess stared into the black and white tile mosaic of the floor. 'You know, of course, that you won't be seeing my business again.'

Robert barely suppressed a smile.

'Can I give you a check?'

'Cash or charge only.'

'Naturally.' Jess pulled out her wallet and handed over her charge card, thinking that what was probably even more remarkable than the number of the murders that occurred every year in Chicago was the fact that there weren't more.

'Ladies and gentlemen of the jury,' Jess began, her eyes making brief contact with each of the eight women and six men who made up the jury and their alternates in what the press was calling the Crossbow murder trial, 'on June the second of this year, Terry Wales, the defendant, shot his wife through the heart with a steel-tipped arrow from a crossbow, in the middle of the intersection at Grand Avenue and State Street. No one here disputes that. It is a fact, pure and simple.

'The defense will try to convince you that nothing about this case is simple, that there is little that is pure,' she said, borrowing Greg Oliver's clever phrase. 'But facts are facts, ladies and gentlemen, and the fact is that Nina Wales, a lovely and intelligent woman of 38, was mercilessly shot down, in a most cruel and horrible way, by the brutal husband she had recently worked up the courage to leave.'

Jess backed away slightly from the jury box, drawing the jurors' eyes toward the defendant, Terry Wales, a relatively innocuous, even mousey-looking man of forty. His frame was slender and wiry, his complexion pale, his thinning hair a colorless blond. It was his lawyer, Hal Bristol, a dark-haired beefy man of maybe sixty, to whom all eyes were naturally drawn. Terry Wales sat beside him looking meek and overwhelmed, his face a mask of bewilderment, as if he couldn't believe the words he was hearing, or the predicament he found himself in.

Perhaps he couldn't, Jess thought, her eyes drawn to the Bible Terry Wales twisted nervously in his hands. Criminals, like teenagers, thought they were invincible. No matter how great their crime, no matter how obvious their motives, no matter how clear the crumbs of the trail they left behind, they never actually thought they'd be caught. They always believed they would get away with it. And sometimes they did. Sometimes all it took was the help of a well-trained lawyer and a well-thumbed copy of the New Testament. Would the jury fall for such a cheap bit of theatrics? Jess wondered, cynically.

'Don't be fooled by the carefully coached picture of pious innocence and regret you see before you, ladies and gentlemen,' Jess admonished, momentarily veering away from her planned speech, watching as Hal Bristol shook his head. 'Don't be tricked into thinking that just because a man clutches a Bible, he understands what's inside it. Or even cares.

'Where was his Bible when Terry Wales regularly battered his wife over the course of their eleven-year marriage? Where was it when he threatened to kill her if she tried to leave? Where was it when he bought a crossbow the day before the killing? Where was the Bible Terry Wales is clutching in his hand when he took that crossbow and used it to shoot down his wife as she emerged from a taxi on her way to see her lawyer? That Bible was nowhere in sight, ladies and gentlemen. Terry Wales had no use for Bibles then. Only now. And only because you're watching him.'

Jess returned to her prepared script. 'The defense will try to tell you that the cold-blooded, premeditated murder of Nina Wales was, in fact, a crime of passion. Yes, they will concede, Terry Wales did purchase the crossbow and arrow; yes, he did shoot his wife. But don't you understand? He didn't really mean to hurt her. He only wanted to scare her. He loved her, they'll try to convince you. He loved her, and she was leaving him. He'd tried reasoning with her; he'd cajoled; he'd begged; he'd pleaded. He'd even threatened. He was a man in pain, a man in turmoil. He was beside himself with grief over the thought of losing his wife.

'They will also try to convince you that Nina Wales was not entirely without blame in her own demise. She was cheating on her husband, they'll assert, although for that we have only the word of the man who killed her.

'They will tell you that Nina Wales taunted her husband about his failings as a lover, that she ridiculed his manhood, baited him relentlessly for his failure to satisfy her voracious needs.

'Finally, the defense will tell you that Nina Wales not only threatened to leave her husband, she threatened to take him for everything he owned, that she threatened to take his children away, turn them against him for ever, leave him with nothing, not even his self-respect.

'And still he loved her, they will tell you. Still he pleaded with her to stay. And still she refused.

'I ask you,' Jess said simply, her eyes travelling across the double rows of jurors, 'what's a man supposed to do? What other choice did Terry Wales have but to kill her?'

Jess paused, giving her words time to sink in, turning in a small circle, taking in the room at a single glance. She saw Judge Harris, whose face registered the same interested yet impassive look it always did during a trial; she saw the prosecutor's table where Neil Strayhorn sat hunched forward in his seat, his head nodding silent encouragement; she saw the crowded rows of spectators, the reporters scribbling notes, the television news artists sketching hurried portraits of the accused.

She saw Rick Ferguson.

He was sitting in the second row from the back of the courtroom, in the third seat in from the center aisle, his hair hanging long behind his ears, his eyes staring straight ahead, his odious Cheshire cat grin firmly in place. Quickly, Jess looked away, her heart pounding.

What was he doing here? What was he trying to prove? That he could intimidate her? That he could harass her at will? That he wouldn't be controlled, couldn't be stopped?

Don't lose it, Jess told herself. Concentrate. Concentrate on the speech you're giving to the jury. Don't let one killer prevent you from bringing another killer to justice. Deal with Terry Wales now, and with Rick Ferguson later.

Jess turned back toward the jury, saw that they were anxiously waiting for her to continue. 'Take a good look at the defendant, ladies and gentlemen,' Jess instructed, again veering from her prepared text. 'He doesn't took like a cold-blooded killer, does he? Actually, he looks pretty harmless. Mild, maybe even a little meek. Pretty skinny for a guy who regularly beat his wife, you're probably thinking. But once again, ladies and gentlemen, don't be fooled by appearances.

'The fact is, and the prosecution will always be bringing you back to the facts of this case, the fact is that Terry Wales has a black belt in karate; the fact is that we have hospital records that will show a history of broken bones and bruises inflicted on Nina Wales by her husband over the years. The fact is that Terry Wales was a wife-beater.

'Let me ask you something, ladies and gentlemen of the jury,' Jess continued, resolutely confining her gaze to the jury box. 'Is it reasonable to expect us to believe that Terry Wales shot his wife in a fit of passion when they hadn't seen each other in several days? Is it reasonable to expect us to believe that there was no premeditation involved even though Terry Wales purchased the murder weapon the day before he shot his wife down? That there was no preconceived plan? That there was no expectation that when he fired the steel-tipped arrow into his wife's chest that she might die?

'Because that's exactly what defines an act of first-degree murder,' Jess explained, feeling Rick Ferguson's eyes burrowing into the back of her head. She spoke with deliberate slowness, making sure the jury heard and appreciated every word, reciting the statute from memory. ' "If the murder was committed in a cold, calculated and premeditated manner pursuant to a preconceived plan, scheme or design to take a human life by unlawful means, and the conduct of the defendant created a reasonable expectation that the death of a human being would result therefrom." That is the definition of murder in the first degree.

'The defense would have you believe that Terry Wales, thoroughly emasculated by his wife, yet distraught at the thought of losing her, was only trying to frighten her when he aimed that crossbow at her heart. They want you to believe that he was actually aiming for her leg. They would have you believe that Terry Wales, an already broken man, "snapped" after his wife taunted him once too often, that he was only trying to shake her up a little when he fired that crossbow into the middle of a busy intersection, that Terry Wales is as much a victim in this case as his wife.

'Don't be fooled, ladies and gentlemen. Nina Wales is the victim here. Nina Wales is dead. Terry Wales is very much alive.'

Jess pushed herself away from the jury box, forced her eyes back to the spectators' benches. Rick Ferguson smiled back from his seat in the second to last row.

'The prosecution will prove,' Jess stated firmly, turning back to the jury, 'that Terry Wales regularly beat his wife. We will prove that he threatened, on more than one occasion, to kill her if she ever tried to leave him. We will prove that after Nina Wales did just that, after she worked up the courage to take her children and run, Terry Wales purchased a crossbow in his local sporting goods store. We will prove that he used that crossbow to shoot Nina Wales through the heart as if she were a deer in a forest.

'He didn't care about her suffering; he *wanted* her to suffer. There was no compassion here, ladies and gentlemen. And this was no crime of passion. This was murder, pure and simple. Murder beyond a reasonable doubt. Murder in the first degree. Thank you.'

Jess smiled sadly at the eight women and six men. Three were black, two of Spanish extraction, one Asian, the rest white. Most were middle-aged. Only two were in their twenties. One woman was perhaps sixty. All looked solemn, prepared to do their duty.

'Mr. Bristol,' Judge Harris was saying as Jess returned to the prosecutor's table.

Hal Bristol was speaking even before he got to his feet, his voice booming across the courtroom, grabbing the jurors by their collective throat. 'Ladies and gentlemen of the jury, Terry Wales is not an educated man. He's a salesman, like some of you. He sells household appliances. He's very good at it, and he makes a good living. He's not a rich man, by any means. But he *is* a proud man.

'Like you, he's had to tighten his belt in these recessionary times. Not so many people out there buying. Especially high ticket items, like appliances. Not as many new homes going up. Not as many people needing new stoves and microwave ovens. Commissions are scarce. We're living in uneasy times. Not a lot to count on.'

Jess sat back in her chair. So this was to be the defense's approach. The killer as someone we could all identify with. The killer we could understand because his reflection mirrors our own. The killer as Everyman.

'Terry Wales thought he could count on his wife. He married her eleven years ago with the understanding that both would continue to work for several years before they started a family. But Nina Wales had a different understanding. After they got married, she decided she wanted children right away. She didn't want to wait. She'd continue to work, she assured him. She certainly had no intention of giving up her job. But soon after their first child was born, Nina Wales quit work. She wanted to be a full-time mother, and how could my client argue with that, especially when she quickly became pregnant again?

'But Nina Wales wasn't an easy woman to satisfy. No matter how much she had, no matter how much her husband could comfortably provide her with, Nina Wales was a woman who always wanted more. So, of course, there were fights over the years. There were occasionally even violent fights. Terry Wales is certainly not proud of his part in them. But spousal violence can happen in the best of marriages – and does. Especially when times get tough.

'Now I don't believe in blaming the victim,' Hal Bristol intoned, and Jess had to admire that the words escaped his mouth without the slightest trace of irony, 'but we all know it takes two to tango. My client is not a violent man. He had to be pushed pretty hard to react in a violent fashion.

'And Nina Wales knew just what buttons to push.'

Jess let her eyes drift toward the rear of the courtroom, feeling the bile rise in her throat. Was that what Rick Ferguson was doing here? Pushing her buttons?

Rick Ferguson stared straight ahead, seemingly mesmerized by what the defense attorney was saying. Occasionally he nodded his head in agreement. One Everyman killer to another. Damn him, Jess thought. Why was he here?

'Nina Wales was an expert at pushing buttons,' Hal Bristol continued. 'She constantly chided her husband over his sagging commissions; she berated him for failing to provide her with greater creature comforts. We have witnesses who will testify to hearing Nina Wales publicly embarrass her husband on more than one occasion. Facts, as the prosecution told you. Not just the word of the defendant. And we have witnesses who will testify that Nina Wales threatened, again on more than one occasion, to take her children and disappear, leaving him with nothing.

'Terry Wales is a proud man, ladies and gentlemen, although his wife made him feel as if there was little to be proud of. And nothing was sacred. Even their sex life became a target for public consumption and ridicule. Nina Wales made fun of her husband's performance in bed, and taunted him at every opportunity about his failure to satisfy her. She even told him she'd taken a lover, and although this may not have been true, Terry Wales believed her.

'Then she left, refused to let her husband even speak to his children. She informed him she was seeing a lawyer, was preparing to take him for everything he had, for everything he'd worked for all his life. Terry Wales was distraught. Destroyed. He was no longer thinking either clearly or rationally. He was desperate. And desperate men, in desperate times, sometimes do desperate things.

'So, he bought a crossbow. A crossbow, ladies and gentlemen. Not a gun, even though he holds several marksman's degrees. Even though a gun, for someone planning to murder his wife, would have been the more logical weapon of choice, much easier to use, more difficult to trace, far more likely to result in the death of the victim.

'No, Terry Wales bought a crossbow. An instrument that was far more likely to create a stir than it was to cause serious harm.

'Which was exactly what he meant to do.

'Terry Wales wanted to scare his wife. He didn't want to kill her.

'If you were planning to murder someone, ladies and gentlemen of the jury, would you choose a weapon as old-fashioned and conspicuous as a crossbow? Would you commit that murder in the middle of the day, in the middle of a busy downtown intersection, with at least half a dozen witnesses to identify you? Would you sit down on the sidewalk afterward, sobbing, and wait for the police? Do these sound like the actions of a rational man, a man who the prosecution claims callously and deliberately plotted the cold-blooded murder of his wife?'

Hal Bristol strode across the courtroom to the prosecutor's

table. 'The defense and the prosecution are in agreement on one thing,' he said, looking directly at Jess. 'My client *is* responsible for the death of his wife.' He paused, striding purposefully back toward the jury box. 'But it is our contention that Terry Wales never meant to kill his wife, that his only intention was to frighten her, bring her back to her senses, bring her back to their home. However misguided, however irrational those intentions may have been, they do not constitute cold, calculated, and premeditated murder.

'During the course of this trial, I'd like you to put yourself in Terry Wales's shoes. We all have our breaking point, ladies and gentlemen. Terry Wales reached his.' Hal Bristol paused dramatically before concluding. 'What would it take to reach yours?'

Jess pictured herself standing in front of the ivory lace curtains of her living room, staring out at the street below, gun in hand. Would she actually have been able to use it? We all have our breaking point, ladies and gentlemen, she thought, turning toward the back of the courtroom, seeing Rick Ferguson pop a piece of gum into his mouth and start to chew.

'Is the prosecution ready to proceed?' Judge Harris asked.

'The prosecution requests a ten-minute recess,' Jess said quickly.

'We will recess for ten minutes,' Judge Harris agreed.

'What's up, Jess?' Neil Strayhorn asked, obviously caught off guard.

But Jess was already on her way toward the back of the courtroom. If she expected Rick Ferguson to jump to his feet, he didn't. In fact, he didn't even look her way, forcing her to speak over the heads of the two people next to him. 'There's an easy way to do this,' she began, 'and a hard way.'

Still, he didn't look at her.

'The easy way is that you stand up and walk out of here now of your own volition,' she continued, unprompted.

'And the hard way?' he asked, eyes focused on the empty Judge's chair.

'I'll call the bailiff, and have you thrown out.'

Rick Ferguson stood up, shuffled past the two men beside him to where Jess stood. 'I just wanted to see what I might have been up against if that old lady hadn't disappeared the way she did,' he said, lowering his eyes to hers. 'Tell me, counsellor, you as good in bed as you are in court?'

'Bailiff!' Jess called loudly.

'Hey, the easy way, remember?' Rick Ferguson turned and walked from the room.

Jess was still shaking ten minutes later when the Judge called the court to order.

An armed Sheriff's deputy escorted Jess to the parking garage across from the Administration Building at almost seven o'clock that night.

She had spent the two hours after court was dismissed conferring with Neil and Barbara about the day's events and tomorrow's strategy, and trying to reach her ex-husband, but his office said he'd been out all afternoon and they weren't sure what time he'd be back. ('Jess, is that you?' the polite voice had inquired as she was about to hang up. 'Haven't heard from you in a long time. Why don't you try him at home later? You still have the number?')

'I'm on level three,' Jess told the deputy. Fully armed Sheriff's deputies always escorted prosecutors to their cars after dark.

'Finally got your car back,' the young man said, his blond hair peeking out from beneath his dark blue cap, his hand near his holster as he led Jess through the outdoor parking lot to the multi-storied garage. Jess told him the sad saga of her red Mustang as they waited for the elevator to arrive.

'At least they washed it,' Jess said as the elevator doors opened and they stepped inside.

'Something good comes from everything, I guess,' the deputy told her philosophically, and Jess nodded, though she was far from sure she agreed. 'God, what's that smell?' he said, as they stepped out at the third level. 'Stinks like an outhouse up here.'

Jess grimaced, the unpleasant odor filling her nostrils and

throat, making her want to gag. She motioned to where she'd parked her car, not wanting to open her mouth, in case whatever was in the air settled on her tongue.

'Jesus, it's getting worse.'

They turned the corner.

'My God,' the guard exclaimed, automatically pulling his gun from the holster and spinning round.

'There's nobody here,' Jess said, surprisingly calm, staring at her car. 'He's long gone.'

'Don't tell me this is your car,' the guard stated, though Jess was sure he already knew the answer. 'Jesus, what sick bastard would do something like this?'

Jess stared at her Mustang, which only this morning had been freshly washed and as good as new. Now it stood, smeared from top to bottom with what was unmistakably excrement, its windows streaked, its new windshield wipers broken and twisting out from the middle of large clumps of feces. Jess felt her eyes sting, and covered her nose and mouth, turning away.

The guard was already on his walkie-talkie, radioing for help. Jess returned to the elevator and sank down onto the cement floor beside it. 'Shit,' she muttered, thinking her choice of expletives remarkably apt, dissolving into peals of helpless laughter. She could laugh or she could cry, she decided.

She'd save the crying for later.

Chapter Twelve

'Walter! Walter, for God's sake, you left the front door unlocked again!' Jess pounded on the door to the second-floor apartment of the three-story brownstone, wondering whether she could be heard over Miles Davis's trumpet.

'Hold your horses, I'm coming,' came the darkly masculine voice from inside. An instant later, the door opened, and the short, roundish systems analyst who was her downstairs neighbor stood before her, wearing a green silk bathrobe and sipping a glass of red wine. He examined her quickly from head to toe. 'Jess, you're beautiful. And you're hysterical. Would you like to come in for a drink?'

'I'd like you to make sure you keep the front door locked,' Jess told him, in no mood for anything as civil as a glass of red wine.

'Oh, did I forget to lock it again?' Walter Fraser appeared resolutely nonchalant. 'I was bringing in the groceries, and I had to keep making trips to the car. It was just easier to leave the door unlocked.'

'Easier, and a lot more dangerous.'

'Bad day, huh?' Walter asked.

'Just keep it locked,' Jess said again, heading up the last flight of stairs to her apartment.

The phone started ringing as soon as she opened her door. What now? she wondered, knocking against the side of the bird cage as she hurried into the kitchen to answer it, hearing the canary chirp in frightened protest. 'Sorry, Fred,' she called, frantically grabbing for the phone . 'Hello.' Her voice was a shout.

'Ouch! Somebody's not happy.'

'Don, is that you?'

'My office said you've been trying to reach me. Something wrong?'

'Nothing that seeing your client in the electric chair wouldn't cure.'

'I assume we're talking about Rick Ferguson,' Don said calmly.

'Excellent assumption. How about this one? Your client shows up in my courtroom today and several hours later my car, which I've just spent over four hundred dollars repairing, turns up covered in shit. What assumptions would you make there?'

'Hold on a minute. You're saying that your car was literally covered in . . .?'

'Excrement, probably human. At least that's what the cops think it is. They've taken samples for analysis, and they're trying to dust the car for prints. Not that that will accomplish a hell of a lot. I'm sure rubber gloves were the order of the day.'

'Jesus Christ,' Don muttered.

'Just tell your client that if he ever sets foot in my courtroom again, I'll have him arrested. I don't care what for.'

'I've already warned him to stay the hell away from you.'

'Just keep him away from my courtroom.'

'You won't see him there again.'

Jess could hear the confusion in her ex-husband's voice, despite his even tone. She knew he was fighting to keep a safe distance between his professional and personal lives, that she was making it next to impossible for him.

'Look,' he said, after a long pause, 'it's almost nine o'clock. Knowing you, you haven't eaten.'

'I'm not very hungry.'

'You need to eat. Come on. I can be there in twenty minutes. We'll go out, grab a steak.'

'Don, I just spent two hours with a car that looks like a shit sandwich. I don't have much of an appetite.' She felt him smile. 'I'm sorry. Another time?'

'Anytime. Get some sleep.'

'Thanks.'

'Oh, and Jess.'

'Yes?'

'The state of Illinois doesn't execute criminals in the electric chair anymore. I believe lethal injections are the order of the day.'

She laughed. 'Thanks for the update.'

They hung up without saying goodbye.

Almost immediately, Jess felt her stomach growl. 'Great. Perfect timing.' Jess looked at the phone, decided against calling Don back. She was too tired, too aggravated, too fed-up to go out. She'd only drag Don down. Besides, why eat steak when she had nice, hard, frozen pizzas right in her very own freezer?

She removed two from their cellophane wrappers and popped them into the microwave, then grabbed a can of Coke from the fridge and pulled open its metal tab, taking a long sip directly from the can. More gas that way, she thought, taking another sip, thinking of her brother-in-law, his new no soft drinks rule. ('I think you're jealous,' Barry had said. 'Because your sister has a husband and a family, and she's happy. And what have you got? A freezer full of frozen pizzas and a goddamn canary!')

Was he right? Was she jealous of her sister's happiness? Could she possibly be so petty?

For the first time in years, Maureen hadn't invited her over for Thanksgiving dinner. She'd said something about having dinner with Barry's parents for a change, but probably she was just fed up. They were all fed up. Even her father had stopped suggesting opportune times for her to meet his new love. He appreciated how busy she was these days, he'd told her, citing all the publicity surrounding her current case. He'd wait for the trial to be over.

What was she doing to her father? Was she jealous of his happiness too? Did she want everyone who loved her to live the same sort of isolated lonely life she'd designed for herself? Could she believe her father's interest in another woman was somehow a betrayal of her mother, even now, after all these years?

Jess buried her head in her hands. No, she realized slowly. It was more that by allowing himself to love another woman, her father was, in some symbolic, but very real way signing her mother's death certificate.

Jess lifted her head from her hands, stared up at the ceiling, tears falling the length of her cheeks. Could it be that she still half expected her mother to come walking back into their lives? Is that what she was waiting for, hoping for, longing for? Even now, after eight years? Was she still waiting for her mother to appear on her doorstep, sweep her faithful daughter into her arms, smother her face with kisses, tell her all was forgiven, that she wasn't responsible for her disappearance, that she'd been found not guilty.

Was she still waiting for her moment of absolution? Could her life not proceed without it?

The microwave oven beeped to announce that dinner was ready, and Jess snapped back to reality, carefully lifting the two steaming pizzas onto a blue-flowered plate. She carried the plate and the can of Coke into the living room and sat down on the sofa, aware for the first time of the sixties music emanating from the radio. *Monday, Monday*, the Mamas and the Papas sang in harmony, and Jess shrugged. Monday, Monday was right! What a day.

'And how was your day, Freddy?' she asked her canary, blowing across the tops of the pizzas, trying to cool them down. 'Better than mine, I hope.' She took an enormous bite from one piece, pulling almost all of the top coating of cheese into her mouth.

The phone rang.

Jess shoved the piece of pizza to the left side of her mouth with her tongue. 'Hello.'

'Is this Jess Koster?'

The man's voice was only vaguely familiar.

'Who's calling?' Jess asked, her body poised, on alert.

'Adam Stohn.'

'Adam Stohn?'

'From Shoe-Inn. The boots you ordered – they came in late this afternoon. I tried to call you at work. They said you were in court. You didn't tell me you were a lawyer.'

Jess felt her heart start to race, the pizza stick to the side of her mouth. 'I didn't get a message.'

'I didn't leave one.'

Silence.

'So, my boots are in,' Jess said after what felt like an eternity.

'You can pick them up any time.'

'That's great. Thank you for letting me know.'

'Or I could drop them by,' he volunteered.

'What?'

'Save you the trip down. You could just give me a check, made out to Shoe-Inn, of course.'

'When?'

'I could come by now, if that's convenient.'

'Now?' *What? When? Now?* Jess heard herself repeat. When had she turned into such a sparkling conversationalist?

'They're calling for snow tomorrow.'

'Are they?'

'Actually, I haven't had dinner yet. How about you? Feel like splitting a pizza?'

Jess promptly spat the half-chewed lump of cheese still in her mouth onto the plate. 'That sounds great.'

'Good. Why don't you tell me where you live?'

'Why don't we just meet somewhere?' Jess suggested in return.

'Name the place.'

Jess named a small Italian restaurant on Armitage Avenue, within easy walking distance.

'Fifteen minutes?'

'See you there.'

'You're early,' he said, sliding into the red vinyl booth at the back of the small family-operated restaurant. He wore blue jeans and a black bomber jacket over a grey turtleneck.

'I'm always early. Bad habit,' she told him, studying his face, thinking him better-looking than she remembered. Was he having similar thoughts about her? She wished now that she'd changed into something more interesting than a plain black sweater and pants. Probably a touch more make-up wouldn't have hurt either. All she'd done was splash some cold water on her face, brushed her teeth, applied a little lipstick, and dashed out of the house.

'Hello, Signorina,' the middle-aged proprietress greeted Jess, laying two stained paper menus on the table. 'Nice to see you again.'

'Nice to see you,' Jess agreed, smiling at the dark-haired, moon-faced woman. 'Carla makes the best pizzas in the world.'

'In the DePaul area anyway,' Carla qualified. 'Can I bring you a carafe of Chianti while you look over the menu?'

'Sounds good,' Adam said, taking a quick glance at the items listed.

'I already know what I want,' Jess said eagerly. 'I'll have the special pizza. It's my all-time favorite thing to eat in the entire world.'

'In that case, make it a large,' Adam said quickly. 'We'll share.' Carla retrieved the menus from the table and headed for the kitchen. 'Incidentally, your boots are in the car. Don't let me forget to give them to you.'

'Don't let me forget to write you a check.

'God, the pressure.' He laughed. 'I take it you come here often.'

'I live just down the street. And I'm not much of a cook,' Jess added.

'I would guess that you don't have a lot of time for cooking.'

'I don't, but I wouldn't anyway.'

He looked surprised. 'A matter of principle?'

'We lawyers do have them,' she said and smiled.

'There was never a doubt in my mind.'

'My mother used to cook all the time,' Jess explained. 'She hated it, so she never taught us how. Maybe she figured if my sister and I didn't know how to cook, we'd never get trapped into doing it.'

'Interesting theory.'

'Not that it worked.'

He looked puzzled.

'My sister has lately turned into Julia Child.'

'And you don't approve?'

'I'd rather not talk about my sister.'

Carla returned with the carafe of Chianti and two wineglasses. 'I was reading about that crossbow killer in the paper tonight,' Carla said, pouring some dark red wine into each glass. 'They mentioned your name and everything. Very impressive.'

Jess smiled. 'Winning would be impressive.'

Carla made a dismissive gesture with her hands. 'No question. You win. No question.' She rubbed her hands against the hospital green apron that stretched across her ample bosom, then made her way to the front of the restaurant. There were five booths and perhaps ten tables crowded into the small room, about half of them currently occupied. The walls were covered with bright, hand-painted scenes of Italy. Plastic grapes hung at irregular intervals from the ceiling.

'So I'm having dinner with a celebrity,' Adam stated, lifting his glass to hers in a toast.

'Just an over-worked, underpaid prosecutor, I'm afraid.' They clicked glasses. 'Health and wealth, as my brother-in-law would say.'

'To your imminent victory.'

'I'll drink to that.' They did. 'So, what about you? How long have you been selling shoes?'

'At Shoe-Inn, since the summer. Before that, for about a year.'

'And before that?'

'Odd jobs. This and that. Itinerant salesman. You know.'

'My father was a salesman.'

'Oh?'

'Then he owned his own store. A couple, actually. Now, he's retired.'

'And driving your mother crazy?'

Jess took a long sip of her drink. 'My mother's dead.'

Jess watched Adam's jaw drop. 'Oh, sorry. That was a bit clumsy. When did she die?'

'Eight years ago. I'm sorry – would you mind if we talked about something else?'

'Anything you want.'

'Tell me more about you. Are you from Chicago?'

'Springfield.'

'I've never been to Springfield.'

'Pretty city.'

'Why'd you leave?'

'Time for a change.' He shrugged. 'And you? Chicago born and bred?'

She nodded.

'No desire to try somewhere else?'

'I'm pretty much of a homebody.'

'You went to law school here?'

'Northwestern.'

'From which you graduated in the top third of your class?' he guessed.

'I stood fourth.'

He smiled into his glass. 'And from there you turned down all offers of lucrative private practice to become an overworked, underpaid prosecutor in the State's Attorney's office.'

'I didn't want to find myself in the litigation department of some big firm, where the only litigation I'd ever see was a war of memos crossing my desk. Besides, the State's Attorney was one of my law professors and he ran for office and was elected, and he hired me. The only question he asked me was whether or not I'd be able to ask for the death penalty.'

'You obviously gave him the right answer.'

Jess laughed. 'They don't want any liberals in the State's Attorney's office.'

'So what's it like there?'

'Honestly?'

'Only if you insist.'

She laughed. 'I love it. At least I do now. In the beginning, it was pretty dry. They started me out in traffic court. That's not wildly exciting, but you have to pay your dues, I guess. I was there for about a year, then I went into the First Municipal

Division, which prosecutes misdemeanors, anything from property damage to aggravated assault. Those are pretty much bench trials, only a few actual jury trials, the sort of stuff that's always serious to the victims, but not to anybody else. Does that sound callous?'

'I'd imagine you'd have to develop a pretty hard shell working in the State's Attorney's office.'

The image of a headless turtle popped itself into Jess's line of vision. 'I stayed at First Municipal Division for another year,' Jess said, speaking quickly. 'Then I went to Felony Review. That was a lot more interesting.'

'What made it more interesting?'

'It involves real investigative work, getting out there and talking to the victims and the witnesses. You work pretty closely with the police. You see, what most people don't realize is that the cops can't actually charge anyone. Only the State can bring charges. The cops investigate, but it's the Assistant State's Attorney who decides whether to approve the charges and put the case into the system.'

'Your first taste of real power.'

Jess took another long sip of her wine. 'My brother-in-law claims that when a woman gets a little power, she loses her sense of humor.'

'Hey, you laughed at my condom joke.'

'Actually, I have a joke for you,' Jess said, hurriedly trying to organize her thoughts. 'One of the secretaries at work told it to me.' She paused, trying to recall the exact phrasing. 'What do you get when you have a hundred rabbits in a row, and suddenly ninety-nine of them take one step back?'

'I don't know. What do you get?'

'A receding *hare*line!' Jess laughed, then stopped abruptly. 'That was terrible. That was a terrible joke.' She shook her head in disbelief. 'I can't believe I told you that joke.'

'It was a totally terrific joke, told with great flourish, I might add,' Adam said, chuckling quietly. 'Next time you see your brother-in-law, tell him he's full of shit.'

Jess pictured first her brother-in-law, then her shit-covered automobile. 'Could we talk about something else, do you think?'

'So you stayed in Felony Review for another year,' he said without missing a beat.

'Seven months.'

'Then on to the Trial section?'

Jess looked surprised. 'How'd you know that?'

'What else is left?' he asked simply.

'Each courtroom has three assistant State's Attorneys assigned to one particular judge, usually for about a year, maybe more. The most senior of those assistants is called the first chair. That's me.' Jess paused, finished the wine in her glass. 'How'd we get on to all this?'

'I believe I asked what it was like in the State's Attorney's office.'

'Well, you can't say I didn't tell you.' Jess looked toward her lap. 'Sorry, I didn't mean to get carried away. I guess it's pretty dry.'

'Not at all.' He poured more wine into her glass. 'Tell me more.'

Jess lifted the glass to her mouth, grateful to have something to do with her hands, breathing in the heavy aroma of the wine, trying to see beyond the warm brown of Adam's eyes. She wondered if he was as interested in the details of her career as he seemed. She wondered what he was really doing here. She wondered what *she* was doing here. 'Well,' she hesitated before continuing, 'I'm responsible for everything that goes on in that courtroom. I prosecute the major cases. I decide what cases to let my second and third chair try. I'm sort of the teacher, or the guidance counsellor, if you will. And I'm the one who takes the heat if they mess up. If something goes wrong in my courtroom, I'm the one responsible.'

'And how many cases do you prosecute in any given year?'

'Anywhere from twelve to twenty. That's in front of a jury. The majority of cases are disposed of through bench trials or plea negotiations.' She laughed. 'It gets very hectic at this time of year. There's usually a race to see which judge can dispose of the most number of cases before Christmas.'

The pizza arrived, steaming and hot, its four different cheeses spilling over the sides of the aluminum pan, a variety of vegetables and sausages spread across its face. 'Looks fabulous,' Adam remarked, cutting a piece for each of them and smiling as Jess immediately lifted her piece into her hands and stuffed the end into her mouth.

Adam laughed. 'You look just like a little kid.'

'I'm sorry. I should have warned you. I'm a total slob when I eat. I have no shame.'

'It's a pleasure to watch you.'

'I could never understand how people can eat pizza with a knife and fork,' she continued, then stopped short, a long string of cheese stretching between her mouth and plate. 'Now you're going to tell me that you always use a knife and fork, right?'

'I wouldn't dare.' Adam lifted his piece of pizza into his large hands and carried it to his mouth.

'It's wonderful, isn't it?'

'Wonderful,' he agreed, his eyes never leaving hers. 'So, tell me more about Jess Koster, assistant State's Attorney.'

'I think I've probably said more than enough. Don't all the books advise women to let men do the talking? You know, find out what his interests are? Fake interest in same?' She paused, the pizza in her hand suspended in mid-air. 'Or is that what you're doing with me?'

'You don't think you're interesting?'

'Just because I find the law fascinating doesn't mean everybody else will.'

'What is it about the law that fascinates you?'

Jess lowered her pizza to her plate, giving serious thought to his question, choosing her words carefully. 'I guess that it's so complicated. I mean, most people like to think of the criminal justice system as a fight between right and wrong, good and evil, the whole truth and nothing but. But it isn't like that at all. It's not black and white. It's varying shades of grey. Both sides subvert the truth, try to use it to their own advantage. A good attorney will always put a "spin" on a bad act, so that it doesn't come out sounding so bad.'

'Lawyers as spin doctors?'

Jess nodded. 'The sad truth is that truth is almost irrelevant in a court of law.' She shrugged. 'Sometimes it's easy for lawyers to lose sight of basic moral and ethical considerations.'

'What's the difference?'

'Morality is internal,' Jess said simply. 'Ethics are defined by a professional code of responsibility. Did that sound as hopelessly pompous as I think it did?'

'It sounded charming.'

'Charming? I sounded charming?' Jess laughed.

'That surprises you?'

'Charming is rarely a word I hear used to describe me,' she answered honestly.

'What words do you hear?'

'Oh . . . intense, serious, intense, dedicated, intense. I hear a lot of intense.'

'Which is probably what makes you such a good prosecutor.'

'Who said I was any good?'

'Asked she who stood fourth in her graduating class.'

Jess smiled self-consciously. 'I'm not sure one thing has anything to do with the other. I mean, you can memorize precedents and procedures, you can study the law books backwards and forwards, but you really have to have a *feeling* for what the law is. It's a little like love, I guess.' She looked away. 'A matter of ghosts and shadows.'

'Interesting analogy,' Adam commented. 'I take it you're divorced.'

Jess reached for her wine glass, lifted it to her mouth, then lowered it without taking a drink. 'Interesting assumption.'

'Two interesting people,' Adam told her, once again clicking his glass against hers. 'How long were you married?'

'Four years.'

'And how long have you been divorced?'

'Four years.'

'Nice symmetry.'

'And you?'

'Married six years, divorced three.'

'Any children?'

He finished his wine, poured the rest of the bottle into his glass, and shook his head.

'Are you sure?' Jess asked, and laughed. 'That was a very pregnant pause.'

'No children,' he repeated. 'And you?'

'No.'

'Too busy?'

'Too much of a child myself, I guess.'

'I doubt that,' he told her. 'You look as if you have a very old soul.'

Jess disguised her sudden discomfort with nervous laughter. 'I guess I need more sleep.'

'You don't need a thing. You're very beautiful,' he said, suddenly focusing all his attention on his pizza.

Jess did the same. For several awkward seconds, nobody spoke.

'I didn't mean to embarrass you,' he said, still concentrating on his plate.

'I'm not embarrassed,' Jess said, not sure what she was.

'So, did your being a prosecutor have anything to do with your divorce?' Adam asked, suddenly shifting gears.

'I'm sorry?'

'Well, being a trial lawyer is a little like being a racehorse, I suspect. You're trained to be a thoroughbred. You hear the bell, you come out running. You've got a big ego, which you need because it's always on the line. And the worst thing is losing. When you're in the middle of a trial, I would think it's very hard to just turn all that off. Basically you're married to the trial for its duration. Am I wrong?'

Jess shook her head. 'You're not wrong.'

'What did your husband do?' Adam cut them each another slice of pizza.

Jess smiled. 'He's a lawyer.'

'I rest my case.'

Jess laughed. 'What about your ex-wife?'

'She's an interior decorator. Last I heard she'd remarried.' Adam took a deep breath, lifted his hands into the air, as if to indicate he'd exhausted himself on the subject. 'Anyway, enough about past lives. Time to move on.'

'That was quick.'

'Nothing much to tell.'

'You don't like talking about yourself much, do you?'

'No more than you do.'

Jess was incredulous. 'What do you mean? I've been talking about myself since I got here.'

'You've been talking about the law. Whenever the questions get more personal, you clam up as tightly as if you were a hostile witness on the stand.'

'I'll make you a deal,' Jess said, surprised to find herself so transparent. 'I won't tell you my secrets if you don't tell me yours.'

Adam smiled, his brown eyes impenetrable. 'Tell me no secrets, I'll tell you no lies.'

There was a long pause.

'Sounds good,' Jess said.

'For me too.'

They resumed eating, finishing off the rest of the pizza in silence.

'Why did you call me tonight?' Jess asked, pushing away her empty plate.

'I wanted to see you,' he answered. 'Why did you accept?'

'I guess I wanted to see you too.'

They smiled at each other across the table.

'So, what's an ambitious lawyer like you doing out with a simple shoe salesman like me?' He signalled for the check.

'I get the feeling there's nothing simple about you.'

'That's because you're a lawyer. You're always looking for things that aren't there.'

Jess laughed. 'And I hear it's going to snow tomorrow. I could use a new pair of winter boots.'

'I have just the thing in the back seat of my car. Can I offer you a ride home?'

Jess hesitated, wondered what was she afraid of?

Carla approached with the bill. 'So, how was everything? You like the pizza?' she inquired of Adam.

'Without doubt, the best pizza in the De Paul area.'

Jess watched Adam take a twenty-dollar bill from his pocket, thought of offering to split the cost of the dinner, then thought better of the idea. Next time, she decided, dinner would be on her.

If there was a next time.

Jess was sleeping, the kind of deep, dreamless, luxurious sleep that had eluded her for weeks. Suddenly, she was awake, her body upright, her hands shooting forward, as if she were falling through the air. All around bells were ringing, alarms were going off.

It was the phone, she realized, reaching across the bed and lifting the receiver cautiously to her ear. The illuminated dial of her digital clock announced it was 3 a.m. No good news ever came at three o'clock in the morning, she knew. Only death and despair thought nothing of waking people up in the middle of the night.

'Hello,' she said, her voice alert and in control, as if she'd been waiting for the phone to ring.

She expected to hear the police on the other end, or possibly the office of the Medical Examiner. But there was only silence.

'Hello?' she repeated. 'Hello? Hello?'

No answer. Not even the courtesy of some token heavy breathing.

She hung up, her head falling back onto her pillow with a gentle thud. Just a stupid nuisance call, she thought, refusing to consider other possibilities. 'Go back to sleep,' she muttered. But sleep had deserted her, and she lay awake, watching as snow silently cascaded outside her bedroom window, until it was time to get up.

Chapter Thirteen

'So, all in all, how would you say it went today?' Jess looked across her desk at Neil Strayhorn and Barbara Cohen, both of whom were fighting off various stages of cold and flu bugs. Neil's cold had been dragging on for so long now, the Kleenex that moved continually between his hand and his long, aquiline nose seemed a permanent fixture. Barbara's red-rimmed eyes were the consistency of runny eggs, threatening to spill over onto her flushed cheeks. Jess swivelled her chair toward the window, concentrating on the mixture of snow and rain that cut diagonally through the dark sky.

'I thought it went pretty well,' Neil said, his voice wandering helplessly through congested nasal passages. 'We made some important points.'

'Such as?' Jess nodded toward Barbara Cohen.

'Ellie Lupino testified that she'd heard Terry Wales threaten to kill his wife if she ever tried to leave him.' Barbara coughed, had to clear her throat in order to continue. 'She swore that Nina Wales wasn't having an affair.'

'She swore that, *to the best of her knowledge*, Nina Wales wasn't having an affair,' Jess clarified.

'She was Nina's best friend for almost ten years. Nina told her everything,' Neil offered. 'Surely that will carry a lot of weight with the jury.'

'Ellie Lupino also admitted that she heard Nina Wales publicly disparage her husband's performance in bed on more than one occasion, that she threatened to take him for everything he had,' Jess reminded them.

'So?' Barbara asked, the word triggering a minor coughing spasm.

'So, that goes to the heart of the defense's case. If they can convince the jury that Nina Wales provoked her husband into an uncontrollable fury–'

'. . . then she was responsible for her own murder!' Barbara sneezed in indignation.

'Then at best we're looking at murder two.'

'So what if Nina Wales taunted her husband with the fact he was lousy in bed? So what if she threatened to leave him? He beat her with his *fists*. Words were the only weapon that she had!' Barbara Cohen clutched at her chest, stubbornly swallowing another coughing fit, which made her sound as if she was choking.

'We have motive, we have malice aforethought, we have cold, calculated premeditation,' Neil rhymed off, punctuating his sentence with a loud blowing of his nose.

'The whole question is one of provocation,' Jess reiterated over the growing cacophony of bronchial histrionics. 'There was a recent case in Michigan where a jury found the husband of a judge guilty only of manslaughter when he killed his estranged wife in her own courtroom. The jury found that the break-up provoked him to kill her. In another case in New York City, a Chinese-American was put on probation, *on probation*, after he bludgeoned his wife to death with a hammer. The wife had been unfaithful, and the judge ruled that because of the husband's cultural background, the infidelity constituted provocation.' She took a deep breath, trying not to inhale the germs lingering almost visibly in the air. 'The only question those jurors are going to be asking themselves is whether, under similar circumstances, they might be capable of the same thing.'

'So what are you saying?' Barbara asked, a lone tear escaping her watery eyes.

'I'm saying that it all boils down to how well Terry Wales performs on the witness stand,' Jess told them. 'I'm saying that we better know everything Terry Wales is going to say to that jury before he does, and not only be ready to call him on it, but to tear him to shreds. I'm saying that it's not going to be easy to win this case. I'm saying that you guys better get out of here and get into bed.'

Neil sneezed three times in rapid succession.

'Bless you,' Jess said automatically.

'You don't have to say bless you when someone has a cold,' Barbara informed her. 'That's what my mother always says,' she explained sheepishly, heading for the door.

'I thought Judge Harris was looking a little rough around the edges today,' Neil said, right behind her.

'Probably too much Thanksgiving turkey,' Jess said, closing the door after them, collapsing into the nearest chair, feeling a nervous tickle at the back of her throat. 'Oh no,' she said, 'don't you get sick now. You do not have time to get sick. Tickle, be gone,' she ordered, returning to her own seat behind her desk, peering over the notes she'd made in court that afternoon, glancing menacingly at the phone.

So what if a week had passed and Adam hadn't called? Had she really expected him to? Their evening together had ended on a very businesslike note – he'd handed over the boots, she'd handed over the check. He'd deposited her in front of her brownstone without so much as a peck on the cheek. She hadn't invited him in; he hadn't asked. They'd said goodbye. No 'Can I see you again?' No 'I'll call you.' Nothing. So why had she been expecting more?

Had she really thought he might call, suggest they spend Thanksgiving together? Two virtual strangers sharing turkey and cranberry sauce? The assistant State's Attorney from Cook County and the shoe salesman from Springfield! What bothered her more? The fact he was a shoe salesman or the fact he hadn't called?

She'd ended up having Thanksgiving dinner with the gay systems analyst from the apartment downstairs, and eight of his friends, pretending she wasn't listening through the ceiling for her phone to ring. After a few glasses of wine, she'd immersed herself in Charlie Parker and Jerry Mulligan, and joined the others in giving thanks for their good fortune at being together, for their sheer good luck at being alive, when so many of their friends had perished.

She drank too much and Walter had to escort her back

upstairs. At least she hadn't had to drive home, she thought now.

She lowered her head into her hands, thinking of her car, vandalized beyond all recognition. A gift from her parents after her acceptance into Northwestern University, it had withstood law school, marriage, divorce, and four years with the State's Attorney's Office.

Only it couldn't withstand this last assault to its dignity. It couldn't withstand Rick Ferguson.

Jess hadn't immediately noticed the slashed tires, hadn't absorbed the gutted upholstery, or the brake pedal ripped from the floor. It was days before she learned the full extent of the damage. A total write-off, of course. No point in trying to put the pieces back together again. Much too difficult. Much too expensive, even with insurance. She was already out over four hundred dollars.

They hadn't found any prints, nothing to link Rick Ferguson to the murder of her car. So, he'd shown up in her courtroom that very day. So what? Nobody had seen him in the parking garage. Nobody had seen him anywhere near her car. Nobody ever saw him anywhere. People disappeared; property was destroyed; Rick Ferguson went on smiling.

Jess picked up the phone and called the office of the Medical Examiner. 'Good, you're still there,' she said when she heard Hilary Waugh's voice.

'Just getting ready to leave,' the woman told her. Jess understood that what she was really saying was, it's late, let's make this quick.

'I take it no one's come in resembling Connie DeVuono,' Jess began, as if Connie might still be alive, as if she had somehow wandered into the office of the Chief Medical Examiner of her own accord.

'No one.'

'You got the dental records I sent over?'

'I got them. They're here, ready and waiting.'

'That should speed things up.'

'Yes, it should. I really have to get going now, Jess. I'm not feeling so hot. I think I might be coming down with something.'

'Welcome to the club,' Jess said, wishing Hilary Waugh a speedy recovery. She replaced the receiver, then immediately picked it up again, needing to hear a friendly voice. She hadn't heard from her sister since before Thanksgiving. It wasn't like Maureen not to call, no matter how busy she was. Jess hoped she was well, that she hadn't been felled by the flu bug that seemed to be sweeping through the city.

'Hello.' The smile in Maureen's voice was audible. Jess felt instantly reassured.

'How are you?' Jess asked.

'I'm fine,' Maureen answered, the smile quickly fading, leaving her voice cold, matter-of-fact. 'Tyler's got the sniffles, but the rest of us are okay. How are you?'

'I'm okay. How was Thanksgiving dinner?'

'Great. Barry's mother's a gourmet cook. But you're not really interested in that.' There was an uncomfortable pause. 'So, you've been busy, as usual?'

'Well, this is a real heater case I'm trying.'

'Heater case?'

'Lots of publicity. I'm sure you've been reading about it.' Jess stopped when she remembered that Maureen didn't read the front pages anymore.

'Actually, yes, I have been following it. I guess it's quite a coup for you to have a case this big.'

'Only if I win it.'

There was silence.

'I haven't heard from you in a while,' Jess ventured, suddenly aware that it had always been her sister who'd made sure they kept in frequent touch.

'I thought that was how you wanted it.'

'How I wanted it? Why would you say that?'

'Oh, I don't know. Maybe because you're always so busy. Too busy to meet Dad's friend, anyway. Too busy to make dinner at Bistro 110. Too busy to keep your appointment with Stephanie Banack.'

'I kept my appointment.'

'Technically, yes, I guess you did. Look, Jess, I'm really not interested in pursuing this. I can appreciate that you're busy. Believe me, I do understand something about what that's like. But don't try to tell me that you're so busy you don't have any time for your family. Don't insult my intelligence that way. If you don't want to be part of this family, that's up to you. I guess I'm going to have to accept it.'

'It's not that I don't want to be with you, Maureen.'

'It's that you don't want to be with my husband.'

'We just don't get along. It happens. It's not the end of the world.'

'And Dad? How long are you going to keep shutting him out?'

'I'm not shutting him out.'

'No. Just the woman he loves.'

'Don't you think you're being overly dramatic?'

'I think Dad's going to marry this woman, Jess.'

Another silence. 'Did he say that?'

'He didn't have to.'

'Well, I'll worry about that when the time comes.'

'Why do you have to worry about it at all?' Maureen demanded. 'Why can't you just be happy for him? Why can't you at least pay him the courtesy of meeting her?'

Jess stared out the window into the encroaching night. It wasn't quite six o'clock and already so dark. 'I better go, let you get dinner ready.'

'Sure. It's what I do best.'

'Maureen—'

'Bye, Jess. Keep in touch.'

The phone went dead before Jess had a chance to say goodbye. 'Great. Just great.' She returned the phone to its carriage, thought of calling her father, decided against it. She could only bear the sound of so much disappointment.

What was she doing to her family? Why couldn't she just reconcile herself to the fact that her brother-in-law was an ass, her sister was Total Woman, her father was in love? When had she grown so intolerant, so inflexible? Did everyone have to live their lives according to her dictates? Was she doing such a great job with her own life?

The door to her office opened. Greg Oliver stood on the other side. The pungently sweet odor of Aramis raced toward her desk.

Just what she needed, Jess thought, acknowledging his presence with a sigh that stretched to the tips of her toes.

'Why aren't I surprised to find you here,' he stated rather than asked.

'Maybe because you heard me talking on the phone?'

'Was that you whining?'

Jess exhaled another deep breath of air. 'That was me.'

'Sounds like you could use a drink.'

'I just need a good night's sleep.'

'That too can be arranged.' He winked.

Jess rolled her eyes, stood up. 'How's the O'Malley trial coming along?'

'In the bag. Should be wrapped up by the end of the week. And the famous crossbow avenger?'

'Hopefully, it'll be in the jury's hands by Friday.'

'I heard they offered to make a deal.'

'Murder two, ten years in prison? Possibility of parole in four? Some deal.'

'You really think the jury's decision will be any different?'

'I can dream,' Jess told him.

Greg Oliver's sly grin curved toward a genuine smile. 'Come on, I'll drive you home.'

'No, thank you.'

'Don't be silly, Jess. Your car is dead and buried; you're never going to find a cab; you call for one now, you'll be here another hour at least, and I'm offering you a ride to wherever you want to go: Vegas, Miami Beach, Graceland?'

Jess hesitated. She knew he was right – a cab would take for ever to get here at this hour. And after her last excursion, she refused to take the El. She could call Don, even though she hadn't heard from him since she'd turned down his offer to spend Thanksgiving with him and Mother Teresa. No, she couldn't call Don. It wouldn't be right. He was her ex-husband, not her chauffeur.

'All right,' Jess agreed. 'But right home.'

'Whatever you say. I'm here to take the lady wherever she wants to go.'

Greg Oliver's black Porsche pulled to a halt outside Jess's three-story brownstone. He turned the engine off. The loud rock music which had accompanied them on the drive, mercifully making conversation all but impossible, came to an abrupt stop. 'So, this is where you live.'

'This is it.' Jess reached for the door handle, eager to escape the smell of his cologne. 'Thanks, Greg. I really appreciate the ride.'

'Aren't you going to invite me in?'

'No,' Jess said simply.

'Come on, Jess. You wouldn't let me buy you a drink. The least you can do is offer me something for my long trip home.'

'Greg, I'm tired; I have an itchy throat; and I have a date,' she added, the lie settling on her tongue like a bitter pill.

'It's half past six; take two aspirin; and you haven't had a date in fifty years. I'm coming up.' In the next instant, he was out of the car.

Jess threw her head back against the dark leather seat. What had she expected? She opened the car door, lifting both legs to the sidewalk simultaneously, and boosting herself out of the car's low frame with her hands.

'You did that very well,' Greg commented. 'A lot of women don't know how to get out of these cars properly. They throw one leg out at a time.' He laughed. 'Of course, it's a lot more fun that way for those on the sidewalk.'

'Greg,' Jess began, walking quickly ahead of him toward her front door, 'I'm not inviting you up.'

'You can't mean that,' he persisted. 'Come on, Jess. All I want is one little drink. What are you so afraid of? What is it you think I'm going to do?'

Jess stopped at her front door, fishing in her purse for her key. Why hadn't she thought to get it ready earlier?

'You think I'm going to come on to you? Is that it?'

'Isn't it?'

'Shit, Jess, I'm a happily married man. My wife just bought me a Porsche. Why would I come on to a woman who obviously hates my guts?'

'Because she's there?' Jess located her key and unlocked the door.

'You're funny,' he said, pushing the door open and stepping into the foyer. 'That's why I put up with all your crap. Come on, Jess. We're colleagues, and I like to think we could be friends. Is that so awful?' He knelt down suddenly, scooping up some letters that lay on the floor under the mail slot, casually rifling through them. 'Your mail.' He deposited the letters in her waiting hand.

'One drink,' Jess told him, too tired to argue further.

He followed her up the three flights of stairs, like a dog at her heels. 'Trust you to live on the top floor,' he said as they reached the door to her apartment.

She unlocked the door. Greg was inside almost before she was.

'You leave the radio on all day?' he asked, his dark brown eyes quickly assessing, then dismissing, the contents of her living room.

'For the bird.' Jess threw her purse and the mail on the sofa, silently debating whether or not to remove her coat and boots. Although it was her apartment, she didn't want to do anything that might encourage Greg to prolong his visit.

Greg Oliver cautiously approached the bird cage, peered through the bars. 'Male or female?'

'Male.'

'How do you know? You look up its feathers?'

Jess walked to the kitchen, located a few beers toward the

back of the fridge, and uncapped one, returning with it to the living room. Greg had already made himself at home on her sofa, his coat thrown across the dining room table, his tie loosened, his shoes off. 'Don't get comfortable,' Jess warned, handing him the beer.

'Don't get cranky,' he countered, patting the seat beside him. 'Come on, sit down.'

Jess hung her coat in the hall closet, leaving her boots on, and quickly took stock of the situation. She'd allowed a man she could barely tolerate, a man obviously on the make, to drive her home. That man was currently sitting on her living room sofa, drinking the beer she'd handed him herself. She was a smart woman, she thought, hearing herself scoff. How had she managed to put herself in this position?

'Listen, Greg,' she told him, walking back toward the sofa, 'just so we set the record straight: I don't want to create a scene; I don't want to make it impossible for us to work in the same department; I don't want to make your life – or mine – any more difficult than it already is.'

'Is there a point to this speech?' he asked, taking a long sip of his beer directly from the bottle.

Jess realized she'd forgotten to give him a glass. 'The point is that I'm very uncomfortable with your being here.'

'You'd be a lot more comfortable if you'd sit down.' Again, he patted the seat beside him. Jess watched her mail bounce toward the next cushion.

'I have no intention of going to bed with you,' Jess said, deciding the direct approach was probably best.

'Who said anything about going to bed with me?' Greg Oliver managed to looked both surprised and offended.

'Just so we understand each other.'

'We do,' he said, though his eyes said otherwise.

Jess sat down on the arm of the sofa. 'Good, because I'm really not in the mood for anything as tacky as date rape. I know the system sucks and even if I weren't too embarrassed to report it, you'd probably get away with it. So I want you to know that I have a loaded gun in the end table beside my bed, and if you so much as lay a hand on me, I'll blow your fucking head off.' She smiled sweetly, watching Greg Oliver's mouth drop into the vicinity of his knees. 'I just wanted to set the record straight.'

Greg sat for several seconds in stunned silence. 'This is a joke, right?'

'No joke. You want to see the gun?'

'Jesus, Jess, no wonder you haven't had a date in fifty years!'

'Drink up and go home, Greg. Your wife is waiting.' She stood up and walked toward the door.

'Why the hell did you invite me up here?' His voice radiated righteous indignation.

Jess could only shrug. Why was she surprised? 'I'm too old for this,' she muttered.

'You're constipated, is what you are,' Greg told her, reaching for his coat. 'Constipated and uptight and what the boys in the school yard used to call a real tease.'

'I'm a tease?' Jess couldn't disguise the fury in her voice.

'If the shoe fits,' he said, impatiently stuffing his feet inside his Gucci loafers. He thrust the beer bottle in the direction of her chest. Jess grabbed for it, the cold liquid splashing across her white blouse. 'Thanks for the hospitality,' he said, already at the door, slamming it shut after him.

'That was cute,' Jess said, watching her canary flit from perch to perch. 'Real cute.' She rubbed her forehead, wondering at what point exactly she had started losing control of her life. She, who meticulously hung each item of clothing in her closet according to color, who carefully placed her freshly laundered panties beneath those not yet worn, who made lists for everything from important appointments to when it was time to wash her hair, and then carefully crossed each item off that list as each was accomplished. When had she lost control of her life?

She walked back to the sofa, leafed through her mail. The heavy scent of Greg's cologne still clung to the cushion where he'd been sitting. Jess took the letters to the window, opening the window slightly to allow a breath of fresh night air inside. The antique lace curtains swelled in gentle surprise.

The mail consisted mostly of bills. A few more requests than usual for donations, not unexpected at this time of year. A notice about Individual Retirement Accounts. Jess looked each over hurriedly, then tossed them aside, concentrating on the stained white envelope that remained. No return address. Her name printed in awkward scrawl, as if by a child. Maybe an early Christmas card from her nephew, Tyler. No stamp. Obviously hand delivered. She tore it open, extricated the single blank sheet of discolored paper from inside, turned it over in her hands, then lifted it gingerly to her nose.

The stale smell of urine mingled with the scent of Greg's cologne.

Jess quickly stuffed the paper back inside the envelope, letting it fall, watching as the breeze carried it, dipping and turning like an expert dance partner, to the floor. It landed silently, effortlessly. She watched as little black specs tumbled from the envelope, like ashes from a lit cigarette, almost disappearing into the hardwood floor.

Slowly, she knelt down, brushing what appeared to be short, wiry black threads into the palm of her hand. Hair, she realized with growing revulsion. Pubic hair. Immediately she swept the hairs back into the envelope.

Pubic hair and urine.

Charming.

There was a knock at her door.

'Oh, great,' she whispered, rising to her feet, closing the window. Pubic hair, urine, and Greg Oliver. What more could a girl want? 'Go home, Greg,' she called sharply.

'Do I have to go home if my name is Adam?'

Jess dropped the offending letter onto her dining room table, not sure she had heard correctly. 'Adam?'

'I see you're wearing your new boots,' he said as she opened the door. 'Were you expecting me?'

'How did you get in?' Jess asked, angry and more than a little embarrassed by how glad she was to see him.

'The front door was open.'

'Open?'

He shrugged. 'Maybe Greg didn't close it properly on his way out.' He leaned against the doorway. 'Get your coat.'

'My coat?'

'I thought we could grab a bite to eat, maybe take in a movie.'

'And if I'm too tired?'

'Then tell me to go home, Adam.'

Jess stared at Adam Stohn, his brown hair falling carelessly across his forehead, his posture maddeningly self-assured, his face as unreadable as a suspect in a police line-up. 'I'll get my coat,' she said.

Chapter Fourteen

They went to a revival of *Casablanca*, despite the fact that each had seen the movie several times on television. They sat near the back and, at Jess's insistence, on an aisle. They said little on the short drive to the movie, nothing at all once seated, and only a few words as they walked to the restaurant afterwards. They never touched.

The restaurant, located on North Lincoln Avenue, was small, dark, and noisy, specializing in roast beef. They sat at a tiny table for two near the back, and only after they had given their orders to the waiter, who wore a thin gold earring through his nose, did they make a few tentative stabs at conversation.

'I read somewhere,' Jess said, 'that when they started filming *Casablanca*, they didn't have a finished script, and the actors were never sure who they were or what they were supposed to be doing. Poor Ingrid Bergman apparently kept asking the director who it was she was supposed to be in love with.'

Adam laughed. 'Seems hard to believe.'

Silence. Adam's eyes drifted toward the deep wine-colored walls. Jess grabbed a warm roll from the bread basket, tore it in half, stuffed it into her mouth.

'You have a good appetite,' he commented, although his eyes were still directed elsewhere.

'I've always been a good eater.'

'Mother tell you to eat everything on your plate?'

'She didn't have to.' Jess swallowed, tore off another piece of the roll.

'You must have a high metabolic rate.'

'I find that frequent hysteria helps keep the pounds off,' Jess told him, popping the bread into her mouth, wondering why they were so ill at ease with each other. They'd had better rapport when they were virtual strangers. Instead of relaxing more with one another, each fresh exposure produced only greater stiffness, as if they were succumbing to an emotional rigor mortis. Probably self-inflicted.

'I don't like the word "hysterical",' he said, after a long pause.

'What's not to like?'

'It has such a negative connotation,' he explained. 'I prefer "high energy".'

'You think they're the same thing?'

'Two sides of the same equation.'

Jess thought it over. 'I don't know. All I know is that ever since I was a little girl, people have been telling me to relax.'

'Which only reinforced this negative image you have of yourself as an hysterical person.' He finally looked her square in the face. Jess was startled by the sudden intensity of his gaze. 'When people tell you to relax, it usually means *they're* the ones having problems with your high energy, not you. But they've made *you* feel guilty. Neat, huh?'

'Another of your interesting theories.'

'I'm an interesting guy, remember?' He grabbed a breadstick, bit off its end.

'So what are you doing selling shoes?'

He laughed. 'Does that bother you, that I sell shoes?'

'Why would it bother me?'

'The fact is that I like selling shoes,' he said, pushing back his chair, extending his legs their full length alongside the table. 'I go to work at ten o'clock every morning. I leave at six. Except Thursdays. On Thursdays, I come in at one, go home at nine. No taking my work home with me. No hours of preparation for the next day. No hassles. No responsibility. I come in; I sell shoes; I go home. Vini; vidi; vinci. Or whatever.'

'But it must be very frustrating for you if someone takes up hours of your time, then leaves with only one pair of shoes or, worse, none at all.'

'Doesn't bother me.'

'Aren't you on commission?'

'Part salary, part commission, yes.'

'Then your livelihood is affected.'

He shrugged, straightened up in his chair. 'I'm a good salesman.'

Jess felt her feet warm in her new winter boots. 'Well, I can certainly attest to that.' She was gratified when he smiled. 'What about intellectually?'

He seemed puzzled. 'What do you mean?'

'You're obviously a very smart man, Mr Stohn. It can't be very intellectually stimulating doing what you do all day.'

'On the contrary. I meet all sorts of bright, interesting people, doing what I do all day. They give me all the intellectual stimulation I require at this point in my life.'

'What exactly *is* this point in your life?'

He shrugged, 'Haven't a clue.'

'Where did you go to school?'

'Springfield.'

'I meant college.'

'Who says I went to college?'

'I do.'

He smiled, an obvious strain. 'Loyola University.'

'You graduated from Loyola University, and now you're selling shoes?'

'Is that a crime in Cook County?'

Jess felt her cheeks flush. 'I'm sorry. I must sound very presumptuous.'

'You sound like a prosecutor.'

'Ouch.'

'Tell me about the crossbow killer,' he said, suddenly changing topics.

'What?'

'I've been following your exploits in the paper this past week.'

'And what do you think?'

'I think you're going to win.'

She laughed, an open, happy sound, feeling strangely grateful for his vote of confidence.

'Are you going to ask for the death penalty?'

'If I get the chance,' Jess said simply.

'And how is the state killing people these days?'

The waiter appeared with two glasses of red Burgundy.

'Lethal injection.' Jess quickly raised her glass to her lips.

'I think I might let that breathe for a few minutes,' the waiter cautioned.

Jess obediently lowered the glass to the table. She found the unintentional combination of wine breathing and lethal injections ironically compelling.

'So, lethal injections, is it? Disposable needles for disposable people. I guess there's a certain justice in that.'

'I wouldn't waste too many tears on the likes of Terry Wales,' Jess told him.

'No sympathy for the criminal underclass at all?'

'None whatsoever.'

'Let me guess, your parents were lifelong Republicans.'

'Are you opposed to the death penalty?' Jess asked, not sure whether she had the strength to engage in a long debate over the pros and cons of capital punishment.

There was silence.

'I think some people deserve to die,' he said finally.

'You sound like you have someone particular in mind.'

He laughed, though the sound was hollow. 'No, no one.'

'Actually, my father is a registered Democrat,' Jess told him after another long pause.

Adam brought his glass of wine to his nose and inhaled, though he didn't drink. 'That's right, you told me your mother passed away.'

'There's a park near here,' Jess said, speaking almost to herself. 'Oz Park. My mother used to push me there in my carriage when I was a baby.'

'How did your mother die?' he asked.

'Cancer,' Jess said quickly, gulping at her wine.

Adam looked surprised, then dismayed. 'You're lying. Why?'

The glass in Jess's hand started to shake, several drops of red wine spilling over onto the thick white tablecloth, like drops of blood. 'Who says I'm lying?'

'It's written all over your face. If you'd been hooked up to a lie detector, the needle would have been all over the page.'

'You should never take a lie detector test,' Jess told him, steadying her glass on the table with both hands, grateful for the digression.

'I shouldn't?'

'They're way too unreliable. A guilty person can beat them, and an innocent person can fail. If you're innocent and you *fail* the test, it's assumed you're guilty. If you're innocent and you *pass* the test, it still doesn't eliminate you as a suspect. So you have nothing to gain and everything to lose by taking the test – that's if you're innocent.'

'And if I'm guilty?' he asked.

'Then you might as well give it a shot.' Jess patted her lips with her napkin, although they were dry. 'Of course, we're very big on lie detector tests at the prosecutor's office, so you didn't hear any of this from me.'

'Any of what?' Adam asked, and Jess smiled. 'Why won't you tell me what happened to your mother?'

Her smile immediately vanished. 'I thought we had a deal.'

'A deal?'

'No secrets, no lies. Remember?'

'Is there something secret about the way your mother died?'

'Just that it's a long story. I'd rather not get into it.'

'Then we don't get into it.'

The waiter approached with their dinners. 'Careful, the plates are hot,' he cautioned.

'Looks good,' Jess said, surveying the prime cut of rare roast beef, swimming in its own dark juices.

'Butter on your baked potato?' the waiter asked.

'And sour cream,' Jess told him. 'Lots.'

'The same,' Adam agreed, watching as Jess cut into her roast beef. 'I like a woman who eats,' he said, and laughed.

They ate for several minutes in silence.

'What was your wife like?' Jess asked, digging into her baked potato.

'Always on a diet.'

'Was she overweight?'

'I didn't think so.' He cut a large piece of meat, stuffed it into his mouth. 'Of course, what I thought didn't count for very much.'

'Doesn't sound like you're on very friendly terms.'

'One of the main reasons we got divorced.'

'I'm friends with my ex-husband,' Jess offered.

Adam looked skeptical.

'We are. Very good friends, as a matter of fact.'

'Is this the famous Greg? As in "Go home, Greg"?'

Jess laughed. 'No. Greg Oliver is a fellow prosecutor. He gave me a ride home.'

'You don't drive?'

'My car had a slight accident.'

A hint of worry fell across Adam's eyes.

'I wasn't in it at the time.'

He looked relieved. 'Well, that's good. What kind of accident?'

Jess shook her head. 'I'd rather not talk about it.'

'We're rapidly running out of things to talk about,' he said.

'What do you mean?'

'Well, you don't want to talk about your car or your mother or your sister or your brother-in-law, and I can't remember, was your father off limits as well?'

'I get the point.'

'Let's see. The ex-husband was relatively safe. Maybe we should stick with him. What's his name?'

'Don. Don Shaw.'

'And he's a lawyer, and you're great buddies.'

'We're friends.'

'So, why the divorce?'

'It's complicated.'

'And you'd rather not talk about it?'

'Why did *you* get divorced?' Jess asked in return.

'Equally complicated.'

'What's her name?'

'Susan.'

'And she's remarried and a decorator and she lives in Springfield.'

'And we're starting to cover familiar territory.' He paused. 'Is this it? We get no further than surfaces?'

'You have something against surfaces? I thought that's why you liked selling shoes.'

'Surfaces it is. So, tell me, Jess Koster, what's your lucky number?'

Jess laughed, took another bite of her roast beef, chewed it well.

'I'm serious,' Adam said. 'If we're going to stick with surfaces, I want them all covered. Lucky number?'

'I don't think I have one.'

'Pick a number from one to ten.'

'All right – four,' she said impulsively.

'Why four?'

Jess giggled, feeling like a small child. 'I guess because it's my nephew's favorite number. He likes it because it's Big Bird's favorite. Big Bird is a character on *Sesame Street*.'

'I know who Big Bird is.'

'Shoe salesmen watch *Sesame Street*?'

'Shoe salesmen are an unpredictable lot. Favorite color?'

'I've never really given it much thought.'

'Think about it now.'

Jess lowered her fork to her plate, looked around the dark room for clues. 'I'm not sure. Grey, I guess.'

'Grey?' He looked stunned.

'Something wrong with grey?'

'Jess, nobody's favorite color is grey!'

'Oh? Well, it's mine. And yours?'

'Red.'

'I'm not surprised.'

'Why not? Why aren't you surprised?'

'Well, red's a strong color. Forceful. Dynamic. Outgoing.'

'And you think that describes my personality?'

'Doesn't it?'

'Do you think grey describes yours?'

'This is getting more complicated than my divorce,' Jess said, and they both laughed.

'What about favorite song?'

'I don't have one. Honestly.'

'Nothing that you turn up the volume for when it comes on the radio?'

'Well, I like that aria from the opera *Turandot.* You know, the one where the tenor is out in the garden by himself.'

'I'm afraid I'm very ignorant when it comes to opera.'

'Knows *Sesame Street*, but not opera,' Jess mused aloud.

'And what else do you like?'

'I like my job,' she told him, aware how adept he was at turning the discussion away from himself. 'And I like to read when I have the time.'

'What do you like to read?'

'Novels.'

'What kind?'

'Murder mysteries mostly. Agatha Christie, Ed McBain, people like that.'

'What else do you like to do?'

'I like jigsaw puzzles. And I like to take long walks by the water. And I like to buy shoes.'

'For which I am eternally grateful,' he conceded, laughter in his eyes. 'And you like movies.'

'And I like movies.'

'And you like an aisle seat.'

'Yes.'

'Why?'

'Why?' Jess repeated, trying to hide her sudden discomfort. 'Why does anybody like an aisle seat? More room, I guess.'

'The needle just went off the page again,' Adam said.

'What?'

'The lie detector. You failed.'

'Why would I lie about liking an aisle seat?'

'You didn't lie about liking an aisle seat; you lied about why you like it. And I don't know why you'd lie. You tell me.'

'This is silly.'

'So aisle seats join the list of forbidden topics.'

'There's nothing to say about them.'

'Tell me why you insisted that you sit on an aisle.'

'I didn't insist.'

His mouth formed a boyish pout. 'Did too.'

'Did not.'

They both laughed, although a certain amount of tension remained.

'I don't think I like being called a liar,' Jess said, fussing with the napkin on her lap, watching it fall to the floor.

'I really wasn't trying to insult you.'

'A lawyer's good word, after all, is the only currency she has.' Jess bent over to retrieve her napkin.

'You're not in court now, Jess,' Adam told her. 'And you're not on trial. I'm sorry if I've overstepped in any way.'

'If I tell you,' Jess said suddenly, surprising them both, 'you'll think I'm a total wacko.'

'I already think you're a total wacko,' Adam said. 'I mean, come on, Jess, anybody who's favorite color is grey . . .'

'I was afraid I'd be sick,' Jess said.

'Sick? As in throw up?'

'I know it sounds silly.'

'Were you feeling queasy?'

'No. I felt fine.'

'But you were afraid you'd throw up if you didn't sit on the aisle?'

'Don't ask me why.'

'Have you *ever* thrown up when you didn't have an aisle seat?' he asked, logically.

'No,' she admitted.

'Then why think you might start now?'

He waited. She said nothing.

'Do I make you that nervous?'

'You don't make me nervous at all,' she lied, then immediately backtracked. 'Well, no, actually, you do make me a little nervous, but you had nothing to do with my thinking I might throw up.'

'I don't understand. '

'Neither do I. Can we talk about something else?' She lowered her head guiltily, another topic eliminated. 'It's just that it doesn't really seem like the right thing to be discussing when we're trying to eat dinner.'

'Let me see if I have this straight,' he said, ignoring her plea. 'You like an aisle seat because you think if you sit, say, in the middle of the theater, you might throw up, even though you've never thrown up in a movie theater before. Right?'

'Right.'

'How long have you had this phobia?'

'Who said I have a phobia?'

'What would you call it?'

'Define phobia,' she instructed.

'An irrational fear,' he suggested. 'A fear that has no basis in reality.'

Jess listened, absorbing his words like a sponge. 'Okay, I have a phobia.'

'What other phobias do you have – claustro, agora, arachna?'

She shook her head. 'None.'

'Other people are afraid of heights or spiders; you're afraid of throwing up in a movie theater if you don't have an aisle seat.'

'I know it's ridiculous.'

'It isn't ridiculous at all.'

'It isn't?'

'It's just not the whole story.'

'Still think I'm holding out on you?' Jess asked, hearing the quiver in her voice.

'What are you really afraid of, Jess?'

Jess pushed away her plate, fighting the urge to flee, her appetite gone. She forced herself to stay in her seat. 'I get these panic attacks,' she said quietly, after a long pause. 'I used to get them a lot a number of years ago. Eventually, they went away. A little while ago, they started coming back.'

'Any reason?'

'Could be any number of things,' Jess said, wondering whether her half-truth would send the needle of the invisible lie detector machine to which she was connected into orbit. 'My heart starts to pound. I get short of breath. I can't move. I feel sick to my stomach. I try to fight it.'

'Why?'

'Why? What do you mean?'

'Why fight it? Does it do any good?'

Jess conceded that it didn't. 'What am I *supposed* to do?'

'Why not just go with the attacks?'

'Go with them? I don't understand.'

'It's simple. Instead of wasting all that energy trying to fight the anxiety, why not just give in to it? Go with the flow, as they say. Look, you're in the theater,' he continued, obviously sensing her confusion, 'and you feel one of these attacks coming on, instead of holding your breath or counting to ten or jumping up from your seat, whatever it is you do, just go with the panic, give in to the feeling. What's the worst that can happen?'

'I'll be sick.'

'So, you'll be sick.'

'What?'

'You'll throw up. So what?'

'I hate throwing up.'

'That's not what you're afraid of.'

'It isn't?'

'No.'

Jess looked around impatiently. 'You're right. Actually what I'm afraid of is not getting any work done tonight if I stay out much longer. I'm afraid I won't get enough sleep if I stay out too late, and I'll come down with this cold I've been fighting, and be a disaster in court tomorrow. I'm afraid I'll lose this case and a cold-blooded killer will walk away with less than five years in jail. I'm afraid I really have to get going.' She checked her watch for emphasis, half rose in her seat. Once again, her napkin fell to the floor.

'I think you're afraid of death,' Adam said.

Jess froze. 'What?'

'I think what you're afraid of is death,' he repeated as she slowly lowered herself back into her seat. 'That's all most phobias come down to, in the end. A fear of death.' He paused. 'And, in your case, the fear is probably justifiable.'

'What do you mean?' How many times tonight had she asked that question?

'Well, I imagine you receive your fair share of threats from people you've put away. You probably get hate mail, obscene phone calls, standard stuff. You deal with death every day. With brutality and murder and man's inhumanity to man.'

'More usually man's inhumanity to women,' Jess qualified, wondering how he knew about all this 'standard stuff'.

'It's only natural for you to be afraid.'

Jess reached down to scoop up her napkin, tossing it carelessly over her plate, like a sheet over a corpse, she thought, watching the brown juices seep through the white cloth. 'Maybe you're right. Maybe that's what it all boils down to.'

Adam smiled. 'So, I make you nervous, do I?'

'A little,' she said. 'Actually, a lot.'

'Why?'

'Because I don't know what you're thinking,' she said truthfully.

His smile turned shy, circumspect. 'Isn't it more interesting that way?'

Jess said nothing. 'I really should get going,' she said finally. 'I have a lot to do to get ready for tomorrow. I probably shouldn't have gone out at all tonight.' Why was she babbling?

'I'll take you home,' he said. But all Jess could hear was, 'I think what you're afraid of is death.'

Chapter Fifteen

The following Saturday Jess enrolled in a self-defense course.

The week had been a strange one. Tuesday saw the wrap-up of the prosecution's case against Terry Wales. A succession of witnesses – police officers, medical authorities, psychologists, eyewitnesses, friends and relatives of the deceased – had all testified. They had proved beyond a reasonable doubt that Terry Wales had murdered his wife. The only question remaining, the stubborn question that had been there from the beginning, was one of degree. Would Terry Wales be able to convince the jury that it had all been a tragic mistake?

He'd certainly made a successful start. Terry Wales had taken the stand Wednesday morning in his own defense, and answered his lawyer's careful questions slowly and thoughtfully. Yes, he had a temper. Yes, he and his wife had engaged in occasionally violent arguments. Yes, he had once broken her nose, and blackened her eyes. And yes, he had threatened to kill her if she tried to leave him.

But no, he never really meant it. No, he never meant to hurt her. No, he was not some unfeeling, cold-blooded killer.

He loved his wife, he'd said, his pale blue eyes focused on the jurors. He'd always loved her. Even when she verbally abused him in front of his friends. Even when she flew at him from across the room, determined to scratch his eyes out, forcing him to fight back in self-defense. Even when she threatened to take him for everything he had. Even when she threatened to turn his own children against him.

He'd only meant to scare her when he fired that arrow into the busy intersection. He'd had no idea his aim would prove so deadly. If he'd wanted to kill her, he would have used a gun. He had several, was an expert shot, whereas he hadn't fired a bow and arrow since he was a kid at camp.

Terry Wales finished the day in tears, his voice hoarse, his skin mottled and pale. His lawyer had to help him from the stand.

Jess and her two partners had stayed up half that night reviewing the testimony of each witness, poring over the police reports, searching for anything they might have overlooked, anything that might help in Jess's cross-examination of Terry Wales the next morning. After Neil and Barbara went home, sneezing and wheezing their way down the hall, Jess had stayed up the rest of the night, returning to her apartment at six the next morning only to shower and change her clothes before heading right back to her office.

She appeared in court on Thursday to find Judge Harris recessing the case till the following Monday. The defendant, it appeared, wasn't feeling too well, and the defense had requested a postponement of several days. Judge Harris coughed his agreement, and court was dismissed. Jess spent most of the day talking to police detectives, encouraging them to use this delay to ferret out additional evidence that might benefit the prosecution's case.

Friday saw the arrival of her annual Christmas card from the Federal Penitentiary. WISHING YOU ALL THE BEST FOR THE HOLIDAY SEASON, it read in letters of bright gold decorated with sprigs of holly. *Thinking of you*, it said at the bottom, as if from a close friend, followed by the simple signature, *Jack*.

Jack had murdered his girlfriend in a drunken argument over where he'd put his car keys. Jess had sent him to prison for twelve years. Jack swore he'd come visit her when he got out, thank her in person for her generosity.

Thinking of you. Thinking of you.

Jess had spent the rest of Friday researching self-defense classes in the city, found one on Clybourn Avenue, not too far from where she lived and right on a subway line. Two hours on Saturday afternoon for three consecutive weeks, the delicate Asian voice on the telephone informed her. One hundred and eighty dollars for the course. Something called Wen-Do. She'd be there, Jess told the woman, recalling what Adam had said. Was it really death she was afraid of? she wondered, unwittingly conjuring up her mother's face, hearing her mother assure her she would be all right.

Thinking of you. Thinking of you.

And then it was Saturday, cloudless, sunny and cold.

The classes were held in an old two-storey building. WEN-DO, the sign proclaimed in black letters almost as large as the structure itself.

'Please to give me your coat, then please to put this on and please to go inside,' the young Oriental woman behind the reception counter instructed, as Jess exchanged her long winter coat for a short, dark blue cotton robe and matching sash. Jess was wearing a loose sweatshirt and pants, as she had been advised over the telephone. They were grey, she noted, suppressing a smile, her favorite color. 'You are early,' the young woman giggled, her high black ponytail bouncing with the gentle movement of her shoulders. 'Nobody else here yet.'

Jess smiled and half bowed, not sure of the proper protocol. The young woman waved her toward a curtain to her right, and Jess, bowing again, stepped through.

The room she stepped into was twice as long as it was wide, and empty except for a series of dark green mats stacked in one corner of the well-scuffed wood-planked floor. Jess caught her reflection in the wall of mirrors that ran along the left side of the room, lending it a depth it didn't have. She looked ridiculous, she thought, a cultural hybrid in her American sweats and Oriental robe. She shrugged, pulling back her hair and securing it with a wide elastic band.

What was she doing here? What exactly was it she hoped to learn? Did she really think she could protect herself from . . . from what? From the elements? From the inevitable?

She heard a shuffle behind her, turned to see a woman with a noticeable limp emerge from between the green flowered curtains. 'Hi,' said the woman, who was probably the same age as Jess. 'I'm Vasiliki. Call me Vas, it's easier.'

'Jess Koster,' Jess said, stepping forward to shake the woman's hand. 'Vasiliki is a very interesting name.'

'It's Greek,' the woman said, checking out her reflection in the mirrored wall. She was tall and big-boned, her dark hair framing her olive complexion and ending bluntly at her square jaw. Aside from her limp, she looked quite formidable. 'I was attacked over a year ago by a gang of thirteen-year-old boys. Thirteen years old! Can you believe it?' Her tone indicated that she couldn't. 'They were after my purse. I said, "Go ahead, take it. There's nothing in it." So they took it, and when they saw I only had ten dollars, 'cause I never carry around much cash, they started beating me, shoved me to the ground, kicked me so hard, they broke my knee cap. I'm lucky to be walking at all. I decided as soon as my therapy was over, I was enrolling in a self-defense course. Next time anybody comes at me, I'm going to be ready.' She laughed bitterly. 'Of course, it's a bit like locking the barn door after the horse has escaped.' She tied an extra knot in the sash at her waist.

Jess shook her head. Juvenile crime had reached epidemic proportions in the city of Chicago. A whole new building was being erected to deal with these violent young offenders. As if a building could do any good.

'What about you? What brought you here?' Vas was asking.

Fear of the unknown, fear of the known, Jess answered silently. 'I'm not sure,' she said out loud. 'I just thought it was probably a good idea that I learn how to defend myself.'

'Well, you're smart. I tell you, it isn't easy being a woman these days.'

Jess nodded, wishing there was a place to sit down.

Again the curtains parted, and two black women stepped inside, their eyes warily scanning the room.

'I'm Vasiliki. Call me Vas,' Vas stated, nodding in their direction. 'This is Jess.'

'Maryellen,' the older and lighter-skinned of the two women said. 'This is my daughter, Ayisha.'

Jess estimated Ayisha's age as seventeen, her mother closer to forty. Both were very pretty, although a faded purple bruise was visible under the mother's right eye.

'I think it's neat, you taking this course together,' Vas was saying as the curtains parted again and another woman, short, plump and middle-aged, her hair noticeably salted with grey, entered the room, tugging nervously at her blue robe. 'Vasiliki, call me Vas,' Vas was already saying. 'This is Jess, Maryellen, and Ayisha.'

'Catarina Santos,' the woman said, her voice tentative, as if she wasn't sure.

'Well, we're a regular little United Nations,' Vas quipped.

'Here to learn the ancient Oriental art of Wen-Do,' Jess added.

'Oh, there's nothing ancient about it,' Vas corrected. 'Wen-Do was developed only twenty years ago by a couple in, of all places, Toronto, Canada. Can you beat that?'

'We're learning a martial arts system developed in Canada?' Jess asked incredulously.

'Apparently it combines physical techniques drawn from both karate and aikido. Anybody know what aikido is?' Vas asked.

Nobody did.

'Wen-Do's guiding ideas are awareness, avoidance and action,' Vas continued, then laughed self-consciously. 'I memorized the brochure.'

'I'm all for action,' Ayisha mumbled as Catarina shrank back against the mirrored wall.

Once more the curtains parted and a young man with a dark pompadour and a healthy strut approached the loose circle of women. He was short and the muscles of his well-sculpted arms could be discerned even beneath his blue robe. His face was well scrubbed and boyish, a small scar, probably the result of a childhood case of chicken pox, sat in the bridge of his nose beside his right eyebrow. 'Good afternoon,' he said, speaking clearly from his diaphragm. 'I'm Dominic, your instructor.'

'Funny,' Vas whispered to Jess, 'he doesn't look Wen-Doish.'

'How many of you think you could fend off an attacker?' he asked, hands on his hips, chin thrust forward.

The women hung back, said nothing.

Dominic slowly sauntered toward Maryellen and her daughter, Ayisha. 'What about you, Mama? Think you could break an attacker's nose if he went after your daughter?'

'He'd be lucky to get away with his head still attached,' Maryellen said forcefully.

'Well, the experience of Wen-Do,' he said, 'is realizing that you are as valuable as any child in your life that you love. Valuable,' he continued, pausing carefully for effect, 'but not vulnerable. At least not as vulnerable as before. You may be weaker than your potential attackers,' he said, backing away from Maryellen and addressing each of the women in turn, 'but you are not all-weak and your attackers are not all-powerful. It's important that you don't think of your attackers as huge, impenetrable hulks, but think of them instead as a collection of vulnerable targets. And remember,' he said, looking directly at Jess, 'anger works a lot better than pleading in most cases. So don't be afraid to get angry.'

Jess felt her knees trembling, was grateful when he turned away, concentrated on someone else. Jess surveyed the faces of the different women, the mini United Nations, as Vas had accurately described them, so representative of all the changes that had occurred in the city in the last twenty years. So different from the Chicago of her childhood, she thought, escaping momentarily into the lily whiteness of her past, being pulled back into the present by the force of Dominic's voice.

'You have to learn to trust your sense of danger,' he was saying. 'Even if you're not exactly sure what you're afraid of, even if you don't know what's making you nervous, even if you're afraid of embarrassing a man who may or may not be a threat to you, the best thing you can do is remove yourself from the situation as quickly as you can. Denial can be very costly. Trust your instincts,' he said. 'And get out as fast as you can.'

If you can, Jess added silently.

'Running away is what works best most often for women,' Dominic concluded simply. 'Okay, line up.'

The women exchanged nervous glances, shuffled warily into a straight line. 'Up against the wall, motherfuckers,' Vas whispered to Jess, then giggled like a small child.

'Give yourself plenty of room. That's right. Spread out a little bit. We're gonna be moving around a lot here in a few minutes. Roll your shoulders back. Loosen up. That's right. Swing your arms. Get nice and relaxed.'

Jess swung her arms from side to side and up and down. She rotated her shoulders backwards, then forwards. She rolled her neck from side to side, heard it crack.

'Don't forget to breathe,' Dominic instructed, and Jess gratefully expelled a deep breath of air. 'Okay, straighten up. Now pay close attention. The first line of defense is called *kiyi.*'

'Did he say kiwi?' Vas asked, and Jess had to bite down on her tongue to keep from laughing.

'*Kiyi* is a great yell, a roar from the diaphragm. *Hohh!*' he shouted, and the women flinched. '*Hohh!*' he yelled again. '*Hohh!*'

Ho, ho, ho, Jess thought.

'The purpose of *kiyi,*' he explained, 'is to wipe out the picture the attacker has of you as being quiet and vulnerable. It also helps ensure that you don't freeze up with fear. *Hohh!*' he shouted yet again, and the women jumped back in alarm. 'Also, it has the element of surprise. Surprise can be a very useful weapon.' He smiled. 'Now, you try it.'

Nobody moved. After several seconds, Ayisha and then Vas started to giggle. Jess wasn't sure whether she wanted to laugh or cry. How could she trust her instincts, she wondered, when she wasn't even sure what her instincts were.

'Let's hear it!' Dominic encouraged. '*Hohh!*'

Another second of silence, then a weak, tentative 'Hohh!' from Maryellen.

'Not "hohh", *hohh!*' Dominic emphasized. 'This is not the time and place to be polite. We want to scare our attacker, not encourage him. Now, come on, let me hear you. *Hohh!*'

'Hohh!' Jess ventured meekly, feeling totally ridiculous. Similar sad sounds echoed throughout the room.

'Come on!' Dominic urged, clenching his fists for emphasis. 'You're women now, not ladies. Let me hear you get angry. Let me hear you make a lot of noise. I know you can do it. I was raised with four sisters. Don't tell me you don't know how to yell.' He approached Maryellen. 'Come on, Mama. There's a man attacking your daughter.'

'*Hohh!*' screamed Maryellen.

'That's more like it.'

'*Hohh!*' Maryellen continued. '*Hohh! Hohh!*' She smiled. 'Hey, I'm starting to like this.'

'Feels good to assert yourself, doesn't it?' Dominic asked, and Maryellen nodded. 'What about the rest of you? Let's hear you put that would-be attacker on the alert.'

'Hohh!' the voices began, still tentative, then louder, gaining strength, '*Hohh! Hohh!*'

Jess tried to join in, but even when she opened her mouth, no sound emerged. What was the matter with her? Since when had she been afraid of asserting herself?

Think anger, she told herself. Think about your car. Think about Terry Wales. Think about Erica Barnowski. Think about Greg Oliver. Think about your brother-in-law. Think about Connie DeVuono. Think about Rick Ferguson.

Think about your mother.

'*Hohh!*' Jess screamed into the suddenly silent room. '*Hohh!*'

'Perfection,' Dominic enthused, clapping his hands. 'I knew you had it in you.'

'Well done,' Vas told her, squeezing her hand.

'Now, if *kiyi* doesn't frighten off a potential attacker, you've got to learn to use whatever weapons are around, starting with your hands, your feet, elbows, shoulders, fingernails. Fingernails are good, so any of you who bite your nails, stop right now. The eyes, ears and nose are among the targets.' Dominic made his fist into a hook, his fingers like talons. 'Eagle claws through the attacker's eyes,' he said, demonstrating. 'Zipper punch to the nose, using those bony knuckles. Hammer fist down on the nose.' Again he illustrated. The women watched with something approaching awe. 'I'm gonna show you how to do all that later,' he told them. 'Believe me, it's not hard. The important thing is not to expect that you're going to be able to match your force against your attacker's, which just isn't going to happen. Instead, what you've got to do is learn to use the attacker's force against him.'

'I don't understand,' Jess said, surprised she had spoken.

'Good. Speak up loud and clear when you don't understand something. Speak up loud and clear even when you do.' He smiled. 'And don't forget to breathe.'

Jess gratefully expelled another deep breath of air.

'That's right, from the diaphragm. You gotta remember to breathe or you're gonna run out of steam pretty fast. Anybody here who smokes, you should give it up. Breathe deeply instead. That's all you're really doing when you smoke anyway. Breathing deeply in and out. You just gotta learn to do it without the cigarette. What is it you don't understand?' he asked Jess, returning abruptly to her question.

'You said we have to use the attacker's force against him. I don't understand what you mean.'

'Okay, let me explain.' He paused for a minute, his eyes narrowing in thought. 'Use the image of circularity,' he began, drawing a circle in the air with his index finger. 'If someone pulls you toward him, instead of resisting and pulling back, which is what we tend to do in that sort of situation, use that attacker's force to be pulled into his body, and then strike when you get there.'

He grabbed Jess's arm. Instinctively, she pulled back.

'No,' he said. 'Exactly wrong.'

'But you told us to trust our instincts.'

'Trust your instincts when they *warn* you of danger. Remember that recognizing danger and getting away as fast as you can always comes first. But when you're already *in* danger, then it's a different story. Your instincts can mislead you. You have to educate your instincts. Now, come here, I'm going to use you to illustrate what I mean.'

Jess reluctantly stepped forward.

'I'm going to pull you toward me, and I want you to resist, the way you did before.' Dominic suddenly lunged forward, his hand clamping down on Jess's wrist, pulling her toward him.

Her adrenaline immediately in overdrive, Jess pulled back, trying to steady her feet against the wood floor, to gain some traction. She was no pushover, she decided, feeling the tugging at her arm, the pain shooting its way to her elbow. She pulled back harder, her breathing becoming shallow.

In the next instant, she was on the floor and Dominic was looming over her.

'What happened?' she panted, not sure how she had gone from two feet on the floor to flat on her back in less than a second.

Dominic helped her to her feet. 'Now, let's try it the other way. Don't fight me. Don't put up any resistance. Let my force pull you close to me. Then use that momentum to push me away.'

Again Jess braced herself. Again Dominic's hand encircled her wrist. But this time, instead of resisting, instead of struggling, she allowed herself to be pulled toward him. Only when she felt their bodies connect did she suddenly use the full force of her weight to push into him, throwing him off balance, and sending him upended to the floor.

'Way to go, Jess!' Vas cheered.

'That's it, girl, you did it,' chimed in Maryellen.

'Awesome,' Ayisha agreed.

Catarina nodded shyly.

Dominic slowly rose to his feet. 'I think you understand now,' he said, dusting himself off.

Jess smiled. '*Hohh!*' she said.

'Hohh, hohh, hohh!' Jess whispered to herself, emerging from the subway near the Magnificent Mile. She felt stronger than she had in weeks, maybe months. Empowered. Good about herself. 'Hohh!' she laughed, drawing her coat tight around her, walking toward Michigan Avenue.

Who said she had to wait for Adam to phone her? This was the nineties, after all. Women didn't sit around waiting for guys to call. They picked up the phone and did the dialing themselves. Besides, it was Saturday, she had no plans for the evening, and

Adam would probably be delighted to see her take the initiative. 'Hohh!' she said, more loudly than she had intended, catching the nervous attention of a passer-by.

The woman picked up her speed. That's right, lady, Jess told her silently. Your instincts tell you danger, get away fast. 'Hohh!' she said again, almost singing, approaching the front window of Shoe-Inn and peering inside.

'Is Adam Stohn here today?' she asked the salesman in the ill-fitting toupee who ran to greet her as soon as she stepped through the front door.

The salesman's eyes narrowed until they all but disappeared. Did he remember her from their last encounter?

'He's with a customer.' His chin directed Jess to the rear of the store.

Adam was standing beside a young woman, his hands full of shoes, her face full of laughter. Jess approached quietly, not wanting to disturb him in the middle of a sale.

'So, you don't like any of these shoes. Well, let me see. Can I interest you in a glass of water instead?' Adam was saying.

The young woman laughed, her long blond hair falling across her carefully rouged cheek as she shook her head.

'How about a candy?'

Jess watched Adam reach into his jacket pocket for a red- and white-striped mint, saw the young woman consider it before refusing the offer.

'How about a joke? You look like a woman who appreciates a good joke.'

Jess felt tears sting her eyes, and quickly backed away, deciding not to hang around for the punch line. She was the joke, after all.

'Did you find him?' the salesman with the ill-fitting toupee asked as she strode toward the front of the store.

'I'll speak to him later. Thank you,' Jess said, wondering what she was thanking him for. Women were so quick to say thank you, to be grateful. 'I'm sorry,' she said, stepping out of another woman's way, the other woman also apologizing. And what are we all so sorry about?

Damn it, she thought, feeling embarrassed and confused. What had possessed her to come here? Why did she think that just because she was feeling good and wanted to share that feeling with somebody, that Adam would be interested in fulfilling that role? So what if she felt empowered? So what if she'd learned to turn her fist into an eagle's claw? Who cared whether she could execute a zipper punch to the nose? Why would he be interested in *kiyi*? He was interested in selling shoes, in earning his commission. Why had she thought she was any different from any of the other hundreds of women whose feet he fondled in any given week? And why was she so disappointed?

'Hohh!' she said, standing alone in front of the store. But her heart wasn't in it, and the word fell to the sidewalk, to be trampled on by a parade of passing feet.

'Well, hi, stranger,' Don was saying, his voice an oasis, even over the phone. 'This is a pleasant surprise. I was beginning to think you were still mad at me.'

'Why would I be mad at you?' Jess pulled the door of the public phone booth closed.

'You tell me. All I know is you've barely said two words to me since our little disagreement at the police station.'

'Sure I have.'

'All right, maybe two words, both of them no: when I asked you over for Thanksgiving, and another time when I invited you out for a steak dinner.'

'Which is exactly why I'm calling,' Jess began, grateful to have been handed such a convenient segue. 'I'm downtown, and I haven't had a good steak in ages, and I thought maybe if you weren't doing anything tonight . . .' Her voice trailed off, leaving only silence. 'You're busy,' Jess said quickly.

'God, Jess,' Don said, his voice an apology, 'any other time, you know I'd jump at the chance, but—'

'But it's Saturday night and Mother Teresa is waiting.'

Another silence. 'Actually Trish is out of town this weekend,'

Don said easily. 'So I accepted an offer to have dinner over at John McMaster's. You remember John.'

'Of course.' John McMaster was one of Don's partners. 'Say hello for me.'

'I'd invite you—'

'I wouldn't go.'

'But you wouldn't go.'

Jess laughed, finding it suddenly hard to catch her breath. Did she really expect her ex-husband to be waiting by the phone every time she felt lonely or depressed and in need of a little friendly support?

'I have a great idea,' he was saying.

'What's your great idea?' Jess felt she was choking, that no air was reaching her lungs. She pulled at the folding door of the phone booth, but it refused to open.

'Why don't I drop over tomorrow morning with some bagels and cream cheese, and you can make me some coffee and tell me who died.'

Jess struggled with the door to the phone booth, numbness teasing at her fingers. She couldn't breathe. If she didn't get out of this damn phone booth soon, she would faint, possibly suffocate. She had to get out. She had to get some air.

'Jess? Jess, are you there? That was a joke. Don't you read the obituaries any more?'

'I really have to go now, Don.' Jess pounded against the door with her fist.

'How does ten a.m. sound?'

'Fine. Sounds great.'

'See you tomorrow morning.'

Jess dropped the phone, letting it dangle from its long cord, watching it sway back and forth as if the victim of a lynching, all the while pushing and pulling at the door of the phone booth in a desperate effort to free herself. 'Goddamn it, let me out of here!' she screamed.

Suddenly the door opened. A grey-haired old lady, not more than five feet tall, stood on the other side, her deeply veined hands clutching the side of the door. 'These things can be tricky sometimes,' she said with an indulgent smile before shuffling on down the street.

Jess shot out of the phone booth, sweat streaming down her face, despite the near freezing temperatures. 'How could I do that?' she whispered into her numbed hands. 'I forgot everything I learned today. How am I going to defend myself against anybody when I can't even get out of a goddamn phone booth?'

It was several minutes before the numbness left her hands, and she was able to hail a cab to take her home.

Chapter Sixteen

Dinner consisted of Stouffer's macaroni and cheese, two pieces of Pepperidge Farm frozen vanilla cake with strawberry icing, and a large bottle of Coca-Cola. 'Nothing like a good dinner,' Jess muttered to her canary as she returned her empty plates to the kitchen, depositing them in the sink, too tired to stack them in the dishwasher.

She shuffled back into the living room, her slippered feet too weary to lift themselves off the floor, reminding Jess of the old woman who had freed her from the phone booth that afternoon. 'She'd probably do better against an attacker than I would,' Jess said, debating whether to continue with the self-defense course for the rest of its two-week duration. 'I might as well. I paid for it,' she conceded, turning off her stereo and covering the bird's cage for the night. She turned off the light and shuffled toward her bedroom, pulling off her grey sweatshirt as she walked, and discarding it and her sweatpants in the laundry hamper, although she had no idea when she'd actually get around to washing them. She'd made it a habit lately to buy only clothes whose labels proclaimed DRY CLEAN ONLY. More expensive, maybe, but much less time-consuming.

She pulled a long, pink- and white-flowered flannelette nightgown over her head, then carefully laid out her clothes for the following day: a pair of blue jeans, a red turtleneck sweater, heavy red socks, and fresh underwear. Just waiting for her to climb inside. Her sneakers sat on the floor by the chair, ready for her to step into. All was right with the world, she thought, slouching toward the bathroom to wash her face and brush her teeth. She couldn't wait to get into bed.

It was barely nine o'clock, she realized with some surprise as she turned off the bedroom lamp and crawled in between the covers. She should probably be doing some work in preparation for the resumption of the Terry Wales trial on Monday, but her eyes were already closing. It had been a long day, and an exhausting one. She'd been disappointed by two men in one afternoon. She'd found power, only to lose it. That was enough to wear anybody out.

'Good night, Moon,' she whispered, recalling the children's book of that name she'd bought for her nephew, listening to vague noises from the apartment downstairs. Walter must be having another party, Jess thought, as she drifted off to sleep.

In her dream, she was facing a jury wearing only her pink and white flannelette night-gown and her tatty pink slippers.

'We love your pyjamas,' one of the female jurors told her, reaching across the jury box to stroke the soft arm of Jess's night-gown. But her hand was an eagle's claw and it ripped through the material as easily as sharp scissors through paper, drawing blood.

'Let me take care of that,' Don offered, vaulting over the defense table and reaching for her bleeding arm.

Jess allowed him to draw her close, feeling their bodies connect, then suddenly pushed her full weight against him, throwing him off balance and to the floor.

Judge Harris banged his displeasure with his gavel. 'Order in the court,' he demanded in Adam Stohn's voice. 'Order in the court.' Then, 'Jess, are you there? Jess? Jess?'

Jess sat up in bed, not fully awake, foolishly grateful to find herself in her bedroom and not in court. Trust me, she thought, clutching at pieces of her dream even as the dream evaporated, to rebuff the one person trying to help.

'Jess,' the voice from her dream continued, 'Jess, are you there?'

The banging of the gavel continued. Only not a gavel, but someone knocking on the door to her apartment, Jess realized, coming fully awake and reaching across her bed to the night table. She pulled open the drawer and reached inside for her gun, alarmed, even as she lifted the gun into her hands, at how easily she did so.

'Who's there?' she called back, sliding into her slippers and steadying the gun as she walked to the door, the floor vibrating beneath her feet from the loud music below.

'It's Adam,' came the response from the other side.

'What are you doing here?' Jess asked without opening the door.

'I wanted to see you.'

'Haven't you ever heard of the telephone?'

'I've seen enough telephones,' he said, and laughed. 'I wanted to see you. It was an impulse thing.'

'How did you get in the house?'

'The front door was open. There's quite a party going on downstairs. Look, I really hate yelling through the door this way. Are you going to let me in?'

'It's late.'

'Jess, if you've got someone else there . . .'

She opened the door. 'There's no one else here.' Jess motioned him inside with a wave of her gun.

'Jesus Christ, is that thing real?'

Jess nodded, thinking he looked wonderful, wondering if she looked as ridiculous as she felt in her pink- and white-flowered flannelette night-gown, fuzzy pink slippers and Smith & Wesson revolver. 'I'm wary of late-night visitors,' she told him.

'Late? Jess, it's ten-thirty.'

'Ten-thirty?'

'You could get a peephole for that door, you know. Or a chain.' He stared nervously at the gun. 'Think you could put that away now?' He took off his jacket, threw it over the arm of the sofa, as if, now that he was here, he intended to stay, and stood before her in a rumpled white sweater and pressed black jeans. It was only then she noticed the bottle of red wine in his hands. 'Tell you what,' he continued, 'you get rid of the gun; I'll open the wine.'

Jess nodded, not sure what else to do. She moved, as if on

automatic pilot, back to her bedroom, returned the gun to its drawer in the night table, and retrieved a pink quilted bathrobe from her closet. By the time she returned to the living room, Adam had opened the wine and poured them each a glass.

'Chateauneuf du Pape,' he said, depositing a glass in her right hand and guiding her toward the sofa. 'What shall we drink to?' he asked as they sat down, their knees touching briefly before Jess pulled away, tucking her legs beneath her.

Jess recalled her brother-in-law's favorite toast. 'Health and wealth?' she offered.

'How about to good times?'

'I'm all for good times.'

They clicked glasses, inhaled the aroma, then raised their glasses to their lips, though neither drank.

'It's nice to see you,' Adam said.

Jess concentrated on his lips, aware of a slight trace of alcohol already on his breath, and wondered where he'd been before he arrived on her doorstep. Out with the customer she'd seen him with this afternoon? Had their date ended early, leaving him with nothing but time and a bottle of wine on his hands?

Jess found herself getting angrier with each new thought. Now that she was fully awake, she was less charmed by his spontaneity than she was angered by his presumptuousness. What was he doing knocking on her door after ten o'clock on a Saturday night and scaring her half to death? Did he really think he could ignore her all week, then show up unannounced any time he felt like it? Did he assume she would just let him in, drink his wine, then take him gratefully into her bed? He was lucky she hadn't shot him!

'What are you doing here?' Jess asked, surprising them both with the suddenness of her question.

Adam took a long sip of his drink, playing with it in his mouth for several seconds before swallowing it. 'Why do you think I'm here?'

'I don't know. That's why I asked.'

He took another drink, this time throwing the liquid against the back of his mouth as if it were a shot of whiskey. 'I wanted to see you,' he said, though his eyes looked just past her, refusing to focus.

'When did you decide that?'

Adam fidgeted on the sofa, took another long sip of his drink, refilled his glass to the top, in no rush to answer her question. 'I don't understand.'

'At what time did you decide you wanted to see me?' Jess probed, impatient now. 'Two o'clock this afternoon? Four? Seven? Ten?'

'What is this, Jess? An interrogation?'

'Why didn't you phone first?'

'I already told you. It was an impulse.'

'And you're just an impulsive kind of guy.'

'Sometimes. Yes. I guess so.'

'Are you married?'

'What?'

'Are you married?' Jess repeated, seeing the situation clearly for the first time, wondering why she hadn't realized it before. 'Simple enough question. Requiring only a simple yes or no answer.'

'What makes you think I'm married?'

'Are you married? Yes or no?'

'The witness will please answer the question,' Adam said, sarcastically.

'Are you married?' Jess said again.

'No,' Adam proclaimed loudly. 'Of course I'm not married.'

'You're divorced.'

'I'm divorced.'

'From Susan.'

'Yes, from Susan.'

'Who lives in Springfield.'

'Who lives on Mars, for all I care.' He finished the wine remaining in his glass in one gulp.

'Then why don't you ever call? Why do you just show up on

my doorstep at all hours of the night?'

'Jess, for Christ's sake, it's ten-thirty!'

'You've already made your commission,' she said, still smarting from the little scene she'd witnessed in the shoe store that afternoon, her cheeks flushing with embarrassment. Had the toupeed salesman told Adam of her visit? 'What are you doing here?'

'You think I'm trying to sell you another pair of boots?'

'I'm not sure what you're trying to sell me.'

He poured himself more wine, drank it down in two gulps, then emptied what remained of the bottle into his glass. 'I'm not married, Jess. Honest.'

There was a long pause. Jess stared into her lap, her anger spent, more relieved than she cared to acknowledge.

'Did we just have our first fight?' he asked.

'I don't know you well enough to fight with you,' Jess answered.

'You know me as well as necessary.' He finished the wine, stared dumbfounded into the bottom of his empty glass, as if just realizing he'd drunk almost an entire bottle of wine in less than ten minutes.

'Necessary for me or for you?'

'I just don't like to plan things too far in advance.'

Jess laughed.

'What's funny?' he asked.

'I plan everything.'

'And just what does planning everything accomplish?' He leaned back against the sofa, shaking his shoes from his feet, lifting his legs off the floor, and casually stretching them across Jess's lap.

'It gives me an illusion of control, I guess,' Jess answered, feeling his weight across her thighs. Her body tensed, then relaxed, welcoming the contact. It had been so long since she'd been with a man, so long since she'd allowed herself the pleasure of a man's caress. Had he been right in his assumptions after all?

'And this illusion of control is important to you?' he was saying.

'It's all I've got.'

Adam leaned his head against the pillow, adjusted his hips so that he was almost lying down. 'I think I may have had too much to drink.'

'I think you're right.' There was a long pause. 'Why did you come here, Adam?'

'I don't know,' he said, his eyes closing, his words heavy, unwilling. 'I guess I shouldn't have.'

Don't say that, Jess said silently. 'Maybe you should go,' she said out loud, fighting the urge to cradle him in her arms. 'I better call you a cab. You're in no shape to drive.'

'Ten minutes' sleep is all I need.'

'Adam, I'm going to call for a taxi.' Jess tried lifting his legs, but they were like dead weights. 'If you'll just shift your feet a bit.'

He did, drawing his knees toward his chest in a semi-fetal position, turning fully on his side. If anything, he felt even heavier than before.

'Great,' Jess said, tickling the bottoms of his feet, trying to get him to move. But her fingers generated no response at all. 'Adam, I can't sit here like this all night,' she said, finding herself close to tears. 'No, this is silly!' she exclaimed. 'I will not be a prisoner in my own apartment. I will not spend the night sitting on my sofa with some comatose drunk sprawled across my lap. I need my sleep. I need to get to bed. *Hohh!*' she shouted, but Adam didn't move.

With renewed determination, Jess tugged at Adam's feet, managing, after a few minutes, to lift them just high enough so that she could slide out from under. Adam's feet returned to the sofa with a gentle plop.

Jess stood over him for several minutes, watching him sleep. 'Adam, you can't stay here,' she whispered, then louder, 'Adam, I'm going to call for a taxi.'

And tell them what? That you have a man passed out on your

sofa and you want someone to pick him up and carry him down three flights of stairs, and then take him home, except that you have no idea where he lives? Oh yes, right. They'll fight over that fare.

Face it, Jess, she told herself, covering him with his jacket. Adam Stohn isn't going anywhere. At least not tonight.

She studied his face, all traces of turmoil hidden by the peaceful mask of sleep. What secrets was he hiding? she wondered, brushing some hair away from his eyes, her fingers tingling at the contact. How many lies had he told her?

Jess tiptoed away from the sofa, wondering whether she was doing the right thing in letting him stay. Would she wake up in the middle of the night to find him looming over her with her gun in his hand? Was he some psychotic sociopath on the lookout for lonely prosecuting attorneys?

She was almost too tired to care.

Trust your instincts, Jess heard her Wen-Do instructor repeat as she crawled back into bed. Trust your instincts.

But just in case her instincts were wrong, she removed the gun from the top drawer of her end table and tucked it carefully underneath her mattress before allowing herself the luxury of sleep.

She awoke the next morning to find him staring at her from her bedroom door.

'Do you always lay out your clothes so neatly?' he was asking. 'Even on a Sunday?'

'How long have you been standing there?' she asked, ignoring his question, sitting up in bed, gathering her duvet around her.

'Not long. A few minutes, maybe.'

Jess looked toward her clock. 'Nine-thirty!' she gasped.

'Shouldn't drink so much,' he said and smiled sheepishly.

'I can't believe I slept till nine-thirty!'

'You were obviously exhausted.'

'I have so much to do.'

'First things first,' he said. 'Breakfast is ready.'

'You made breakfast?'

He leaned against the doorway. 'It wasn't easy. You weren't lying when you said you don't cook. I had to run out and buy some eggs and vegetables.'

'How'd you get back in?'

'I borrowed your key,' he said simply.

'You went into my purse?'

'I put it back.' He approached her bed, held out his hand. 'Come on, I've been slaving over a hot stove all morning.'

Jess threw back her covers and stepped out of bed, ignoring the offer of his hand, not sure she liked the idea of his having gone into her purse. 'Let me just wash my face and brush my teeth.'

'Later.' He grabbed her hand, pulled her through the hallway to the dining area. The table was set, orange juice already poured into glasses.

'I see you found everything.' So, he'd been through her kitchen cupboards as well.

'You don't have any dishes that match,' he said and laughed. 'You're a strange woman, Jess Koster. Interesting, but strange.'

'I could say the same about you.'

He smiled, cryptically. 'I'm not really that interesting.'

It was her turn to laugh. Jess felt herself relax instantly with the sound. If he was some psychotic sociopath who was going to kill her, he'd obviously decided to do it after breakfast, so she might as well enjoy the meal he'd prepared. Trust her instincts. 'What's on the menu?' she asked, her stomach rumbling at the thought of a half-decent breakfast.

'The best Western omelet in the De Paul area,' he answered, sliding one of two perfectly shaped omelets onto her plate, the other onto his, garnishing each with a sprig of parsley.

'You even got parsley. I'm really impressed.'

'That was the general idea. Don't let it get cold,' he said, pouring her a cup of coffee. 'Cream? Sugar?'

'Black.'

'Eat up.'

'It looks wonderful. I can't believe you did all this.'

'It was the least I could do after the way I behaved last night.'

'You didn't do anything last night.'

'Precisely. I finally get to spend the night with a beautiful woman, and what do I do? I drink myself into a stupor and pass out on her sofa.'

Jess ran a self-conscious hand through her tangled hair.

'No, don't do that,' he said, bringing her hand back to the table with his own. 'You look lovely.'

Jess slid her hand away from his, poked at her omelet with her fork.

'So, what's the verdict?' He waited while she took her first mouthful of food.

'Fabulous,' Jess said, enthusiastically. 'Definitely the best omelet in the DePaul area.'

They ate for several minutes in silence.

'I took the cover off the bird cage,' Adam said, 'and I brought in your morning paper. It's on the sofa.'

Jess looked from the bird cage to the sofa. 'Thanks.' She paused. 'Anything else you did that I should know about?'

He leaned across the dark mahogany table and kissed her. 'Not yet.'

Jess didn't move as Adam leaned forward to kiss her again. Her lips were tingling; her heart was pounding. She felt like a teenager. She felt like a blushing bride. She felt like an idiot.

Was she really such a pushover? Were a glass of orange juice, a cup of coffee, and a Western omelet all that was necessary to get into her heart and into her bed?

And now he was kissing her lips, her cheeks, her neck, back to her lips. His arms wrapped around her, pulled her against him. How long had it been, she wondered, since a man had kissed her in this way? Since *she* had kissed a man in this way?

'I shouldn't be doing this,' she said, as his kisses became deeper, as her kisses responded in kind. 'I have so much work to do to be ready for tomorrow.'

'You'll do it,' he assured her, burying his lips in her hair.

'Most murder trials only last a week to ten days,' she

whispered, trying to talk herself out of her ardor, 'but the defendant got sick . . .'

Adam covered her mouth with his own, his hands reaching for her breasts.

She tried to protest, but a grunt of pleasure was the only sound that emerged.

'Murders are actually among the easiest cases to try,' she continued stubbornly, wondering which was stranger – what she was doing or what she was saying. 'Except when they involve the death penalty, as this one does . . .'

Again he silenced her with his mouth. This time she surrendered to the almost unbearably pleasant sensation of his lips on hers, his hands on her body.

Suddenly, a buzzer sounded. It beeped once, then again.

'What's that!' Adam asked between kisses.

'The intercom,' Jess answered, wondering who it could be. 'Someone's downstairs.'

'They'll go away.'

The buzzer sounded again, three times in rapid succession. Who was it? Jess wondered. Now, of all times. Ten o'clock on a Sunday morning!

'My God!' Jess said, pulling out of Adam's embrace. 'It's my ex-husband! I forgot all about him. He said he'd drop by this morning.'

'He's as good as his word,' Adam said as the buzzer sounded again.

Jess went quickly to the intercom by the door and spoke into it.

'Don?'

'Your bagels have arrived.' His voice filled the apartment.

'This should be interesting,' Adam said, grabbing his coffee mug and flopping down on the living room sofa, obviously enjoying the situation.

'Oh God,' Jess whispered, hearing Don's footsteps on the stairs and opening the door before he could knock. 'Hi, Don.'

He was wearing a heavy parka over dark green corduroy

pants, his arms filled by two large bags of bagels.

'It's freezing out there,' he remarked. 'What kept you? Don't tell me you were still asleep!' He took two steps inside the apartment, then froze at the sight of Adam on the sofa. 'Sorry,' he said immediately, confusion evident in his face as he extended his hand toward Adam. 'I'm Don Shaw, an old friend.'

'Adam Stohn,' Adam replied, shaking Don's hand. 'A new one.'

There was silence. No one seemed to breathe.

'There's coffee,' Jess offered.

Don looked toward the dining room table. 'Looks like you've already eaten.'

'Jess forgot to tell me you were dropping by,' Adam explained, his voice a smile. 'I'd be happy to whip up another omelet.'

'Thank you, but maybe some other time.'

'Let me hang up your coat.' Jess held out her arms.

Don dropped the bags of bagels into them. 'No. I think I'll get going. I just wanted to get these to you.' He headed for the door. 'You should probably put them in the freezer.'

The phone rang.

'Busy place,' Adam said.

'Don, wait a minute. Please,' Jess urged. Don waited by the door while Jess went to the kitchen to answer the phone. When she came back a minute later, she was pale and shaking, her cheeks streaked with tears. Both men moved instantly toward her. 'That was the Medical Examiner's office,' she said quietly. 'They found Connie DeVuono.'

'What? Where? When?' Don asked, the words emerging like pellets from a gun.

'In Skokie Lagoons. An ice fisherman stumbled across her body late yesterday afternoon and called the police. They brought it to Harrison Street by ambulance.'

'They're sure it's her?'

'Dental records don't lie.' A cry caught in Jess's throat. 'She'd been strangled with a piece of wire rope, so tight she was almost decapitated. Apparently, the body was quite well preserved because of the cold.'

'I'm so sorry, Jess,' Don told her, drawing her into his arms.

Jess cried softly against his shoulder. 'I have to go see Connie's mother. I have to tell her.'

'The police can do that.'

'No,' Jess said quickly, seeing Adam tiptoe toward the door, his jacket over his arm. 'I have to do it. Jesus, Don, what can I say to her? What can I say to her little boy?'

'You'll think of just the right words, Jess.'

Jess said nothing as Adam opened the door and threw her a delicate kiss good-bye. The door closed softly after him.

'Where does Connie's mother live?' Don asked. If he was aware of Adam's departure, he said nothing.

'Miller Street. I have the exact address written down somewhere.' Jess wiped the tears away from her eyes.

'Go take a shower and get dressed. I'll drive you over.'

'No, Don, you don't have to do that.'

'Jess, you don't have a car, and there's no way I'm letting you go through this alone. Now, please, don't argue with me on this one.'

Jess reached over and stroked her ex-husband's cheek. 'Thank you,' she said.

Chapter Seventeen

'Are you all right?' he was asking.

'No.'

Jess was crying. She'd started the minute she heard the Medical Examiner's voice, and hadn't stopped. Couldn't. Even in the shower, her tears hadn't abated. She'd cried as she slipped into her jeans and red sweater, cried as she slid into the front seat of Don's Mercedes, cried as they pulled up in front of Mrs Gambala's modest duplex in Little Italy.

'You have to stop crying,' Don had urged gently. 'Otherwise she'll know before you even open your mouth.'

'She'll know anyway,' Jess had told him. And she had been right.

The front door had opened before Jess reached the top step of the elaborate little red brick porch. Mrs Gambala stood in the doorway, a small woman dressed from head to toe in black, her grandson peeking out warily from behind her ample hips. 'They found her,' Mrs Gambala said, accepting the truth even as she shook her head from side to side in denial.

'Yes,' Jess had admitted, her voice catching, unable to continue.

Steffan had taken one look at Jess, one look at his grandmother, then raced up the narrow staircase to his room, his door slamming in painful protest.

They'd gone inside where Jess had explained the details to Mrs Gambala, promising to tell her everything as soon as the coroner's report came in, assuring her that the man responsible would be quickly apprehended and brought to trial. She stared at Don, as if daring him to contradict her.

'Are you going to issue a warrant for Rick Ferguson's arrest?' Don had asked as they were returning to the car.

There was nothing Jess wanted to do more, but she knew that until she learned the details of the way Connie DeVuono died, she was smarter to hold off. She had to know exactly what, if any, physical evidence there was to link Rick Ferguson to Connie's death. 'Not yet. Are you going to call him?'

'What reason would I have for calling him if you're not going to arrest him?' he'd asked in exaggerated innocence. 'Besides, it's Sunday. I don't work on Sundays.'

'Thank you,' Jess told him, then started crying again.

'Are you all right?' he was asking now.

'No,' she said, folding her top lip under the bottom in an effort to stop them from quivering.

Don reached across the front seat and took her hands in his. 'What are you thinking about?'

'I'm thinking about how Mrs Gambala keeps all her furniture covered in plastic wrap,' Jess told him, releasing a deep breath of air.

Don laughed, clearly surprised. 'You don't see much of that any more,' he agreed.

'Connie told me about it once. She said that Steffan didn't like waiting for her at his grandmother's house because she kept all the furniture in plastic and there wasn't anywhere comfortable to sit down.' A sob caught in Jess's throat. 'And now, that's where he'll grow up. In a house full of plastic covers.'

'In a house full of love, Jess,' Don reminded her. 'His grandmother loves him. She'll take good care of him.'

'Connie said her mother was too old to look after him, that her English was poor.'

'So, he'll teach her English, and she'll teach him Italian. Jess,' Don said, giving her hands an extra squeeze, 'you can't worry about everything. You can't absorb everyone else's pain. You have to pick and choose, or you'll make yourself nuts.'

'I always thought it would be better to know,' Jess confided, after a long pause. 'I always thought it would be better, no matter how awful, to know the truth, for there to be a resolution. Now, I'm not so sure. At least before today, there was hope. Even if it was false hope, maybe that's better than no hope at all.'

'You're talking about your mother,' Don said quietly.

'All these years I thought that if only I'd known one way or the other what happened to her, then I could get on with my life.'

'You *have* gotten on with your life.'

'No, I haven't. Not really.' She looked out the car window, noticed for the first time that they were travelling east on I-94.

'Jess, what are you talking about? Look at all you've accomplished.'

'I know what I've accomplished. That's not what I mean,' she told him.

'Tell me what you mean,' he directed gently.

'I mean that eight years ago, I got stuck. And no matter what I've done, no matter what I've accomplished, emotionally, I'm still stuck back on the day my mother disappeared.'

'And you think that if you'd known what happened to her, that if someone much like yourself had approached you then and given you the same sort of news you delivered to Connie's son today, you would have been better off?'

'I don't know. But at least I would have been able to deal with it once and for all. I would have been able to grieve. I would have been able to go on.'

'Then you've answered your own question,' he told her.

'I guess I have.' Jess wiped the tears away from her eyes, rubbed at her nose with the backs of her fingers, stared out the side window of the car. 'Where are we going?'

'Union Pier.'

'Union Pier?' Jess immediately conjured up the image of the small lakeshore community approximately seventy miles outside Chicago where Don maintained a weekend retreat. 'Don, I can't. I have to get ready for court tomorrow.'

'You haven't seen the place in a long time,' he reminded her. 'I've made some changes, incorporated some of the ideas you once suggested. Come on, I promise to have you back by five o'clock. You know you aren't going to be able to think clearly before then anyway.'

'I don't know.'

'Give yourself a break, Jess. We both know you're as prepared for tomorrow as anyone could possibly be.'

They continued in silence, Jess following the scenery, watching as the few drops of rain that had started falling turned gradually to snow. Buildings gave way to open fields. They took the Union Pier exit, continued east toward Lake Michigan. *Elsinor Dude Ranch*, a large wooden sign announced over an arched wrought-iron gate. *Horse trails and Lessons. Inquire inside. Driving range*, another sign proclaimed half a mile down the road, oblivious to the fact it was the wrong season for golf. Jess remembered her father teasing her mother about teaching her to play golf after he retired.

Union Pier Gun Club, another large wood sign stated, as they continued east, the snow becoming heavier, more insistent. Jess sat up straight in her seat, all her senses on instant alert.

'What's the matter?' Don asked.

'Since when did they have a gun club out here?' Jess asked.

'Since for ever,' Don reminded her. 'Why? You feel like working off some frustration? Although I'm pretty sure you have to be a member,' he continued when she failed to respond.

'Do they have an archery range?'

'What?'

'An archery range,' Jess repeated, not exactly sure where her thoughts were headed.

'I wouldn't think so. Why the sudden interest in archery?' He stopped abruptly. 'The crossbow killer?' he asked.

'Terry Wales swore on the stand that he hadn't fired a bow and arrow since he was a kid in camp. What if I can prove he did?'

'Then I'd say you have a clear shot at murder one.'

'Can I use your phone?'

'The whole point of this trip was for you to relax.'

'This *is* how I relax. Please.'

Don lifted the car phone off its receiver, handed it to Jess. She quickly dialed Neil Strayhorn at home.

'Neil, I want you to find out about all the archery clubs within a two-hour drive of Chicago,' she said without unnecessary preliminaries.

'Jess?' Neil's voice filled the car over the speaker phone.

'I want to know if Terry Wales is a member of any of them, if he's even been near an archery range in the last thirty years. Detective Mansfield can probably help. There can't be that many archery clubs around. Tell him we need the information by tomorrow morning. I'll call you later.' She hung up before he could object or ask questions.

'You're a hard taskmaster,' Don told her, turning left onto Smith Road.

'I had a good teacher,' Jess reminded him, bracing herself as the car bounced along the unpaved, bumpy, one-lane road.

Summer cottages lined the secluded route. Despite the fact that the homes along the Bluff had roughly quadrupled their value in the last decade, the residents obviously considered repairing the potholes in the road a low priority. Jess held tightly to the door handle as the car bounced toward Don's pinewood cottage, finding it increasingly difficult to see out the front window.

'It looks so forbidding,' Jess said, as snow swirled everywhere around them.

'I'll light a fire, open a bottle of wine, it won't look so bad.'

'It's really starting to snow.'

'I'll race you to the front door,' Don said, and Jess was off and running.

'I'd forgotten how beautiful it is here.' Jess stood by the large glass window that made up the back wall of the cottage and stared through the snow at the small garden she had planted herself many years ago. The Bluff stood just beyond, a series of steps carved right into its steep side, leading down to the lake. Large spruce trees lined the borders of Don's property, separating him from his neighbors on either side, guarding his privacy. Behind her, a fire roared in the large brick fireplace. Don sat on the white shag rug between the fireplace and one of two old-style colonial chesterfields, the remains of the picnic lunch he'd prepared spread out before him.

'We miss you,' Don said quietly. 'The garden and I. Do you remember when you planted those shrubs?'

'Of course I do. It was just after we got married. We argued about what kind of bushes would grow the fastest, be the prettiest.'

'We didn't argue.'

'All right, we *discussed.*'

'And then we compromised.'

'We did it your way,' Jess said, and laughed. 'This was a nice idea, coming here. Thank you for thinking of it.' She returned to the white shag rug, lowered herself to the floor, leaned back against the brown- and ochre-striped sofa.

'We had a lot of nice times here,' he said, his voice steeped in nostalgia.

'Yes, we did,' she said. 'I think I liked May the best, when everything was just starting to bud, and I knew I had the whole summer to look forward to. By the time June came around, I was already starting to worry that summer would be over soon and winter would be coming.'

'And I always liked winter best because I knew that no matter how cold it got outside, I could come up here and build a fire and make a picnic lunch, and be warm and happy. What more could anyone ask for than to be warm and happy?'

'Sounds so simple.'

'It doesn't have to be difficult.'

'Do you bring Trish here often?' she asked.

'Not often.'

'Why not?'

'I'm not sure.'

'Are you in love with her?' Jess asked.

'I'm not sure,' Don said again. 'What about you?'

'I'm definitely not in love with her.'

Don smiled. 'You know what I mean. You gave me quite a surprise this morning.'

'It wasn't the way it looked,' Jess said quickly.

'How did it look?'

'I guess like we'd spent the night together.'

'You didn't?'

'Well, in a manner of speaking, I guess we did. Adam had a little too much to drink and passed out on my couch.'

'Charming.'

'He's really a very nice man.'

'I'm sure he is, or you wouldn't be interested in him.'

'I'm not sure I am. Interested in him.' Jess wondered if she was protesting too much.

'How long have you known him?'

'Not long. Maybe a month,' she said. Maybe less, she thought.

'But he obviously feels comfortable enough to pass out on your couch. And you obviously feel comfortable enough to let him.'

'What choice did I have?'

'I couldn't answer that.'

'Neither can I,' Jess admitted.

'What does he do?'

Jess could hear the strain in Don's voice from trying to sound casual, and was touched by it. 'He's a salesman.'

'A salesman?' He didn't bother to hide his surprise. 'What does he sell?'

'Shoes.' Jess cleared her throat. 'Don't be a snob, Don,' she said quickly. 'There's nothing wrong with selling shoes. My father started out as a salesman, you know.'

'Adam Stohn seems a little old to be starting out,' Don said.

'He likes what he does.'

'So much that he has to drink himself into a drunken stupor and pass out?'

'I don't know that one thing has anything to do with the other.'

'Why do *you* think it happened?'

'Objection. Calls for a conclusion.'

'Objection overruled. Witness will answer the question.'

'I'm not in love,' Jess stated.

'The witness may step down,' Don said, and Jess bowed her head in gratitude.

'So, what's it like these days in the prestigious law firm of Rogers, Donaldson, Baker and Shaw?' she asked, picturing Adam Stohn as he waved good-bye to her from the doorway of her apartment that morning.

'It's all right.'

'You don't sound very enthusiastic.'

'The place has changed.'

'Really? How?'

'Well, when I first came on board, there were only ten of us,' he explained. 'Now, there are over two hundred. That's quite a change right there.'

'But you always wanted the firm to grow, to be the biggest and the best,' she reminded him.

'The best, yes. Not necessarily the biggest.'

'So bigger isn't necessarily better?'

'That's right. Haven't Masters and Johnson taught you anything?'

She laughed. 'Did you know they got divorced?'

'Masters and Johnson?'

'Shocking, isn't it?' Jess, wondering how they got on to the subject of sex, stared out the window at the steady downfall of heavy snow.

'So, aside from the size, what else about your firm aren't you happy with?'

'Everything's far more dollar orientated than it used to be, which I guess is only natural these days,' he began. 'Nobody really cares about anything except getting their dockets out. I think the personality of the firm has changed over the years. Not for the better.'

Jess smiled. What he was really saying was that the firm no longer reflected his own strong personality, the way it had in the beginning, when he was one of ten, not two hundred.

'So, how would you change things?'

Don lowered his chin against his chest, the way he did whenever he was giving a matter serious thought. 'I don't think they *can* be changed. The firm's too big. It's a law unto itself. The only way to change it would be to leave it.'

'Are you prepared to do that?'

'I've been thinking about it.'

'What would you do?'

'Start up again,' he said, his voice warming to the idea. 'Take a few of the top guns with me, recruit a few others. Form a small firm in a family neighborhood, you know the kind, with interior brick walls and plants hanging from stucco ceilings. A couple of secretaries, a couple of bathrooms, one small kitchen at the back. You interested?'

'What?'

'I may have just talked myself into a very interesting idea. What about it, Jess? How does Shaw and Koster sound to you?'

Jess laughed, but only because she wasn't sure what else to do.

'Think about it.' Don stood up and walked to the window. 'It doesn't look like we're going to be able to get out of here this afternoon.'

'What?' Jess was instantly on her feet behind him.

'The snow's not letting up at all. If anything, it looks like it's getting worse. The wind's picking up. I'd hate to get caught in a white-out on the highway.'

'But I have to get back.'

'I'll get you back. Just not this afternoon. We may have to wait until after dinner.' He walked toward the large open pine kitchen to his left and opened the freezer. 'I'll defrost a couple of steaks, open up another bottle of wine, and call the highway patrol, find out how bad weather conditions are on the roads. Jess, stop worrying,' he told her. 'Even if worst comes to worst and we can't get out of here tonight, I'll have you back in time for court in the morning, I promise. Even if I have to carry you back on snowshoes. Okay? Does that set your mind at rest?'

'Not really,' she told him.

'That's my girl,' he said.

Jess spent the rest of the afternoon on the phone.

The Medical Examiner had nothing new to report. The autopsy on Connie DeVuono hadn't been completed; it would be a few days until they could interpret all their findings.

Neil Strayhorn had contacted Barbara Cohen and Detective Mansfield. They had managed to find the names of two archery clubs in the Chicago area and another four within a hundred-mile radius of the city. The police were already on their way to question the management. Luckily, all the clubs were open on Sundays, although two had closed early because of the storm, and couldn't be reached. Messages had been left on their answering tapes to call the police first thing in the morning. Neil would call her as soon as they had any news.

Jess went over in her mind the list of questions she had prepared for Terry Wales. Don was right, she acknowledged, watching him as he busied himself in the kitchen preparing dinner. She was as ready as she was ever going to be. She didn't need her notes. She'd already memorized her questions and the likely responses they'd elicit. The only thing that she had to do now was show up in court on time.

'The radio just said they expect the snow to stop by midnight,' Don told her, depositing a glass of red wine in her hand before she could protest the news. 'I say we stay here overnight, get a good night's sleep, and head back around six. That way we're in the city by seven-thirty at the latest, and you still have plenty of time to get ready for court.'

'Don, I can't.'

'Jess, I don't think we have any choice.'

'But what if the snow doesn't stop by midnight? What if we can't leave here in the morning?'

'Then Neil will ask for a continuance,' Don said simply. 'Jess, the weather isn't your fault.'

'And if we leave now?'

'Then we'll probably spend the night in a snowbank. But if that's what you want, I'm willing to gamble.'

Jess stared out the back window at a blizzard in full rage. She had to acknowledge the insanity of trying to go anywhere in weather like this. 'How soon till dinner?' she asked.

'That was Detective Mansfield,' Jess said, pushing the phone off the white shag rug, absently watching the flames as they danced, like cobras ready to strike, in the fireplace. 'None of the four archery clubs they were able to contact has any record of Terry Wales being a member.'

'Did they show his picture around?'

Jess nodded. 'No one knew him.'

'That still leaves a couple of places, doesn't it?'

'Two. But we can't reach them till morning.'

'Then there's nothing to do but get a good night's sleep tonight.' Don, sitting beside Jess on the floor, reached over to twist the long wire cord of the telephone around his fingers, returning the phone to the small pine table between the two couches.

Jess followed the motion of his hands, mesmerized by the slow, circular movement. When she spoke, her voice was equally slow, as if emerging from a deep trance. 'Did I tell you that the coroner said the wire was twisted around Connie's neck so tightly she was almost decapitated?'

'Try not to think about that now, Jess,' Don said, wrapping his arms around her. 'Come on, you've had a good dinner and some excellent wine, and now isn't the time to—'

'It's my fault,' she told him, feeling the wire as it sliced its way into Connie's throat.

'Your fault? Jess, what are you talking about?'

'If I hadn't convinced Connie that she had to testify, she'd still be alive.'

'Jess, that's ridiculous. You can't know that. You can't blame yourself.'

'It must have been so awful,' Jess continued, a shudder racing through her body, pushing her tighter into Don's arms, 'feeling that wire cutting into her neck, knowing she was going to die.'

'Jesus, Jess.'

Jess's eyes overflowed with tears, spilled down across her cheeks. Don quickly moved to brush them aside, first with his fingers, then his lips.

'It's all right, baby,' he was saying. 'Everything will be okay. You'll see. Everything will be all right.'

His lips felt gentle, soothing against her skin as he traced the line of her tears from her cheeks to the sides of her mouth, then followed the tears as they ran between her lips, his mouth softly covering her own.

Jess closed her eyes, picturing Adam as he'd reached across her dining room table to kiss her, felt herself respond, knowing she was responding to the wrong man, but unable to stop herself.

It had been so long, she thought, her arms moving to encircle Adam's waist even as Don's hands disappeared under her red sweater, tugged at the zipper of her jeans. It was Adam's caresses she experienced as Don's weight fell across her, Adam whose fingers and mouth knowingly brought her to a gentle climax even before he penetrated her.

'I love you, Jess,' she heard Adam say, but when she opened her eyes, it was Don she saw.

Chapter Eighteen

The dream began as it always did, in the waiting room of the doctor's office, the doctor handing her a phone, telling her her mother was on the line.

'I'm starring in a movie,' her mother told her. 'I want you to come and see me. I'll leave tickets at the box office.'

'I'll be there,' Jess assured her, arriving at the theater within seconds, asking for her tickets from the gum-chewing ticket taker.

'No one left any tickets for you,' the girl told her. 'And we're all sold out.'

'Are you looking for a ticket?' Mrs Gambala asked. 'I can't go. My daughter swallowed a turtle and she died, so I have an extra ticket.'

The theater was dark, the movie about to start. Jess located an empty seat on an aisle, sat down, waited. 'I found a lump in my breast,' her mother was saying as Jess looked toward the screen. But a huge pillar totally obstructed her view. No matter how frantically she tried, how stubbornly she persisted, Jess couldn't see round it.

'It's my fault,' she whispered to Judge Harris, who was sitting beside her. 'If I'd gone to the doctor with her that afternoon like I promised, she wouldn't have disappeared.'

In the next instant she was on the street, about to climb the front steps of her parents' house, when a white car pulled up at the corner and a man got out and started walking toward her, his face in shadows, his arms outstretched. He was right behind her as she raced up the stairs and tore open the door, her fingers frantically searching for the lock. But the lock was broken. She felt the tug at the screen door, felt her fingers losing their grip, knew that Death was only inches away.

Jess sat up with a start, her entire body bathed in sweat, her breath coming in painful, uneven gasps.

It took her a moment to assess where she was. 'Oh, God,' she moaned, seeing Don sleeping peacefully beside her on the white shag rug, the remains of the once grand fire flickering meekly behind the black wire mesh screen. 'Oh, God,' she whispered again, throwing off the blanket he had obviously covered them with. She gathered her clothes around her, wondering how she could have allowed what had happened between her and Don.

'I love you,' she could still hear him say.

I love you too, she wanted to tell him now, but she couldn't, because she didn't, not in the same way he loved her. She'd used him, used his feelings for her, his deep commitment to her, used the love he felt for her, the love he'd always felt for her. For what? So that she could feel better for a few minutes? Feel less alone? Less frightened? So that she could hurt him all over again? Disappoint him anew? The way she always hurt and disappointed everyone who'd ever loved her.

Her hands shaking, she slipped into her panties and bra, shivering now, straining to breathe, as if a giant boa constrictor had wrapped itself round her and was slowly tightening its coils. She staggered to her feet, pulling her sweater over her head, trying desperately to get warm.

Falling back onto the chesterfield behind her, she brought her knees to her chest and hugged them, an uncomfortable numbness seeping through her body. 'No,' she cried softly, not wanting to wake Don, selfishly wishing that he would awake on his own and surround her with his arms, make her demons go away.

Take deep breaths, she told herself, as the invisible snake continued its deadly embrace, extending its wide coils from her toes to her neck, cutting off all hope of air. She stared into the snake's cold eyes, saw its jaws open in eager anticipation, felt a final squeeze at her ribcage.

'No,' she gasped, fighting to keep from throwing up, struggling with her imaginary tormentor. 'No!'

And suddenly she saw Adam's face, and heard his voice. 'Don't fight it,' he was telling her. 'The next time you have one of these attacks, just go with it. Let yourself go.'

What did he mean?

'What's the worst thing that can happen?' he'd asked.

'I'll throw up,' she'd answered.

'So, you'll throw up.'

I'm afraid, she thought now.

'I think what you're afraid of is death.'

Help me. Please help me.

'Go with the flow,' he was saying. Don't fight it. Just go with it.'

The same advice, Jess realized, as her self-defense instructor had given her.

When faced with an attacker, don't fight him, go with him.

Strike when you get there.

'Go with it,' she repeated over and over. 'Go with it. Don't fight it. Go with it.'

What's the worst that can happen?

So you'll throw up.

So you'll die.

She almost laughed.

Jess stopped fighting, letting the panic fill her body. She closed her eyes against the dizziness that enveloped her, threatened to send her sprawling to the floor. She felt light-headed and sick to her stomach, sure that at any second she would lose consciousness.

But she didn't lose consciousness.

She didn't die.

She wasn't even going to throw up, she realized with growing amazement, feeling a loosening at her chest, the giant snake slowly losing interest and slithering away. A few minutes later, the numbness vanished and her breathing returned to normal. She was all right. She hadn't died. Nothing had happened to her at all.

She'd gone with her panic, flowed with her anxiety, and

nothing of any consequence had happened to her. She hadn't thrown up all over herself. She wasn't paralyzed. She wasn't dead.

She'd won.

Jess sat for several minutes on the striped couch without moving, savoring her victory. 'It's over,' she whispered, feeling suddenly confident and happy, wanting to wake Don, tell him the news.

Except she knew it wasn't Don she wanted to tell.

Jess pushed herself to her feet and rummaged gently under the blanket for her socks. She found them, put them on, then quickly slid into her jeans. She walked to the window and stared out through the darkness at the Bluff beyond.

'Jess?' Don's voice was full of sleep.

'It's stopped snowing,' she told him.

'You're dressed.' He propped himself up on one elbow, and reached across the rug for his watch.

'I was cold.'

'I would have warmed you.'

'I know,' she told him, an unmistakable note of melancholy creeping into her voice. 'Don . . .'

'You don't have to say anything, Jess.' He slipped the watch over his wrist, snapped it shut, massaged the back of his neck. 'I know you don't have the same feelings for me that I have for you.' He tried to smile, almost succeeded. 'If you want, we'll just pretend that last night never happened.'

'The last thing I ever wanted to do was hurt you again.'

'You haven't. Honestly, Jess. I'm a big boy. I can deal with last night if you can.' He paused, checked the time. 'It's only four o'clock. Why don't you try to sleep for a few more hours?'

'I wouldn't be able to sleep.'

He nodded. 'Do you want me to make you a cup of coffee?'

'How about I make you one back at my apartment?'

'Are you saying you want to leave now?'

'Would you mind very much?'

'Would it matter?'

Jess knelt on the rug beside her ex-husband, and gently stroked his cheek, feeling the early morning stubble. 'I *do* love you,' she said.

'I know that,' he told her, placing his hand over one of hers. 'I'm just waiting for *you* to figure it out.'

It was almost seven o'clock in the morning before they arrived back in the city. The drive home was slow and treacherous. A couple of times, they'd slid on a hidden patch of ice and almost veered into a ditch. But Don hadn't panicked. He'd merely gripped the wheel tighter and continued resolutely on, although it often felt to Jess as if she could have walked back to Chicago faster.

She was on the phone the instant she arrived back in her apartment.

'Anything?' she asked Neil instead of hello.

'Jess, it's seven o'clock in the morning,' he reminded her. 'The clubs don't even open till ten.'

Jess replaced the receiver, watched Don as he tidied up the remains of the breakfast Adam had prepared for her yesterday. Was it really only yesterday? Jess wondered, thinking it felt like so long ago. 'You don't have to do that,' Jess said, taking the dish Don was washing out of his hand and laying it on the kitchen counter.

'Yes, I do. There isn't a clean dish in the place.' He lifted it off the counter and ran it under the tap.

'There's coffee,' Jess said, shaking the coffee pot. 'I can just pop a couple of mugs in the microwave.'

Don took the coffee pot out of Jess's hands and poured its muddy brown contents down the sink. 'You and your microwave,' he said. 'Now get out of here. *I'll* make the coffee; *you* take a shower.'

Jess walked into the living room. 'Hello, Fred,' she said, bringing her nose up against the narrow bars of his cage. 'How are you doing, fella? I'm sorry I didn't come home last night to cover you up. Did you miss me?'

The bird hopped from perch to perch, oblivious to her concern.

'Why don't you get a dog or a cat?' Don called from the kitchen.

'That thing doesn't care whether you're here or not.'

'I like Fred. He's low-maintenance,' she said, thinking of the black vinyl boots she had purchased from Adam. Definitely a worthwhile investment, she thought now, seeing them by the front door, the snow melting off their toes onto the hardwood floor. No salt rings. No water marks. Satisfaction guaranteed or your money back.

She thought about Adam, wondered what he was doing now, where he'd gone after he left her apartment. What he'd made of the morning's confusing events. What he'd say if he knew about last night.

Jess shook her head as she headed down the hall toward her bedroom, trying to shake loose such disconcerting thoughts. She'd started the day by almost making love to one man, and ended it by making love to another. One was little more than a stranger, a man she knew virtually nothing about; the other was her ex-husband, about whom she knew virtually everything. One was here now, was always here when she needed him; the other dropped by whenever he felt the urge.

Was that what she found so appealing about Adam Stohn? she wondered. The fact that she was never sure from one moment to the next when, or even if, she might see him again?

The room was as she'd left it, the bed unmade. Jess hated unmade beds, the way she hated anything left unfinished. She quickly set about making it, fluffing the pillows and tucking in the sheets. Then she went into the bathroom and ran the shower, pulling off her sweater and jeans, tucking them neatly in the closet, selecting her grey suit and pink blouse for today's appearance in court, laying them neatly across the white wicker chair.

She pulled a pair of skin-colored pantihose from the top drawer of her dresser, along with a fresh pink lace bra and panties, laying them carefully on top of her suit, about to discard the underwear she had on when she noticed a rip in the crotch of the pink lace panties. 'Great. How did that happen?' she asked, examining the uneven tear that split the crotch of her panties from seam to seam.

She tossed them into the waste paper basket, retrieved another pair from the top drawer, casually looking them over, her eyes quickly fixating on the jagged tear at the crotch. 'My God, what's going on here?' With growing panic, Jess examined all her underwear, discovering all her panties had been slashed in exactly the same way. 'My God! Oh, my God!'

'Jess?' Don called from the other room. 'What are you muttering about?'

'Don!' she cried, unable to say anything else. 'Don! Don!'

He was instantly at her side. 'What is it? What's the matter?'

Wordlessly, she handed him her torn underwear.

'I don't understand.'

'They're ripped! They're all ripped!' She scrunched the delicate fabric of the panties in her hand between trembling fingers.

He looked as confused as Jess felt. 'Your panties are ripped . . . ?'

'*All* my panties are ripped,' she said, finally finding her voice. 'Every last one of them. Look. It's like they've been slashed with a knife.'

'Jess, that's crazy. They must have gotten torn in the washing machine.'

'I wash them by hand,' Jess snapped, losing patience. 'Rick Ferguson's been here, Don. Rick Ferguson did this. He's been here. He's been in my things.'

It was Don's turn to lose patience. 'Jess, I can understand your being upset, but don't you think you're flying a little fast and loose with the assumptions here?'

'Who else could it be, Don? Who else *would* it be? It has to be Rick Ferguson. Who else could get in here as easily as if he had a key?' She broke off abruptly.

'What?' Don asked.

Adam had borrowed her key, she thought. Borrowed it when he went out to buy groceries while she'd been asleep. Had he had another key made? Had he used it to get back into her apartment when she was away?

'It had to be Rick Ferguson,' Jess continued, immediately pushing aside such unpleasant thoughts. 'He broke into Connie's apartment without any problem. Now, he's broken into mine.'

'We don't know who broke into Connie's apartment,' Don reminded her.

'How can you keep defending him?' Jess demanded.

'I'm not defending him. I'm just trying to get you to be reasonable.'

'He used to work in a locksmith's shop!'

'A summer job. When he was a teenager, for God's sake.'

'It explains how he's able to get into apartments without any sign of forced entry.'

'It explains nothing. Jess,' Don persisted. 'Anyone could get into this apartment without much trouble.'

'What are you talking about?'

He led her back toward the front door. 'Look at this lock. It's useless. I could pick it open with my credit card. Why don't you have a dead bolt, for God's sake? Or a chain?'

Hadn't Adam asked her almost the same thing? Why don't you get a peephole? Or a chain? he'd asked as she stood before him, gun in hand.

Her gun! Jess thought, almost knocking Don over as she raced back toward her bedroom. Had whoever broke into her apartment and slashed her underwear also stolen her gun?

'Jess, for God's sake, what are you doing now?' Don called after her.

The goddamn gun, she thought, pulling at the bedcovers she had recently tucked in. Had he stolen her gun?

The gun was exactly where she'd left it. She pulled it out from underneath the mattress with a deep sigh of relief.

'Jesus Christ, Jess! Is that loaded?'

She nodded.

'You're sleeping with a loaded gun under your mattress? Are you trying to kill yourself? What if you moved funny and the damn thing went off? Are you nuts?'

'Please stop yelling at me, Don. It's not helping.'

'What the hell are you doing sleeping with a loaded gun under your mattress?'

'I usually keep it in the drawer.' She indicated the night table with a nod of her head.

'Why?'

'Why? You're the one who gave me the damn thing in the first place. You're the one who insisted I have it.'

'And you're the one who insisted she'd never use it. Would you put the damn thing away before you shoot somebody!'

Jess deposited the gun gently in the top drawer of her night table. 'I've been threatened,' she reminded him, closing the drawer. 'My car's been vandalized and destroyed. I've received strange letters in the mail.'

'Letters? What kind of letters?'

'Well, just one letter,' she qualified. 'Soaked in urine, full of pubic hair clippings.'

'Jesus, Jess. When was this? Did you tell the police?'

'Of course I told them. There's nothing they can do. There's no way of proving who sent the letter. Just like there'll be no way of proving who slashed my panties or broke into my apartment. Just like they couldn't prove who broke into Connie's apartment, or who killed and mutilated her son's pet turtle.'

'Jess, we don't know that there's any connection between the break-ins at Connie's place and yours. We don't even know that there was a break-in here,' he said.

'What does that mean?' Jess asked, anger swelling her throat, making it hard to speak.

'Who is this Adam Stohn anyway, Jess?'

'What?' Had he been able to reach inside her brain, read her most secret thoughts? Tell me no secrets, I'll tell you no lies, she thought.

'Adam Stohn,' Don repeated. 'The man who passed out on your sofa Saturday night. The man who was making you breakfast Sunday morning. The man who could easily have gone through your things while you were sleeping, maybe had a little fun with one of your kitchen knives.'

'That's ridiculous,' Jess protested, trying not to remember he'd also gone into her purse, borrowed her key.

'He's the wild card here, Jess. Just who is this man?'

'I already told you. He's a guy I met, a salesman.'

'A shoe salesman, yes, I know. Who introduced you?'

'No one,' Jess admitted. 'I met him at the shoe store.'

'You met him at the store? Are you saying you picked him up when you went to buy shoes?'

'It's legal, Don. I didn't do anything wrong.'

'Not wrong, maybe. But certainly stupid.'

'I'm not a little kid, Don.'

'Then stop acting like one.'

'Thank you. This is just what I needed this morning. A lecture on dating by my ex-husband.'

'I'm not trying to lecture you, goddamn it. I'm trying to protect you!'

'That's not your job!' she reminded him. 'Your job is defending men like Rick Ferguson. Remember?'

Don slumped down on the bed. 'This is getting us nowhere.'

'Agreed.' Jess plopped down on the bed beside him, several pairs of panties scattering to the floor. 'It's so hot in here,' she said, realizing she was still in her underwear. 'Jesus Christ, the shower!'

She hurried into the bathroom, steam rushing to escape the small room as she fought her way through the rush of hot water to turn off the taps. She returned to the bedroom, sweat pouring off her face, her hair wet and dripping into her eyes, her shoulders slumped forward in defeat. 'How am I supposed to go to court looking like this?' she asked, near tears.

'It's not even seven-thirty,' Don told her gently, 'so you still have lots of time. Now, first things first. The first thing we're going to do is call the police.'

'Don, I don't have time to deal with the police now.'

'You can tell them what happened over the phone. If they think it's necessary, they can come over later and dust for prints.'

'That won't do any good.'

'No, I don't think it will. But you have to report the incident anyway, you know that. Get it on the record. Including your suspicions about Rick Ferguson.'

'Which you don't share.'

'Which I *do* share.'

'You do?'

'Of course I do. I'm not a complete idiot, even where you're concerned. But suspicions are one thing, assumptions are another.' He underlined his words with a nod of his head. 'The second thing I want you to do,' he continued, 'is take your shower and get dressed. Forget the underwear for the time being. I'll call my secretary and have her drop something off for you before you go to court.'

'You don't have to do that.'

'As soon as you're dressed, I want you to pack a suitcase. You're moving into my apartment until this whole thing gets straightened out.'

'Don, I can't move into your apartment.'

'Why not?'

'Because this is where I live. Because all my things are here. Because of Fred. Because . . . I just can't.'

'Bring your things. Bring Fred. Bring whatever, *whoever*, you want. Separate bedrooms,' he told her. 'I won't come anywhere near you, Jess, if that's the way you want it. I just want you safe.'

'I know you do. And I love you for it. But I just can't,' she said.

'Okay, then, at the very least, I want that lock replaced,' he told her, obviously recognizing there was nothing to be gained by continuing the argument. 'I want a deadbolt and a chain installed.'

'Fine.'

'I'll arrange for it this morning.'

'Don, you don't have to arrange everything. I can do it.'

'Really? When? When you're in court? How about while you're cross-examining Terry Wales?'

'Later. When I get home.'

'Not later. This morning. I'll have my secretary come over, stay with the locksmith.'

'Is this the same secretary who's bringing me my underwear?'

'Things are a little slow at the office.'

'Sure they are.'

'Lastly,' he continued, 'I want you to consider a bodyguard.'

'A what? For whom?'

'For Santa Claus. Who do you think, Jess? For you!'

'I don't need a bodyguard.'

'Someone just broke into your apartment and slashed your underwear, probably the same someone who destroyed your car and sent you a urine-soaked letter in the mail. And you don't think you need protection?'

'I can't be guarded twenty-four hours a day indefinitely. What kind of life is that?'

'Nobody said anything about indefinitely. A few weeks, then we'll see.'

'That's silly. Why can't we just hire a detective to keep tabs on Rick Ferguson instead?'

'Agreed,' he said quickly. 'I'll take care of it this morning.'

'What? Wait a minute, I'm having trouble keeping track here. How can you do that? Is it ethical? Hiring a detective to spy on your own client?'

'I almost hired one after your car was destroyed. I should have, dammit, then maybe this wouldn't have happened. Anyway, if he's innocent, he has nothing to worry about.'

'That's my line.'

'Jess, I love you. I'm not going to take a chance on anything happening to you.'

'But won't it be expensive, hiring a detective?' she asked, steering the conversation away from the personal.

'Consider it my Christmas present. Will you do that for me?' he asked, and Jess marvelled at how he could make it sound as if she'd be doing him the favor by accepting his generous offer.

'Thank you,' she said.

'I'll tell you one thing,' he told her solemnly. 'If it *is* Rick Ferguson who's been harassing you, then client or no client, I'll shoot the bastard myself.'

Chapter Nineteen

'Could you state your full name for the jury, please?'

'Terrence Matthew Wales.'

Jess rose from her seat behind the prosecutor's table and approached the witness stand, eyes fastened on the defendant. Terry Wales stared back steadily, even respectfully. His hands were folded in his lap, his posture bent slightly forward, as if he didn't want to miss a word she might say. The impression he created, in his dark grey suit that curiously complemented her own, was that of a man who had tried all his life to do the right thing, that he was as sorry and surprised as anyone for the way things had worked out.

'You live at twenty-four twenty-seven Kinzie Street in Chicago?'

'Yes.'

'And you've lived there for six years?'

'That's correct.'

'And before that you lived at sixteen Vernon Park Place?'

He nodded.

'I'm afraid the court stenographer requires a yes or no, Mr. Wales.'

'Yes,' he said quickly.

'Why did you move?' Jess asked.

'I beg your pardon?'

'Why did you move?' Jess repeated.

Terry Wales shrugged. 'Why does anybody move?'

Jess smiled, kept her voice light. 'I'm not interested in why anybody moves, Mr Wales. I'm interested in why *you* moved.'

'We needed a bigger house.'

'You needed more space? More bedrooms?'

Terry Wales coughed into the palm of his hand. 'When we moved to the house on Vernon Park Place, we only had one child. By the time we moved to Kinzie, we had two.'

'Yes, you already stated your wife was in a hurry to have children. Tell me, Mr Wales, how many bedrooms did the house on Vernon Park Place have?'

'Three.'

'And the house on Kinzie Street?'

'Three,' he said quietly.

'Sorry, did you say three?'

'Yes.'

'Oh, the same number of bedrooms. Then I guess it was the house in general that was bigger.'

'Yes.'

'It was three square feet bigger,' Jess told him matter-of-factly.

'What?'

'The house on Kinzie Street was three square feet bigger than the house on Vernon Park Place. Approximately this size,' she explained, pacing out a three-foot square in front of the jury.

'Objection, Your Honor,' Hal Bristol called from his seat at the defence table. 'Relevance?'

'I'm getting to that, Your Honor.'

'Get there fast,' Judge Harris instructed.

'Isn't it true, Mr Wales, that the reason you left your house on Vernon Park Place was because of repeated complaints about your conduct by your neighbors to the police?' Jess asked quickly, her adrenaline pumping.

'No, that's not true.'

'Isn't it true that the neighbors reported you to the police on several occasions because they feared for your wife's safety?'

'We had one neighbor who called the police every time I played the stereo too loud.'

'Which just happened to coincide with every time you beat your wife,' Jess stated, looking at the jury.

'Objection!' Hal Bristol was on his feet.

'Sustained.'

'The police were called to your house on Vernon Park Place the night of 3 August 1984,' Jess began, reading from her notes, though she knew the dates by heart, 'the night of 7 September 1984, and again the nights of 22 November 1984, and 4 January 1985. Is that correct?'

'I don't remember the exact dates.'

'It's all on file, Mr Wales. Do you dispute any of it?'

He shook his head, then answered, looking toward the court stenographer. 'No.'

'On each of those occasions when the police were called, your wife showed obvious signs of beatings. Once she even had to be hospitalized.'

'I've already testified that our fights often got out of hand, that I'm not proud of my part in them.'

'Out of hand?' Jess said. 'More like out of *fist*. Your fist.'

'Objection!'

'Sustained.'

Jess walked to the prosecutor's table, exchanged one police report for another. 'This report states that on the night of 4 January 1985, the night your wife was hospitalized, Nina Wales had bruises to over forty per cent of her body and was bleeding internally, that her nose and two ribs were broken, and that both eyes were blackened. You, on the other hand, had several scratch marks on your face, and one large bruise on your shin. That doesn't sound like a very fair fight, Mr Wales.'

'Objection, Your Honor. Is there a question here?'

'Isn't it true that your wife had recently given birth to your second child?'

'Yes.'

'A little girl?'

'Rebecca, yes.'

'How old was she on the night of 4 January 1985?'

Terry Wales hesitated.

'Surely you remember your daughter's birthday, Mr Wales,' Jess prodded.

'She was born on December 2nd.'

'December 2nd, 1984? Just four weeks before the fight that put your wife in the hospital?'

'That's right.'

'So, that would mean that all these other attacks—'

'Objection!'

'All these other *incidents,*' Jess corrected, '3 August 1984, 7 September 1984, 22 November 1984, they all occurred while your wife was pregnant. Is that correct?'

Terry Wales dropped his head toward his chest. 'Yes,' he whispered. 'But it isn't as one-sided as you make it out to be.'

'Oh, I know that, Mr Wales,' Jess told him. 'Who among us could forget that bruise on your shin?'

Hal Bristol was on his feet again, his eyes rolling toward the ceiling. 'Objection, Your Honor.'

'Withdrawn,' Jess said, retrieving yet another police report from Neil Strayhorn's outstretched hand, then returning to the witness stand. 'Jumping ahead a few years, if we could, to the night of 25 February 1988, you put your wife in the hospital again, didn't you?'

'My wife had gone out and left the kids alone. When she came back home, it was obvious to me she'd been drinking. Something inside me just snapped.'

'No, Mr Wales, it was something in your wife that got snapped,' Jess immediately corrected. 'Specifically her right wrist.'

'She'd left the kids alone. God knows what could have happened to them.'

'Are there any witnesses to the fact that she left the children alone, Mr Wales?' Jess asked.

'I came home and found them.'

'Was anyone with you?'

'No.'

'So we have only your word that your wife went out and left the children by themselves?'

'Yes.'

'Well, I don't know why we wouldn't believe you,' Jess stated, bracing herself for the objection she knew would follow.

'Ms Koster,' Judge Harris warned, 'can we please skip the sarcasm and get on with it.'

'I'm sorry, Your Honor,' Jess said, smoothing her skirt,

suddenly reminded of the new underwear Don's secretary had brought over just prior to the start of court. The events of the morning, of the day before, crowded into her mind. The discovery of Connie's body, the break-in at her apartment, the destruction of her underwear all swirled in her brain, fuelled her anger, propelled the words out of her mouth. 'What about the nights of 17 October 1990, 14 March 1991, 10 November 1991, 20 January 1992?'

'Objection, Your Honor,' Hal Bristol said. 'The witness has already admitted his part in these domestic disputes.'

'Overruled. The witness will answer the question.'

'The police were called to your house on each of those occasions, Mr Wales,' Jess reminded him. 'Do you remember that?'

'I don't remember specific dates.'

'And your wife ended up in the hospital on two of these occasions.'

'I believe we both ended up in the hospital.'

'Yes, I see that on the night of 10 November 1991, you were treated at St Luke's for a bloody nose and then released. Your wife, on the other hand, stayed on till morning. I guess she just needed a good night's sleep.'

'Ms Koster.' Judge Harris warned.

'Sorry, Your Honor. Now, Mr Wales, you told the jury that the reason for most of these fights was because you were provoked.'

'That's right.'

'It doesn't take much to provoke you, does it, Mr Wales?'

'Objection.'

'I'll rephrase that, Your Honor. Would you say you have a quick temper, Mr Wales?'

'These last few years have been difficult ones in the retail business. They took their toll. On occasion, I was unable to control my temper.'

'On many occasions, it would seem. Including long before we entered into these tough economic times. I mean, 1984 and 1985 were pretty good years, businesswise, weren't they?'

'Businesswise, yes.'

'I see you posted record commissions those years, Mr Wales,' Jess stated, again exchanging one piece of paper for another.

'I worked very hard.'

'I'm sure you did. And you were amply rewarded. And yet, police records show you beat your wife. So it would appear that your temper really didn't have anything to do with how well you were doing at work. Wouldn't you agree?'

Terry Wales took several seconds before answering. 'No matter how well I was doing, it wasn't enough for Nina. She was constantly complaining that I wasn't making enough money, even before the recession hit. These last few years have been hell.'

'Your income took a substantial drop?'

'Yes.'

'And your wife resented the fact there was less money coming in?'

'Very much.'

'I see. How exactly did your drop in income affect the household, Mr Wales?'

'Well, the same way everybody else has been affected, I guess,' Terry Wales answered carefully, glancing at his attorney. 'We had to cut down on entertaining, eating out, buying clothes. Stuff like that.'

'Stuff that affected your wife,' Jess stated.

'That affected all of us.'

'How did it affect you, Mr Wales?'

'I don't understand.'

'Objection. The witness has already answered the question.'

'Get to the point here, Ms Koster,' Judge Harris advised.

'You were the sole supporter of your family, isn't that right? I mean, you made quite a point earlier of telling us that it was your wife who insisted she give up her job.'

'She wanted to stay home with the children. I respected that decision.'

'So, the only money Nina Wales had access to was the money that you gave her.'

'As far as I know.'

'How much money did you give her every week, Mr Wales?'

'As much as she needed.'

'About how much was that?'

'I'm not sure. Enough for groceries and other essentials.'

'Fifty dollars? A hundred? Two hundred?'

'Closer to a hundred.'

'A hundred dollars a week for groceries and other essentials for a family of four. Your wife must have been a very careful shopper.'

'We had no choice. There was simply no money to spare.'

'You belong to the Eden Rock Golf Club, do you not, Mr Wales?'

A slight pause. 'Yes.'

'How much are the yearly dues?'

'I'm not sure.'

'Would you like me to tell you?'

'I think they're just slightly over a thousand dollars,' he answered quickly.

'Eleven hundred and fifty dollars, to be exact. Did you give that up?'

'No.'

'And the Elmwood Gun Club. You're a member there as well, aren't you?'

'Yes.'

'How much are the yearly dues there?'

'About five hundred dollars.'

'Did you give that up?'

'No. But I paid out a lot of money to join those clubs in the first place. It would have meant losing my initial investment.'

'It would have meant a saving of over fifteen hundred dollars a year.'

'Look, I know it was selfish, but I worked hard; I needed some sort of outlet.'

'Do you belong to any other clubs, Mr Wales?' Jess asked and held her breath. She was still waiting for this morning's police report to come in.

'No,' came the immediate reply.

'You don't belong to any other sports clubs?'

Jess watched for a look of hesitation in Terry Wales's eyes, but there was none. 'No,' he said clearly.

Jess nodded, looking toward the rear of the courtroom. Where was Barbara Cohen? Surely they must have heard from the police by now.

'Let's go back to the night of 20 January 1992,' Jess stated, 'the last time police were called to your house to investigate a domestic dispute.' She waited a few seconds to allow the jury to adjust to her change in topics. 'You testified that was the night your wife first told you she had a lover.'

'That's right.'

'How exactly did that come about?'

'I don't understand.'

'When did she tell you? At dinner? When you were watching television? When you were in bed?'

'It was after we'd gone to bed.'

'Please go on, Mr Wales.'

'We'd just finished making love. I reached over to take her in my arms.' His voice cracked. 'I just wanted to hold her. I . . . I know I wasn't always the best husband, but I loved her, I really did, and I wanted everything to be all right between us.' Tears filled his eyes. 'Anyway, I reached for her, but she pulled away. I told her that I loved her, and she started to laugh. She told me I didn't know what love meant, that I didn't know what *making* love meant. That I didn't know how to make love. That I was a joke. That I had no idea what it took to satisfy a woman, to satisfy her. And then she told me that it didn't matter, because she'd found someone who *did* know how to satisfy her. That she had a lover, someone she'd been seeing for months. That he was a *real* man, a man who knew how to satisfy a woman. That maybe one night she'd let me watch them together so that I could learn a thing or two.' Again his voice cracked. 'That's when I lost it.'

'And you beat her.'

'And I hit her,' Terry Wales qualified. 'And she started

pounding on me, scratching at me, telling me over and over again what a loser I was.'

'And so you hit her, over and over again,' Jess said, using his words.

'I'm not proud of myself.'

'So you've said. Tell me, Mr Wales, what was your wife's lover's name?'

'I don't know. She didn't say.'

'What did he do for a living?'

'I don't know.'

'Do you know how old he was, how tall? Whether or not he was married?'

'No.'

'Did you have any suspicions as to who it might be? A friend, perhaps?'

'I don't know who her lover was. It wasn't the sort of thing she would confide in me.'

'And yet she *did* tell you she had a lover. An interesting thing to confide in an often abusive husband, wouldn't you say?'

'Objection, Your Honor.'

'Sustained.'

'Did anyone else hear your wife confess to having a lover?'

'Of course not. We were in bed.'

'Did she ever talk about him when you had company?'

'No. Only when we were alone.'

'And since her friends have already testified that she never confided any such news to them,' Jess went on, 'it seems that once again we have only your word.'

Terry Wales said nothing.

'So, your wife told you she had a lover; you beat her to a bloody pulp, and the neighbors called the police,' Jess summarized, feeling Hal Bristol object even before the word was out of his mouth.

'Your wife *did* end up in the hospital that night, didn't she?' Jess said, rephrasing her question.

'Yes.'

'How long after that did your wife tell you she was leaving you?'

'She was always threatening to leave me, to take my kids away from me, to take me for everything I had.'

'When did you know she meant it?' Jess asked.

Terry Wales took a deep breath. 'The end of May.'

'You've testified that your wife told you that she'd consulted a lawyer and was moving out.'

'That's correct.'

'You testified that you begged and pleaded with her to change her mind.'

'That's right.'

'Why?'

'I don't understand.'

'You've told us that your wife told you she'd taken a lover, that she repeatedly called your manhood into question, told you you were a lousy lover, a lousy husband, a lousy provider, that she made your life a living hell. Why would you beg and plead with her to stay?'

Terry Wales shook his head. 'I don't know. I guess that, despite everything we did to each other, I still believed in the sanctity of marriage.'

'Till death do you part,' Jess stated sardonically. 'Is that the general idea?'

'Objection, Your Honor. Really.'

Judge Harris waved away the objection with an impatient hand.

'I never meant to kill my wife,' Terry Wales said directly to the jury.

'No, you were just trying to get her attention,' Jess said, watching the rear door of the courtroom open, and Barbara Cohen walk through. Even from a distance of thirty feet, Jess could see the glint in her assistant's eye. 'Your Honor, may I have a minute?'

Judge Harris nodded and Jess strode to the prosecutor's table.

'What've we got?' she asked, taking the report from Barbara's hands, and quickly scanning the pages.

'I'd say just what we need,' Barbara Cohen answered, not even trying to suppress her smile.

Jess had to bite down on her lower lip to keep from laughing out loud. She spun round, then held back, careful not to appear too eager. Move in slowly, she told herself, as she inched forward. Then move in for the kill. 'So, you were distraught and emasculated and desperate, is that right?' she asked the defendant.

'Yes,' he admitted.

'And you decided you wanted to do something that would shake your wife up, make her come to her senses.'

'Yes.'

'So you went out and you purchased a crossbow.'

'Yes.'

'A weapon you hadn't shot since you were a kid in camp, is that right?'

'Yes.'

'What camp was that?'

'Sorry?'

'What was the name of the camp you went to where you first learned to shoot a bow and arrow?'

Terry Wales looked toward his lawyer, but Hal Bristol's subtle nod directed him to answer the question. 'I believe it was Camp New Moon.'

'How many years did you attend Camp New Moon?' Jess asked.

'Three, I believe.'

'And they taught you how to shoot a bow and arrow?'

'It was one of the activities offered.'

'And you won several medals, did you not?'

'That was almost thirty years ago.'

'But you did win several medals?'

Terry Wales laughed. 'They gave medals to all the kids.'

'Your Honor, would you please instruct the witness to answer the question,' Jess asked.

'A simple yes or no will suffice, Mr Wales,' Judge Harris told the defendant.

Terry Wales lowered his head. 'Yes.'

'Thank you,' Jess said, and smiled. 'And until you fatally shot your wife through the heart on June the second of this year, it had been almost thirty years since you'd fired a bow and arrow?'

'Twenty-five or thirty,' Terry Wales qualified.

Jess checked the folder in her hand. 'Mr Wales, have you ever heard of the Aurora County Bowmen?'

'I'm sorry, the what?' Terry Wales asked, a slight flush blotching his cheeks.

'The Aurora County Bowmen,' Jess repeated. 'It's an archery club located about forty-five miles southwest of Chicago. Do you know it?'

'No.'

'According to the brochure I have, it's a non-profit organization formed in 1962 with the purpose of providing facilities where archers can pursue their sport. "No matter what area of archery your interest lies in",' Jess continued reading, '"be it hunting, competitive target or pleasure shooting, using the longbow, recurve, compound or *crossbow*, the Aurora County Bowmen offers ideal facilities for practising throughout the year."'

Hal Bristol was on his feet and moving toward the Judge's bench. 'Objection, Your Honor. My client has already stated he has no knowledge of this club.'

'Interesting,' Jess said immediately, 'since club records show Terry Wales has been a member there for the past eight years.' Jess held up a faxed copy of the club membership. 'We'd like this entered as State's Exhibit F, Your Honor.'

Jess handed the records to Judge Harris who looked them over before passing them down to Hal Bristol's waiting fist. Hal Bristol scanned the evidence, nodded angrily, then returned to his seat, glaring openly at his client.

'Do you remember the club now, Mr Wales?' Jess asked pointedly.

'I joined the club eight years ago and hardly ever used it,' Terry Wales explained. 'Frankly, I'd forgotten all about it.'

'Oh, but they didn't forget you, Mr Wales.' Jess was careful to keep the gloat out of her voice. 'We have a signed affidavit from a Mr Glen Hallam, who's in charge of the equipment at Aurora County Bowmen. The police showed him your picture this morning, and he remembers you very well. Says you've been a regular there for years, although, oddly enough, he hasn't seen you since the spring. I wonder why that is,' Jess mused, offering the statement as State's Exhibit G. 'He says you're quite a shot, Mr Wales. Bull's-eye nearly every time.'

A collective gasp emanated from the jury box. Hal Bristol looked toward his lap. Terry Wales said nothing.

Bull's-eye, Jess thought.

Chapter Twenty

'I understand you pulled off quite a coup in court today,' Greg Oliver greeted Jess as she walked past his office at the end of the day.

'She was brilliant,' Neil Strayhorn exclaimed, a step behind Jess, Barbara Cohen at his side. 'She laid her trap, then stood back and let the defendant strut inside and slam the door behind him.'

'The case isn't over yet,' Jess reminded them, unwilling to rejoice too early. They still had other witnesses to cross-examine, final arguments to deliver, and the unpredictability of the jury to contend with. One could never get too cocky.

'My favorite moment,' Neil was saying as they settled in behind their desks, 'was when you asked him if he'd ever heard of the Aurora County Bowmen.'

'And he didn't move,' Barbara continued, 'but you could see his cheeks kind of sink in.'

Jess permitted herself a loud, raucous laugh. That had been her favorite moment too.

'Well, well, the ice maiden cracks.' Greg leaned in from the doorway, one hand on either side of the frame.

'What can we do for you, Greg?' Jess felt her good mood about to evaporate.

Greg ambled toward Jess's desk, shaking a loosely clenched fist, as if he were about to toss a dice. 'I've got a present for you.'

'A present for me,' Jess repeated dully.

'Something you need. Very badly.' His voice all but spun with innuendo.

'Is it bigger than a breadbox?' Neil asked.

'I could really use a breadbox,' Barbara stated.

Jess looked Greg coolly in the eye and waited. She said nothing.

'No guesses?' he asked.

'No patience,' Jess told him, gathering up her things. 'Look, Greg, I want to get a bit more work done here, then I'm going home. It's been a very long day.'

'Need a ride?' Greg's lips curved into a wavy line, like a small, thin snake.

'I've already offered to drive Jess home,' Neil said quickly, and Jess smiled gratefully.

'But I've got what you need,' Greg persisted, opening his fist and dropping a set of keys onto the desk in front of Jess. 'The keys to Madame's apartment.'

Jess reached for the new set of keys, the stale scent of Greg's cologne bouncing off the shiny metal. 'How did you get these?'

'Some woman delivered them this afternoon. Kind of cute actually, except that her thighs were in two different time zones.'

'You're a class act,' Barbara told him.

'Hey, I'm the sensitive new man of the nineties.' He sauntered back to the door, his fingers waving good-bye, then disappeared down the hall.

'Where's my crossbow?' Barbara asked.

'They're never around when you need them.' Jess glanced over the list of witnesses who would be testifying the next day, and jotted down a few notes before feeling her eyes cross with fatigue. 'How're things coming on the Alvarez case?'

'Examination for discovery is coming up next week,' Barbara told her. 'I'm almost finished taking depositions, and it doesn't look like McCauliff is in the mood to bargain.'

'McCauliff loves nothing better than the sound of his own voice echoing in a crowded courtroom. Be careful. He'll try to intimidate you by using lots of big words nobody understands,' Jess warned them. 'Think you can handle him?'

'I've got my dictionary ready,' Neil told her, and smiled.

Jess tried to smile back, but her mouth was too tired to cooperate, and she managed only a slight twitch. 'That's it for me, gang. I'm gonna call it a day.'

Barbara checked her watch. 'You feeling all right?'

'I'm exhausted.'

'Don't get sick on us now,' Barbara pleaded. 'We're entering the home stretch.'

'I don't have time to get sick,' Jess agreed.

'Come on, you heard me tell Oliver I was driving you home,' Neil volunteered.

'Don't be silly, Neil. It's way out of your way.'

'You trying to make a liar out of me?'

'When are you going to give in and buy a new car?' Barbara asked.

Jess pictured her once proud red Mustang, battered and broken, covered in excrement. 'As soon as I get Rick Ferguson behind bars,' she said.

The phone was ringing when she got to her apartment. 'Just a minute,' she called out, fiddling unsuccessfully with her new key, twisting it in the lock. 'Damn it, come on. Turn, for God's sake.'

The phone continued to ring, the key still refusing to connect properly. Had Greg Oliver given her the wrong set of keys? she wondered, then asked herself whether such an error would have been deliberate or accidental. Or maybe the fault lay with Don's secretary. Maybe she'd mixed up Jess's keys with her own. Or possibly the locksmith had made the mistake. Maybe the keys were defective. Maybe she'd never get inside her apartment. Maybe she'd grow old and die right here in her hallway without ever seeing the inside of her apartment again.

Maybe if she just calmed down and stopped trying so hard.

The key turned in the lock. The door opened. The phone stopped ringing.

'At least you're inside,' Jess said, acknowledging her canary with a wave of her fingers, uncomfortably bringing Greg Oliver to mind. She set her briefcase down, pulled off her boots, and rifled through the mail she'd carried upstairs in her coat pocket. Nothing interesting, she thought gratefully, tossing both the letters and her coat across the sofa. 'So, Fred, I had quite a day today. A woman I hardly know bought me some new panties, and I got new keys, and look here, brand new locks.' She walked back to the door, locking and unlocking it several times until she felt the key turn easily, playing with the deadbolt as if it were a shiny new toy. 'And I was positively amazing in court,' she continued. 'Let me tell you about how my brilliant hunch paid off.'

She stopped.

'This is pathetic,' she said out loud. 'I'm talking to a goddamn canary.' She walked into the kitchen, looked toward the phone. 'Ring, damn you.'

The phone was stubbornly silent. This is silly, Jess thought, impatiently grabbing the phone from its receiver. The phone works both ways. Who said she had to wait until someone called her?

Except who would she call? She didn't really have any friends outside of the office. Judging from the lack of jazz riffs emanating from the apartment below, Walter Fraser wasn't home. She had no idea where to reach Adam. She was afraid to call her father. Her sister was barely speaking to her.

She could call Don, she thought, *should* call Don, share with him the news of her day, thank him for insisting that she come with him to Union Pier yesterday. If she hadn't, she would never have seen the sign for the Union Pier Gun Club, would never have thought to seek out archery clubs in the Chicago area, would never have had the chance to shine so brilliantly in court today. Not to mention, she should thank him for everything else he had done for her – the new underwear, new locks, new set of keys.

Which was precisely why she didn't want to call him, she understood. Like a spoiled child who has received too much and is in danger of being overwhelmed, she was tired of saying thank you, weary of being grateful. She couldn't share the news of her triumph in court today with Don without sharing at least part of the credit, and she wasn't ready to do that. 'You're getting very selfish in your old age,' she admonished herself aloud, then thought she was probably no more selfish now than she'd always been. 'What witnesses from the past could we dredge up to testify against you?' she asked, the image of her mother's tear-streaked face filling her mind before she had a chance to block it.

'The hell with this nonsense,' Jess growled, quickly dialing her sister's number in Evanston, waiting while it rang six times. 'I'm probably taking her away from the babies,' she muttered, debating whether or not to hang up when a strange voice answered the phone.

The voice was somewhere between a croak and a rasp, unidentifiable as to gender. 'Hello?' it said painfully.

'Who is this?' Jess asked in return. 'Maureen, is that you?'

'It's Barry,' the voice whispered.

'Barry! What's the matter?'

'Terrible cold,' Barry said, pushing the words out of his mouth with obvious effort. 'Laryngitis.'

'My God. Do you feel as bad as you sound?'

'Worse. The doctor put me on antibiotics. Maureen just went to the drugstore to pick up the prescription.'

'So, now she has four children to look after, not three,' Jess said without thinking.

There was a moment's silence.

'I'm sorry,' Jess apologized quickly. Hadn't she intended this call as a conciliatory gesture? 'I didn't mean to say that.'

'You just can't help yourself, can you?' Barry asked hoarsely.

'I said I was sorry.'

Another long pause. The sound of an almost other-worldly voice. Slow. Deliberate. 'Did you get my letter?'

Jess froze. The image of a urine-soaked piece of paper pushed itself in front of her eyes and under her nose. 'What letter?' Jess asked, hearing a baby cry in the distance.

'Shit, they're waking up,' Barry exclaimed, his voice surprisingly close to normal. 'I've got to go, Jess. We'll have to talk about this some other time. I'll tell Maureen you called. Always a pleasure talking to you.'

A busy signal assaulted her ears. Jess quickly hung up the

phone, then didn't move. Could she really be thinking what she was thinking? Could her brother-in-law, *her sister's husband*, for God's sake, father of her nephew and twin nieces, a respected *accountant*, of all things, could he really be the person responsible for that disgusting letter she'd received in the mail?

Certainly, he disliked her. They'd been at each other's throats almost since the wedding. She didn't like his values; he didn't like her attitude. He thought she was spoiled and humorless and deliberately provocative; she found him small-minded, controlling, and vengeful. She'd accused him of undermining her sister's autonomy; he'd accused her of undermining his parental authority. *One of these days, Jess, you'll go too far*, he'd told her that night at dinner. Had that been a threat or simply an acknowledgment of the way things were? She remembered how Barry had gloated about stealing a client away from his former partner and supposed friend. *I never forget*, he'd boasted. *I get even.*

Was the urine-soaked letter Barry's way of getting even? Had he sent her clippings of his public hair in order to prove some perverse point? Had she alienated him to such a loathsome degree?

How *many* men had she managed to alienate in her young life?

Jess massaged the bridge of her nose. The list of candidates was endless. Even after she eliminated all the men she'd helped send to prison, there were the countless number of other men she'd prosecuted, defence lawyers she'd offended, fellow workers she'd tangled with, potential suitors she'd scorned. Even her relatives weren't immune to her peculiar charm. Any one of a hundred men could have sent her that letter. She'd made enough enemies to keep the post office busy for weeks.

A buzzer sounded. Jess immediately picked up the phone, realizing as soon as she heard the busy signal that it wasn't the phone at all, but someone at the downstairs door. She approached the intercom by the front door cautiously, wondering who was there, not sure whether she wanted to find out.

'Who is it?' she asked.

'Adam,' came the simple response.

She buzzed him up. Seconds later, he was outside her door.

'I tried to phone,' he said as soon as he saw her. 'First, no one answered; then the line was busy. Are you going to invite me in?'

He's the wild card here, Jess. Just who is this man? she heard Don say.

'You must have been very close by.' Jess stood in the doorway, blocking his entrance. 'I wasn't on the phone that long.'

'I was around the corner.'

'Delivering shoes?'

'Waiting for you. Are you going to invite me in?' he asked again.

He's the wild card here, Jess.

Her mind raced back to when she'd first met Adam Stohn. The vandalization of her car, the urine-soaked letter, the torn underwear, all had taken place since their first meeting. Adam Stohn knew where she worked. He knew where she lived. He'd even spent the night on her sofa.

All right, so he'd had the opportunity to do these things, Jess acknowledged silently, losing herself momentarily in the soft stillness of his brown eyes. But what possible motive could he have for wanting to terrorize her?

Her mind rifled through old mental files. Was it possible she'd prosecuted him once? Sent him to prison? Maybe he was the brother of someone she'd sent to jail. Or the friend. Maybe he was someone's hired gun.

Or maybe he was the reincarnation of Al Capone, she scoffed. Maybe she could spend the rest of her life questioning the motives of every man who showed her even the most casual of interest. He doesn't want to kill you, for God's sake, she thought, stepping back and letting Adam inside her apartment.

He wants to get you into bed.

'I was curious about what happened yesterday,' he told her, taking off his jacket and throwing it over her coat, as if their coats were lovers.

Jess told him about having to break the news of Connie DeVuono's death to her mother and son, and about today's triumph in court. She left out that in between the two events she'd spent the night with her ex-husband.

'He's still in love with you, you know,' Adam said, twisting the dials on her stereo until he found a country music station. Garth Brooks was singing cheerfully about his father shooting and killing his mother in a jealous rage.

'Who?' Jess asked, knowing full well whom he meant.

'The bagel man,' Adam told her, pacing restlessly about her apartment, lifting the bag of bagels from the dining room table and holding them up. 'You forgot to put these in the freezer.'

'Oh, damn. They'll be hard as rocks.'

Adam redeposited the bag on the table, walked slowly back toward her. 'How do you feel?'

'Me? A little tired, I guess.'

'How do you feel about your ex-husband?' he qualified.

'I told you, we're friends.' Jess ached to sit down, was afraid to.

'I think there's more to it than that.'

'Then you're wrong.'

'I called you last night, Jess,' he told her, very close now. 'I called you till quite late. I think it was three in the morning when I finally gave up and went to sleep.'

'I wasn't aware I had to answer to you.'

Adam stopped, took two steps back, hands in the air. 'You're right. I have no business asking you these questions.'

'Why are you?'

'I'm not sure.' He looked as puzzled as she felt. 'I guess I just want to know where I stand. If you're still involved with your ex-husband, just say the word. I'm out of here.'

'I'm not involved,' Jess said quickly.

'And the bagel man?'

'He understands how I feel.'

'But he's hoping to change your mind.'

'He's involved with someone else.'

'Unless you change your mind.'

'I won't.'

They stared at each other for several seconds without speaking.

He's the wild card here, Jess.

In the next second, they were in each other's arms, his hands in her hair, her lips on his.

Just who is this man?

His hands reached down, drew her hips toward his, his lips moving down her neck.

Who is this Adam Stohn anyway, Jess? she heard Don ask again, feeling her ex-husband still inside her. How could she have let last night happen? How could she allow one man to make love to her one night, and another the next? Wasn't this the nineties? The age of AIDS? Wasn't promiscuity an outdated relic of more innocent times?

She almost laughed at the correlation of promiscuity with innocence. She was a lawyer all right, she thought. She could put a spin on anything.

'I can't do this,' she said quickly, pulling out of the embrace.

'Can't do what?' His voice sounded almost as hoarse as Barry's.

'I'm just not ready for this yet,' she told him, searching the room for invisible, disapproving eyes. 'I don't even know where you live.'

'You want to know where I live? I live on Sheffield,' he said quickly. 'A one-bedroom apartment. A five-minute walk from Wrigley Field.'

And suddenly they were laughing, great wondrous whoops of laughter straight from the gut. Jess felt the tension of the last few days break up and dissolve. She laughed for the sheer joy of it, for the miraculous release it provided. She laughed so hard her stomach ached and tears spilled from her eyes. Adam quickly kissed the tears away.

'No,' she said, pulling just out of his reach. 'I really can't. I need time to think.'

'How much time?'

'I could think over dinner,' she heard herself say.

He was already at the door. 'Where would you like to go?'

Again they were laughing; this time so hard Jess could barely stand up. 'How about I just make us something here?'

'I didn't think you cooked.'

'Follow me,' she told him, laughing her way toward the dining area, where she picked up the bag of bagels and carried it into the kitchen. 'One or two?' she asked, popping open the door of the microwave oven.

He held up two fingers. 'I'll open the wine.'

'I don't think there is any,' she said sheepishly.

'No wine?'

She opened the fridge. 'And no pop either.'

'No wine?' he said again.

'We can have water.'

'Bread and water,' he mused. 'Where'd you learn your culinary skills? The federal penitentiary?'

Jess stopped laughing. 'Have you ever been to prison?' she asked.

He looked startled, then amused. 'What kind of question is that?'

'Just trying to make conversation.'

'This is your idea of small talk?'

'You didn't answer me.'

'I didn't think you were serious.'

'I'm not,' Jess said quickly, putting four bagels on a plate and sticking them in the microwave.

'I've never been to prison, Jess,' Adam told her.

She shrugged, as if the matter were of absolutely no consequence. 'Not even to visit a friend?' The forced note of casualness sounded jarring even to her own ears.

'You think I consort with convicted felons? Jess, what am I doing here?'

'You tell me,' Jess said, but Adam's only answer was a smile.

'So you were an only child,' Jess said as they sat on the floor in front of the sofa finishing their dinner.

'A very spoiled only child,' he elaborated.

'My sister always says that children aren't apples – they don't spoil.'

'What else does your sister say?'

'That you can't spoil a child with too much love.'

'She sounds like a very good mother.'

'I think she is.'

'You sound surprised.'

'It's just not what I expected from her, that's all.'

'What did you expect from her?'

'I'm not sure. A brilliant career, I guess.'

'Maybe she thought she'd leave that to you.'

'Maybe,' Jess agreed, wondering how the conversation always reverted back to her. 'You and your wife never wanted children?'

'We wanted them,' he said. 'It just never worked out.'

Jess understood from the way his voice dropped that it was a topic he didn't wish to pursue. She finished the last of her bagel, lifted the glass of water to her lips.

'What was your mother like?' he asked suddenly.

'What?' Jess's hand started to shake, the water spilling from the glass onto the floor. She scrambled to her feet. 'Oh my God.'

His hand was immediately on her arm, gently pulling her back down. 'Relax, Jess, it's only water.' He used his napkin to wipe up the spill. 'What's the matter?'

'Nothing's the matter.'

'Then why are you shaking?'

'I'm not shaking.'

'What did your mother do to you?'

'What do you mean, what did she do?' Jess snapped angrily. 'She didn't do anything. What are you talking about?'

'Why won't you talk about her?'

'Why should I?'

'Because you don't want to,' he said evenly. 'Because you're afraid to.'

'Another one of my phobias?' Jess asked sarcastically.

'You tell me.'

'Anybody ever tell you you'd make a good lawyer?'

'What happened to your mother, Jess?'

Jess closed her eyes, saw her mother standing before her in the kitchen of their home, tears falling down her cheeks. I *don't need this, Jess, she was saying I don't need this from you.* Jess quickly opened her eyes. 'She disappeared,' she said finally.

'Disappeared?'

'She'd found a small lump in her breast, and she was pretty scared. She called the doctor, and he said he'd see her that afternoon. But she never showed up for her appointment. Nobody ever saw her again.'

'Then it's possible she's alive?'

'No, it's not possible,' Jess snapped. 'It's not possible.'

He reached for her, but she pulled away from his reach.

'She wouldn't abandon us just because she was scared,' Jess continued, speaking from somewhere deep inside her. 'I mean, even if she was scared, and I know she was, that doesn't mean she'd run out on us. She wasn't the kind of woman who would just walk out on her husband and daughters because she couldn't face reality. No matter how scared she was. No matter how angry.'

'Angry?'

'I didn't mean angry.'

'You said it.'

'I didn't mean it.'

'What was she angry about, Jess?'

'She wasn't angry.'

'She was angry at you, wasn't she?'

Jess looked toward the window. Her mother's tear-streaked face stared back at her through the antique lace curtains. *I don't need this, Jess. I don't need this from you.*

'I came downstairs and found her all dressed up,' Jess began.

'I asked her where she was going, and at first she wouldn't tell me. But eventually it came out that she'd found this lump in her breast, and she was going to see her doctor that afternoon.' Jess tried to laugh, but the laugh stuck in her throat, like a piece of bagel she could neither swallow nor cough up. 'It was just like my mother to get all dressed up in the morning when she didn't have to be somewhere till late in the afternoon.'

'Kind of like someone who selects the clothes she's going to wear the next day the night before.'

Jess ignored the implication. 'She asked me if I'd go with her to the doctor. I said, sure. But then we got into an argument. A typical mother-daughter kind of thing. She thought I was being headstrong. I thought she was being overprotective. I told her to stay out of my life. She told me not to bother taking her to the doctor's. I said, have it your way, and slammed out of the house. By the time I got back, she'd already left.'

'And you blame yourself for what happened.' It was more statement than question.

Jess pushed herself to her feet, walked to the bird's cage with exaggerated strides. 'Hi, Fred, how're you doing?'

'Fred's doing great,' Adam told her, coming up behind her. 'I'm not so sure about his owner. That's a shitload of guilt you've been carrying around all these years.'

'Hey, whatever happened to our pact?' Jess asked, swiping at her tears, refusing to look at him, concentrating all her attention on the small yellow bird. 'No secrets, no lies, remember?' She made awkward chirping noises against the side of the cage.

'Do you ever let him out?' Adam asked.

'You're not supposed to let canaries out of their cages,' Jess said loudly, hoping to still the shaking in her body with the sound of her voice. 'They're not like parakeets. Parakeets are domestic birds. Canaries are wild. They aren't meant to be let out of their cages.'

'So you never have to worry about him flying away,' Adam said softly.

This time the implication was too blatant to ignore. Jess spun round angrily. 'The bird is a pet, not a metaphor.'

'Jess—'

'Just when did you give up psychiatry for selling shoes?' she demanded bitterly. 'Who the hell are you, Adam Stohn?'

They stood facing one another, Jess shaking, Adam absolutely still.

'Do you want me to go?' he asked.

No, she thought. 'Yes,' she said.

He walked slowly to the door.

'Adam,' she called, and he stopped, his hand on the doorknob. 'I think it's probably a good idea if you don't come back.'

For an instant she thought he might turn round, take her into his arms, confess all. But he didn't, and in the next instant, he was gone and she was alone in a room full of ghosts and shadows.

Chapter Twenty-One

By the end of the week, the Medical Examiner's report on Connie DeVuono was in and the jury in the Terry Wales murder trial was out.

Connie DeVuono had been raped, then beaten and strangled with a piece of thin magnetic wire that had sliced through her jugular and almost severed her head from her body. Forensics had determined that the wire that caused her death was identical to wire found in the factory that employed Rick Ferguson. A warrant had just been issued for Rick Ferguson's arrest.

'How long do you think the jury will be out?' Barbara Cohen was asking when the phone rang on Jess's desk.

'You know better than that,' Jess told her, reaching for the phone. 'Could be hours. Could be days.'

Barbara checked her watch. 'It's already been over twenty-four hours.'

Jess shrugged, as anxious as her assistant but reluctant to admit it. She picked up the phone, brought the receiver to her ear. 'Jess Koster.'

'He's disappeared,' Don said instead of hello.

Jess felt her stomach lurch. She didn't have to ask who Don was talking about. 'When?'

'Probably sometime in the middle of the night. My guy just called. He's been watching the house all night and when he didn't see Ferguson leave for work this morning at the usual time, he got suspicious, waited awhile, finally did some snooping around. He could see Ferguson's mother either asleep or passed out in bed; Ferguson was nowhere to be seen. My guy called the warehouse, and sure enough, Ferguson hasn't shown up. It looks like he picked up on the tail, figured the police were about to arrest him, and climbed out one of the back windows while it was still dark.'

'The irony is that the police *were* about to arrest him,' Jess admitted. 'We issued a warrant this morning.'

Don's tone became instantly businesslike, no longer the concerned ex-husband but the ultimate professional, carefully attuned to the rights of his client. 'What've you got?' he asked.

'The wire used to kill Connie DeVuono was the same kind of wire found in the warehouse that employs Rick Ferguson.'

'What else?'

'What else do I need?'

'More than that.'

'Not to bring him in.'

'Any prints?'

'No,' Jess admitted.

'Just a flimsy piece of wire?'

'Strong enough to kill Connie DeVuono,' Jess told him. 'Strong enough to convict your client.'

There was a slight pause. 'Okay, Jess, I don't want to get into all this now. We can talk about the case against my client as soon as the police bring him in. In the meantime, I've asked my guy to keep an eye on you.'

'What? Don, I told you I don't want a baby-sitter.'

'*I* want,' Don insisted. 'Indulge me, Jess. Just for a day or two. It won't kill you.'

'And Rick Ferguson might?'

His sigh echoed against her ear. 'You won't even know you're being watched.'

'Rick Ferguson knew.'

'Just do this for me, will you?'

'Any ideas where your client went?'

'None.'

'I better go,' Jess told him, already thinking ahead to what she would tell the police.

'I take it the jury's still out in the Crossbow case?'

'Over twenty-four hours.'

'Word on the street says your closing argument was a classic.'

'Juries are notably impervious to classics,' Jess said, anxious now to get off the phone.

'I'll call you later.'

Jess hung up without saying goodbye.

'Detective Mansfield just called,' Neil told her. 'Apparently Rick Ferguson's skipped. They're issuing an APB for his arrest.'

The phone rang on Jess's desk.

'Looks like it's going to be one of those days,' Barbara said. 'You want me to get that?'

Jess shook her head, answered the phone. 'Jess Kcster.'

'Jess, it's Maureen. Is it a bad time?'

Jess felt her shoulders slump. 'Well, it's not the best.' She could almost see the disappointment in her sister's face. It seeped into the air around her, like an invisible, poison gas. 'I can spare a few minutes.'

'Barry just told me this morning that you called on Monday,' Maureen apologized. 'I'm so sorry.'

'Why should you apologize for Barry's mistakes?'

There was silence.

'Sorry,' Jess said quickly. Couldn't she ever leave well enough alone?

'He's been so sick all week. He could hardly think straight, he was so stuffed up. The doctor was afraid it might be pneumonia, but whatever it was, the antibiotics killed it. He went back to work this morning.'

'I'm glad to hear he's feeling better.' Jess immediately pictured the urine-soaked letter filled with pubic hair she had received in the mail, wondering again whether Barry could have sent it.

'Anyway, he just remembered about your phone call as he was walking out the door this morning. I almost killed him.'

'A lot of killing going on in your house these days,' Jess remarked absently.

'What?'

'So, how've *you* been?'

'Me? I don't have time to get sick,' Maureen said, sounding

very much like her younger sister. 'Anyway, I know how busy you are, and how you don't like to be interrupted at work, but I didn't want you to think I was ignoring your phone call. I'm really so glad that you phoned . . .' Her voice threatened to dissolve into tears.

'How's Dad?' Jess asked, realizing she hadn't spoken to her father in weeks, feeling the familiar pattern of guilt and anger. Guilt that she hadn't spoken to him, anger for her guilt.

'He's really happy, Jess.'

'I'm glad.'

'Sherry's very good for him. She makes him laugh, keeps him on his toes. They're coming for dinner next Friday night. We're going to put up the Christmas tree and decorate the house and everything.' She paused. 'Would you like to join us?'

Jess closed her eyes. How long could she go on hurting the very people who meant the most to her? 'Sure,' she said.

'Sure?'

'Sounds great.'

'Great?' Maureen repeated, as if she needed the confirmation of her own voice to accept what she was hearing. 'Yea,' she agreed, 'it will be great. We've missed you. Tyler hasn't stopped playing with that toy airplane you bought him. And you won't believe how much the twins have grown.'

Jess laughed. 'Really, Maureen, it hasn't been that long.'

'Almost two months,' Maureen reminded her, catching Jess off guard. Had two months really elapsed since the last time she'd seen her family?

'I better go now,' Jess told her.

'Oh, sure. You must be swamped. I heard on the news that the jury in that Crossbow killing thing retired yesterday. Any word?'

'None yet.'

'Good luck.'

'Thanks.'

'See you next week,' Maureen said.

'See you next week,' Jess agreed.

'Something wrong?' Barbara asked as Jess replaced the receiver.

Jess shook her head, pretended to be studying a file on her desk. Almost two months! she thought. Two months since her last visit to her sister's house. Two months since she'd hugged her nephew and cradled her infant nieces in her arms. Two months since she'd seen her father.

How could she have let that happen? Weren't they all she had left? What was the matter with her? Was she so self-centered, so self-absorbed, that she couldn't see past her own narrow little world? Was she so used to dealing with scum that she no longer knew how to act around decent people who loved her, whose only crime was in wanting to live their lives as they saw fit? Wasn't that all she'd ever wanted – no, demanded – for herself?

Wasn't that exactly what she'd been fighting about with her mother on the day her mother disappeared?

Jess threw her head back, feeling the muscles in her shoulders cramp. Why couldn't she stop obsessing on her mother? Why was she still a prisoner of something that had happened eight long years ago? Why did everything ultimately have to hark back to the day her mother had vanished?

Damn Adam Stohn, she thought, the cramping in her shoulders spreading to the other muscles in her back. He was responsible for her current malaise. He'd gotten her to open up, to talk about her mother. He'd unleashed all the anguish and the sadness and the guilt she'd been suppressing for so long.

It wasn't Adam's fault, she knew. He couldn't have known the emotional minefield he was walking into when he'd asked his simple questions, the raw nerves he was exposing. You can't put a band-aid on a cancer, she thought, and expect it to heal. Pull the band-aid off after years of benign neglect, and you had a full-scale malignancy raging out of control.

No wonder he hadn't wanted to stick around, that he'd been in such a hurry to leave. 'Do you want me to go?' he asked, and she'd said, 'I think it's probably a good idea if you don't come back.' And that was that, she thought now, remembering that she'd also once told him that a lawyer's good word was the only currency she had.

He was only being as good as her word.

'Damn you, Adam Stohn,' she whispered.

'Did you say something?' Barbara asked, looking up from her desk.

Jess shook her head, an acute sense of unease creeping into her chest, toying with her breathing, playing havoc with her equilibrium. She felt dizzy, light-headed, as if she might topple from her chair. Oh no, she thought, automatically stiffening, the world around her disappearing into a cloud of anxiety. Don't fight it, she told herself quickly. Go with it. Go with it. What's the worst that can happen? So you fall off your chair. So you land on your ass. So you throw up? So what?

Slowly, she released the air in her lungs and floated into the center of the large, miasmal mist. Almost immediately, it began evaporating around her. Her dizziness subsided and her breathing returned to normal, the muscles in her shoulders relaxing, surrendering their tension. Familiar sounds filtered to her ears – the hum of the fax machine, the clicking of computer keys, the ringing of the telephone.

Jess watched Neil walk over and pick up the phone on her desk. How long had it been ringing? 'Neil Strayhorn,' he pronounced clearly, his eyes locked on Jess. 'They are? Now?'

Jess took a deep breath, rose quickly to her feet. She didn't have to ask. The jury was in.

'Ladies and gentlemen of the jury, have you reached your verdict?'

Jess felt the familiar surge of adrenaline race through her body, though she was holding her breath. She both loved and hated this moment. Loved it for its drama, its suspense, the knowledge that victory or defeat was just a word away. Hated it for the same reasons. Hated it because she hated to lose. Hated it because, in the end, winning or losing was really what it was all about. One lawyer's truth against another's, justice relegated to the role of hapless observer. No such thing as the whole truth.

The foreman cleared his throat, checked the paper in his hand before speaking, as if he might have forgotten the decision the jury had reached, as if he wanted to make absolutely sure what it said. 'We, the jury,' he began, then cleared his throat again, 'find the defendant, Terry Wales, guilty of murder in the first degree.'

Immediately the courtroom erupted. Reporters ran from the room; briefcases snapped shut; friends and relatives of the deceased hugged each other in tearful abandon. Judge Harris thanked, then dismissed the jurors. Jess embraced her partners, accepted their congratulations, caught the look of resignation in Hal Bristol's eyes, the sneer of scorn on the defendant's lips as he was led away.

Outside the courtroom, the reporters thronged around her, pushing microphones up against her mouth, waving notebooks in front of her face. 'Were you surprised at the verdict? Did you expect to win? How do you feel?' they asked as cameras clicked and flash strobes exploded.

'We have great faith in this country's jury system,' Jess told the reporters, walking toward the elevators. 'We never doubted the outcome for a minute.'

'Are you going to ask for the death penalty?' someone called out.

'You bet,' Jess answered, pressing the button for the elevator, hearing Hal Bristol tell another reporter he intended to appeal.

'How does it feel to win this case?' a woman shouted from the back of the throng.

Jess knew she should remind the reporters that what was important here wasn't winning but the truth, that a guilty man had been convicted of a heinous crime, that justice had been served. She smiled widely. 'It feels great,' she said.

'Hey, was that your picture I saw in the paper this morning?' Vasiliki watched as Jess pulled her hair into a ponytail in front of the long mirror of the Wen-Do instruction hall.

'That was me,' Jess acknowledged shyly, her head still thumping from too many beers at Jean's Restaurant the night before. Normally she didn't frequent Jean's after work, unlike many of the prosecuting attorneys to whom Jean's was a second home. But everyone kept telling her a celebration was in order, and in truth, she'd felt like a nice long pat on the back.

She'd called her father right after she got back to her office, but he wasn't home, phoned her sister, but she was busy with the babies and had time for only the briefest of congratulations.

She'd called Don, told him of her victory, heard him mumble his apologies about not being able to take her out for a celebration dinner, something about a prior commitment. A prior commitment named Trish, Jess thought but didn't say, wondering what she expected from the man.

Then she'd done something she'd never done before, never permitted herself the luxury of doing before: she'd gone into the washroom, locked herself in a cubicle, closed her eyes, and just stood there. 'I won,' she'd said softly, allowing the ghost of her mother to pull her into a proud embrace.

The celebration at Jean's lasted until the early hours of the morning. Her trial supervisor, Tom Olinsky, had driven her home, walking her right to her door and making sure she got inside safely. Jess never saw the man Don had hired to watch out for her, but she knew he was there, and was grateful in spite of herself.

She'd fallen into a deep sleep, hadn't even heard her alarm clock go off, and was almost late for her self-defense class, arriving just seconds before everyone else, her hair not even brushed.

And now here she stood, her stomach empty and her head pounding, and she was expected to yell and execute eagle claws and zipper punches and hammer fists. 'Use those bony knuckles!' she could hear Dominic shouting even before he entered the room.

'You didn't tell us you were some hot-shot district attorney,' Vasiliki scolded as the other women circled round her.

'State's attorney,' Jess corrected automatically.

'Whatever, you're a celebrity!'

Jess smiled, uncomfortable with her new status. The other women stared at her with open curiosity.

'I read you're gonna ask for the death penalty,' Maryellen said. 'Think you'll get it?'

'I'm keeping my fingers crossed.'

'I don't believe in the death penalty,' Ayisha stated.

'She's young,' her mother whispered.

The curtains parted and Dominic entered the room. 'Good afternoon, everybody. Are you ready to kick ass?'

The women responded with a variety of grunts and raised hammer fists.

'Good. Let's all spread out now. Give yourselves lots of room. That's right. Now, what's the first line of defense?'

'*Kiyi,*' Vasiliki shouted.

'*Kiyi*, that's right. And what is *kiyi*?' Dominic stared directly at Jess.

'It's a cry,' she began.

'Not a cry. A great yell,' he corrected. 'A roar.'

'A roar,' Jess repeated.

'Women cry too easily. They don't roar nearly enough,' he instructed. 'Now, what is *kiyi*?'

'A roar,' Jess responded, the word reverberating against her brain.

'So, Jess, let me hear you roar,' Dominic instructed.

'Just me?' Jess asked.

'These women probably aren't gonna be with you when someone tries to grab you off the street,' he told her.

'You don't seem to have any trouble roaring in the courtroom,' Vasiliki reminded her slyly.

'Come on,' Dominic ordered. 'I'm coming at you. I'm big and I'm dangerous and I want your ass.'

'Hohh!' Jess yelled.

'Louder.'

'Hohh!'

'You can do better than that.'

'*Hohh!*' Jess roared.

'That's better. Now I'm having second thoughts about messing with you. What about you?' Dominic turned his attention to Catarina.

Jess smiled, pushing her shoulders back proudly, listening to the sound of women roaring.

'Okay, let's see those eagle claws through the attacker's eyes,' Dominic told them, once again starting with Jess. 'That's right. A little more defined,' he told her, fitting his fingers over hers, shaping them into an eagle's talon. 'Now, go for my eyes.'

'I can't.'

'If you don't, I'll cut you into little pieces,' he warned. 'Come on. Go for my eyes.'

Jess lunged at her instructor's eyes, watching with relief as he ducked out of her way.

'Not bad. But don't worry about me. I can take care of myself. Try it again.'

She did.

'Better. Next,' he continued, again working his way down the line.

They worked on their eagle claws and zipper punches and hammer fists until they were fluid motions. 'Don't be afraid to drive the bone from your attacker's nose right up into his brain.'

'In that case,' Vasiliki quipped, 'shouldn't we be aiming for below the belt?'

The women laughed.

'Hey, why is it that women don't have any brains?' Vasiliki asked teasingly, her hands on her wide hips.

'Why?' Jess asked, giggling already.

'Because we don't have penises to keep them in!'

The women hooted.

'I got another one,' Vasiliki continued quickly. 'Why can't men ever tell when women have orgasms?'

'Why?' they all asked.

'Because they're never there!'

The women roared.

'Ouch!' their instructor yelled. 'That's enough. I give up. You got me, ladies. I'm a dead man. You can put away those hammer fists. You don't need 'em.'

'What's that small piece of flesh at the end of a penis?' Vasiliki whispered to Jess as the women rearranged themselves in a straight line.

Jess shrugged her shoulders.

'A man!' Vasiliki shouted.

'Okay, okay,' Dominic said, 'let's start putting some of that hostility and aggression to good use, shall we?' He paused to make sure he had their undivided attention. 'Now, I'm gonna teach you some other moves that are designed to help you fend off an attacker. Say you're walking home alone, and some guy grabs you from behind. Or some guy lurches out of the bushes and grabs you. What's the first thing you do?'

'Kiyi!' Maryellen answered.

'*Hohh!*' her daughter said at the same time.

'Good,' Dominic told them. 'Start screaming! Anything that's gonna get attention. Doesn't have to be "Hohh!" but it does have to be loud. Now, what happens if he's got his hand round your mouth, or a knife at your throat? You're not gonna scream. What are you gonna do?'

'Faint,' Catarina said.

'No, you're not gonna faint,' Dominic assured her. 'You're gonna . . . what?'

'Go with him,' Jess stated. 'Don't resist. Use the attacker's force against him.'

'Good. Okay, let's try a few moves.' He motioned to Jess. 'I'm gonna grab you and I want you to pretend to go with me.' He reached out and grabbed Jess's hand, pulling her toward him in slow motion. 'Come with me, that's right. Okay, now you're here, push hard against me. That's right. Use my own weight against me. Use the force of my pulling you in to push me off. Push. Good.' He let go of Jess's hand. 'Once you've got the bastard off balance, remember to use whatever weapon is at hand, including your feet. Kick, bite, gouge, trip. We've gone over some of the things you can do with your hands. Now here's some moves you can do with your feet.'

Jess watched carefully while Dominic executed a few choice maneuvers.

'What about flips? Can we flip 'em into the air?' Vasiliki asked.

They learned flips, how to use their shoulders to lead the attack, carry the weight. At the end of almost two hours, the women were breathing hard and fighting harder.

'Okay, let's see you put this together,' Dominic told them. 'Divide up into twos. Vas, you and Maryellen pair up; Ayisha, go with Catarina. You,' he said, pointing at Jess, 'come with me.'

Jess took several tentative steps toward Dominic. Suddenly he reached out and grabbed her, pulling her toward him. *'Hohh!'* she screamed loudly, hearing the word fill the room, as she instinctively pulled back. Damn, she thought, how many times did she have to be told? Go with him. Don't resist. Go with him.

She allowed herself to be pulled forward, fell against him, then pushed her full weight into him, quickly using her feet to trip him and her shoulder to upend him before falling with him to the ground.

She'd done it, she thought triumphantly. She'd gone with her attacker, used his superior strength against him, flipped him flat on his rear end, proved she wasn't so vulnerable after all. She threw her head back and laughed out loud.

Suddenly she felt a tapping at her forehead, turned to see Dominic smiling at her, the index and middle fingers of his right hand pressed against her temple like the barrel of a gun. His thumb snapped down, then up, as if pulling an imaginary trigger. 'Bang,' he said calmly. 'You're dead.'

Chapter Twenty-Two

'Goddamn, son-of-a-bitch.' Jess was still muttering as she walked along Willow Street. What the hell was she doing wasting her time, her Saturday afternoons, for God's sake, one of the very few free afternoons she had, for God's sake, trying to learn how to defend herself, pretending she was invulnerable, for God's sake, when in truth, she was no match for anyone really determined to do her harm. A well-timed 'Hohh!' wouldn't do much good against a crossbow; an eagle's claw to the eyes was no match for a bullet to the brain.

Here she'd been roaring away, feeling invincible, in control, all-powerful, and all it took was a couple of fingers to rip her illusions into pathetic shreds. There was no such thing as control. She was as vulnerable as anyone else.

Next week, Dominic had assured them, next week he'd show them how to disarm a knife-wielding or gun-toting attacker. Great, Jess thought now, crossing the road. Something to look forward to.

She saw him as soon as she turned the corner onto Orchard Street. He was coming down her front steps, the collar of his bomber jacket turned up against the cold. She stopped, not sure whether to continue or whether to turn on her heels and run as fast as she could in the other direction. Recognizing danger and getting away from it came first on the list of priorities, she had been taught. Running was what worked most often for most women.

She didn't run. She just stood there, stood waiting in the middle of the sidewalk until he turned and saw her, stood there while he walked toward her, stood there as he reached for her, drew her into his arms.

'We need to talk,' Adam said.

* * *

'I grew up in Springfield,' he was saying, leaning across the small table of the Italian restaurant they had gone to their first evening together. It was still early. The restaurant was almost empty. Carla hovered nearby, although she made no move to approach them, as if she understood there were things that needed to be said before anyone could even think of food. 'I think I already told you that I'm an only child,' Adam continued. 'My family is quite well off. My father is a psychiatrist,' he said, and laughed softly, 'so you weren't so far off the mark when you asked me when I'd given up psychiatry for selling shoes. I guess some things are in the genes.

'My mother is an art consultant. She has a thriving little business she runs out of their home. A very large home, I might add, filled with expensive antiques and modern paintings. I grew up with the best of everything. I learned to expect the best of everything. I thought I was entitled to the best of everything.'

He stopped. Jess watched his hands fold and unfold on the top of the table. 'Things always came pretty easily for me: school, grades, girls. Everything I wanted, I more or less got. And for a long time I wanted a girl named Susan Cunningham. She was pretty and popular and as spoiled as I was. Her father is H. R. Cunningham, if you know anything about the construction business.'

Jess shook her head, focusing on his mouth as he spoke.

'Anyway, I wanted her, I set my sights on her, and I married her. Needless to say, since we are now divorced, it was not a marriage made in heaven. We didn't have a thing in common except we both liked looking in the mirror. What can I say? We were two very self-absorbed people who thought everything we did and said deserved a round of applause. When we didn't get it, we pouted and argued and generally made life miserable for one another.

'The only thing we did right was Beth.'

Jess looked from his mouth to his eyes, but Adam quickly looked away. 'Beth?'

'Our daughter.'

'You have a daughter? You said—'

'I know what I said. It wasn't the truth.'

'Go on,' Jess directed softly, holding her breath.

'Beth was born a few years after we got married, and she was the sweetest little thing you ever saw. She looked like a china doll, one of those porcelain figurines that are so beautiful and so delicate you're almost afraid to touch them. Here,' he said, shaking hands fumbling for the wallet in his pocket, removing a small color photograph of a blond, smiling, little girl in a white dress with bright red smocking across the top.

'She's lovely,' Jess agreed, trying to still his hand with her own.

'She's dead,' Adam said, returning the picture to his wallet, stuffing the wallet back into the pocket of his jeans.

'What?! My God! How? When?'

Adam looked across the table at Jess, but his eyes were unfocused and Jess knew he didn't see her. When he spoke again, his voice was strained, distant, as if he was speaking to her from some faraway place. 'She was six years old. My marriage was pretty much over. Susan claimed I was married to my work, I claimed she was married to hers. We both claimed that neither one of us spent enough time with our daughter. We were both right.

'Anyway, my father could see what was going on and he suggested counselling, and we tried it for awhile, but our hearts weren't really in it. Her parents could see what was going on too, but their approach was a little different. Instead of therapy, they bought us a cruise to the Bahamas. They thought that if we could just spend a few weeks alone together, maybe we could sort through our differences. They offered to take care of Beth. We said okay, what the hell, why not?

'Beth didn't want us to go. Kids sense when things aren't right, and I guess she was afraid that if we left, one of us might not come back, I don't know.' He stared toward the door, saying nothing for several seconds. 'Anyway, she started having tantrums, stomach aches, that sort of thing. The morning we were leaving, she complained about a stiff neck. We didn't pay too much attention. She'd been complaining about one thing or another for several days. We just figured it was her way of trying to get us to stay home. We took her temperature, but she didn't have a fever, and Susan's parents assured us that they'd take good care of her, whisk her off to the doctor at the first sign of any real problems. So we left on our cruise.

'That night she developed a slight fever. Susan's parents called the doctor who told them to give Beth a couple of Children's Tylenol and bring her to his office in the morning if she wasn't any better. By the middle of the night, her fever had spiked to almost a hundred and five and she was delirious. My father-in-law bundled her up and took her to the hospital, but it was too late. She was dead before morning.

'Meningitis,' Adam said, answering the question in Jess's eyes.

'My God, how awful.'

'They called us on the ship, arranged for us to get home, but of course there was no home. The only thing that had been keeping us together was gone. We tried grief counselling, but we were far too angry with each other for it to work. Basically, we didn't want it to work. We wanted to blame each other. We wanted what happened to be somebody's fault.

'I thought of suing the doctor, but we had no case. I even thought of suing my in-laws. Instead, I sued for divorce. And then I ran. Gave up my job, gave up my home, gave up everything. What does anything mean anyway when you lose a child? So I took off. Came to the big city. Got a job selling men's ties at Carson, Pirie, Scott and Company. Then I discovered women's shoes and the rest is history.'

He looked from Jess to the door to the table and back to Jess. 'I met a lot of women but I stayed clear of any involvements. I flirted; I played games; I sold lots of shoes. But no way would you catch me drifting into another relationship. No sir. Who needs that kind of heartache?

'And then you walked into the store, and you were banging the heel of that shoe into the palm of your hand so hard it was only a matter of time before one or the other broke. And I looked at you, and I looked into your eyes, and I thought, this person is as wounded inside as I am.'

Jess felt tears fill her eyes and looked briefly away.

'I wasn't going to call you,' he continued, his voice drawing her eyes back to his. 'The last thing I was looking for was to get involved in somebody else's problems, although, who knows, maybe that's exactly what I was looking for. At least that's what my father would probably say. Maybe it was just time, I don't know. But when those damn boots came in, I knew I had to see you again. And so I called and asked you out, although I kept telling myself it would be a one-shot deal. I certainly had no intention of calling you again.

'But I kept finding myself at your door.

'And all this past week, I've been thinking about you, and that even though you told me not to come back, that I had to see you, and I haven't sold a single goddamn pair of shoes . . .'

Jess found herself laughing and crying at the same time. 'And your parents?' she asked.

'I haven't seen them since I left Springfield.'

'That must be very hard on you.'

He looked surprised. 'Most people would have said hard on *them*, but yes, it's been hard on me too,' he admitted.

'Then why do it?'

'I guess I just haven't been ready to face them,' he said. 'I speak to them occasionally. They're trying to understand, give me the time and space I need, but, you're right, I guess it doesn't make much sense anymore. Just that you get into patterns. Dangerous patterns sometimes.'

'You didn't sell shoes back in Springfield, did you?' she asked, knowing the answer but asking anyway.

He shook his head.

'What did you do?'

'You don't want to know.'

'I have this awful feeling I already do,' she stated. 'You're a lawyer, aren't you?'

He nodded guiltily. 'I wanted to tell you, but I kept thinking that since I wasn't going to call you again, what difference did it make?'

'And here I went on and on about the law, about how the legal system works.'

'I loved it. It was like a refresher course. It made me realize how much I've missed the practise of law. Your enthusiasm is contagious. And you're a great teacher.'

'I feel like such an idiot.'

'I'm the only idiot at this table,' he corrected her.

'What kind of law did you practice?' She started laughing even before she heard his answer.

'Criminal,' came the expected response.

'Of course.'

Jess rubbed her forehead, thinking she should have run when she had the chance.

'I really never intended to lie to you,' he reiterated. 'I just never thought it would get this far.'

'How far is it?' Jess asked.

'Far enough for me to know I didn't want to lose you. Far enough for me to think you deserved to know the truth. Far enough for me to think I'm falling in love,' he said softly.

'Tell me about your daughter,' Jess said, reaching across the table and taking his hands in hers.

'What can I say?' he asked, his voice shaking.

'Tell me some of the nice things you remember.'

There was a long pause. Carla approached, then caught the look in Jess's eye, and backed away.

'I remember when she was four years old, and she was all excited because it was her birthday the next day,' Adam began. 'Susan had bought her a new party dress and she couldn't wait to wear it. She'd invited a bunch of kids over for a party, and we'd arranged for a magician and all that stuff you do at kids' parties. Anyway, we went to bed, I'm sound asleep, and all of a sudden I felt this gentle tap on my arm, and I opened my eyes, and there was Beth standing there looking at me. And I said, "What is it, sweetie?" And she said in this very excited little voice, "It's my birthday." And I said, "Yes it is, but go back to bed now, honey, it's three o'clock in the morning." And she said, "Oh, I thought it was time to get up. I got all dressed and everything." And there she was, she'd put on her party dress all by herself, and her shoes and her white frilly socks, and she was standing there all ready to go at three o'clock in the morning, and I remember thinking how wonderful it was to be that excited about something. And I got up and I walked her back to her room, and she got back into her pyjamas, and I tucked her into bed, and she fell right off to sleep.'

'I love that story,' Jess told him.

Adam smiled, tears forming in the corners of his eyes. 'One time at nursery school, she must have been all of three, she told me there was this little boy who was bothering her in class, that he was calling her names and she didn't like it. So I asked her what names the little boy was calling her, and she said, in this sweet, innocent little voice, "He calls me a fucker and a sucker."'

Jess burst out laughing.

'Yes, that was my reaction too, I'm afraid,' Adam said, laughing now as well. 'And of course that only encouraged her. And she looked at me with those enormous brown eyes and said, "Will you come to school with me today, Daddy? Will you tell him not to call me a fucker and a sucker again?"'

'And did you?'

'I told her I was sure she could handle the little bugger all by herself. And I guess she must have, because we never heard about him again.'

'You sound like you were a good daddy.'

'I like to think I was.'

'Were you a good lawyer?' Jess asked after a pause.

'Springfield's finest.'

'Ever think of going back to it?'

'To Springfield, never.'

'To the law.'

He paused, signalled for Carla, who hesitated, then approached cautiously. 'We'll have the special pizza and two glasses of Chianti, please.'

Carla nodded her approval, then left without speaking. 'You didn't answer my question,' Jess reminded him.

'Do I ever think about going back to the law?' he repeated, measuring out each word. 'Yes, I think about it.'

'Would you do it?'

'I don't know. Maybe. My knees are getting a little tired of the shoe business. Maybe if an inspiring case came along, I might be persuaded. Who knows?'

Carla brought their drinks to the table. Jess immediately lifted her glass in the air, clicking it against Adam's.

'To sweet memories,' she said.

'To sweet memories,' he agreed.

As soon as they got to her apartment, she knew something was wrong.

Jess stood frozen outside her door, waiting, listening.

'What's the matter?' Adam asked.

'Can you hear that?' she asked.

'I hear your radio, if that's what you mean. Don't you usually leave it on for the bird?'

'Not that loud.'

Adam said nothing as Jess twisted her key in the lock, gently pushing open the door.

'My God, it's freezing in here,' Jess exclaimed immediately, seeing her antique ivory lace curtains billowing into the air.

'Did you leave the window open?'

'No,' Jess said, hurrying toward the window and bringing it quickly shut. The curtains collapsed around her, covering her face like a shroud, as the music swelled. Opera, she realized, shaking off the curtains as she would a giant spider's web, and rushing to the stereo, turning the music down. *Carmen*. The March of the Toreadors.

'Maybe we should call the police,' Adam was saying.

Jess spun round on the heels of her boots. Except for the open window and the stereo, nothing appeared to have been touched. 'Nothing seems to be missing.' She started toward her bedroom.

'Don't go down there, Jess,' Adam warned.

Jess stopped, turning toward him. 'Why not?'

'Because you don't know what, or who, might be waiting for you,' he reminded her. 'Christ, Jess, you, of all people, should know better. What's the first thing the police advise when you think your place has been burglarized? They tell you not to go inside,' he continued without waiting for her response. 'And why do they tell you that?'

'Because whoever broke in might still be there,' Jess answered quietly.

'Let's get out of here and call the police,' he said again.

Jess took two steps toward him, then stopped dead. 'My God!'

Adam spun round, then back to Jess. 'What? What's the matter?'

'Fred,' she said, her voice shaking, her hand pointing toward the bird cage.

For an instant, Adam looked confused, unable to focus.

'He's gone,' Jess shouted, running to the bird cage, peering in through the bars, checking the inside to make sure the small canary wasn't hidden underneath the paper that lined the bottom. But the bird was definitely gone. 'Somebody opened the cage door and let him out,' Jess cried. 'He must have flown out the window.'

Even as she spoke, Jess realized the unlikelihood of the canary having successfully navigated its way through the billowing curtains without someone's firm hand to guide it, the virtual certainty of its having frozen to death once tossed into the hostile night. Tears once again filled her eyes and she started to cry. 'Why would anyone do that? Who would want to hurt a poor little bird?' Jess moaned into Adam's arms, the unwanted image of a small boy's mutilated pet turtle appearing before her eyes.

They called the police from Walter Fraser's apartment, waited there while the police looked through her apartment.

'They won't find anyone,' Jess said as Walter fixed her a cup of tea, and insisted that she drink it. 'He's long gone.'

'You sound like you know who it is,' Adam commented.

'I do,' Jess nodded, telling them briefly about Rick Ferguson. 'Did you hear anyone go up the stairs, Walter?' Jess asked. 'Or see anyone suspicious?'

'Just your friend here,' Walter remarked, winking at Adam, fitting his round body into a green velvet tub chair.

Jess looked toward Adam.

'He was pacing around outside,' Walter continued. 'Waiting for you, I guess.'

'What about the music?' Adam asked quickly. 'Do you know what time the volume went up?'

'Well, I was out most of the afternoon,' Walter told them, his eyes tracing back through the events of his day, 'and when I came home, the music was already blaring. I thought it was unusual, but then I thought, who am I to complain? Besides, it was Placido Domingo, so it wasn't exactly hard to take.'

'You didn't hear anyone walking around upstairs?' Jess asked.

'If I did, I guess I assumed it was you.' He tapped her hand reassuringly. 'Drink your tea.'

The police asked the same questions, received the same answers. They'd found no one in Jess's apartment. Nothing in the other rooms appeared to have been touched.

'You're sure you didn't leave the window open yourself?' one of the officers, a young woman with short red hair and a razed complexion, inquired, pad and pencil ready to jot down Jess's response.

'I'm very sure.'

'And the stereo and the bird cage, there isn't a chance—'

'No chance,' Jess replied testily.

'We can send someone over to dust for prints,' the older male officer, whose name was Frank Metula, offered.

'Don't bother, Frank,' Jess told him, thinking him greyer than the last time she'd seen him. 'He didn't leave any prints.' Jess told them of her suspicions, that there was already a warrant out for Rick Ferguson's arrest.

'Would you like an officer to watch the house tonight?' Frank asked.

'There's already somebody keeping an eye on me,' Jess told

them. 'A detective my ex-husband hired.'

'He's been watching the house?' Adam asked.

'No, unfortunately. He's been following me, so he wouldn't have seen anything.'

'We'll drive by every half-hour or so anyway,' Frank Metula volunteered.

'He won't be back,' Jess told them. 'At least not tonight.'

'I'll stay with her,' Adam said, his voice brooking no arguments.

'That gun in the night table by your bed,' the female officer remarked, 'I assume you have a license for it?'

Jess said nothing as the young woman followed her older partner out the door.

She lay on top of her bed, wrapped in Adam's arms.

Several times, she drifted off to sleep, wandering in and out of strange, unsettling dreams where everything was larger than life and nothing was as it seemed. The dreams would disappear as soon as she opened her eyes. Each time she moved, she felt Adam's arms tighten around her.

After the police left, she and Adam had returned to her apartment, stumbling toward her bedroom, collapsing on top of the bed, fully clothed. There'd been no fumbling for buttons, no attempt at romance. They'd simply lain there in each other's arms, Jess occasionally closing her eyes, opening them to find Adam watching her.

'What?' she asked now, sitting up, rubbing at the sleep in her eyes, brushing some hair away from her face with her hands.

'I was thinking how beautiful you are,' he said, and Jess almost laughed.

'I have no make-up on,' Jess told him. 'I've been wearing the same sweats all day, and I've been crying half the night. How can you say I'm beautiful?'

'How can you think you're not?' he asked in return, gently massaging the muscles in her back.

Jess arched her back, pressed against his hands. 'I keep hearing those damn toreadors marching through my brain,' she said, referring to the music that had been playing when they'd first come home. 'It's funny, I never really liked *Carmen*.'

'No?'

'Another uppity woman doesn't respond the way a man wants, so he kills her. I get enough of that at work.'

Adam's expert fingers worked their way into her sore muscles. 'Try not to think about any of that now. Just relax. Try to get some sleep.'

'Actually, I'm hungry,' Jess said, surprising herself. 'I can't believe how no matter what happens, I'm always hungry.'

'Want me to fix you one of my special omelets?'

'Too much trouble. How about I just pop a few frozen pizzas in the microwave?'

'Sounds wonderful.

She pushed herself out of bed and shuffled toward the kitchen, hearing her mother call after her to pick up her feet when she walked. Adam was right behind her as she opened the freezer door and pulled out the package of frozen pizzas.

'Just one for me,' he said.

Jess placed three small frozen pizzas on a plate, feeling Adam's arms encircle her waist. She fell back gently against his chest, letting his weight support her, confident he wouldn't let go. She felt his lips in her hair, on her neck, the side of her cheek. Slowly, reluctantly, she pulled out of his embrace, carried the plate of pizzas to the microwave oven, pulled open its door.

Immediately, she felt a giant wave of revulsion sweep through her body, filling her stomach and threatening to drown her from within. She brought her hand to her mouth, gasping in silent horror at what she saw.

The small canary lay stiff on its side, its spindly feet extended straight ahead, its yellow feathers charred and blackened, its eyes glassy in death.

'Oh, my God,' Jess sobbed, falling backward, her body caving forward, nausea causing her head to spin and her legs to wobble.

'What is it?' Adam asked, rushing to catch her before she fell.

Jess opened her mouth to speak, but no words came. In the next instant, she was vomiting all over the floor.

Chapter Twenty-Three

She woke up to the smell of fresh coffee.

Adam was sitting at the foot of her bed, extending a full mug of black coffee toward her. 'I wasn't sure if you'd feel like eating,' he said, shrugging apologetically, 'so I didn't make anything.'

Jess took the mug from his hand, downed a long sip of coffee, swishing it gently against the sides of her mouth, trying to rid herself of the unpleasant taste that still lingered. She vaguely remembered Adam washing her off, getting her out of her wet clothes and into her night-gown, insisting she lie down, tucking her into bed.

'How do you feel?' he asked.

'Like I've been hit by a train,' Jess said. 'Like someone's knocked the stuffing right out of me.'

'Someone did,' he reminded her.

'Oh God,' Jess moaned. 'My poor Fred.' A sob caught in her throat, as she watched her hands start to shake. Adam reached over to steady them with his own, lifting the coffee mug from her grasp and placing it on the night table beside her. 'That was some night,' Jess remarked, and almost laughed. 'I mean, when was the last time you had an evening like last night? You take a woman to dinner, and next thing you know, you're being interviewed by the police and scraping roasted canaries out of microwave ovens.' Jess bit back a fresh onslaught of tears. 'Not to mention your date throws up all over you.'

'Actually, you missed me,' he said softly.

'Really? You must have been the only thing I missed.'

'Just about.'

'Oh God, the thought of cleaning up that mess . . .'

'It's already done.'

Jess stared at him with a gratitude that was almost palpable. 'And Fred?' she whispered.

'He's taken care of,' Adam said simply.

Jess said nothing for several seconds, her sniffling the only sound in the still apartment. 'I'm a real treat,' she said finally, swiping at her tears with the back of her hand. 'Stick with me.'

'I intend to,' Adam said, leaning forward, kissing Jess gently on the lips.

Jess pulled back self-consciously, hiding her mouth behind her hands. 'I should take a shower, brush my teeth.'

He backed away. 'I'll see what I can rustle up for breakfast. Think you could eat anything?'

'I'm ashamed to say, yes.'

He smiled. 'You see, it wasn't so bad after all, was it?'

'What?'

'Throwing up. The very thing you feared the most. You did it – spectacularly, I might add – and you lived to tell the tale.'

'I still hated it.'

'But you survived it.'

'Temporarily.'

'Go take your shower. You'll feel a lot better.' He kissed the tip of her nose, then left the room.

Jess sat for several minutes in bed, staring toward the window, imagining the cold air pressing its face against the pane, like a small child eager to come inside where it was warm. It looked to be a beautiful day, she thought, clear and sunny, only a hint of wind rattling the bare upper branches of the trees. She wondered what fresh terrors the cold sun was hiding. Look at me too long, it seemed to say as she approached her bedroom window, and you'll go blind. Get too close and I'll reduce you to a pile of ashes. '*Hohh!*' she barked, but the sun held fast, undaunted.

She'd never realized before how quiet her apartment was without the subtle song of her canary. That song had always been there, she realized, heading into her bathroom, starting the shower, slipping out of her clothes. Such a gentle sound, she thought, closing the bathroom door, hearing Adam busy in the kitchen, stepping inside the tub, pulling the shower curtain closed. So soothing, so constant, so life-affirming.

Now silenced.

'Goddamn you, Rick Ferguson,' she whispered.

He was getting closer, cleverly orchestrating his every move in order to achieve the maximum effect, Jess realized, positioning herself directly under the hot spray of the shower. Exactly what he'd done with Connie DeVuono. The effortless, unseen break-ins, the mounting campaign of terror, the sadistic slaying of innocent pets, scaring the hapless woman half to death before moving in to finish her off. So, he was still pulling the wings off butterflies, Jess thought, recalling the smile that had sent shivers through her body the first time she'd seen him. The smile had said it all.

'*Hohh!*' Jess cried, spinning round quickly, her fingers twisting into sharp claws, slicing through the steam. Her heel slipped on the bottom of the tub. She skidded, lost her balance, fell forward, her arms shooting forward, the wrist of her left hand smacking sharply against the tile wall, her right hand grabbing for the clear plastic shower curtain, pulling on it, hearing it snap, break away from its hooks, then miraculously holding, supporting her weight, permitting her to regain her footing. 'Goddamn it,' she said, throwing her head back, her wet hair whipping against the top of her spine, taking several deep breaths, filling her lungs with hot air.

She reached for the soap, rubbing it harshly across her body and into her hair. She didn't have the patience for shampoo. Soap would do just as well, she thought, feeling the lather growing between her fingers as she worked it into her hair, suddenly reminded of the shower scene from Alfred Hitchcock's *Psycho*.

In her mind she watched a hapless Janet Leigh begin her innocent ablutions, saw the bathroom door creak slowly open, the strange shadowy figure approach, the large butcher's knife rise into the air as the shower curtains were pulled open, the knife coming down against the screaming woman's flesh, again and again and again.

'Jesus Christ,' Jess exclaimed loudly, impatiently rinsing the soap out of her hair. 'Are you trying to do Rick Ferguson's job for him? What's the matter with you?'

And then she heard the bathroom door open and saw Rick Ferguson walk through.

Jess held her breath, trying to force a scream from her mouth, to make any kind of sound at all. *Hohh!* she thought wildly, but no sound emerged. Rick Ferguson stood watching her for several seconds from the doorway as Jess reached over and twisted the shower taps to Off. The water trickled to a stop. And suddenly he was striding toward the tub, his arms extended, reaching for the curtain. Where was Adam? Jess wondered, fumbling for whatever weapons were at hand, seizing on the soap, preparing to hurl it at Rick Ferguson's head. How had he gotten inside? What had he done to Adam?

Hands grabbed the shower curtain, pushed it aside. Jess lunged forward. '*Hohh!*' she cried loudly, hurling the soap at her attacker's head. He flinched, fell backward against the sink, his hands raised to protect his face.

'Jesus Christ, Jess,' she heard him yell. 'Are you nuts? Are you trying to kill me?'

Jess stared at the man cowering in front of her. 'Don?' she asked meekly.

'Jess, are you all right?' Adam called, racing into the room.

'I'm not sure,' Jess told him honestly. 'What are you doing here, Don? You scared the life out of me.'

'I scared you?' Don demanded. 'I almost had a heart attack, for God's sake.'

'I told you to wait until she had finished her shower,' Adam said, not doing a very good job of hiding his growing smile.

'What are you doing here?' Jess asked again.

Don looked from Jess to Adam and then back to Jess. 'Can I talk to you for a few minutes alone?'

Jess pushed some wet hairs away from her forehead, realizing suddenly that she was standing naked in front of two men, one of whom was her ex-husband, the other her would-be lover.

'Could somebody please hand me a towel,' she asked, trying to sound casual.

Adam immediately wrapped her in a large peach-colored bath towel, helping her out of the tub and onto the bathmat. Jess found herself squeezed between the two men, not sure how she wound up in situations like this one, wondering whether it was all another of her silly dreams. The small bathroom, barely big enough for one, was threatening to explode with three.

'It's okay, Adam,' Jess assured him.

Adam looked toward Don, then gave the smile that had been playing with the corners of his mouth full rein. 'We have to stop meeting like this,' he told Don before leaving the room.

'What's going on, Don?' she asked.

'Suppose you tell me.'

'You're the one who barged into my bathroom,' she reminded him.

'I didn't barge in. I called your name a couple of times. I thought I heard you say something. I assumed you said to come in. So I did. Next thing I know I'm getting beaned with a bar of soap.'

'I thought you were Rick Ferguson.'

'Rick Ferguson?'

'My imagination's in overdrive these days,' she told him. 'Do you mind if we go into the bedroom. I'm feeling a little ridiculous talking to you dressed in a towel.'

'Jess, we used to be married, remember?'

'You still haven't told me what you're doing here.'

Jess walked past him into her bedroom, pulling on her housecoat and using the towel to dry her hair.

'I was worried about you,' he said. 'The guy I hired to watch you said there was some excitement here with the police.'

'That was last night.'

'I didn't get home till this morning,' he admitted sheepishly.

Jess looked at him with mock reproach. In truth, she felt enormous relief.

'I came right over. Your boyfriend,' he said, almost choking on the words, 'let me in. He said you were in the shower, but—'

'But you wanted to see for yourself. Well, you certainly did.'

'What happened last night?' Don asked.

Jess told him about returning home, meeting Adam outside, finding the window in her apartment open, the bird missing. About waking up in the night hungry, deciding on a snack, opening the door to the microwave oven, finding her dead canary inside.

'Jesus, Jess. I'm so sorry.'

Jess wiped away a few stray tears, amazed at her seemingly endless supply. 'He was such a sweet little bird. He just liked to sit in his cage and sing all day. What kind of sick mind . . . ?'

'There are a lot of sick people out there,' Don said sadly.

'One in particular.'

'I have something to tell you,' Don stated. 'Something that should put your mind at rest. If that's possible.'

'What's that?'

'Rick Ferguson walked into the police station at eight o'clock this morning and turned himself in.'

'What?' Jess ran immediately to her closet, started fumbling for some clothes.

'He claims he had no idea the police were looking for him. He'd been with a woman he'd met.'

'Sure he was. He just doesn't happen to remember her name.'

'I don't think he asked.'

Jess pulled on some underwear, followed quickly by her jeans and a heavy blue sweater. 'How long have you known about this?'

Jess noted the sadness that registered in Don's eyes. 'There were two messages on my service when I got home this morning,' he said evenly. 'One concerned you and what went on here last night; the other was from Rick Ferguson, telling me he'd been home, talked to his mother, found out the police were looking for him, and that he was headed for the station to turn himself in. I'm on my way down there now. I think I might be able to persuade him it's in his best interests to cooperate with the State's Attorney's office.'

'Good. I'm going with you.' Jess pulled her wet hair into a ponytail.

'What about Chef Boyardee?'

Jess looked through the bedroom wall toward the kitchen. 'Breakfast will have to wait till I get back.'

'You're going to leave the man alone in your apartment?' Don's voice was incredulous. 'Jess, need I remind you that the last time he was here, you woke up to find all your panties slashed to ribbons.'

'Don, don't be ridiculous.'

'Was it just a coincidence that he turned up here last night, Jess?' Don asked, impatiently. 'Hasn't it even occurred to you that it might have been Adam who broke into your apartment? That it might have been Adam who killed your canary? You caught him leaving the scene, for God's sake!'

'I didn't catch him,' Jess protested, her voice hollow. 'He was here looking for me. He hadn't been upstairs.'

'Says who?'

'He does,' Jess stammered.

'And you believe everything he tells you? You don't even admit the possibility that he might be lying?'

'Tell me no secrets, I'll tell you no lies,' Jess said quietly, not realizing she was speaking out loud.

'What?'

Jess snapped back into the present. 'It doesn't make sense, Don. Why would Adam be doing these things? What motive could he possibly have?'

'I have no idea. I only know that ever since you met this guy, a lot of strange things have been happening to you. Strange and dangerous.'

'But Adam has no reason to hurt me.'

The look on Don's face changed from concern to sadness. 'Are you falling in love with him, Jess?' he asked.

Jess released a deep sigh. 'I don't know.'

'Jesus, Jess, he's a shoe salesman, for God's sake. What are you doing with this guy?'

'He isn't a shoe salesman,' Jess said quietly.

'What?'

'Well, he is, I guess,' Jess corrected herself. 'Not that it matters.'

'What are you trying to say, Jess?'

'He's a lawyer.'

'What?'

'He's a lawyer.'

'A lawyer,' Don repeated.

'Something happened. He got disillusioned, so he gave it up . . .'

'And found fulfillment selling shoes, is that what you're seriously trying to tell me?'

'It's a very long story.'

'And a very tall one. Jess, are you so enamored of this guy that you can't recognize a crock of shit when it hits you in the face.'

'It's very complicated.'

'Only lies are complicated,' Don told her. 'The truth is usually very simple.'

Jess looked from the floor to the ceiling, then over to the window, anywhere but at her ex-husband, refusing to consider the possibility he might be right.

'You know I only want what's best for you, don't you?' Don was saying.

Jess nodded, tears returning to her eyes. She brushed them angrily away.

'That's all I've ever wanted,' he added quietly.

Jess nodded. 'We should get over to the station,' she said. 'I have a few questions I want to ask your client.'

Rick Ferguson was slumped into the same chair, in the same interrogation room, in almost the same position, as when Jess had questioned him the last time. Two plain clothes detectives sat off to one corner. For an instant, Jess felt as if she'd never left.

He was wearing the same brown leather jacket, the same blue jeans, the same spike-toed black boots. The same superior attitude clung to his posture. As soon as Jess walked in the room, he stiffened, following her movement with his hooded, cobra-like eyes. Slowly, he uncoiled his body, as if preparing to strike. Then immediately, he relaxed, opening his legs wide, as if deliberately exposing the bulge at his crotch. 'I like your hair,' he drawled at Jess, scratching lazily at the inside of his high. 'Wet suits you. I'll have to remember that.'

'Shut up, Rick,' Don ordered, following Jess into the room. 'And sit up straight in the chair.'

Rick Ferguson pushed his body up into something vaguely resembling a sitting position though he kept his legs wide apart. His long hair hung loose to his shoulders. Absently, he reached up to flick it behind his ears. Jess noted the presence of an earring in his left ear.

'Is that new?' she asked, pointing to the small gold loop.

'How observant you are, Jess,' Ferguson remarked. 'Yes, it's new. I also got a new tattoo. The scales of justice.' He laughed. 'On my ass. Want to see it?'

'Cut the shit, Rick,' Don told him succinctly.

Ferguson looked surprised. 'Hey, what are you getting so bent out of shape about? You're *my* lawyer, remember?'

'Not if you keep this up.'

'Hey, man, what's going on here?' His eyes travelled rapidly between Don and Jess. 'You got something going with the pretty prosecuting attorney?'

'You said you'd answer a few of Ms Koster's questions,' Don said, his voice sharp. 'I'll tell you if there's anything I think you shouldn't answer.'

'Hey, my life's an open book. Fire away, counsellor.'

'Did you kill Connie DeVuono?' Jess asked immediately.

'No.'

'Where were you on the day she disappeared?'

'What day was that?'

She gave him the exact date and appproximate time.

He shrugged. 'I think I was home with my mother that afternoon. She hadn't been feeling too well.'

'You work where?'

'You know where.'

'Answer the question.'

'Ask me nicely.'

Jess glanced at her ex-husband.

'Answer the question, Rick. You agreed to cooperate.'

'She doesn't have to be rude.' Rick Ferguson's hand rubbed at the crotch of his jeans.

'You work at the Ace Magnetic Wire Factory, is that correct?'

'Bingo.'

'Can you describe your job for me, Mr Ferguson?'

'Mr Ferguson?' he repeated, sitting up tall. 'I think I like the way you say that.'

'Tell her what you do, Rick,' Don advised.

'She knows what I do. Let her tell me.'

'You operate a forklift that transfers spools of wire from the warehouse down to the dock, is that right?'

'That's right.'

'Before that, you were a press man, someone who presses out the wire.'

'Right again. You've obviously done your homework, Jess. I had no idea you were so interested in me.'

'What do you make of the fact that the wire you take down to the dock every day is the same wire that was used to kill Connie DeVuono?'

'Don't answer that,' Don said quickly.

Rick Ferguson said nothing.

'Where have you been the last few days?'

'Nowhere special.'

'Can you be more specific?'

'Not really.'

'Why did you sneak out of the house in the middle of the night?'

'I never snuck out of the house.'

'Your house was being watched. You were seen entering it on the night of 9 December. You were not seen leaving. You didn't show up for work the next morning.'

'I took a few days' sick leave. I'm entitled. And hey, if you didn't see me walk out of my front door, that's your fault, not mine.'

'You didn't run off?'

'If I'd run off, why would I have come back? Why would I voluntarily turn myself in?'

'You tell me.'

'There's nothing to tell. I didn't run off. Hey, as soon as I heard you guys were looking for me, I rushed right over. I had no reason to run away. You got nothing on me.'

'On the contrary, Mr Ferguson,' Jess told him, 'I have motive, I have opportunity, I have access to the murder weapon.'

Rick Ferguson shrugged. 'You got nothing,' he repeated.

'You never answered my questions about where you've been the past several days.'

'Yes, I did. It just wasn't the answer you wanted to hear.'

'What about yesterday?'

'What about it?'

'Where were you yesterday? Surely, you can remember that far back?'

'I can remember. I just don't see where it's any of your business.' He looked at his lawyer. 'What's where I was yesterday got to do with why I'm being arrested?'

'Answer the question,' Don told him, and Jess thanked him with an almost imperceptible nod of her head.

'I was with a girl I met.'

'What's her name?'

'Melanie,' he said.

'Last name?'

'I never asked for her last name.'

'Where does she live?'

'I have no idea. We went to a motel.'

'Which motel?'

'The one that was closest.'

Jess looked from the blood-red concrete floor to the acoustic tile ceiling in exasperation. 'In other words, you can't prove where you were yesterday.'

'Why should I have to?' Again, Rick Ferguson turned to Don,

his eyes squinting into a question. 'What does where I was yesterday have to do with this DeVuono dame's murder?'

'Ms Koster's apartment was broken into sometime between two in the afternoon and seven in the evening yesterday,' Don told him.

'Gee, that's too bad,' Rick Ferguson said, his voice a smile. 'Anything missing?'

Jess pictured the open window and empty bird cage that greeted her upon her return to her apartment. 'You tell me,' she said, her voice flat, void of emotion.

'What – you think I did it?' A look of reproach filled Rick Ferguson's face.

'Did you?' Jess asked.

'I already told you. I was with a girl named Melanie.'

'We have witnesses who can place you at the scene,' Jess lied, wondering whether Don would object, grateful when he didn't.

'Then your witnesses are mistaken,' Rick said calmly. 'Why would I want to break into your apartment? That wouldn't be very smart.'

'Nobody claimed you were very smart,' Jess told him.

Rick Ferguson clutched at his chest. 'Ouch! You sure know how to hurt a guy, Jess.' He winked. 'Maybe some day I can return the favor.'

'Rick,' Don said before Jess could respond, 'have you ever met a man named Adam Stohn?'

Jess's head snapped toward her ex-husband.

'What's that name again?' Rick Ferguson was asking.

'Adam Stohn,' Don repeated.

Jess turned her attention back to Rick Ferguson, reluctantly waiting for his reply.

'Is he one of your supposed witnesses?' Rick Ferguson asked, then shook his head. 'I'm afraid the name doesn't ring a bell.' He smiled. 'But then, you know how I am with names.'

'This is getting us nowhere,' Jess said impatiently. 'You're saying you know absolutely nothing about Connie DeVuono's murder? Is that what you're telling us?'

'That's what I'm telling you.'

'You've just been playing games with us,' Jess said angrily.

'I've just been telling you the truth.'

'In that case,' Jess told him, 'consider yourself under arrest for the murder of Connie DeVuono.' She turned and strode briskly from the room.

Don was right behind her. 'Jess, wait a minute, for Christ's sake. Think about what you're doing.' The officers in the outer area looked discreetly away.

'There's nothing to think about.'

'You don't have a case, Jess.'

'Stop telling me I don't have a case. I have motive. I have opportunity. I have the murder weapon. What more do I need?'

'Some fingerprints on the murder weapon would be nice. Some hard DNA evidence linking Connie DeVuono to my client, which I know you don't have. A few witnesses who might have seen my client and the victim together around the time she disappeared, which you also don't have. A bridge between the dead body and Rick Ferguson, Jess, something to connect the two.'

'I'll connect them.'

'I wish you luck.'

'I'll see you in court.'

Chapter Twenty-Four

Jess was arguing with her trial supervisor right up to the moment of Rick Ferguson's preliminary hearing the following Friday.

'I still think it was a mistake not to take this before the Grand Jury,' Jess told Tom Olinsky as she walked beside him through the mistletoe-laden corridors, paying scant attention to the Christmas and Channukah decorations that covered the walls.

'And I told you that we don't have a strong enough case to take before the Grand Jury.'

Tom Olinsky walked very quickly for such a big man, Jess thought, having to take very long strides just to keep up.

'Your ex-husband has already hit us with a motion *in limine.*'

'Damn him,' Jess muttered, still smarting over Don's move to limit the state's introduction of evidence.

'He's just doing his job, Jess.'

'And I'm trying to do mine.'

They pushed their way through a reception area that was all but overwhelmed by a huge, tinsel-draped, popcorn-swaddled Christmas tree, into the exterior hall, heading toward the elevators.

'A Grand Jury would have rubber-stamped the indictment,' Jess continued. 'We'd have a trial date set by now.' Jess also wouldn't have had to face her ex-husband in court so early, she admitted to herself, since the defense wasn't present at Grand Jury proceedings, and no cross-examination of witnesses was allowed. The prosecution simply presented its case to the twenty-three members of the Grand Jury and asked them to find a 'true bill', which held the defendant over for trial.

When a case was shaky, and everyone but Jess seemed to agree this case was shaky, the prosecutor's office usually went the route of a preliminary hearing. That way, the onus was on the judge, and not the State's Attorney, to decide whether there was sufficient evidence to hold a person over for trial. It was a very political decision, Jess recognized, a way to get the case out of the system. The State's Attorney's office didn't like to prosecute a case when there was a good chance the state might lose. A preliminary hearing let the prosecutor's office off the hook by forcing the judge to decide whether or not there was probable cause to hold a person over for trial. The whole procedure could take as little as twenty minutes.

Jess was reminded of Don's longstanding advice to think of the criminal justice system as a game: in a preliminary hearing the state put forth its evidence in as general terms as possible, careful to reveal the least amount of evidence in hand, just enough to produce a finding of probable cause; the defense, meanwhile, tried to uncover as much information about the prosecution's case as possible.

If the prosecutor's office was successful, an arraignment would follow three weeks after the preliminary hearing, wherein the accused would appear before the Chief Judge for the criminal division of the circuit court of Cook County to hear the charges read aloud. According to the unwritten rules of the game, this right was usually waived by the defense counsel, and the accused then entered a plea of either guilty or not-guilty.

The accused *always* pleaded not guilty, Jess acknowledged, following Tom Olinsky into the elevator, suppressing a smile as the three people who were already inside took a giant collective step back to give him room.

The Chief Judge then used a computer to randomly assign which judge would try the case. A court date was selected, and the case now became one of approximately 300 cases on a judge's call. Murder cases generally took anywhere from a few months to a year to hit court, and this was where the game started to get really interesting.

The state could no longer be coy with its evidence. It was obliged to reveal the full extent of its case against the defendant. This was done through a series of 'discoveries'. Any evidence that would be helpful to the accused, all police reports, experts' statements, documents, photos, names and addresses of witnesses, prior convictions, and so on, would have to be handed over to the defense. The defense, in turn, was obligated to disclose its own list of witnesses, along with whatever medical and scientific reports it planned to introduce into evidence, and to reveal its main strategy of defense, be it alibi, consent, self-defense, or varying degrees of insanity.

If the defendant was denied bail, the state had 120 days to bring him to trial, if this was the defendant's wish. It always was. If the accused was out on bond, the state had 160 days to bring him to trial, if the defendant so demanded. He almost never did.

Even if the accused wanted to go to trial right away, the lawyer would need time to review all the state's evidence. Still, part of the poker game on the part of the defense was to keep the demand for trial running. That tended to unnerve the state, occasionally forcing the prosecutor's office to trial before it was ready. Justice delayed, after all, was justice denied.

If after 160 days the prosecution still wasn't ready, the defense could bring a speedy trial discharge motion before the judge and have the case thrown out of court. This was the worst thing that could happen to an assistant state's attorney, Jess knew, stepping off the elevator at the ground floor ahead of Tom Olinsky, although he quickly passed her as they marched through the corridor that connected the Administration building to the Court House.

But all that was later, Jess reminded herself, her heels clicking along the granite floor. First she had to make it through the preliminary hearing.

The preliminary hearing was being held in one of the smaller, more modern courtrooms on the second floor. 'Let's take the stairs,' Tom Olinsky suggested, walking between the tall, brown, Doric-style pillars, past the bank of ten elevators, to the stairwell. For a man of his girth, he was amazingly spry, Jess thought, thinking she would be exhausted before she even set foot in the courtroom.

Jess smelled the food emanating from the various lunch rooms on the first floor as they made their way up the stairs, and she wondered if Don and Rick Ferguson were having coffee in the room reserved for defendants and their lawyers, the room that the State's Attorney's office not so affectionately referred to as the gang-bangers' lounge.

She hadn't seen Don all week, hadn't even spoken to him since he'd filed his motion *in limine*. She knew, as even Adam had reminded her, that her ex-husband was only doing his job, but it made her furious anyway. Did he have to be so damn *good* at his job?

As for Adam, she hadn't seen him all week either, although she'd spoken to him every night over the phone. He was in Springfield, visiting his parents for the first time in almost three years. He'd be back in Chicago tomorrow. Meanwhile, he called every night at ten o'clock to wish her a good night's sleep. And to tell her he loved her.

Jess hadn't yet spoken of her feelings. She wasn't sure quite what they were. Certainly she was attracted to him; certainly she liked him enormously; certainly she understood the pain he'd been through. Did she love him? She didn't know. She was afraid to let herself go enough to find out.

Go with it, she heard distant voices murmur. Go with it. Go with it.

Maybe after the preliminary hearing was over. Maybe after she'd succeeded in getting Rick Ferguson bound over for trial, she could let go of the nagging doubts about Adam that Don had planted in her brain, concentrate on letting whatever was developing between them progress naturally.

Trust your instincts, the voices purred. Trust your instincts.

'After you,' Tom Olinsky said, pulling open the door and allowing Jess to step inside first. An odd time for chivalry, Jess thought, looking around the circular, windowless courtroom.

The courtrooms on the second, third and fourth floors reminded Jess of small spaceships. Once inside the outer doors, one found oneself in a sparse, predominantly grey, glass-enclosed space, where spectators waited in a semi-circular area on the other side of the glass from the actual proceedings. The judge's bench was directly opposite the outer doors, the jury box either to the judge's left or right, depending on the courtroom. In this courtroom, the jury box, which would remain empty during the preliminary hearing, was to the judge's left, and Jess's right.

After four o'clock in the afternoon, these courts handled nothing but drug cases. They were always busy.

The various clerks were likewise busy at their stations as Jess and Tom Olinsky stepped up to the prosecutor's table where Neil Strayhorn was already settled in. Jess deposited her briefcase on the floor, perusing the room to see whether any of her witnesses had yet arrived.

'No one's here,' Neil told her.

'You checked with the police to make sure they got their notification of trial?' Tom Olinsky asked, sitting down beside Neil, his wide hips spilling over the sides of the wooden chair.

'At 7:45 this morning,' Jess answered, wondering why he was asking her such a basic question. Obviously she had checked with the police to make sure they'd be here. She'd also called the crime lab to go over the analysis of the physical evidence in the case, and conferred with Hilary Waugh about the questions she'd be asking her on the stand. Connie's mother, Mrs Gambala, would also be testifying, along with one of Connie's co-workers and Connie's closest friend.

They would corroborate the state's contention that Connie was deathly afraid of Rick Ferguson because of threats he'd made against her life if she proceeded with the assault charges against him, thereby providing the state with the motive for the murder.

'Tom, you don't have to stay,' Jess told her trial supervisor. 'Neil and I will be fine.'

'I want to see how this one goes down,' he said, leaning back into the chair, his weight lifting its front legs off the floor.

Jess smiled, realizing she was grateful for his show of support. He'd given her a hard time all week, fretted openly that he thought the state's case too circumstantial, but in the end he'd gone along with her intense desire to proceed.

'I have a feeling this one's looking for you,' Tom said as the door to the courtroom opened and an older woman, dressed all in black, tentatively poked her head inside.

'Mrs Gambala,' Jess said warmly, approaching her and taking hold of both her hands. 'Thank you for coming.'

'We put that monster away?' Mrs Gambala said, her statement curling into a question.

'We'll put that monster away,' Jess assured her. 'You remember my associate, Neil Strayhorn. And this is Tom Olinsky, my trial supervisor. Tom, this is Connie's mother, Mrs Gambala.'

'Hello, Mrs Gambala,' he said, slowly rising to his feet. 'Hopefully, we'll have you out of here pretty quickly.'

'You see that justice is done,' Mrs Gambala said in return.

'You'll have to wait outside until you're called as a witness,' Jess explained, leading her back into the hallway. 'You can sit here.'

Jess pointed to a bench along the wall. The older woman remained on her feet. 'You understand what I'm going to ask you on the stand? You're comfortable with the questions I'm going to ask?'

Mrs Gambala nodded. 'I tell the truth. Connie, she was terrified of that man. He threatened to kill her.'

'Good. Now, don't worry. If you don't understand a question, or you don't understand anything that's going on, anything the defense attorney asks you, just say so. Take all the time you need.'

'We put that monster away,' Mrs Gambala said again, walking toward the window at the end of the corridor, staring out at the cold grey day.

The other witnesses arrived soon after. Jess spoke briefly with the police and the forensics expert, thanked Connie's friend and her co-worker for being so prompt. She guided them toward the bench and told them they would be called shortly. Then she returned to the courtroom.

The spectator section was filling up, mostly lawyers and their clients awaiting their turn before the judge. Don and Rick Ferguson had yet to arrive. Was it possible that Don was planning some last minute pyrotechnics?

The court clerk loudly cleared his throat before calling the court to order and introducing Judge Caroline McMahon. Caroline McMahon was a woman in her early forties, whose round face belied her angular frame. She had short dark hair and a pale complexion that blushed deep red whenever she lost her patience, a not infrequent occurrence.

Don pushed through the doors of the courtroom with appropriate dramatic flourish just as the clerk was reading Rick Ferguson's name aloud.

'Here, Your Honor,' Don said loudly, leading his client to the defense table.

'Is the defense ready?' Caroline McMahon asked, a trace of sarcasm evident in her voice as she peered over her reading glasses at the tardy attorney for the defense.

'Yes, Your Honor.'

'And the state?'

'The state is ready, Your Honor,' Jess answered, almost eagerly.

'I'm going to reserve judgement on your motion, Mr Shaw,' Caroline McMahon announced immediately, 'until I see where the prosecution's case is going. Ms Koster, you may proceed.'

'Thank you, Your Honor,' Jess stated, walking toward the empty witness stand. 'The state calls Detective George Farquharson.'

Detective George Farquharson, tall and fair-skinned and balding, marched through the outer doors of the court, through the already crowded spectator section, through the glass doors that split the courtroom in half, to the stand. He was duly sworn in and seated, stating his name and rank clearly and loudly, a man obviously comfortable with himself and the job he was about to do.

'On the afternoon of 5 December,' Jess began, 'did you have occasion to investigate the death of Connie DeVuono?'

'I did.'

'Can you tell us about it?'

'My partner and I drove out to Skokie Lagoons in response to a telephone call from a Mr Henry Sullivan, who'd been ice-fishing and come across Mrs DeVuono's body. It was obvious as soon as we saw the body that she'd been murdered.'

'How was it obvious?'

'The piece of wire was still wrapped round her neck,' Detective Farquharson answered.

'And what did you do after you saw the body, Detective Farquharson?'

'We cordoned off the area and called the Medical Examiner's office. Then the body was placed in an ambulance and sent over to Harrison Street.'

'Thank you, Detective.'

Don rose briefly. 'Did you find any evidence at the scene, Detective Farquharson, other than the wire round Mrs DeVuono's neck?'

'No.'

'No footprints? No cigarette butts? No clothing?'

'No, sir.'

'So there was nothing at the scene linking my client to the deceased?'

'No, sir.'

'Thank you.' Don returned to his seat.

'You may step down, Detective Farquharson,' Judge McMahon told him.

'The state calls Dr Hilary Waugh.'

Hilary Waugh wore a royal blue pantsuit and a simple strand of pearls, her dark hair pulled into her trademark French braid.

'Dr Waugh,' Jess said, as Hilary Waugh settled into the witness stand, 'what were the results of the post-mortem on Connie DeVuono?'

'We found that Connie DeVuono died of asphyxiation as the result of being strangled with a piece of magnetic wire. The wire also severed her jugular, but that was after death.'

'Was there evidence Connie DeVuono had been beaten?'

'Yes. Her left wrist had been broken as well as several ribs, and her jaw had been dislocated.'

'Was there evidence of sexual assault?'

'Yes. The body was nude, and the vagina showed signs of trauma.'

'How long had Mrs DeVuono been dead before she was found, Doctor?'

'Approximately six weeks. We identified her through her dental records.'

'Thank you.

'Was there any sperm found in the vagina?' Don asked, quickly jumping to his feet.

'We found no traces.'

'Any bite marks?'

'Just from animals.'

'Any traces of blood that weren't Connie DeVuono's?'

'No.'

'Traces of saliva?'

'None that we could find at this time. Mrs DeVuono had been dead for about six weeks and was in a state of advanced decomposition.'

'Yet, due to the severe cold, the decomposition hadn't advanced as much as it would normally. Isn't that correct?'

'Yes.'

'And yet you found no blood samples, no teeth marks other than animal, no saliva traces, nothing of any real significance. Certainly nothing that would help you identify the perpetrator of this crime.'

'No,' the doctor admitted.

'Thank you, Doctor.'

'The state calls Dr Rudy Wang,' Jess said immediately following Hilary Waugh's exit from the stand.

An expert in forensics, Dr Wang was short, grey-haired, and, despite his Oriental-sounding name, of Polish extraction. He wore a brown pinstripe suit and a worried expression that made him look as if he had forgotten to wear his glasses.

'Dr Wang, did you have a chance to examine the wire that

was used to strangle Connie DeVuono?' Jess asked, approaching the witness stand.

'Yes, I did.'

'Could you describe it, please?'

'It was a magnetic wire, steel-grey, eighteen inches long and approximately a quarter of an inch round. Very strong, very sturdy.'

'You also examined a similar piece of wire taken from the Ace Magnetic Wire Factory where the defendant works, did you not?'

'I did. They were identical.'

'Thank you, Dr Wang.'

Don was on his feet and in front of the witness before Jess had a chance to return to her table. 'Dr Wang, were there any fingerprints on the wire that was found round Connie DeVuono's neck?'

'No.'

'Partial prints? Anything?'

'No. Nothing.'

'And how common would you say this type of wire is?'

Rudy Wang shrugged. 'Pretty common, I guess.'

'You could buy it in any hardware store?'

'You might be able to find it in a hardware store, yes.'

'Thank you.'

'You may step down,' the judge directed.

Don smiled over at Jess before returning to his seat.

'I hate it when defense lawyers look so happy,' Tom Olinsky whispered to Jess.

'The state calls Mrs Rosaria Gambala,' Jess said loudly, anger gripping her hands, twisting them into tight fists.

Mrs Gambala, in a long-sleeved black sweater over a long black skirt, ambled slowly from the back of the courtroom toward the witness stand, swaying from side to side as she walked, as if she was in danger of tipping over. She steadied herself against the front of the witness stand as she was sworn in, her dark eyes nervously scanning the room, stumbling when she saw the defendant. A muffled cry escaped her lips.

'Are you okay, Mrs Gambala?' Jess asked. 'Do you need a glass of water?'

'I'm okay,' the woman said, her voice surprisingly strong.

'Can you state your relation to the deceased?' Jess asked.

'I'm her mother,' the older woman answered, speaking of her daughter in the present tense.

'And when did you first report your daughter missing, Mrs Gambala?'

'On 29 October 1992, when she didn't pick up Steffan after work.'

'Steffan being her son?'

'Yes. My grandson. He comes to my house after school, till Connie is finished working. She always calls before she leaves work.'

'And on the afternoon of 29 October, your daughter called and said she was on her way, but then she never showed up, is that right?'

'I called the police. They say I have to wait twenty-four hours. I call you. You no home.'

'Why did you call me, Mrs Gambala?'

'Because you were her lawyer. You were supposed to help her. You knew her life was in danger. You knew about the threats he made.' She pointed an accusatory finger at Rick Ferguson.

'Objection!' Don called out. 'Hearsay.'

'This is a preliminary hearing,' Jess reminded her ex-husband. 'Hearsay is admissible.'

'I'm going to allow it,' the judge ruled. 'Proceed, Ms Koster.'

Jess returned her attention to Rosaria Gambala. 'Rick Ferguson made threats against your daughter's life?'

'Yes. She was so afraid of him. He say he's going to kill her.'

'Objection,' Don called again. 'Your Honor, can we approach the bench?'

The two lawyers moved directly toward the judge.

'Your Honor, I believe now would be a good time to rule on my motion to limit the evidence introduced in this case on the grounds that almost all the evidence against my client is hearsay, and highly prejudicial,' Don began, taking the initiative.

'Which is perfectly admissible in a preliminary hearing,' Jess said again.

'Your Honor, there is no direct evidence that my client ever threatened Connie DeVuono.'

'The state will call two more witnesses in addition to Mrs Gambala who will testify that Connie was scared to death of the defendant, that he threatened to kill her if she proceeded with her plans to testify against him in court.'

'Your Honor, such hearsay evidence is not only prejudicial, but irrelevant.'

'Irrelevant?' Jess asked, hearing her voice bounce off the surrounding glass. 'It goes to motive, Your Honor. Connie DeVuono had accused Rick Ferguson of raping and beating her—'

'Something that was never proved in a court of law,' Don reminded her.

'Because Connie DeVuono never made it to court. She was murdered before she could testify.'

'Your Honor,' Don argued, 'my client has always claimed to be innocent in the attack on Mrs DeVuono. In fact, he has an airtight alibi for the time of the alleged attack.'

'I will call several police officers to testify that Connie DeVuono positively identified Rick Ferguson as the man who beat and raped her,' Jess offered.

'Hearsay, Your Honor,' Don stated flatly. 'And since Connie DeVuono didn't say anything to the police about Rick Ferguson until three days after she was attacked, her statement cannot be classified an "excited utterance", and therefore is not an exception to the hearsay rule. The only person, Your Honor, who can identify my client as her assailant, who can testify that he threatened her life, is dead. Since it was never proved that my client had anything to do with the attack on Mrs DeVuono, I must ask that you disallow the introduction of such highly inflammatory and prejudicial evidence against my client.'

'Your Honor,' Jess stated quickly, 'the state contends that this evidence, while admittedly hearsay, is definitely probative. It goes to the heart of the state's case against Mr Ferguson.'

'The fact is that the state has nothing that links my client to the dead woman except a series of unsubstantiated, second-hand claims.'

'Judge McMahon,' Jess said, noting the judge's cheeks were now brushed with broad strokes of crimson, 'the state intends to call Connie's best friend and a co-worker to the stand. Both women will testify that Connie DeVuono was terrified of Rick Ferguson, that she told them he'd threatened to kill her if she testified against him.'

'Your Honor, we're just going round in circles here.' Don raised his arms in exasperation.

'What is going on?' Mrs Gambala cried from the witness stand. 'I don't understand.'

Caroline McMahon looked sympathetically toward the older woman leaning forward in the witness stand. 'You may step down, Mrs Gambala,' she told her softly, the color in her cheeks deepening.

'I don't understand,' Mrs Gambala repeated.

'It's okay,' Jess told her, helping her down from the stand. 'You did very well, Mrs Gambala.'

'You don't need to ask me any more questions?'

'Not at the moment.'

'That man doesn't have to ask me questions?' She pointed a trembling finger at Don.

'No,' Jess said quietly, noting the look of defeat on Tom Olinsky's face as Neil Strayhorn led Mrs Gambala out into the hall.

'I'm prepared to rule on your motion now, Mr Shaw,' the judge stated.

Don and Jess drew closer to the bench.

'I'm inclined to side with the defense on this one, Ms Koster,' she began.

'But, Your Honor—'

'The prejudicial effect of the evidence clearly outweighs its probative value, and I will prohibit the state from introducing this evidence at trial.'

'But without this evidence, Your Honor, our hands are tied. The state can't prove motive. We simply don't have a case.'

'I'm inclined to agree,' the judge stated. 'Are you prepared to bring a motion to dismiss?'

Jess looked from the judge to her ex-husband. To his credit, he refrained from visibly gloating.

'It's your move,' he told her.

The next minute, all charges against Rick Ferguson were dismissed.

'How could you do it?' Jess demanded angrily of her ex-husband as she paced back and forth in front of him in the now empty corridor outside the courtroom. Tom Olinsky had gone back to the office; Neil was at the other end of the long hall trying to explain to Mrs Gambala and the other two witnesses exactly what had transpired, why Rick Ferguson would not be charged with murder. 'How could you let that killer walk free?'

'You didn't have a case, Jess.'

'You know he killed her. You know he's guilty!'

'Since when did that count for anything in a court of law?' Don demanded, then immediately softened. 'Look, Jess, I know how much you want Rick Ferguson to be guilty. I know how badly you want him behind bars. Frankly, I'd feel better about him behind bars too, at least until we figure out who's been terrorizing you. But I'm not at all convinced it's Rick Ferguson we have to worry about, and I can't abandon my professional obligation to my client because I happen to be in love with you.' He stopped, his eyes searching hers for a trace of understanding. Stubbornly, Jess refused to comply. 'Look, let's call a truce,' he offered. 'Let me take you out for dinner.'

'I don't think that would be a very good idea under the circumstances.'

'Come on, Jess,' he urged, 'you can't take these things personally.'

'Well, I do. Sorry if that disappoints you.'

'You never disappoint me.'

Jess felt the crest of her anger ebbing. What was the point in being mad at Don when the person she was really angry with was herself? 'I can't tonight, Don. I've already made plans,' she said.

'Adam?'

'My sister,' she said. 'And my brother-in-law. And my father. And his new love. A fitting end to a perfect day. I'll talk to you soon.' She spun round on her heels, found herself face to face with Rick Ferguson. 'Jesus Christ!'

'No,' he said. 'Just me.' He smiled. 'I was hoping we could go out and celebrate,' he said to Don, speaking over Jess's head.

'I'm afraid I can't make it,' Don said coldly.

'Oh, that's too bad.' Rick said, his smile belying his words. 'How about you, Jess? I could show you a real good time.'

'You won't show her so much as your shadow. Ever again,' Don stated. 'Is that clear?'

Rick Ferguson fell back, his hand on his heart, as if he'd been mortally wounded.

'You're a tough man, Mr Shaw,' he said, quickly straightening up, 'but hell, if that's the way you want it, that's the way you'll have it. I'm just feeling so good right now, I wanted to spread some of that good feeling around.'

'Go home, Rick,' Don said. He grabbed Rick roughly by the elbow and guided him toward the elevators, one obligingly opening as they neared. But just as they were about to step inside, Rick Ferguson scrambled free of his lawyer's grasp and darted back toward Jess.

Jess held her breath as he approached, determined to stand her ground. Surely he wouldn't do anything to hurt her now, not here in the Court House, not with his lawyer fast approaching.

'Want to know how good I feel, counsellor?' he was asking, staring directly into Jess's eyes and speaking so quietly that only she could hear. 'I feel just like the cat who swallowed the canary.'

For a second, Jess couldn't find her voice, could barely find her breath. 'You bastard,' she whispered.

'You bet,' Rick Ferguson told her. 'And don't worry,' he added, seconds before Don wrestled him to the floor. 'You won't even see my shadow.'

Chapter Twenty-Five

Jess drove her rental car to Evanston, pulling into her sister's driveway at five minutes to six o'clock. Her father's blue Buick was already in the driveway. 'Great,' she whispered, wishing she'd had time for at least one drink before she had to meet the new recruit. 'Now just stay calm. Smile. Look happy.'

She repeated these simple phrases to herself until they became meaningless, and she went on to new ones. 'Be nice. Be gracious. Don't fight.'

'Don't fight,' she said again, nodding her head up and down until it felt in danger of dropping off trying to work up the necessary courage to get out of the car. 'Be nice.' The front doored open and Barry appeared, motioning for her to come inside with a giant sweep of his hands. Could her brother-in-law really have sent her that awful letter?

Don't be ridiculous, she said to herself, careful not to let her lips move. Barry didn't send you that letter. Rick Ferguson sent you it.

Now you're *really* being ridiculous, another voice argued. Rick Ferguson didn't do anything. He isn't guilty, remember? There's simply no hard evidence linking him to any wrongdoing of any kind. You did not prove him guilty. Therefore, he is innocent.

Innocent and out there just waiting for you, she thought, opening her car door, stepping out, then slamming it shut, refusing to be intimidated. Tomorrow she'd attend her final class in self-defense, learn how to disarm a would-be attacker. She doubted Rick Ferguson would do anything before then. That would be too obvious, even for him. If anything happened to her, he'd be the immediate suspect.

Big deal, Jess thought, realizing she had forgotten to bring either a bottle of wine or gifts for the kids. Rick Ferguson had been the immediate, and *only*, suspect in the murder of Connie DeVuono. That had seemed obvious enough too. And yet, the state hadn't been able to produce enough evidence to bring him to trial. Undoubtedly, he'd be just as clever in dispatching her. She'd probably just disappear one day, never to be seen or heard from again.

Like mother, like daughter, she thought, finding a curious comfort in the irony of the situation, as if fate had brought her full circle. She saw her father appear in the doorway behind his son-in-law, and was, for the first time, grateful that he had a new woman in his life. It would make it easier for him when the inevitable happened.

'Christ, Jess,' Barry called out. 'Could you walk any slower? Get the hell in here. It's freezing.'

As if to underline his point, the wind blew an extra gust of cold air in from the water, shaking the bare branches of the trees. Jess noted the blue lights that were laced through the small evergreen shrubs against the front of the house, wondered if they'd turned blue from the cold. They looked mournful, sad. A circular green paper wreath decorated with a bright red bow hung in the middle of the doorway.

'Tyler made it in nursery school,' Barry said proudly as Jess maneuvered her way up the poorly shovelled front steps, feeling as if lead weights had been attached to her ankles. 'Where'd you get the car?'

'I rented it this afternoon,' Jess explained, stepping inside and allowing her father to take her in his arms. 'Hi, Daddy.'

'Hi, sweetheart. Let me look at you.' He pushed her an arm's length away, careful not to let go of his hold on her, then drew her back into his embrace. 'You look wonderful.'

'What kind of car is that?' Barry was asking.

'A Toyota,' Jess said of the small red car she had newly leased, strangely grateful to have something so mundane to talk about.

'Shouldn't be driving Japanese cars,' Barry scolded, helping her off with her coat and hanging it in the closet. Jess caught sight of a black mink coat she knew wasn't her sister's, and wondered fleetingly how mink meshed with Birkenstock sandals. 'The American car industry needs all the support it can get.'

'Which explains your Jaguar,' Jess said, dropping her purse to the floor.

'My next car will be American,' Barry assured her. 'I was thinking of a Cadillac.'

'Cadillac's a good car,' Art Koster said, the look in his eyes imploring Jess to leave it at that.

Jess nodded. 'I'm sorry I've been so busy lately, Daddy,' she apologized, delaying her entry into the main part of the house.

'I understand, sweetie,' her father told her, and Jess could see from the compassion that shaped his soft brown eyes that he did.

'I'm so sorry if I hurt you,' she whispered. 'You know it's the last thing I'd ever want to do.'

'I know that. And it's unimportant. No harm done. You're here now.'

'I'm sorry I forgot to bring anything for anyone,' Jess apologized again, seeing Maureen appear in the foyer holding one of the twins, Tyler wrapped, as tight as cellophane, around her legs. The entire Peppler clan, Jess noted, was dressed in festive red and green. Maureen and the baby were wearing almost identical red velvet dresses; Tyler and his father wore dark green trousers, matching red cardigans and wide murky-green ties. They looked as if they had just stepped off the front of a greeting card. Jess felt distinctly out of place in her black and white argyle sweater and plain black slacks.

'I'm so glad you could make it,' Maureen said, tears in the corners of her eyes. 'I was afraid you might call at the last minute and—' She broke off abruptly. 'Come on inside.'

Art Koster put his arm round his younger daughter and brought her into the living room. The first thing Jess noticed was the enormous Scottish pine Christmas tree that stood in front of the grand piano, waiting to be adorned. The next thing she saw was the Madonna figure sitting next to it on the rose-colored sofa holding a baby in a red velvet dress.

'Sherry,' her father said, leading Jess to the sofa, 'this is my younger daughter, Jess. Jess, this is Sherry Hasek.'

'Hello, Jess,' the woman said, handing the baby to Jess's father as she stood to shake Jess's hand. She was as slim as her father had described and even shorter than Jess had imagined. Her black hair looked surprisingly natural, and was pulled back into a jewelled clasp at the nape of her neck. A large black onyx heart hung from a long gold chain round her neck. She wore a simple white silk blouse and charcoal-grey pants over solid black leather shoes. No Birkenstocks anywhere in sight. Her handshake was firm, though her hands were ice cold, despite the fire roaring in the fireplace.

She's as nervous as I am, Jess thought, telling herself not to cry as she shook the woman's hand. 'I'm sorry it's taken so long for me to meet you,' Jess told her sincerely.

'These things happen,' Sherry Hasek said.

'What can I get you to drink?' Barry asked. 'Wine? Beer? *Coca-Cola*?' he asked pointedly.

'Can I have a Coke?' Tyler asked immediately.

'You can have milk,' Maureen answered.

'I'll have some wine,' Jess said, lifting the baby from her sister's arms, thinking her sister was right – the twins really had grown in the last two months. 'Hello, you sweet little thing. How are you doing?'

The baby stared at her as if she were a creature from outer space, her eyes crossing as she tried to focus on Jess's nose.

'They're really something, aren't they?' Barry said proudly, pouring Jess a glass of white wine and holding it toward her. 'I'll take Chloe,' he said, exchanging the glass of wine for his infant daughter.

'I always wanted twins,' Sherry said. 'And girls. Instead I got three boys. One at a time.'

'My friends all say that boys are more trouble when they're young,' Maureen said, sitting down, a baby in her arms, a small boy clinging to her knees, 'but girls are worse when they hit their teens.'

'What about it, Art?' Barry asked. 'How were your girls as teenagers?'

Art Koster laughed. 'My girls were always perfect,' he said graciously, as Jess fought down the image of her mother's tearful face.

I don't need this, Jess. I don't need this from you.

'I don't think we were perfect,' Jess said, quickly raising her glass to her mouth. 'Cheers, everyone.' She took a long sip, then another.

'Health and wealth,' Barry toasted.

Jess tried to concentrate on Sherry Hasek's oval face. Her eyes were dark and wide apart, but the rest of her features were curiously crowded together, as if there wasn't quite enough room on her face for everything. When she became animated, her mouth seemed to jump all over the place. And she talked with her hands, using her long, manicured fingers for emphasis, creating the impression of an alert, if cluttered, mind.

Not at all like her Mother, Jess thought, superimposing her mother's wider face over that of Sherry Hasek, recalling her mother's blue-green eyes, her soft skin, the nose in perfect proportion to the mouth, her cheekbones high and prominent. It was a face that created the illusion of calm, made those around her feel safe and secure. There had been something so soothing about the delicate balance of her features, as if the serenity she projected was the result of a deep inner peace.

Her mother had always been that way, Jess realized, so comfortable with herself that she had effortlessly been able to make those around her feel comfortable too. She rarely lost her temper, almost never yelled. Yet there was never any question as to how she felt about something. She was never coy, had no patience for second-guessing. She said what she felt and expected the same courtesy from others. She treated everyone with respect, Jess thought now, seeing her mother's face streaked with tears, even when those around her were undeserving of that respect.

'Earth to Jess,' she heard Barry say. 'Come in, Jess. Come in.'

Jess felt the glass of wine slipping through her fingers, and squeezed it tightly before it could fall to the floor, feeling the fragile glass crack and collapse inside her fingers, her hand becoming sticky and wet. She looked down to see her blood mingling with the white of the wine to create a delicate rosé, her ears suddenly open to the sounds of horror and concern that were filling the room.

'Mommy!' Tyler cried.

'My God, Jess, your hand!'

'How the hell did you do that?' Barry rushed a napkin under her hand before she could drip blood on the carpet.

One of the babies started crying.

'I'm all right,' Jess heard herself say, though in truth she still wasn't sure what had happened, and therefore couldn't decide whether she was all right or not.

'That's quite a grip you've got there,' her father was saying, gently opening her fist to examine her injured hand, carefully extricating two small triangles of glass, softly wiping the blood away with his white linen handkerchief.

'My eagle's claw,' Jess said.

'Your what?' Barry asked, patting the carpet down with a bit of soda water.

'I've been taking self-defense classes,' Jess muttered, wondering if she was really having this conversation.

'And they're teaching you how to protect yourself from a glass of white wine?' Barry asked.

'I'll get some antiseptic cream for that,' Maureen said, efficiently depositing both babies into Jolly Jumpers that stood side by side near the doorway. The twins bounced happily as their mother left the room, Tyler, still crying, clinging to his mother's feet.

'I'm really sorry,' Jess said.

'Why?' Sherry asked. 'Did you do it on purpose?'

Jess smiled gratefully. 'It hurts like hell.'

'I'm sure it does.' Sherry examined the small cuts that mingled with the natural lines of Jess's hand. 'You have a good strong life line,' she observed in passing.

'What the hell were you thinking about?' Barry asked, getting to his feet as his wife re-entered the room.

'I thought you didn't allow swearing in the house,' Jess reminded him.

'Here, let me rub some of this on.' Maureen rubbed the soothing salve into her palm before Jess could protest. 'And I brought some gauze.'

'I don't need gauze.'

'Keep your hand above your head,' Barry instructed.

'Really, Barry, the cuts aren't that deep.'

'Maybe we should call a doctor,' Maureen said. 'Just to be on the safe side.'

At the mention of the word 'doctor', Tyler started to wail.

'It's all right, Tyler,' Maureen assured him, reaching down to scoop the frightened child into her arms. 'The doctor's not for you.' She turned to Jess. 'He hates doctors because the last time he was sick, you know, when everybody had colds, the doctor stuck that thing down his throat to have a look, and it made Tyler gag. He just hates throwing up.'

Jess laughed and Tyler cried louder. 'I'm sorry, sweetie,' she said, bending down to her nephew's height while keeping her arm raised, allowing Sherry to wrap the gauze round her injured hand. 'I wasn't laughing at you. It's just that I know exactly how you feel. I don't like throwing up either.'

'Who does?!' Barry asked, reaching for the phone on an end table beside the sofa. 'What about it, Jess? Is medical attention required?'

'Not for me.' She let her father lead her to the sofa where he carefully positioned her between himself and his new love. 'I'm tough. Remember?' But if Barry recalled the details of their last argument, he gave no such acknowledgement.

'Did they ever find out who trashed your car?' Maureen asked.

Jess shook her head, feeling Rick Ferguson's eerie presence in the room, like the ghost of Christmas Past. She shooed it away with the sound of her voice. 'So, I understand you're quite an artist,' she said to the woman sitting beside her.

Sherry laughed. It was a charming laugh, like wind chimes in a warm breeze. Jess heard her mother's more raucous laughter in the distance. 'I just play around really, although I've always had a very deep love of art,' Sherry explained, looking over at Jess's father for approval, something Jess's mother would never have done, Jess thought.

'Is that art or Art?' he asked playfully.

Again Sherry laughed. 'Both, I guess.'

'Do you prefer oils or pastels?' Jess asked, not caring one way or the other, but anxious to get away from the subject of love.

'I'm better with pastels. Your father prefers oils.'

Jess winced. Her mother would never have presumed to speak for her father. And did this woman really feel it necessary to inform her of her own father's preferences?

'Sherry's being overly modest,' her father said, presuming now to speak for Sherry. Were all people in love guilty of such presumption? Jess wondered. 'She's quite a talented artist.'

'Well,' Sherry demurred. 'I'm not too bad at still-life.'

'Her peaches are terrific,' Art stated with a wink.

'Art!' Sherry laughed, reaching across Jess to mockingly slap Art Koster's hand. Jess felt vaguely sick. 'Your father is better at the nudes.'

'Figures,' said Barry.

'I keep offering to paint her picture,' Art said, smiling at Sherry as if Jess wasn't sitting between them. 'But she says she's holding out for Jeffrey Koons.'

Again the sound of wind chimes in the air. Jess supposed she should know who Jeffrey Koons was, but she didn't, although she laughed anyway, as if she did.

Jess wondered what her mother would make of this pleasant little family scene: Maureen standing beside Barry, his arm draped across her shoulder, her own arms wrapped round her son; Jess snuggled on the sofa between her father and the woman he wanted to paint in the nude; the twins bouncing in their Jolly Jumpers, their saucer-like eyes keeping a guarded eye out for their mother. That's right, Jess thought, watching them gently bounce up and down, like human yo-yos, their bootied toes barely touching the floor. Keep an eye on your mother, she warned them silently. Watch out that she doesn't disappear.

'Earth to Jess,' she heard again. 'Earth to Jess. Come in, Jess.'

'Sorry,' Jess said quickly, catching the look of annoyance in Barry's eyes, as if her inattentiveness was somehow a reflection on his abilities as a host. 'Were you saying something?'

'Sherry asked you if you liked to paint.'

'Oh. Sorry. I didn't hear you.'

'That much was obvious,' Barry said, as Jess caught the worried look that suddenly clouded Maureen's eyes.

'It's not important,' Sherry immediately qualified. 'I was just making conversation.'

'Actually I don't know whether I like painting or not,' Jess answered. 'I haven't done it since I was a child.'

'Remember the time you got a hold of those crayons and you drew all over the walls of the living room,' Maureen said, 'and Mom got so mad because they'd just been freshly painted.'

'I don't remember that.'

'I don't think I'll ever forget it,' Maureen said. 'It was the loudest I think I ever heard Mom yell.'

'She didn't yell.'

'She did that day. You could hear her for blocks.'

'She never yelled,' Jess insisted.

'I thought you said you didn't even remember the incident,' Barry reminded her.

'I think I can remember my own mother.'

'I remember lots of times she yelled,' Maureen said.

Jess shrugged, trying to disguise her growing anger. 'Never at me.'

'Always at you.'

Jess stood up, walked to the Christmas tree, her hand throbbing. 'When are we going to decorate this thing?'

'We thought right after dinner,' Barry said.

'You never knew when to let go of things,' Maureen

continued, as if there had been no interruption. 'You always had to have the last word.' She laughed. 'I remember Mom saying that she always loved having you around because it was so nice living with someone who knew everything.'

Everyone laughed. Jess was beginning to hate the sound of wind chimes.

'My boys were like that,' Sherry agreed. 'Each one thought he had all the answers. When they were seventeen, they thought I was the stupidest person on earth. By the time they were twenty-one, they couldn't believe how smart I'd gotten.'

Again, everyone laughed.

'Actually, we had a few very rough years,' Sherry confided. 'Especially just after their father left. Not that he was around that much to begin with. But his leaving kind of made it official, and the boys did a lot of acting out. They were rude and rebellious, and no matter what I said or did, it wasn't right. We always seemed to be fighting about something. I'd turn around, and there I'd be in the middle of a confrontation, and I could never quite figure out how I got there. They said I was too strict, too old-fashioned, too naive. Anything I could be, I was too much of it. It seemed we were always at each other's throats. And then, suddenly they were all grown up, and I found that I was still relatively in one piece. They went off to college, eventually all moved out on their own. I bought a dog. He loves me unconditionally. He sits by the door and waits for me whenever I go out. When I get home, he smothers me with kisses, he's so glad to see me. He doesn't argue with me; he doesn't talk back; he thinks I'm the most wonderful thing on earth. He's the child I always wanted.'

Art hooted with delight.

'Maybe we should get a dog,' Barry said, winking at his wife.

'I think every mother probably goes through periods where she wonders why she bothered,' Maureen said.

Once again, Jess saw her mother's face. *I don't need this, Jess. I don't need this from you.*

'I mean, God knows I adore my children,' Maureen continued, 'but there are moments—'

'When you wish you were back at work?' Jess asked, watching Barry's shoulders stiffen.

'When I wish it were a little *quieter*,' Maureen told her.

'Maybe we *should* get a dog,' Barry said.

'Oh great,' Jess exclaimed. 'Something else for Maureen to take care of.'

'Jess,' Maureen warned.

'Sherry's dog is the cutest little thing,' Art Koster said quickly. 'A toy poodle. Beautiful red coat, a very unusual color for a poodle. When she first told me she had a poodle, I thought, oh no, I can't get involved with a woman who could love a dog like that. I mean, poodles are such a cliché.'

'And then he met Casey,' Sherry interjected.

'And then I met Casey.'

'And it was love at first sight.'

'Well, more like love at first walk,' Art Koster qualified. 'I took the damn pooch out for a walk one afternoon, and I couldn't believe how absolutely everyone we passed came over to pet the damn thing. I never saw so many smiles on so many people in one afternoon in my life. It made me happy just to be part of it. And of course poodles are very smart. Sherry says that when it comes to dogs and intelligence, there's poodles and then there's everything else.'

Jess could barely believe her ears. Was her father really engaged in an avid discussion about a toy poodle?

'Jess was always an animal lover,' her father was saying.

'Really? Do you have any pets?' Sherry asked.

'No,' Jess said.

'She has a canary,' Maureen answered at almost the same moment.

'No,' Jess said again.

'What happened to Fred?' Maureen asked.

'He died. Last week.'

'Fred died?' Maureen repeated. 'I'm so sorry. Had he been sick?'

'How would you know whether or not a canary was sick?' Barry scoffed.

'Don't talk to her in that tone,' Jess said sharply.

'I beg your pardon?' There was more surprise than anger in Barry's voice.

'What tone?' Maureen asked.

'Are the boys coming home for Christmas this year?' Art Koster asked suddenly. For a minute, nobody seemed to know what he was talking about.

'Yes,' Sherry answered, snapping to attention, her voice a touch too loud, a shade too enthusiastic. 'At least, that's the latest word. But you never know what they could decide at the last minute.'

'Where are your boys now?' Jess asked, allowing herself to be drawn back into the conversation. Smile, she thought through tightly gritted teeth. Be nice. Be gracious. Don't fight.

'Warren is a gym teacher at a high school in Rockford. Colin is at the New York Film School; he wants to be a director. And Michael is at Wharton. He's my entrepreneur.'

'Three very bright young men,' Jess's father said proudly.

'Maureen has an MBA from Harvard,' Jess said, her resolve of only seconds ago crumbling.

'Have you met them yet, Dad?' Maureen asked, as if Jess hadn't spoken.

'Not yet,' her father answered.

'I was hoping I could persuade you all to come for Christmas dinner at my place this year,' Sherry proposed. 'That way I could introduce you.'

'Sounds great,' Maureen said immediately.

'Count *us* in,' Barry said, pointedly. 'What about you, Jess?'

'Sounds fine,' Jess concurred, straining for sincerity. Smile, she thought. Be nice. Don't fight. Stay calm. 'Speaking of dinner . . .'

'Ready whenever you are,' Maureen said.

Jess found herself staring at the woman who was poised to take her mother's place. 'Ready or not,' she said.

Chapter Twenty-Six

'This roast is delicious,' Sherry Hasek was saying, delicately patting at the sides of her mouth with her rose-colored napkin. 'It's so rare these days that I eat red meat. I've forgotten what a treat it is.'

'I've tried to wean Maureen away from red meat,' Barry said, 'but she says she was raised on mother's milk and good old-fashioned Chicago roast beef, so what are you going to do?'

'Enjoy it,' Art said.

'I think as long as you don't overdo things, you're okay,' Sherry said. 'Everything in moderation, isn't that what they say?'

'They say so many things,' Maureen continued, 'it's hard to keep track. One minute we're supposed to avoid red meat; the next minute they tell us it's good for us. They keep warning us of the dangers of alcohol, then they tell us a glass of red wine a day prevents heart attacks. Something's good for you one day, bad for you the next. Right now, fiber is in, fat is out. Next year, it'll probably be the reverse.'

'To moderation,' her father toasted, lifting his glass of red wine into the air.

'Health and wealth,' Barry said.

'I was reading an article in the doctor's office the other day,' Art Koster began. 'It was an old magazine, and the reporter was asking this celebrity he was profiling, I didn't know who she was, he asked her to name her favorite drink and state three reasons why she liked it. It's a game. Why don't we try it?'

'My favorite drink?' Barry mused. 'It would have to be red wine. It's tasty; it smells wonderful; and it's intoxicating.'

'I like orange juice,' Maureen followed. 'It's healthy; it's invigorating; and it's refreshing.'

'Sherry?' Art asked.

'I'd have to say champagne,' she answered. 'It's fun; it suggests celebration; and I like the bubbles.'

'Jess?' Barry asked.

'What?'

'It's your turn.'

'Did you say you'd been to the doctor?' Jess asked her father.

'Haven't you been listening?' Barry asked.

Jess ignored her brother-in-law. 'What's wrong, Dad? Haven't you been feeling well?'

'I'm fine,' her father stated. 'It was just my annual check-up.'

Where are you going? Jess asked her mother.

Nowhere, she answered.

Since when do you get so dressed up to go nowhere?

'So, what's your answer?' Barry prodded.

'My answer to what?'

Barry shook his head. 'Really, Jess, I don't know why you bother accepting our dinner invitations if you're not going to take part in the conversations.'

'Barry, please,' Maureen pleaded softly.

'What's your favorite drink?' Art repeated 'And the three reasons why.'

'This is the conversation we're having?' Jess asked.

'It's a game,' Sherry said pleasantly.

'I don't know,' Jess said finally. 'Black coffee, I guess.' She noticed they were all waiting for her to continue. 'Why? Because it wakes me up in the mornings; it's slightly bitter; and it's good to the last drop.' She shrugged, hoping she had fulfilled all expectations.

'Dad?' Maureen asked.

'Beer,' he told them. 'It's simple; it's straightforward; it makes me feel good.'

'So what does it all mean?' Maureen wondered.

'Well,' Art said with appropriate flourish, 'the drink represents sex. In my case, I like it because it's simple, straightforward, and makes me feel good.'

Everyone struggled to remember their three reasons for liking the drink each had selected, laughter breaking out as each realized what had been said.

'So you think sex is tasty, intoxicating and smells wonderful,' Maureen reminded her husband. 'I think I'm flattered.'

'I think I'm lucky,' he answered, looking over at Jess. 'Slightly bitter, huh?'

Jess said nothing. Be nice, she thought. Try to smile. Be gracious. Don't fight.

'And you like the bubbles,' Art said, snuggling up to Sherry.

Jess wondered what her mother would have said. White wine maybe, because it was clear, direct, and to the point. Or maybe cream soda because it was sweet, pretty, and laced with nostalgia. Or maybe even milk, for the same reasons her father liked beer.

'Earth to Jess,' Barry was saying again. 'Earth to Jess. Come in, Jess.'

'The first time was cute, Barry,' Jess said, more sharply than she'd intended. 'Now it's merely tiresome.'

'So is your behaviour. I'm just trying to figure out whether you're simply preoccupied or whether you're being deliberately rude.'

'Barry . . .' Maureen warned.

'Why on earth would I be deliberately rude?' Jess demanded.

'You tell me. I don't profess to have any understanding into what you're all about.'

'Is that so?'

'Jess . . .' her father said.

'I'd say we understand each other pretty well, Barry,' Jess told him, her patience evaporated. 'We hate each other's guts. That's pretty clear, isn't it?'

Barry looked stunned, as if he'd just been slapped across the face. 'I don't hate you, Jess.'

'Oh, really? What about that charming little letter you sent me? Was that a token of your affection?'

'Letter?' Maureen asked. 'What letter?'

Jess bit down on her tongue, tried to stop herself from saying anything further. But it was too late. The words were already pouring out of her mouth. 'Your husband sent me a urine-soaked sample of his esteem, along with the clippings of his pubic hair.'

'What? What are you talking about?' everyone seemed to demand at once.

'Have you flipped out altogether?' Barry was yelling. 'What are you saying, for Christ's sake?'

What *was* she saying? Jess wondered suddenly, aware that their yelling had triggered a fresh onslaught of tears in the twins. Did she really believe that Barry had sent her that letter? 'Are you saying it wasn't you?'

'I'm saying I haven't got the foggiest notion what the hell you're talking about.'

'You're swearing again,' Jess said.

Barry sputtered something unintelligible in response.

'I got an anonymous letter in the mail last month,' Jess expanded. 'It was filled with strands of pubic hair and soaked in urine. When I spoke to you on the phone a little while later, you asked me if I'd gotten your letter. Are you denying it?'

'Of course I'm denying it! The only thing I ever sent you in the mail was a notice about Investment Retirement Accounts.'

Jess vaguely recalled tearing open a letter, seeing something about a registered retirement savings plan, tossing it away without much thought. My God, was that what he'd been talking about on the phone that day? 'That's what you sent me?'

'I'm an accountant, for God's sake,' he told her. 'What else would I send you?'

Jess felt the room starting to spin. What was the matter with her? How could she have accused her own brother-in-law of such a depraved act? Even if she'd believed it, how could she have said it out loud? In the man's own home? At his dinner table? In front of his family?

Her sister was voicing the same sentiments. 'I can't believe you'd say these things!' she was crying, holding her son in her arms. 'I can't believe you'd even think them.'

'I'm sorry,' Jess said helplessly, Tyler wailing at the sight of his mother's tears. The twins shrieked in their Jolly Jumpers.

'Children, can we just calm down,' Art Koster urged, speaking to the grown-ups.

'It's just that Barry and I had just had that big argument,' Jess tried to explain, 'and I knew how angry he was, how he liked to get even, and then I got this letter in the mail, and soon after that, I spoke to Barry and he asked me if I'd gotten his letter . . .'

'So you concluded he was the one responsible! That he could have such a sick, perverted mind. That I could have married such a disgusting individual!'

'You had nothing to do with it. Maureen, this isn't about you.'

'Isn't it?' Maureen demanded. 'When you attack my husband, you attack me too.'

'Don't be silly,' Jess argued.

The twins cried louder; Tyler squirmed out of his mother's arms and ran upstairs.

'You haven't given him a chance from the day we got married,' Maureen yelled, her free arms waving frantically in the air.

'That's not true,' Jess countered. 'I liked him fine until he turned you into Donna Reed.'

'Donna Reed!' Maureen gasped.

'How could you let him do it?' Jess demanded, deciding that now that she was in it, she might as well go all the way. 'How could you give up everything and let him turn you into Superwife?'

'Why don't I take the twins upstairs?' Sherry offered, deftly lifting the girls from their Jolly Jumpers and carrying them upstairs, one under each arm.

'Children, why don't we stop this now before we say things we'll regret,' Art said, then sighed, as if acknowledging it was already too late for that.

'Just what is it exactly that you think I've given up?' Maureen demanded. 'My job? I can always get another job. My education? I'll always have that. Can't you get it through that thick head of yours that I am doing exactly what I want to do? That it was *my* decision, not Barry's, *mine,* to stay home and be with my children while they were young. I respect *your* choices, Jess, even if I don't always agree with them. Can't you respect mine? What is so wrong with what I'm doing?'

'What's wrong with it?' Jess heard herself say. 'Don't you realize that your whole life is a repudiation of everything our mother taught us?'

'What?' Maureen looked as if she had been struck by lightning.

'For God's sake, Jess,' her father said, 'what on earth are you talking about?'

'Our mother raised us to be independent women with lives of our own,' Jess argued. 'The last thing she would have wanted was for Maureen to be trapped in a marriage where she wasn't permitted room to grow.'

Maureen's eyes glowed with red-hot fury. 'How dare you criticize me. How dare you presume to know anything about my marriage. How dare you drag our mother into it! *You* were the one, *not me,'* she continued, 'who was always fighting with Mother over these exact issues. *You* were the one, *not me,* who insisted she was going to get married while she was still in school, even though Mother pleaded with you to wait. *You* were the one who fought with her all the time, who made her cry, who made her miserable. "Just wait till you've finished law school," she kept saying. "Don's a nice man, but he won't give you any room to grow. Just wait till you've finished school," she begged you. But you wouldn't listen. You knew everything then, just like you know everything now. So stop trying to assuage your own guilt by telling everyone else how to live their lives!'

'What do you mean, my own guilt?' Jess asked, almost breathless in her anger.

'You know what I mean.'

'What the hell are you talking about?'

'I'm talking about the fight you had with Mommy the day she

disappeared!' Maureen shot back. 'I'm talking about how I called home from the library that morning, I guess just after you stormed out of the house, and she was crying. And I asked her what was wrong, and she tried to tell me it was nothing, but finally she admitted that the two of you had been going at it again pretty good, and I asked her whether she wanted me to come home, and she said no, she'd be fine, she had to go out anyway. And that was the last time I spoke to her.' Maureen's features looked in danger of melting, her eyes, nose and mouth sliding across her face as she dissolved into a flood of frustrated tears.

Jess, who had risen to her feet at some point during the confrontation, sank back into her seat. She heard voices yelling, looked around, saw not her sister's living room but the kitchen of her mother's house on Burling Street, saw not her sister's tear-streaked face, but her mother's.

'You're all dressed up,' Jess observed, coming into the kitchen, and noting her mother's fresh white linen suit. 'Where are you going?'

'Nowhere.'

'Since when do you get so dressed up to go nowhere?'

'I just felt like putting on something pretty,' her mother said, then added casually, 'and I have a doctor's appointment later on this afternoon. What are your plans?'

'What kind of doctor's appointment?'

'Nothing special.'

'Come on, Mom. You know I can always tell when you're not telling me the truth.'

'Which is one of the reasons you'll make a great lawyer.'

'The law has nothing to do with the truth,' Jess told her.

'Sounds like something Don would say.'

Jess felt her shoulders tense. 'Are you going to start?'

'I wasn't trying to start anything, Jess. It was just an observation.'

'I'm not sure I appreciate your observations.'

Laura Koster shrugged, said nothing.

'So, what kind of doctor's appointment is it?'

'I'd rather not say until I know for sure whether I have anything to worry about.'

'You're worried already. I can see it in your face. What is it?'

'I found a little lump.'

'A lump?' Jess held her breath.

'I don't want you to worry. It's probably nothing. Most lumps are.'

'Where is this lump?'

'In my left breast.'

'Oh, God.'

'Don't worry.'

'When did you find it?'

'This morning, when I was taking a shower. I called the doctor and he's sure it's nothing. He just wants me to come down and let him have a look at it.'

'What if it's not nothing?'

'Then we'll cross that bridge when we come to it.'

'Are you scared?'

Her mother didn't answer for several seconds. Only her eyes moved.

'The truth, Mom.'

'Yes, I'm scared.'

'Would you like me to come to the doctor's with you?'

'Yes,' her mother said immediately. 'Yes, I would.'

And then the conversation had somehow veered off track, Jess recalled now, seeing her mother at the kitchen counter making a fresh pot of coffee, offering Jess some fresh blueberry buns she'd purchased from a nearby bakery.

'My appointment's not till four o'clock,' her mother said. 'Will that ruin your plans?'

'No,' Jess told her. 'I'll call Don. Tell him our plans will have to wait.'

'That would be wonderful,' her mother said, and Jess understood immediately that her mother wasn't simply referring to the plans they'd made for the afternoon.

'What is it you have against Don, Mother?' she asked.

'I have absolutely nothing against him.'

'Then why are you so against my marrying him?'

'I'm not saying you shouldn't marry the man, Jess,' her mother told her. 'I think Don is a lovely man. He's smart. He's thoughtful. He obviously adores you.'

'So, what's the problem?' Jess demanded.

'The problem is that he's eleven years older than you are. He's already done all the things you've yet to try.'

'Eleven years is hardly a major age difference,' Jess protested.

'It's eleven years. Eleven years that he's had to figure out what he wants from his life.'

'He wants me.'

'And what do you want?'

'I want him!'

'And your career?'

'I'll have my career. Don is very intent on my becoming a successful lawyer. He can help me. He's a wonderful teacher.'

'You want a partner, Jess. Not a teacher. He won't give you enough room to grow.'

'How can you say that?'

'Honey, I'm not saying you shouldn't marry him,' her mother repeated.

'Yes, you are. That's exactly what you're saying.'

'All I'm saying is wait a few years. You're only in first year law school. Wait till after you pass the bar exams. Wait till you've had a chance to find out who you are and what you want.'

'I know who I am. I know what I want. I want Don. And I'm going to marry him whether you like it or not.'

Her mother sighed, poured herself a cup of freshly brewed coffee. 'You want a cup?'

'I don't want anything from you,' Jess said stubbornly.

'Okay, let's just drop it.'

'I don't want to drop it. You think that you can raise all these issues, and then say, let's drop it just because you don't feel like discussing it anymore?'

'I shouldn't have said anything.'

'You're right. You shouldn't have.'

'Sometimes I forget you know it all.'

'Oh, that's rich, Mother. Really rich.'

'I'm sorry, honey. I shouldn't have said that. I guess I'm a little nervous today, and maybe more upset than I realized.'

'No, you can't use that excuse,' Jess said mercilessly. 'Don't start laying any guilt trips on me.'

'I'm not trying to lay any guilt trips.' Tears filled her mother's eyes.

'And don't you dare cry,' Jess warned. 'I'm not the bad guy here.'

'I never said you were the bad guy.'

'Stop trying to live my life.'

'That's the last thing I want, Jess,' her mother said, tears falling the length of her cheek. 'I want you to live your life.'

'Then stay out of it!'

Her mother shook her head, dislodging more tears. 'I don't need this, Jess,' she said. 'I don't need this from you.'

And then what? Jess wondered now, feeling like a large wind-up toy, unable to stop spinning until its battery ran out. More careless words. More angry protestations.

'You don't have to take me to the doctor's. I can get there on my own.'

'Have it your way.'

Storming out of the house.

The last time she saw her mother alive.

Jess jumped to her feet, raced toward the foyer, stumbling into the Jolly Jumpers, almost knocking them over, taking a few seconds to right them.

'I'm sorry, Jess,' Maureen was crying after her. 'Please don't go. I didn't mean to say those things.'

'Why not?' Jess asked, stopping abruptly, turning toward her sister, seeing her mother's face. 'They're all true. Everything you said is true.'

'It wasn't your fault,' Maureen told her. 'Whatever happened to our mother wasn't your fault.'

Jess shook her head in disbelief. 'How can you say that?' she asked. 'If I'd taken her to the doctor's like I promised, she would never have disappeared.'

'You can't know that.'

'Of course I know that. And you know it too. If I had gone with her to the doctor's, she'd still be here today.'

'Not if someone was stalking her,' her father said, crowding into the foyer, Barry by his side. 'Not if someone was determined to do her harm. You know as well as I do that it's next to impossible to stop someone if they're really out to get you.'

Jess thought immediately of Rick Ferguson.

The phone rang.

'I'll get it,' Barry said, crossing into the living room. No one else moved.

'Why don't we go back into the dining room and sit down?' Maureen offered.

'I really think I should leave,' Jess told her.

'We never talked about what happened,' Maureen said. 'I mean, we talked about the facts; we talked about the details. But we never really talked about how we felt. I think we have a lot to talk about. Don't you?'

'I want to,' Jess told her, her voice like a small child. 'I just don't think I can. Not tonight anyway. Maybe another day. I'm so tired. I just want to go home and crawl into bed.'

Barry appeared in the hallway. 'It's for you, Jess.'

'Me? But nobody knows I'm here.'

'Your ex-husband knows.'

'Don?' Jess vaguely recalled having told her ex-husband she was having dinner at her sister's.

'He says it's very important.'

'We'll be in the dining room,' Maureen said, allowing Jess her privacy as she walked, trancelike, toward the phone.

'Has something happened?' she asked instead of hello. 'Did Rick Ferguson confess?'

'Rick Ferguson is on his way to Los Angeles. I bought him a ticket and put him on the plane myself at seven o'clock this evening. It's not Rick Ferguson I'm concerned about.'

'What are you concerned about?' Jess asked.

'Are you seeing Adam tonight?'

'Adam? No, he's out of town.'

'Are you sure?'

'What do you mean, am I sure?'

'I want you to stay over at your sister's house tonight.'

'What?! Why? What are you talking about?'

'Jess, I had my office do some checking on this guy. They called the State Bar. They've never heard of any lawyer named Adam Stohn.'

'What?'

'You heard me, Jess. They never heard of the guy. And if he lied to you about who he is and what he does, then there's a good chance he's lying about being out of town. Now, do me a favor, and stay over at your sister's, at least for tonight.'

'I can't do that,' Jess whispered, thinking of everything that had happened tonight, the things that had been said.

'Why not, for God's sake?'

'I just can't. Please, Don, don't ask me to explain.'

'Then I'm coming over.'

'No! Please. I'm a big girl. I have to take care of myself.'

'You can start taking care of yourself when we know everything's okay.'

'Everything *is* okay,' Jess told him, feeling numb from head to toe, as if she had been injected with an overdose of Novocaine. 'Adam isn't going to hurt me,' she mumbled, speaking away from the receiver.

'Did you say something?'

'I said not to worry,' Jess told him. 'I'll call you in the morning.'

'Jess—'

'I'll speak to you tomorrow.' She hung up the phone.

Jess stood by the telephone for several seconds and tried to make sense of what Don had told her. No record of a lawyer named Adam Stohn? No one by that name registered to practice law in the state of Illinois? But why would he have lied? And did that make everything else he'd told her a lie as well? Was there nothing in her life that added up? Nothing that made any sense?

Jess stared at the bare Christmas tree waiting patiently for adornment, heard the quiet voices emanating from the dining room. 'I think we have a lot to talk about,' her sister had said. And she was right. There was a lot that needed to be said, a lot that needed to be dealt with. Together and alone. Maybe she'd call Stephanie Banack on Monday morning, see if the therapist might consider seeing her again. She had to stop acting as her own judge and jury, she realized, creeping quietly into the foyer. It was time to let go of the suffocating guilt that had coated her for the past eight years, like a second skin.

Grabbing her purse but abandoning her coat to the hall closet, Jess silently opened the front door and stepped into the bitter night air. In the next instant, she was behind the wheel of her rented car, speeding south along Sheridan Road, tears streaming down her cheeks, music blasting from the radio, wanting only to crawl into her bed, pull the covers up over her head, and disappear until morning.

Chapter Twenty-Seven

She was still crying when she arrived home.

'Stop crying,' she admonished herself, turning off the car's ignition, silencing Mick Jagger's misogynistic boasting. *Under my thumb*, he wailed after her as she raced through the cold toward her three-story brownstone. 'What are you still crying about?' she asked herself, pushing her key into the lock, feeling the front door give way, locking it again securely behind her. 'Just because you acted like a total idiot tonight, because you called your sister Donna Reed and your brother-in-law a pervert, because you made the impression of a lifetime on your father's new girlfriend, because you snuck out of the house like a thief in the night, because Adam Stohn isn't who he claims to be, because Rick Ferguson gets to go to California instead of the electric chair . . . No,' she reminded herself, taking the stairs two at a time, 'they don't fry people in Illinois any more. They put them to sleep. Like dogs,' she added, mindful of the last line from Kafka's *Trial*, crying even harder.

There were no trumpets or saxophones to accompany her up the final flight of stairs, no light creeping out from underneath Walt Fraser's door. Probably away for the weekend, she thought, thinking that maybe she'd call Don when she got inside her apartment, suggest a few days in Union Pier. Forget about Adam Stohn. Or whoever the hell he really was.

She unlocked the door to her apartment and stepped over the threshold, allowing the silence and the darkness to draw her in, like old friends at a party, warmly greeting the late arrival. No need anymore to leave the radio or the lights on all day. No more innocent, sweet melodies to welcome her home. She double locked her door.

The street lights filtered in through the antique ivory lace curtains, casting an eerie glow on the empty bird cage. She hadn't had the courage to put it away, the will to consign it to the back of a closet, the strength to tote it down to the street, the good sense to give it to the Salvation Army. Poor Fred, she thought, giving in to a fresh onslaught of tears.

'Poor me,' she whispered, dropping her purse to the floor, slouching toward her bedroom.

He came at her from behind.

She didn't see him, didn't even hear him, until the wire was around her throat, and she was being rudely yanked backward into oblivion. Her hands automatically flew to her neck as she frantically sought to dig her fingers in between the wire and her flesh. The wire cut into her bandaged hand, and she felt the stickiness of fresh blood on her fingers, heard herself gagging, gasping for air. She couldn't breathe. The wire was cutting off her supply of oxygen, slicing into the flesh at her throat. She lost control of her legs, felt her toes being lifted off the floor. With everything in her, she fought to stay erect, to pull herself away from her attacker.

And then, somewhere inside the panic, she remembered – don't pull away; don't fight it; go with it. Use the image of circularity. If someone pulls you, rather than resist and pull back, use the attacker's force to be pulled into his body. Strike when you get there.

She stopped fighting. She stopped resisting, although it went against every instinct she had. Instead, she allowed her body to go limp, felt her back cave in against her assailant's chest as he pulled her toward him. Her neck throbbed in pain, like a giant pulse. For a terrifying instant, she thought it might be too late, that she was in danger of blacking out. She found the idea surprisingly seductive and was momentarily tempted to give in to the sensation. Why prolong what was clearly inevitable? Blackness was swirling around her. Why not dive into the thick of it? Why not simply disappear inside it forever?

But then suddenly, she was fighting back, fighting her way out of the darkness, using her assailant's weight against him, allowing the force of her body to knock her attacker to the ground. She fell with him, her hands shooting wildly into the air, knocking against the side of the bird cage, sending it crashing to the floor. Her assailant yelled as he lost his balance, and she quickly used her feet to kick at his legs, her nails to scratch at his arms, her elbows to jab at his ribs.

She felt the wire around her throat loosen just enough for her to break free. She scrambled to her feet, gasping for breath, her body on fire, trying desperately to suck air into her lungs, almost collapsing with the effort. She felt the indent of the wire still pressing into her throat, digging deeper into her flesh, as if it had become part of her, even though it was no longer there. She felt as if she were dangling from a hangman's noose, as if, at any minute, her neck might snap.

Suddenly, she heard him moan, turned, saw his dazed, muscular form sprawled across the floor, took quick note of the black pointed-toed boots, the tight jeans, the dark T-shirt, the brown leather racing gloves covering his large hands, the long dirty blond hair that was whipped across the side of his face, hiding all but his twisted grin.

I am Death, the grin said, even now. *I have come for you.*

Rick Ferguson.

A small cry escaped her throat. Had she actually thought he'd quietly board a plane to California and disappear from her life? Hadn't this night been a foregone conclusion from the moment of their first confrontation several months ago?

A million images flooded her brain as she saw him struggling to regain his footing – eagle claws and zipper punches and hammer fists. Then she remembered – getting away comes first. Forget the heroics and the theatrics. Running away is what works most often for most women.

But Rick Ferguson was already on his feet, lumbering toward her, blocking her way to the front door. Scream, her inner voice commanded. Yell, goddamn you! Roar! '*Hohh!*' she cried, watching him flinch, momentarily startled by the sound. '*Hohh!*' she yelled again, even louder the second time, thinking of the gun that lay in the drawer of the end table beside her bed, wondering if she could get to it, her eyes scanning the dark room for whatever weapon was at hand.

If anything, her outburst seemed to bring him new life. Rick Ferguson's evil grin burst into an outright laugh. 'I like a good fight,' he said.

'Stay away from me,' Jess warned.

'Connie wasn't much of a challenge. She just kind of crumpled up and died. No fun at all. Not like you,' he told her. 'Killing you is gonna be a pure pleasure.'

'Likewise, I'm sure,' Jess said, lunging to the floor and scooping the empty bird cage into her hands, hurling it at Rick Ferguson's head, watching it connect, seeing a thick line of blood race down his cheek from the gash in his forehead. She turned on her heels and ran from the room, her thoughts scrambling to catch up.

Where was she going? What was she going to do when she got there?

Her bedroom had never seemed so far away. She tore through the hall, hearing him only steps behind her. She had to get her gun. She had to get her gun before he was able to lay his hands on her again. She had to use it.

She threw herself at the small end table beside her bed, pulling open the top drawer, her desperate fingers searching for her gun. It wasn't there. 'Goddamn it, where are you?' she cried, throwing the contents of the drawer to the floor.

The mattress! she thought, falling to her knees, reaching under the mattress, though she distinctly remembered Don insisting she not keep it there. Still, what if she was mistaken? What if she hadn't moved it after all?

It wasn't there. Goddamn it, it wasn't there!

'Looking for this?' Rick Ferguson stood in the doorway, dangling the revolver from the end of his gloved fingers.

Jess rose slowly to her feet, her knees knocking painfully together, as he aimed the gun directly at her head. Her heart was pounding wildly; her ears were ringing; tears were falling the length of her cheeks. If only she could get her thoughts together; if only she could stop them from careening around directionless inside her brain, hammering on the inside of her skull, as if they were trying to escape; if she could only stop her legs from shaking . . .

'Nice of you to invite me into your bedroom,' he said, moving slowly toward her. 'Of course, I already know where you keep your panties.'

'Get the hell out of here,' Jess yelled, recalling her torn panties, seeing the blood from her neck smeared across the white of her duvet.

He laughed. 'You sure are a feisty little thing, aren't you? Yea, I gotta say I admire your nerve. Telling a man with a loaded gun to get the hell out. That's real cute. I suppose now you're gonna tell me I'll never get away with this.'

'You won't.

'Sure I will. Don't forget – I've got a very good lawyer.'

Jess looked toward the window. The curtains were parted, the light from the street filling the room with ghosts and shadows. Maybe someone would see inside. Maybe someone was watching them now. Maybe if she could just keep Rick Ferguson talking, if she could somehow distract him long enough to get to the window . . . And then what? Jump? Scream? A scream could only travel so far against a loaded gun. She almost laughed – tomorrow was the day she was supposed to learn how to disarm a would-be assailant. Tomorrow – not much chance of that.

Her forehead grew wet with perspiration, the sweat dripping into her eyes, mingling with her tears. The light from the street lamps blurred, spinning out in all directions like a spotlight, blinding her, like the sun. She thought she heard voices from somewhere outside, but the voices were distorted, like a record being played on the wrong speed. Too slow. Everything too slow. A scene from a movie filmed in slow motion, happening to someone else. So, this was how Connie must have felt, Jess thought. This was what death felt like.

'I thought Don put you on a plane to California,' she heard herself say, as if she were an actress and her lines were being dubbed by someone else.

'Yea. Generous of him, wasn't it? But I decided California

could wait a few days. I knew how bad you wanted to see me. Take off your sweater.'

He said it so casually, the words didn't quite register. 'What?'

'Take off your sweater,' he repeated. 'And your pants too, while you're at it. The fun's about to start.'

Jess shook her head, feeling a word dislodge itself from her throat, tumble out of her mouth. It hit the air, barely audible. 'No.'

'No? Did you say no?' He laughed. 'Wrong answer, Jess.'

She felt as if she were already naked, standing exposed before him, and she shivered with the sudden cold. She imagined his hands pinching her flesh, his mouth biting her breasts, his body pounding cruelly into hers. He would hurt her, she knew, make sure she suffered before she died. 'I won't do it,' she heard herself say.

'Then I'll have to shoot you.' He shrugged, as if this were the only logical alternative.

Jess's heart was beating so furiously, it threatened to burst out of her chest. Like in *Alien*, she thought, amazed her mind could focus on such trivia. She felt as if she was burning up, then was suddenly ice cold again. How could he be so calm? What was going on behind the opaque brown eyes that gave away nothing. 'You'll shoot me anyway,' she said.

'Well, no. Actually, I was planning on using my hands to finish you off. But I'll shoot you if I have to.' His smile grew, his eyes slithering across her body, like an army of tiny snakes. 'In the shoulder. Or maybe the knee. Maybe in the soft part of your inner thigh. Yea, I kind of like that. Just enough to make you a little more cooperative.'

Jess felt the sting of the bullet pierce the flesh of her thigh, though she knew he hadn't fired. She could barely stand for the shaking in her legs. Her stomach cramped, threatened to humiliate her further. If she could just keep him talking, she thought. Isn't that what they always did in the movies? They talked, and then someone came along just in the nick of time to rescue them. She pushed words out of her mouth. 'You shoot, and it'll alert the neighbors.'

He was unimpressed. 'Think so? Didn't look like there was anybody home when I got here. Now, take off your clothes or I'm liable to get bored, and when I get bored, my lovemaking tends to get a bit rough.'

Oh God, Jess thought. Oh God, oh God, oh God.

'How did you get in here?' she asked, wondering where her voice was coming from. It felt detached, as if it had been disconnected and was now floating free form in the room.

'The lock hasn't been made that can keep me out.' He laughed again, clearly enjoying himself. 'I guess I can say the same thing about a woman.' He cocked the trigger of the gun. 'Now, you've got thirty seconds to get those clothes off and lie down on the bed.'

Jess said nothing, her throat suddenly too dry to form words. From somewhere beside her, her alarm clock loudly ticked off the seconds, like a bomb about to explode. So, this is how it ends, she thought, unable to swallow, to draw air into her lungs, terror gnawing at her extremities like a hungry rat.

What would it be like? she wondered. Would there be a white light, a long tunnel, a feeling of peace and well-being, as was often reported by those who claimed to have died and come back? Or would there be blackness? Nothingness? Would she simply cease to be? When it was all over, would she find herself alone, or would her loved ones be there to greet her? She thought of her mother. Would she finally get to see her again, to find out exactly what fate she had met? Had it been this way for her too? My God, Jess thought, her chest aching, as if it were splitting in two, had her mother experienced this same kind of terror and pain before she died? Was this what her mother had gone through?

And what would this do to her father, her sister?

When they didn't hear from her, when they couldn't reach her, Barry would probably assure them that Jess was just too embarrassed to contact them, that she'd merely taken off for a few days, that she was too self-centered to realize the pain she might be causing them, that perhaps, on some subconscious level, she was punishing them. It would be days before they took her disappearance seriously, before the police were called and her apartment searched. Her apartment would show obvious signs of struggle. The blood on her duvet would be analyzed, found to be hers. There would be no signs of forced entry. No revealing fingerprints. Don would point the finger of suspicion at Adam. By the time everything was sorted out, Rick Ferguson would be long gone.

'Don't make me tell you again,' Rick Ferguson was saying.

Jess took a deep breath and pulled her sweater over her head, the delicate hairs along her arms rising in protest. Her skin started to throb, as if she had pulled pieces of it off along with her sweater, as if she'd been skinned alive. The sweater dropped to the floor.

'Very nice,' he said. 'I always liked black lace.' He shook the gun in the direction of her pants. 'Now the rest.'

Jess watched the scene unfold as if from a great distance. Again she recalled the experiences of those who claimed to have died. Didn't they always report leaving their bodies and floating toward the ceiling, watching the events from the air? Maybe that was what was happening to her. Maybe she hadn't escaped from her living room after all. Maybe the wire had sliced through her throat and killed her. Maybe she was already dead.

Or maybe she still had time to save herself, she thought, a renewed surge of adrenaline interrupting her reveries, convincing her she was still alive, that there might be something she could do. Use whatever weapons are at hand, she heard Dominic instruct, as her fingers curled into the elastic waistband of her wool pants. Like what? she wondered, impulses colliding painfully in her brain, causing her head to throb. Her bra? Could she strangle the man with her lace brassiere? How about smothering him in cashmere?

How about her shoes? she wondered, slowly removing her hands from her waist. Rick Ferguson jabbed the gun impatiently into the air. 'I have to take my shoes off,' she stammered. 'I can't get my pants off if I don't take my shoes off first.'

'Hey,' he said, relaxing, 'the nakeder, the better. Just hurry up about it.'

She bent over, wondering what in God's name she was planning to do, slowly removing her left shoe and tossing it casually aside, thinking she was out of her mind, she didn't have a chance, he would kill her for sure, then moving to her right foot, knowing she only had seconds left, lifting the black flat off her foot, making a motion as if tossing the shoe aside, instead gripping it tightly, then hurling it with all her strength toward the gun in his hand.

She missed completely.

'Oh God,' she moaned. 'Oh my God.'

But the sudden action caught Rick Ferguson by surprise, and he jumped back in alarm. What the hell should she do now? Could she push past him toward the front door? Could she possibly survive a jump from a third-floor window? Did she have the strength to disarm him?

It was too late. Already, he'd recovered his equilibrium. Already, the gun was cocked and pointed at her heart. 'I think I'm going to enjoy killing you even more than I enjoyed roasting that damn canary,' he said, tracing an invisible line through the air with his gun, down past her breasts, past her ribs and stomach, stopping at the crotch of her pants.

There was no time left, no choices left. He was going to shoot her. Render her defenseless long enough to rape and sodomize her. Then finish her off with his hands. Oh God, Jess thought, picturing her dead canary, wishing she would faint, knowing he would only force her back to consciousness, make her suffer through every agonizing second. And then without thinking, without even knowing what she was doing until she was already doing it, Jess was leaping across her bed to the window, screaming at the top of her lungs.

The shot exploded into the air around her, and she knew she was as good as dead. It was so loud, she thought, louder than she had ever imagined it could be, like a burst of thunder at her ear. The room assumed an eerie glow, as if the contents had been hit by lightning, the colors newly magnified, the soft peaches now a vivid orange, the greys and blues electric. Her body felt light, suspended in mid-air. She wondered where the bullet had struck her, how long it would take her to fall to the floor.

He'd be waiting to rip the remaining clothes off her near lifeless body, to force himself inside her, smothering her with his weight, overwhelming her with his odors. Already she could feel his fingers tearing at her, his tongue licking at her blood. His would be the last face she would see, his grin the sight she would take with her to her grave.

And suddenly, she was spinning around and Rick Ferguson was coming at her, his hands reaching toward her, his face white with fury, his smile gone. And then he was falling, tumbling toward her, and Jess realized that she was all right, that she hadn't been shot, that it was Rick Ferguson who was plunging to the floor, sprawling across her stockinged feet, that it was Rick Ferguson who was dead.

Darkness swirled around her, like a whirlpool in the middle of an ocean, threatening to pull her into its center, as her eyes absorbed the gaping hole in the middle of his back. The blood spurted from it, like oil from a geyser, soaking his black T-shirt, spilling onto the rug. Jess felt dizzy, faint. She clutched the side of her dresser for support.

And then she saw him in the doorway, the gun dangling from his hand. 'Don!' she gasped.

'I told you if that bastard ever tried to hurt you, I'd kill him myself,' he said quietly. The gun slipped from his fingers to the floor.

Jess rushed into his arms. Immediately they encircled her, pulling her tight against him. She pressed her head against his shoulder, absorbing his clean smell, clinging to the warmth of his body. He felt so good. He felt so safe.

'You're safe now,' he told her, as if reading her thoughts, kissing the side of her face over and over again. 'You're safe. I'm here. I won't ever leave you.'

'He was waiting for me inside the apartment,' Jess began after several minutes, trying to come to grips with everything that had happened. 'He had a wire. The kind he used to kill Connie. He tried to strangle me. But I got away. I ran for my gun, but it wasn't there. He had it. He must have searched the apartment before I got home. He said there wasn't a lock that had been made that could keep him out.'

'It's okay now,' Don said, his voice a salve. 'It's okay. You're safe now. He can't hurt you anymore.'

'I was so scared. I thought he was going to kill me.'

'He's dead, Jess.'

'I kept thinking about my mother.'

'Don't, sweetheart.'

'About what this would do to my father and my sister.'

'It's over now. You're safe.'

'Thank God you got here.'

'I couldn't let you stay alone.'

'He didn't get on the plane,' she said, then laughed, feeling giddy, light-headed. 'I guess that's pretty obvious.'

'I'm just glad I got here in time.' Don hugged her tighter against him.

'I can't believe you did. You're my Prince Charming,' Jess said, and thought that he was. How could she ever have hurt him the way she had? How could she have left him? How could she possibly survive without him? 'It's just like in the movies.' She laughed nervously, recalling all those movies where a monstrous killer erroneously presumed dead rises up to strike again. Her eyes drifted back to the body on the floor. 'Are you sure he's dead?'

'He's dead, Jess.' Don smiled indulgently. 'I can shoot him again if you'd like.'

Jess laughed, surprised at the sound. She'd been savagely attacked with a piece of wire rope, almost raped, almost murdered, and here she was laughing. Probably it was a nervous reaction, a way of coping with what had very nearly been. Her eyes travelled the length of Rick Ferguson's body, and she understood how easily that body could have been hers. If Rick Ferguson had been allowed a few more minutes. If Don hadn't shown up when he did, like a hero from a silent movie, riding in on horseback in the final seconds of the reel to rescue the unfortunate heroine from her fate.

It was uncanny how well Don knew her, Jess thought, burrowing in closer against his chest, how he always knew when she needed him, whatever her protestations to the contrary. She'd told him on the phone that she was all right, that she'd speak to him tomorrow, that she was in no danger tonight. And still he'd come. Still he'd charged in and taken control. Saved her from a gruesome death. Saved her from her own stubborn stupidity.

Was she really surprised? Hadn't he done the same thing throughout their marriage, ignoring her wishes to do what he thought best? She'd gotten angry, railed against him, fought for the freedom to make her own mistakes, demanded her right to be wrong. He'd tried to understand, given lip-service to her pleas, but in the end, he'd done things the way he'd always intended. More often than not, it had proved to be the right way. Like tonight.

As if watching a television rerun, Jess saw herself pushing open the downstairs door, locking it after her, racing up three flights of stairs, entering her apartment, once again locking the door after her, taking several steps inside, suddenly feeling the sharp tug of wire around her throat, struggling with her assailant, momentarily breaking free, seeing the door, wondering if she could get to it, open it, before Rick Ferguson could get to her.

Her mind's eye narrowed in on the locked door of her apartment, as if she were adjusting a kaleidoscope. What's wrong with this picture? a little voice asked, snapping her sharply back into the present. The door to her apartment had been locked, she realized, swallowing a gasp, as was the outside door. How then had Don gotten inside? 'How did you get in?' she heard herself ask.

'What?'

Jess pulled slightly away from his embrace. 'How did you get inside the house?'

'The door wasn't locked,' he said.

'Yes it was,' she insisted. 'I locked it after I came in.'

'Well, it was open when I got here,' he told her.

'And my apartment?' she asked. 'I double locked the door as soon as I got inside.'

'Jess, what is this?'

'A simple question.' She took several steps back, stopped when she felt Rick Ferguson's feet against the backs of her legs. 'How did you get inside my apartment?'

There was a moment's silence, a look of calm resignation, then, 'I used my keys.'

'Your keys? What do you mean? What keys?'

He swallowed, looked toward the floor. 'I had a second set made when you had your locks changed.'

Jess shook her head in disbelief. 'You had a second set made? Why?'

'Why? Because I was worried about you. Because I was afraid something like this might happen. Because you need me to look after you. That's why.'

Jess looked down, saw Rick Ferguson dead at her feet, her gun still inside his open hand. Don had saved her life, for God's sake. Why was she suddenly so angry with him? What difference did it make that he'd had a copy of her keys made? If he hadn't, she'd be a corpse, for God's sake. Was she really going to be angry at him for saving her life?

She felt an annoying tickle at her throat, tried to dismiss it as a byproduct of the injury to her neck, almost succeeded, until she felt the tickle creeping stealthily toward her chest, like a large spider. Picking up both strength and speed, it scurried across her arms and legs, depositing its poison, leaving everything it touched numb. Was she going to have an anxiety attack now? she wondered incredulously. Now when it was all over? When she was safe? When there was no reason for her to panic?

And then she heard Adam's voice. *Go with it*, he said. *Don't fight it. Go with it.*

Adam, she thought. Adam, whom Don distrusted and had tried to warn her against. Adam, whom Don had investigated, who wasn't who he said he was. What did Adam have to do with any of this? 'I don't understand,' she said out loud, staring at Don, wondering if there was more he hadn't told her.

'Don't worry about anything now, Jess. All that matters is that you're safe. Rick Ferguson is dead. He can't hurt you anymore.'

'But it wasn't Rick Ferguson you were worried about,' Jess persisted, remembering his phone call to her sister's, stubbornly trying to make sense of all that had happened. 'It was Adam you claimed was dangerous. You said you'd had him investigated; you said the State Bar had never heard of him.'

'Jess, what's this got to do with anything?'

'But Adam was never a threat to me. It was Rick Ferguson all along. So, why would Adam lie?' Once again the kaleidoscope shifted, its contents scrambling to present yet another picture. 'Unless he didn't lie. Unless it was you who lied to me,' she said, scarcely believing her own ears. Was she really saying these things? 'You didn't call the State Bar, did you? And if you did, then you found out that Adam Stohn is exactly who he says he is. Isn't he?'

There was a long silence. 'He isn't right for you, Jess,' Don said finally.

What was going on? What was Don saying? 'Isn't that for me to decide?'

'Not when it's the wrong decision. Not when it affects me, when it affects us, our future together,' he told her. 'And we *could* have a future together, if you'd only stop fighting me. You need me to take care of you, Jess. You always have. Tonight proved that.'

Jess looked from her ex-husband to the body lying on the floor, then back to her ex-husband, the kaleidoscope in her mind twisting and turning furiously, until the captive bright pieces of multi-colored plastic could no longer differentiate between up and down, right or left, and the kaleidoscope burst apart, scattering the delicate slivers of her reality into the air. 'Why did you come over here tonight?' she asked. 'I mean, you knew Adam was out of town, and you thought Rick Ferguson was on a plane to California, so what made you come over? How did you know to have a gun? How did you know I was in danger . . . unless you set this whole thing up?' she asked, her voice trailing into the air, the sudden realization of what she was saying slicing through her body as painfully, and as easily, as a piece of wire rope. 'You did, didn't you? You set this whole thing up!'

'Jess . . .'

'You coached him, told him what to say, what buttons to push. Right from the beginning.'

'I used him to bring us back together,' Don said simply. 'Was that so wrong?'

'He almost killed me, for God's sake!'

'I would never have let that happen.'

Jess shook her head in disbelief. 'You orchestrated everything. The way he was waiting for me when I got to work that first morning, the way he followed me up the stairs, like he'd stepped right out of my nightmares, nightmares you knew all about, goddamn you! It wasn't a coincidence that he used the word "disappear". You told him about what happened to my mother, didn't you? You knew exactly the effect it would have on me, the anxiety it would produce.'

'I love you, Jess,' Don told her. 'All I've ever wanted is for us to be together.'

'Tell me,' Jess said.

'Tell you what?'

'Everything.'

'Jess, what do details matter? The important thing is that we were meant to be together.'

'You did this so that we could be together?'

'Everything I've done since the day we met has been for that reason.'

'Tell me,' she repeated.

He took a deep breath, releasing it slowly into the space between them. 'What do you want to know?'

'What exactly was your relationship with Rick Ferguson?'

'You know my relationship with him. He was my client; I was his lawyer.'

'Did you know he'd killed Connie DeVuono?'

'I never asked him.'

'But you knew.'

'I suspected.'

'And you offered to get him off if he'd do you a favor in return.'

'Connie was still alive when I agreed to take his case. I had no idea at the time he was planning to kill her.'

'But you knew he'd broken into her apartment, knew he'd raped her, knew he'd beaten her, knew he was harassing her.'

'I knew the charges against him.'

'Don't be coy with me, Don.'

'I knew he was probably guilty.'

'So you suggested a deal?'

'I suggested we might be able to help each other out.'

'You told him all about me, coached him in what to say and do.' Jess's voice was a monotone, her questions flat, as if they'd already been answered.

'Something like that.'

'But why? Why now?'

Don shook his head. 'It was something I'd been thinking about it for a long time, a way to prove to you how much you needed me. And suddenly, there he was, opportunity knocking, as it were. And the idea sort of came together in my mind. Plus, there was something about the symmetry I found appealing – you know, four years together, four years apart. I knew I couldn't afford to wait much longer. And then along came Adam Stohn, and I knew I couldn't afford to wait at all.'

'What exactly did you tell Rick Ferguson to do?'

'Essentially what he did best. I gave him free rein, as long as he didn't hurt you.'

'Hurt me? He almost killed me!'

'I was right behind you, Jess. You were never in any real danger.'

Jess rubbed the front of her neck, felt the blood still damp. 'You told him to break into my apartment and slash my underwear! You told him to destroy my car!'

'I told him to frighten you. I left the details up to him.'

'He killed Fred!'

'A canary, for God's sake. I'll buy you a hundred canaries, if that's what you want.'

Jess felt the tickle of the spider's legs spreading from her arms and legs up toward her brain. Could she really be having this conversation? Could they really be saying these things to one another? Could she really be hearing them?

'And tonight?' she asked. 'What was he supposed to do tonight?'

'I told him that, considering your famous tenacity, you'd never rest until you saw him convicted of Connie's murder. I knew he couldn't resist coming after you, and I wanted to make sure I controlled the time and place, so I simply encouraged him to finish the job as quickly as possible.'

'You sent him here to kill me.'

'I sent him here to be killed!' Don said, and laughed. 'Hell, I even gave him a key.' He laughed again. 'I used him, Jess, to get what we both wanted.'

'What we *both* wanted?'

'Be honest, Jess. Wasn't the death penalty what you were after? The State wasn't going to do it. I did it for them. For you. For us,' he added, the laughter gone.

'So you set him up.'

'The man was an animal. Scum. Your words, remember? He killed Connie DeVuono. He fully intended to kill you.'

'But you called me at my sister's, urged me to spend the night. You begged me not to come home.'

Again Don laughed. 'Knowing you'd do just the opposite. Knowing your pride would send you scurrying back as fast as you could. God forbid you listen to what your husband tells you to do.'

'My *ex*-husband,' Jess quickly reminded him.

'Yes,' he acknowledged. 'Your ex-husband. The man who

loves you, who's always loved you, who never stopped loving you.'

Jess raised her hands to her head in order to stop the sudden spinning. None of this was real, she thought. None of this was actually happening. This was Don, for God's sake. The man who'd always been there for her, who'd been her teacher, her lover, her husband, her friend. The man who'd nursed her through her mother's death and years of crippling anxiety attacks. And now he was telling her that he'd deliberately engineered their return. He was telling her that he'd been behind Rick Ferguson's prolonged campaign of terror. He was telling her that he'd come here tonight to commit murder. All in the name of love. My God, what else was he capable of?

Jess's mind raced backwards through the last eight years. Her anxiety attacks had begun just after her mother's disappearance, had lasted throughout her marriage to Don, abated only after their divorce. Had they been trying to tell her something?

He won't give you room to grow, she heard her mother say.

Her beautiful mother, she thought, slowly approaching Rick Ferguson's body and kneeling over it, hearing her knees crack, wondering if her body was about to break apart. Her eyes quickly passed over the gaping wound in the middle of his back, as she tried to ignore the sickly sweet odor of death that was straining, like a mask soaked in ether, to cover her nose.

'I love you, Jess,' Don was saying. 'No one could ever love you the way I have all these years. I could never let anyone come between us.'

The kaleidoscope in Jess's mind refocused, the last of the pieces falling into place, arranging themselves in front of her eyes with startling clarity, and suddenly she knew exactly what else he was capable of.

Jess swivelled around on her haunches, found herself staring up at her ex-husband, whose brown eyes reflected only his love for her. 'It was you all along,' she said, her voice an alien force that had invaded her body, pushing out thoughts she didn't know she had. 'You killed my mother.' As soon as the words touched the air, Jess understood with absolute certainty they were true. Slowly, she rose to her feet. 'Tell me,' she said, as she had said earlier, the alien's voice low, barely audible.

'You won't understand,' he told her.

'Make me understand,' she said, forcing her voice into a gentle caress. 'Please, Don, I know you love me. I want so much to understand.

'She was trying to keep us apart,' Don said, as if this was all the explanation necessary. 'And she would have succeeded. You didn't know that. But I did. As she was always pointing out, I was a lot older than you. I had a lot more experience. You were so hooked into her, I knew she'd eventually wear you down, convince you that you should wait until you graduated. And I knew that if we waited, there was a chance I might lose you. It was a risk I couldn't take.'

'Because you loved me so much,' Jess said.

'Because I loved you more than anything in the world,' he qualified. 'I didn't want to have to kill her, Jess. Believe it or not, I actually liked the woman. I kept hoping she'd come around. But she never did, and I gradually came to understand that she never would.'

'So you decided to kill her.'

'I knew it had to be done,' he began, 'but I was waiting for the right moment, the right opportunity.' He shrugged, the gesture filled with ironic innocence, as if everything that had happened had been beyond his control. 'Sort of like what happened with Rick Ferguson, I guess.' He shrugged again, and the innocence fell away. 'And then one morning, you called and told me about the fight the two of you had had, about how you'd stormed out of the house, told your mother to find her own way to the doctor's. I could hear the guilt in your voice. I knew that you were already regretting the fight, that if the lump in her breast proved to be malignant, you'd agree to postpone the wedding. I recognized that if I didn't move quickly, it would be too late.

'So, I drove to your house, told your mother you'd called and told me what happened, explained how sorry you were, said I didn't want to be the source of any more problems between you, that I'd back off, talk you into postponing our wedding until after you graduated.'

He smiled, obviously caught up in the memory. 'She was so relieved. Really, she looked like the weight of the world had been lifted off her shoulders. She thanked me. She even kissed me. Said that, of course, she'd never had any objections to me personally, but that, well, you know . . .'

'So you offered to drive her to the doctor's.'

'I *insisted* on driving her to the doctor's,' Don elaborated. 'In fact, I said it was such a lovely day, why didn't we go for a nice drive first. She thought that was a lovely idea.' His smile grew wider. 'We drove to Union Pier.'

'What?'

'I had everything worked out. Once she got in the car, it was easy, really. I said that I wanted her opinion on some renovations I'd been thinking about for the cottage. She was happy to help, even flattered, I think. We walked around the house, she told me what she thought would look nice, then we went out back, stood looking at the Bluffs.'

'Oh, God.'

'She never saw it coming, Jess. One clean shot to the back of the head. And it was all over.'

Jess swayed, almost lost her balance, grasped the floor with her toes, managed to hang on. 'You killed her,' she whispered.

'She was a dying woman, Jess. In all likelihood, she'd have been dead of cancer within five years. Think of the pain I saved her, the years of agony for everyone concerned. Instead, she died on a beautiful sunny day, looking out over the Bluffs, not worrying about her daughter for the first time in months. I know this must be hard for you to understand, Jess, but she was happy. Can't you see? She died happy.'

Jess opened her mouth to speak, but it was several seconds before any sounds emerged. 'What did you do . . . afterward?'

'I gave her a proper burial,' he said. 'Out by the Bluffs. You were looking at her grave a few weeks ago.'

Jess pictured herself standing by the back window of Don's

cottage, staring through the swirling snow toward the Bluffs beyond.

'I thought of telling you the truth then,' he continued. 'To finally put your mind to rest, to let you know that you had nothing to feel guilty about anymore, that your fight with your mother had nothing to do with her death, that her death was a foregone conclusion from the moment she tried to interfere with our plans. But I knew the timing wasn't right.'

Jess recalled the feel of Don's arms around her, the touch of his lips on hers as they'd made love before the fireplace, the false comfort he'd provided. That he'd always provided. Had some deep part of her self-conscious always suspected as much? Surely that was what her anxiety attacks had been trying for years to tell her.

'What about my father? He was against our marriage too.'

'Your father was a pussycat. I knew once your mother was out of the picture, there'd be no problem with your dad.'

'And the gun?' Jess asked. 'What did you do with the gun?'

Again Don smiled, a smile more terrifying than Rick Ferguson's had ever been. 'I gave it to you as a present after you left me.'

Jess clutched at her stomach. She stared down at the small revolver in Rick Ferguson's outstretched hand, the gun Don had insisted she take to protect herself after their divorce, the same weapon he had used to end her mother's life.

'I liked the irony of it,' Don was saying, as if he were commenting on a point of law, not confessing to her mother's murder. When had his obsessiveness crossed the boundary into madness? How had she failed to recognize it for so long?

She had slept with her mother's killer, for God's sake. Was he the crazy one or was she? She felt dizzy, her head lolling backward, as if she might faint.

'Now you understand how much I love you,' he said, 'how all I've ever wanted was to take care of you.'

Jess's head swayed from side to side, her eyes unable to focus. Was he going to kill her too? 'And now what?' she asked.

'And now we'll call the police and tell them what happened. That Rick was waiting for you inside your apartment, that he tried to kill you, that I got here just in time, that I had to shoot him in order to save you.'

Jess's eyes rolled back in her head, her head snapping over her right shoulder.

'And then it'll all be over,' Don continued, reassuringly. 'And you'll come home with me. Back where you belong. Where you've always belonged. And we can be together. Like we were meant to be.'

Nausea swept across Jess's body like a giant wave. It rolled over her, knocking her feet out from under her, sending her crashing to her knees, carrying her out to sea, threatening to drown her. She reached out instinctively for something to grab onto, something to save her, to keep her from being swept away, from going under. Her fingers found a branch, grabbed hold, tightened their grip. The gun, she understood, curling her fingers around its handle, using it to pull herself back to safety, straightening her shoulders as she fought her way free of the deadly current. In one quick and fluid motion, Jess brought the gun up, pointed it directly at her ex-husband's heart, and pulled the trigger.

Don stared at her in surprise as the bullet ripped through his chest. Then he crumpled forward and fell to the floor.

Jess rose slowly to her feet and walked to his side. 'Bull's-eye,' she said calmly.

She wasn't sure how long she stood there, staring down at her ex-husband, the gun pointed at his head, ready to shoot again if he so much as twitched. She wasn't sure when she became aware of other sounds, of traffic outside her window, of laughter echoing down the street, of her phone ringing.

She looked over at the clock. Ten o'clock. It would be Adam, calling to check on how she was, to find out how her day had gone, to wish her a good night's sleep.

She almost laughed. She wouldn't get any sleep tonight, that much was sure. She'd have to deal with the police, contact her family. Tell them about Rick Ferguson, about Don, the truth about what had happened here tonight, the truth about what had happened eight years ago. The whole truth. Would they believe any of it?

Did she?

Jess walked to the phone and picked up the receiver. 'Adam?' she asked.

'I love you,' he answered.

'Could you come home?' Her voice was soft but in control, surprisingly anxiety-free. 'I think I'm going to need a good lawyer.'